Tony Criddle joined a British naval engineering school at age fifteen, and graduated five years later as an Air Electrical Artificer Engineer. A few years later he further educated and trained as a helicopter pilot, and later still a flying instructor.

He reached Central Flying School 'A' category status eventually, and was able to examine both student pilots and instructors. He taught both basic students and operational tactics on larger helicopters over several tours, as well as search and rescue techniques on the Australian Navy's SAR Squadron when seconded on exchange to the RAN Fleet Air Arm at Nowra.

On his return to the UK, Tony taught basic flying on the RN's helicopter training squadron, and also flew for two years with the 'Sharks, the Fleet Air Arm helicopter display team, performing at the various UK air displays. He transferred to the RAN after and conducted another twelve years with them. In his time with the RAN, he was a safety practitioner, XO and CO of a Fleet Support Organization at Jervis Bay and a Project Officer in Canberra. In mid-1991, he suffered a serious injury that was service related, and was discharged six months later in a wheelchair. He did get reasonably mobile again eventually, but completed a Graduate Diploma in Psychology and Counselling while he recovered.

After thirty-six years of operations, including service in combat zones and policing actions, he retired to a Sheep and Cattle farm he'd built up at Bungarby on the Snowy

River. More recently he moved to the Southern NSW Coast to write down some experiences based on fact, before, to quote him, 'he's too bloody old to remember it'.

Dedication

Getting published was already hard enough before the advent of e-books and the electronic media, especially for a first timer. My heartfelt thanks to Austin Macauley, and their professional production team for the guidance and opportunity they provided.

To Dear Bob & Caroline

Fondest Regards

Tony Criddle

X X

Anthony Criddle

IN THE LAP OF THE GODS

AUSTIN MACAULEY PUBLISHERS™

LONDON • CAMBRIDGE • NEW YORK • SHARJAH

A CIP catalogue record for this title is available from the British Library.

ISBN 9781787103771 (Paperback)
ISBN 9781787103788 (E-Book)

www.austinmacauley.com

First Published (2018)
Austin Macauley Publishers Ltd.
25 Canada Square
Canary Wharf
London
E14 5LQ

Acknowledgments

To those who said 'why not give it a go' – Many thanks.

Even if we are prepared to die for a belief, it does not necessarily mean it's true.

Voltaire

Prologue

It was as bleak as sin and as cold as a witch's tit on that Saturday of a Northern winter. Nick Evans flailed mobile arms hard and fast, trying not to shiver, trying not to show it. For the first time in his young life, he felt that his contributions were appreciated here, that his teammates relied on him heavily, and he was eager to show it.

In his younger years, there had been only mindless indifference and unwarranted censure, but although the discipline at the Royal Naval College also tended towards stern, here it was fair. If you did get kicked up the backside, it was because you deserved it. That he could live with, because for him it hadn't always been true. Then again the college was training future Military Leaders, not classifying breakfast cereals.

A player collected the water-logged ball from beyond a sideline, while the forwards shuffled into the resemblance of a scrum on navy's twenty-five yard line. Nick flashed a quick look around to pinpoint the rest of his team. An Iranian cadet on the left wing signalled furtively with a shielded hand. Nick Evans nodded.

Not all the players on the field were from the UK. It was more cost effective for smaller, cash-strapped countries to send their young officers to British Service Academies. Military schools were hellish expensive to operate for a limited number of students, and the skills taught there had been standardised and proven over several violent centuries. No big surprise therefore that the teams contained several players with colouring closer to roasted coffee than dollops of single cream. Then again maybe not. Clinging slime had homogenised normally diverse complexions on that turbulent, vicious day, but origins didn't count much in this match anyway. Only the service you belonged to did.

Navy's left wing, Farhad Amini, had never been into parochial crap much, but a vicious Devonian Saturday got him thinking. Bitter, growling winds burrowed through his saturated, mud-spattered jersey as if it wasn't there, and the goose-bumps on his creamy, wrinkled skin felt almost as big as marbles under the dripping cotton.

Sure, the high sandy plateaus of his own country dished out unforgiving cold or scorching heat at times, but dry chills you could wrap up against and a blistering sun you could shelter from. It was the damp, energy-sapping purgatory of this country's winter that was almost impossible to avoid.

But experience dots the 'I's and crosses the 'T's, and this was Amini's first time in England. He didn't know that the relentless winter of 1965-66 had already been longer and harsher than most the southwest endured. Winters in the West Country were usually short lived, but that year it had been hammered by savage meteorological challenges that left a crust of inches-deep snow blanketing anything even vaguely stationary. It was as if winter had some sort of grudge to settle.

Meanwhile, south of Dartmouth, a confused, wind-lashed sea sent salt-laden moisture crashing into dripping cliff faces, while the aggressive, dark rain clouds rolling above them threw an eerie shroud over the whole of that picturesque river valley. The lower buildings drifted in and out of focus while the higher houses remained totally invisible.

Slightly lower, the imposing red-brick walls and ornate sandstone windows of the naval college spasmodically drifted into view as wispy stratus tumbled across the normally colourful hills. And it was cold, very cold, like the storage room at an abattoir. Anything outside flashed back slick wet shades of white or black.

That playing field was the only one in use on that miserable Saturday, and being the college, it had to be for rugby union. The lack of spectators was not a big surprise either, but half way along a sideline four miserable, oilskin-wrapped bodies watched thirty young men and a referee slog across the quagmire of the field. And as if to emphasis their misery, although huddled together, the managers and trainers were somehow still apart. They deliberately avoided acknowledging each other, let alone speaking. It wasn't a matter of choice to be there. It was expected of them, although no-one else would have been that insane. Surely only the British would play in this sort of weather.

But it was a new sort of patriotism for Farhad Amini. A tradition of the hard kind. And the annual blood match between the army cadets at Sandhurst and youngsters at the naval college would be played even in a raging blizzard.

By then no-one was quite sure when those vicious bouts had started, only that it was some time in the late 1800s. Both teams also played the air force cadets at Cranwell, but that one didn't count as much. This game had become the blood match, part of a tribal tradition, whereas the air force had only been around long enough to develop habits. Inevitably, army and navy thought even those were a shade on the dubious side.

But the fight was hard and bitter, even in that energy sucking weather. It was close to ignoble to lose the derby on your home turf, almost a scandal, but right then it was navy under intense pressure. They were two points down with only three minutes left to play, and worse still, the sailors had been beaten back to their own twenty-five. The ball was buried deep in the middle of a loose ruck, but 'Scrum' was a bit posh for the pile of straining bodies collapsed near the centre of the navy quarter line. The backs from both teams stretched across the field in an arrowhead, all ready for a final desperate effort.

Almost miraculously the navy's scrum-half fielded the ball cleanly from the pile of straining bodies and spun it high to his right. It was agonisingly beyond the reach of a straining three-quarter, but thudded safely into Nick's hands, hovering not far behind. And he was a Welsh-man. Rugby was in his blood. It didn't stay there long.

He needed a short wriggle, almost slipping as he set himself on the correct foot, before punting the ovoid leather towards the touchline near to army's goal. The ball soared high, surprisingly away from, not in front of his own back line, and kicked so hard, it momentarily disappeared into the base of the low, ragged clouds.

And the jink told Farhad Amini what was coming. The grass strips down the wings had escaped much of the churning traffic of mid-field, and a last desperate ploy for just these conditions had been worked out by Evans and his exotic teammate. The Iranian exploded from stationary to full flight in just two steps, like a gazelle from the high desert plateaus of his native homeland. He didn't lose speed or distance by watching the ball either. It would be there or it wouldn't be. Everyone else was caught on the wrong foot.

Farhad Reza Amini, 'Fred' to his mates, didn't look up until close to the opposition's twenty-five. By then the ball was dropping gently, but by Jesus, it was going to be long. It bounced high and true, but several feet ahead of him. 'Fred' threw back his head and lunged in desperation, and fielded it with grasping fingertips. He streaked headlong for the posts.

A desperate army full-back floundering in the wet, sticky mire of mid field got a hand to Amini's ankle, but it was already too late. Amini started to topple but hung onto the ball as if his life depended on it, slithering through the mud for the last few yards and scoring convincingly between the posts. The short kick was superfluous. Navy had won.

It was Nick who hoisted Amini to his feet. "Christ, Fred, I thought it was far too long," he muttered. "That's definitely one I owe you mate."

Chapter One
Ulster - earlier seventies

The persuasion was vigorous and pointed before a 'Five' informer gave up the location of a planned culvert bomb near the A28 from Strabane to Armagh. It was on a rough gravel road paralleling the border with County Monahan and there was a demonic logic to it. That quiet stretch of border was patrolled by the British randomly but often, and the PIRA would know that. A sting was organised and Nick Evans was part of it.

A few days later he got orders to lead another Wessex Mark Five from HMS Sea Eagle, a navy air station in Londonderry, to Newry Barracks in County Down. They forged low level, in loose formation, through the random mists and dripping clouds for twenty-seven miles. The sting would happen just to the west, and Eight Four Five Naval Air Squadron were back-up and contingency.

Just on dusk, the choppers flew a deliberately disjointed patrol above the moorlands and green handkerchief-sized fields, sometimes at 500 feet sometimes lower, sometimes with lights blazing and sometimes without. Occasionally they crossed paths, at others they were miles apart, but they were careful to stay on the British side of the border.

Four Special Boat Service specialists, (SBS) the Royal Marine's equivalent of the SAS, hunkered in jump-seats in the cabin of Nick's machine. Part of the plan was to get them somewhere that overlooked the culvert unseen, and just as dusk was biting, his number two flew overhead with navigation lights on and anti-collision lights flashing brightly. Nick had already picked his spot.

He flipped his night-vision goggles down and virtually auto-rotated into a small, wet vale that meandered towards the border, squeezing as near as he dared to a crop of vague mature trees hugging the sides of the mini-valley. From there the team had a clear line of sight to the culvert and would be between the road and the border. Whiskey Alpha's wheels never got closer than a couple of feet from the ground, and the SBS disappeared before the machine dropped its nose again.

Nick weaved randomly at low level for several miles before he put his lights back on and zoom climbed to join his mate from a random direction. He gave it another fifteen minutes before leading back to Newry.

Job number one for the SBS was to suss out the authenticity of the information. The PROVOS weren't going to risk setting up ambushes until the random patrol had passed for the day, so if it did happen, the SBS would witness it and switch the op on. Their secondary task was to block the PROVOS escape route to the border. Permanently.

The SBS had been there two days when a Royal Marine Land Rover patrolled through just after dawn. Nothing happened right away, but maybe an hour later, three males in a Ute spent time in the culvert. The vehicle drove off after, but two of the males disappeared into a wooded hollow nearby. Game, set and match. The SBS team sent the flash message.

They couldn't see it through the dripping murk, but a watery sun had just cleared the horizon when two long wheel-base Land Rovers with eight Marines aboard sloshed along a by-road from the north. Tension was on the high side. There were several iffy spots on that lonely, wooded tract, and none of them thought their 'flack' jackets were sissy. They kept a rigid fifty metres apart.

The plan called for the vehicles to pause briefly short of the culvert and four of the Marines to sweep through

17

the trees from the north. The terrorists would have to be close to detonate with a cell phone at the right moment, and the SBS were ideally placed to take out any that the patrol missed. With only ten minutes to go, things were on the hairy side.

There was no warning, just a large explosion close to the lead Rover's near-side front wheel. Dirt, flora, flame and scrap metal arced high towards the low, sullen clouds, and even though it was travelling slowly, the lead vehicle canted and flipped onto its side. The blast was ear shattering, and the noise from falling dirt and debris drowned out the screech of abrading aluminum as the vehicle body slid along the gravel track. The driver and passenger up front died instantly, but the two Marines in back were a little luckier. Both were ejected as the vehicle tipped.

One was perforated by shrapnel to go with his broken arm, and the other was badly shaken but functional. Both were covered in grime and body parts.

The driver of the second Rover braked frantically, twisting into a skid as he halted some fifteen metres from the wreck ahead. As they scrambled for cover, the high-pitched whine of Kalashnikovs on rapid fire stuttered into life from behind, causing them to duck even lower. Angry, invisible bullets tore jagged, bright gashes in the aluminum bodywork, and two more Marines got ventilated. One permanently. The troop sergeant and radio operator bailed out unscathed.

Controlled taps of three from the sergeant's SLR thudded into the trees as the radio man dragged the injured driver into the ditch beside the road. Shortly after, another SLR joined in from the ditch, targeting the disembodied wraiths of blue smoke drifting in the undergrowth behind. The sergeant screamed at the trooper to radio in as he rapidly changed magazines. The Royal wiped his mate's blood from his face with a grubby hankie before complying.

That misty dawn was getting towards perfect for covert operations if you didn't have to fly in it. Nick, his wingman and their crewmen perched in Newry ops centre over a brew, talking to someone in a green beret, dark-blue trews and a woolly pulley. The gold bars on his epaulettes held apart by a red flash said he was a navy doctor, but the beret said he had completed a commando course and was attached to a Marine Commando.

The chat was quiet and tense, and with violent action due to kick in, the radio was switched to external speakers. They heard the Marine's company commander chatting to the OIC of the ops centre, but the crisp, controlled broadcast was not what they expected.

"Newry ops, surveillance one, do you read?" A Marine corporal grabbed for the plastic mic and acknowledged.

"I'm relaying for two section. They can't get through on VHF and the truck HF is knackered. They were ambushed over four miles north of our position and both Rovers are out of action. They have three dead including their Sunray (leader), two injured and three in action. An IED took out the lead Rover and they're pinned down by automatic fire. They need help ASAP."

The OIC took the mic. "Are you in a position to assist?"

"Negative on immediate, Newry. We haven't got transport so we'll have to yomp. It'll take nearly an hour with our kit, and we've got to clear the woods in front of us first. The two we saw go in may still be there. It's doubtful, but we can't risk it."

"Roger, stand-by."

But Nick was ahead of him.

"Bernie, flash up Whiskey Alpha for me and then follow in Hotel. Pick up the SBS guys on the road when you get there and fly top cover when I go in. We've got eight boot-necks with their dead and wounded, so I won't have space or weight for anything else. Doc and Chalkie get a med kit, stretchers and some body bags aboard

Alpha, and make sure you've got the light machine gun. I'll be with you in five. Any questions?" They shook their heads. "Okay go." They were out the door almost as soon as Nick finished speaking.

He took the grid references off the major's map, told him what he was going to do, before he started running himself.

Nick could see that the Met-man's report wasn't a furphy as he raced towards the big olive-green Wessex. Sullen, grey clouds collided a few hundred feet above, while insistent drizzle draped everything in dripping, shiny silver. Grey wisps of radiation fog snuck grimy tentacles upwards around his legs.

And Bernie hadn't hung around. Both of Alpha's engines were roaring when Nick raced outside, and the black rotor blades were already beating at close to operational speed. The swirling vortexes from the hefty down-draft were outlined by twisting strands of water vapour. Nick paused, waiting for a thumbs up from his wingman in the co-pilot's seat. He caught the thumbs up from Chalkie on the way in. They were ready to go when he was. Bernie wasn't half way to his own helicopter, forty yards away, when Nick lifted.

He towered out to clear the corrugated fence that stopped aimed shots into the compound, before accelerating north-west just above the swilling radiation fog. The bruised, angry cloud wasn't much more than 200 feet above him when he crossed the twisted, cavorting channels of the Clanrye River, and from there he turned north towards the cross-roads. He latched on to the A28 twenty odd miles from the site.

Nick Evans racked up the speed to max as he tore along the glistening road, looming in and out of the low, rolling cloud base, startling traffic going both ways. The purple bottoms of disjointed cloud forced him to skim even closer to the dirt. Finding Dunmacmay Road was hard at that speed and height, but he was practically driving along the highway, not flying above it by then, so spot it he did. He banked left and a few minutes later a disembodied voice filled his earphones.

"Whiskey Alpha, Whiskey Hotel, confirm tasking over?"

"Whiskey Hotel, pick up the 'boot-necks' and cover me when I go in. I've just passed them about a half a mile up the road from where they were holed up. My crewie has an LMG so I'll brass up our guests before I give it a try. You keep their heads down while I do, over."

"Whiskey Alpha copy that. I'm a few minutes behind you."

A different voice joined in. "Whiskey Alpha, Surveillance One, copy."

Then a different voice again. "Whiskey Alpha, two section copy. We are still under fire, but it's spasmodic and there is some shelter. The road's been cut through a small hillock near the overturned Rover and the banks are four feet high. Slight camber on the road and a drainage ditch either side, Wind northerly five, over."

"Roger two section. We're three minutes out. I'll fly up the left side of the road from the south and spray them first. Confirm hostiles 200 yards behind?"

"That's an affirmative Alpha, out."

Nick released the press-to-transmit. "Standby, Chalkie, two minutes to go. You'll be hard pushed to see a decent target so just pour as much copper in as you can."

"Roger that." Then with some surprise, he yelled "The Doc's at the door with a Stirling. I thought medics were bloody non-combatants boss."

"I've seen God-botherers armed to the frigging teeth when they're with the Marines, Chalkie. Something about not being able to do their Jesus thing if their guys are dead. Just make sure the bugger doesn't shoot you. I'm knocking the speed back a bit. Here we go."

Only seconds later, Nick Evans raised the nose in a flare and eased to the left. From there the road and vehicles were visible, and the firing line clear. By the time he levelled out, his speed was down to a comfortable eighty knots and now he could see the cammoed Marines huddled either side of the decimated lead Rover. Almost immediately after, a thick straggle of trees ahead erupted in a cloud of smoke and tumbling leaf shards.

Nick was surprised he could hear the thump of the LMG and rip of the Stirling filtering above the bedlam of the flight and the confines of his thick flying helmet. A slight whiff of cordite trickled up from the cabin below. That he did expect.

He banked down-wind right as the trees got more attention, and two hefty thumps rocked the machine as he leaned even harder into the turn. A distracted "Fuck" was all he could manage before he lined up for the road. "Whiskey Hotel, Whiskey Alpha, show-time. Landing short of the lead vehicle in two."

Seconds later, Nick raised the nose in a flare and eased right with his front wheels still ten feet above the deck. It was a hot LZ and he wasn't hanging about. The big chopper stopped as the front wheels hit the road and the Doc scrambled to the Marines with his bag. Chalkie emptied a half clip up the road as shadows flitted across the few open yards.

Seconds later, Nick's cab rocked as Whiskey Hotel thundered over-head, spitting copper indiscriminately, and then smoke and debris from an explosion mushrooming high above the trees got his attention. Jesus, that had to be an RPG.

"Whiskey Hotel—Chalkie took out one of the PROVOS on the road. The rest have bugged out towards the border. Was that a bloody RPG?"

"Sure was, Whiskey Alpha. One of the SBS guys had it along in case their targets took off in a vehicle. I'll do another run while you finish the pick-up, over."

"I heard that boss. I'll nip out and give the Doc a hand." Chalkie appeared seconds later, shuffling in a half crouch with the folded stretchers. The helicopter felt strangely lonely with him gone, but the adrenalin was still pumping fiercely as the crewman dropped the litters beside the doctor. Two cautious Marines eased a body from the front Rover, oddly gently under the circumstances. Another covered them from alongside the wreck. The crewman led them back to the chopper, throwing a thumbs up as he did. The Marines returned for the others while Chalkie dragged the corpse to the rear of the cabin.

Nick watched as the Doc readied the wounded, and saw him indicate a stretcher and the chopper. The Marines lifted and shifted. There was a rasp as Chalkie re-connected his headset.

"The Doc's stabilised both of them, boss. About two minutes."

"Roger that." Nick hit the press-to-transmit. "Whiskey Alpha, pulling pitch in two."

"Roger. I'll pass down your port side from ahead, firing as you go. Any further shots?"

"Some random from the left a few minutes ago. One hit us but nothing serious—over."

"Okay. Rolling in hot in one minute."

Whiskey Hotel thundered past as Alpha lifted, and Nick sensed rather than saw another explosion on his left. When he had enough forward speed, he banked hard right and headed for Newry.

"Whiskey Hotel, Alpha. Newry will have dispatched a clean-up team by now. Hang around until they get here."

"Whiskey Alpha, roger. I'll have a look near the border."

Then Chalkie got his in. "The wounds aren't life threatening, boss, but the Doc reckons they'll be painful. We were bloody lucky as well. One of the rounds that hit us was less than an inch from the tail rotor cables."

Nick was finally coming down again. "Okay, Chalkie. I guess we'll save the aerobatics until later then."

They were landing in the compound within fifteen minutes.

Nick Evans presented at the Palace several months later to receive his Distinguished Flying Cross, the one with the diagonal purple and white stripes. The navy now saw him as someone who could be going places, as a possible future leader, and wanted to hang on to him. His squadron CO thought so too, but for him it was more personal. It wouldn't do his own career any harm to retain a genuine hero either. Unfortunately for him, Nick saw through it. He'd been there and done it, and could read body language. The 'chat' went from belligerent to frosty in minutes when Nick realised he was part of someone else's agenda again. In the end, he was cautioned about his attitudes, so to the CO's astonishment Nick saluted and dismissed himself.

Nick gave it some more thought when he was on his own, but it didn't take long. Sure the flying was great, the squadron way of life was satisfying, and the few close friends he'd made were in that narrow, insular world, but the coin had a flip side too. The Marine lieutenant killed in that dubious border clash had been a sometime mess and drinking 'oppo', and he'd operated with the sergeant who'd been injured a few times before. And even closer to home were the dreadful injuries a navy mate suffered in a vicious and indiscriminate car bombing.

It was a nasty little action, with no compassion on either side. Also, it was impossible to tell the good guys from the bad ones over there, yet they all thought God was on their side. It was just like when he was young, when he felt he was everyone's stepping stone into personal agendas. He listened, but a career break point was imminent for Nick, and he took it. He'd had enough of being manipulated.

By then, he'd sorted out his own credos and dreams. There aren't any atheists in trenches, but he kept them to himself. There wasn't much he felt strongly about, nor anyone he felt that close to either. Really, it was part of being alone, about arrested commitment, but he didn't twig it. He became a rolling stone who liked to fly choppers, and it didn't really matter much where. Nick thought he'd survived childhood largely intact, but traumatic experiences slip into a troubled adulthood as sinuously as a viper into a rock bed.

Chapter Two
Selection

Some things seem inevitable when you're a kid, so it was no surprise that a young Nick Evans copped the occasional clip around the ear. He didn't remember any real physical abuse though, and half-hearted clips he could handle. It was a sense of belonging, of family, that he'd never known. He'd always felt he was a pawn in a bigger game, and for him, childhood was more about survival than living.

Nick's father was an argumentative Catholic, his mother a belligerent Baptist, and when he knew about such things, even he wondered why they'd ever had sex, let alone got married. Any topic was good for an argument, even the mundane, allowing them to twist the knife in deeply, but if it was vaguely theological, that was a bonus. What religion he should be brought up in was never resolved, although both tried to influence his views, so he grew up totallyconfused.Their fervent, incomprehensible bickering isolated Nick from their seething, antagonistic world, yet he was always in the middle of the animosity. At first, he tried tears to break it up, but nothing worked. Inevitable, their bitterly, antagonistic marriage imploded, though surprisingly it did go on until his eleventh year. Nick didn't even remember when his father moved out in the end, only that he hadn't been around for a while. The aftermath was more noticeable.

After that, Nick lived with a selection of aloof parents, detached grandparents and the occasional, unfamiliar aunt, for years. He thought about taking off even then, but he was a kid. The threat of boarding school if he didn't shape up was an adequate deterrent.

But a decent set of 'A' levels turned out to be his passport out. When Nick reached his later teens, he realized it was crunch time.

Nick was embedded with his father's sister, a waspish, unhappy spinster in her forties, at the time. She was old before her time, and had turned nagging into an art form. In the end, he trudged off to the local recruiting depot and applied to fly with the navy.

Nick was fascinated by the train ride to *HMS Sultan*, near Portsmouth. It was the only one he could remember going on. For him, it was a long way from his native Cardiff, but senior naval officers sorted out the wheat from the chaff there. He'd booked the trip, but didn't share the knowledge until he was going.

It was on a cold and gusty morning three days before the interviews, when Nick rocked up to Cardiff Central. He encouraged a sense of elation to swallow a sense of nagging apprehension as he moved hesitantly towards the black, greasy locative, but that was short lived. Random swirls of damp, musty steam cavorted eerily around his legs, while the demonic panting from the idling engine mocked his limited years and shallow experience. The realisation hit home hard. He'd made his choices, but now life had plenty of time to throw him the odd curve ball. But for him, failure wasn't an option and he'd done his homework. Travelling early was part of it.

Reading had often been Nick's escape, and one recent book he'd devoured was John Winton's epistle, 'We joined the Navy.' On the journey south he poured over the highlights once again. It was a comical, but fairly accurate, portrayal of naval selection boards around that time, and when he got to Fareham train station, he had a plan. Not surprisingly the trip passed as if someone had hit fast forward.

Nick took a cab to *Sultan*'s wardroom, some ten miles south. The carved sandstone and scrolled iron gateway looked grand enough, manned by the obligatory naval guards, but to his young eyes the ornately pompous officer's mess seemed even more imposing. He paused, his pupils dilated and his mouth slightly ajar, taking in the sandstone and brick façade of early Victorian vintage.

A wrinkled, elderly hall porter guarded the foyer.

"Nick Evans, sir, I'm here for air-crew selection."

"I'm not a sir, sonny, I work for a living. Mister Jenkins will do." The stone-faced retainer handed him a pamphlet on mess rules and regulations, before hefting Nick's light suitcase with a theatrical groan. He led off to a dark, timbered bedroom on the first floor. If he thought Nick was on the early side, he never mentioned it, but then again, he'd stopped being interested in what young officers got up to years before.

Nick was allocated a frugal, wood-panelled room the navy called a cabin. It was small, about the size he expected it to be, and with a swift nod he was left to his own devices. Amen. It didn't take long to stow his gear.

Nick knew it would be Monday morning before the board kicked off, and other hopefuls wouldn't get there until later on Sunday, so he didn't waste time contemplating. With most of the regulars on weekend, the mess was largely his for the next twenty-four hours. Stimulated by curiosity, he ambled through those dark, polished rooms and corridors, perusing and analysing.

He first noticed the jumbo-sized, smoky oils hanging at intervals on the wall-spaces in that dim labyrinth. All different, yet all similar too, depicting sailing ships and seascapes as would be inevitably in a ward-room. The number of masts identified the type, while the intensity of colours, direction of wind, and the rolling sea-states suggested the weather, as Winton had alluded to. The canvases said a lot if you had time to look, and Nick did. No surprises for him on the Monday.

After more intense snooping, one particular room grabbed Nick's attention. A brightly polished brass plate on the thick oak doors advertised it as a conference room, and like other communal spaces, it wasn't locked.

Several upholstered chairs planted precisely down one side of a large, polished table intimidated a single, lonely chair on the other side. Also, it was a tad lower, and less upholstered as well. No surprises there. Obviously it was where the important stuff happened. He took his time, even peering intently through the smeared glass of the panelled windows. But he hadn't finished yet.

Around six on the Saturday evening, Nick wandered into the bar, where a noisy bunch of subalterns grabbed his attention. They were obviously working at getting half-tanked before heading ashore. He joined them by buying a round and then picked the brains of anyone with a view on interview boards. By the time he trudged into dinner, he was feeling confident, but he kept to himself. Some members of the board could be amongst the few older, more senior group dining there.

Metaphorically, he flew through the exams and tests over the next few days, and the navy was glad to get him. Within a few months, he was on his way to the Royal Naval College in Dartmouth.

Chapter Three
BRNC Dartmouth

It was a warm spring day in April when Nick topped the steep descent into that picturesque coastal township. His wheels were an elderly but reliable Hillman Minx. A decent 'banger' had been on his horizon for some time, and he'd held down a paper round and super-market stacking job to pay for it. Nonetheless, he felt pleasantly surprised when his father presented him with it on his eighteenth birthday. True Nick had been getting along better with him since reaching his late teens, but it had still been unexpected.

And although quaint wasn't a word in Nick's dictionary, he couldn't think of anything else to describe the stone, brick and warped wooden façades of that pretty diminutive port. Most of the buildings were ornate and antique, with the River Dart cluttered with moored yachts and motor cruisers swinging haphazardly on a docile, ebbing tide. Antiquated ferries puffed across those quiet, friendly waters, and the harbour was protected by stolid Napoleonic fortresses crouched at its river mouth like guardian gargoyles. If you ignored the cars, it had probably looked much the same 200 years before.

The next day was a Friday and Nick's joining instructions said to report to the parade ground by noon. Again he was taking no chances, and booked a room in a local pub the night before. He'd already checked that an overnight train arrived at Plymouth station mid-morning, so that must allow 'newbies' to be bussed to the college for the weekend joining ritual. Getting oriented and kitted out over the weekend would not be a good time to stand out.

At ten minutes to noon, a hired bus led him through an avenue of blossoming beech onto the tarmacked surface in front and below the imposing, weather-stained college. Several youngsters edged slowly towards the disembarking crowd and elderly chief petty officers, their faces hewn from weathered stone, herded them into a resemblance of an orderly group. It took a while before everyone was assembled with their baggage amid a hum of light-hearted joshing and banter. Nick figured that it was all about to change.

A tall, pale recruit dressed in sports jacket and Calvary twills ran slim, sensitive fingers through his long, unruly hair. He confronted the nearest CPO.

"I say, old chap, can you suggest somewhere local I can put my wife up for a while?"

The other chiefs turned as one, their faces defused and blotchy, and if looks could kill, the recruit would already be putrefying. It took several long seconds before the Chief could trust himself to speak. When he did, his voice was low but vibrant with anger.

"If the navy wanted you to have a wife, it would issue you with one. Now get back in line or I'll break your bloody legs."

It set the tone for the next twelve months.

Chapter Four

Flying helicopters was to be Nick's thing, but it was some time before he climbed into one. Apart from some grading flights in a light fixed wing at an airfield near Plymouth, the college was all about naval traditions, vocational academics and relevant technology. But Nick's stay there wasn't all work. He was a natural sportsman amid a plethora of excellent facilities, and although the extensive boat handling was compulsory, he enjoyed driving the mix of motor and sailing craft he had to qualify on. Truth be known, he became quite good at it, and that wasn't a bad thing at a Naval College. Even so, it was a busy twelve months before he moved to an Air-force Flying School in Yorkshire, and another six months before arriving at the basic chopper training Squadron at a Naval Air-station in Cornwall.

On that squadron, 'seniors' decided whether you would stream to anti-submarine or troop-carrying choppers, and the choice had little to do with your preferences. You headed either for Dorset or Somerset, wherever the navy needed more pilots at the time, and Ulster had become a weeping sore in the British breast again. Nick was funnelled towards Somerset and trooping with the Royal Marines.

Wrestling with the tactical stuff was definitely on the fraught side, but Nick graduated with a good pass on a clear, bitter Friday in the early spring. With several others, he walked into a different office block, as a qualified pilot, on the following Monday. Supposedly, he was one of the big guys now, but soon realised he still had things to learn. His first combat tour was only months away and that was going to be serious.

Nick Evans quickly absorbed everything he was taught, but even so, he was gratified to receive a clearance for all solo flights before they departed. Forty-two Commando Royal Marines was deploying to Ulster a couple of months later, and his squadron was going with them.

Nick's first action in that small, vicious conflict was in some ways what he'd joined for, although the fighting around supposedly religious tenets got him thinking. It was a close re-run of the idiocy of his youth, and Nick could see little justification for it, but his country was knee-deep in jingoism by then, and no-one cared much what he thought about it anyway. Just doing your job satisfied most, but then again, none of them had been where Nick had been either.

A few months after he got back from Ulster, Nick was distracted by a six-month instructional course, followed by a teaching tour in Somerset. It was another two and a half years before he was posted back to the truncated green fields and thick, dangerous hedges of Northern Ireland once more. And this time it was different. This time he was a flight leader and got his say at the planning level too. But that also had a down side. No matter what or where it happened, now he was in the thick of it. The training kicked in a few months later.

Chapter Five
Moving on

Nick had made his later twenties when prospecting with choppers took off in a big way. Owning oil and mineral rights meant big money, and a frantic avarice fostered a myriad of companies to spring up overnight. Finding the black, viscous geysers of oil or the iridescent glitter of minerals became an obsession, an inroad to almost limitless cash and power, and helicopters were just about the perfect machines for doing it. Trained chopper pilots became as rare as rocking horse manure, and it is disgustingly expensive to train them. Most were ex-military.

And these were the guys who'd been there and done it. They knew where a balmy sun shone almost daily, where warm, crystal oceans lapped pristine white sands, and even where conditions were so extreme that they attracted hefty pay cheques. A deployment to an exotic, favoured destination became a casual throw of loaded dice.

So Nick's future prospects didn't worry him much, and the other side of the world was something of a mystery. His service with the Marines had been largely in Europe, so for him, driving rains and bitter, snow-blown winters were the norm. Now he craved something different. Nick saw an opening in a magazine for Helo pilots to support the Argyle Diamond Company. He'd never been to Australia. He took it.

By the time he arrived in Western Australia, Nick's backside felt beyond sore. Pilot or not, he was used to sorties of a few hours duration, not twenty-four of the bloody things. After he'd appeased the humorless paragon inspecting passports, a company car took him to the airport's hotel. There the driver gave him an aircraft ticket for Darwin and a 'Puddle Jumper' pass for the next day. With close to sadistic pleasure, he grinned.

"Only another eight hours flying tomorrow, Nick. You should reach Lake Argyle by six in the evening. I can shout you a meal if you're up to it." Nick groaned and declined. He was crashed within the hour.

The same driver picked him up at eight the next morning.

"Sleep okay?"

"Two frigging hours. I was awake for the rest of the night."

The driver nodded wisely. "Yeh. Jet leg's a bastard, mate. Still, not much longer, eh."

Nick groaned again. "What's out there for God's sake?"

"I've never been there, Nick. Too bloody far for me. Most of the guys work two weeks with a day either side for domestic stuff. There's a couple of weeks off in Perth in between. I coordinate the turn overs and flights from here, and fix up the odd accommodation. The 'Bongs' own the land the mine's on, so a lot of them work there and live in a separate community built by Rio Tinto. That's all I know really."

"What the hell is a Bong?"

"Sorry, mate. An Abbo. A native Australian. I've got several blokes going back up on your flight, and pilots are honchos, so you go Business class. I've stuck a supervisor alongside you. He'll put you in the picture."

Nick nodded and looked out the window. There were a lot of trees and paddocks around even there.

Nick Evans dumped his solitary suitcase, pocketed his boarding parse, and shouldered his backpack. He followed 'Boots' the driver, for that was how he'd introduced himself, to terminal two. Around 100 people mooched or nattered in groups. 'Boots' led towards a group of seven males who stood slightly apart. All were lean and wore jeans and polo tops. Their deeply tanned skins and wrinkles suggested they'd squinted at distant horizons in strong sunlight for a long time. All but one wore base-ball caps. The driver nodded and steered Nick towards the one who was hatless.

"Jack, Nick Evans. He's the new 'Pommie' chopper pilot." He part turned. "Jack Bishop is a motor pool supervisor." The men shook hands.

"I don't know any nitty gritty about the mine, Jack. I told Nick you'd fill him in on the flight."

Jack nodded. "We'll do that on board, Nick." He pointed towards a vending machine. "You've got about fifteen minutes before we board."

'Boots' didn't hang around. He said his good byes and took off as Nick headed for the machine.

"You take the window seat, mate, I've done it heaps of times and there's nothing to see for the next five hours anyway."

Nick looked at him. "Are you serious?"

"Never more so, mate. Have you been to Australia before?"

"Haven't been east of the Mediterranean before, but I looked at the maps."

"It's bloody vast, Nick, and about ninety percent of the population lives within a hundred miles of the coast. There's a half-decent sealed road that goes all the way around, and one up the middle, but many country roads are still dirt. A lot of people visiting for the first time see the pretty pictures, but forget to check the friggin' scale."

Nick looked out the aircraft window. "I can see several roads and towns out there. It seems fairly populated to me."

"We've only been going fifteen minutes, though. Give it another ten. Darwin's northeast, so we won't be following the coast, and we've got three bloody great deserts to cross. Trust me, all you'll see is sand, scrub and a few lumps and bumps for the next four hours."

Nick still looked sceptical. "What about the mine itself?"

Jack Bishop collected his thoughts. "Okay. It only started up a few years ago, on the edge of Lake Argyle in the northeastern Kimberly's. It's still being developed, and looks a bit like South Africa's Kimberly mines, but the volcanic plug is Lamproite, not Kimberlite. It means that a lot of the diamonds are industrial, not gem quality, but so bloody prolific that they're worth digging for. The icing on the cake is that it's one of the few places in the world where you find gem-quality pink and red diamonds, and they are hellish expensive."

"What about the living conditions? Boots said something about two weeks on and two off, and most of you guys live in Perth."

"That's true. Up at the mine, the guys lodge in dormitories for two weeks at a time, while supervisors like me, and specialists like you, get demountable three-room cabins. The department heads get houses, and usually live out there with their wives. Their kids go to boarding school in Darwin."

"So I wouldn't have to commute. I don't know a bloody soul in Perth?"

"Not at all. The mine's on Abbo land, and Rio Tinto built them their own settlement. A lot of them work there, and their women work in the pub and shops. They do things like house cleaning and laundry too. Mind you, Darwin is still about 600 klicks northeast, and the nearest town is Kununurra, nearly 200 klicks north. There isn't much to do but work, get pissed and sleep anyway." Jack paused to think.

"Our shifts are twelve hours long for fourteen days, with one day either end for paperwork and catch-ups. As a chopper pilot you'll have to be flexible, but no weekends off."

Nick looked at him before he spoke. "You don't seem to be a boozer, Jack. What do you do?"

It was Jack's turn to scrutinize. "I'll have a few beers with the boys, but I'm not really into the sauce. I do some amateur archaeology in my spare time." He paused again. "I'm friendly with a couple of elders, and they've okayed me to photograph cave paintings and dig through old middens."

Nick smiled. "Okay, I give in. What's a bloody midden? It was Jack's turn to grin. "Ignorant Pommie prick. Basically, they're rubbish dumps close to old Abbo campsites or caves. Sometimes you can find artefacts or broken tools and spearheads that someone chucked away."

"I'm not much of a drinker myself, mate, but that interests me. Could you take me along to some of it?"

Jack looked at him reflectively before he spoke again. "If you want, I can sort something out, but it's serious shit. Most sacred sites are protected by law, and there are men or women only places that are taboo for whites. Respect them and their beliefs, and you'll get on fine. I get a day to hand over and pack before I fly south, and one when I get back to catch up. That's the only chance I get to nose around. We'll have a look tomorrow if you like."

"Thanks, Jack. I'd really go for that."

"Right. I'm going to get my head down for a while. I suggest you do to. You look like shit."

In didn't take long to collect their baggage before Nick followed to a twin prop King Air. It was being loaded with boxes, and the pilots were already aboard. Nick dumped his case and backpack alongside the stack and was shepherded to adjacent front seats.

"I'll give you the rest when we're airborne and it's quieter."

Nick nodded. Fifteen minutes later, they were on their way. There was no cabin service. First up, it's tropical up there. Six months of wet in the summer, and six months of dry in the winter, and the temperature's between about twenty-five to thirty-five degrees all year round. In the wet, the rivers overflow seriously, the roads go under overnight, and a lot of country becomes totally impassable, People do their travelling in the winter months when the crocs are confined to the coast as the rivers are low. The only reliable way in and out is by air, and the national pastime is getting pissed and punching out anyone who can still stand. I do my nosing around in the dry, obviously, and I suggest you do too. If you do get stuck in the bush in the wet, they probably won't find your body until Autumn. We get the odd cyclone there too, just to spice it up a bit."

"You're putting me down because I'm a Pommie right?"

Jack shook his head. "She's dinkum, mate. It gets as hot and humid as a whore's knickers up there, and the country's unforgiving. Don't take risks and if you're going anywhere, let someone know."

"Any other nasties I should know about?"

Jack grinned. "You're going to think I'm pulling your 'plonk' again, but just about all the wildlife can be pretty dangerous. We've got scorpions and poisonous spiders that can injure or kill, and people can get badly stung by several sorts of jelly fish. There's also lots of sharks and salt water crocodiles that find people tasty, and you can add about a hundred different sorts of snakes to that. Ninety percent of them are venomous, and five of the buggers are in the top ten of the most poisonous on earth. Hunting wild pigs is a sport up there too, put they aren't your farmyard porkers either. They're big, black and permanently pissed off, with tusks several inches long. If you do go hunting, treat them with respect."

"Jesus, if I'd known all that, I probably wouldn't have come."

"It's not that bad really, lad. You just need some common sense. Most people are bitten by snakes when they're trying to kill them, and kids need to be taught not to stick their hands down dark holes or into rocky openings. If you don't camp too close to water either, and hunt with someone who has some experience, you'll be okay. Given the chance, most things will avoid you. You can buy a booklet at one of the mine shops with coloured pictures of all the nasties, and they've also got chapters on first aid. Take a decent first-aid kit when you do go bush, and you'll have it covered."

Nick still wasn't sure if he was being put down. There was a hint of sarcasm in his voice. "Is there anything else I should know about?"

"Just one. Don't knock off anyone's wife or girlfriend, and keep clear of the indigenous women. It's still pretty wild and woolly up there, and revenge is on the harsh side. There is a women's dorm there too, but apart from a couple of secretaries, most of the girls drive eighty-tonne dumpers or monster bulldozers. It's said they've got a lighter touch on the machinery, but most of them have got bigger bloody muscles than you or I put together." He grinned again. "Don't get into a punch up with them either. You're the one who'll end up in the sawdust."

"Well, thanks for that. I think I'll barricade my bloody cabin daily."

Jack's smile just frosted his face. "Twenty minutes to go, mate. The ops: manager will give you a brief and a shack when we get there. I'll show you around in the morning."

The whispering solitude and vast, turbulent pastels of northern Australia were about right for Nick's nomadic soul right then, and he soon discovered a kinship with the ruggedly laconic locals. The pale reds and rich olives of that isolated, unforgiving landscape got his attention for hours on end, and he even appreciated the vivid riot of wildflowers in the wet and the withered burnt browns of the blistering dry. Before long, he was looking for signs of ancient Australians who had been there for maybe 50,000 years. Sometimes with Jack, and sometimes without. He had his friends, and they knew where he was going, but he often went alone.

Nick even got to enjoy the spectacular thunderstorms and savage, ground-battering cyclones in a perverse sort of way. His soul was more artistic than he realized. Later on, he even felt obliged to take out Australian citizenship.

But it didn't last that long. He tried sifting for Sapphires and noodling for Opal in New South Wales and used Darwin for recreation, but even that began to pall. A couple of relationships there hadn't lasted long either. The first woman turned out to be a closet alcoholic, the other on the run from two, not one marriage. When Jack was discharged after a nasty dumper truck accident, and the few alike souls were becoming hundreds who weren't, it was time to pack his bags.

An American exploratory company with a Sydney subsidiary was advertising for helicopter pilots at the time. He'd never been to the Middle East.

Chapter Six
Persia – In the Beginning

Archaeology managed to work out that Persia was settled by small bands of both *Homo sapiens* and Neanderthals long before the start of the last ice age 35,000 years ago. And as the ice retreated, even more clans moved into what were fertile acres at the time. The area is credited with introducing farming in the early Bronze Age. And paradoxically, one of the larger, more warlike tribes were known as Iranians.

As the population exploded, so did the conflicts amongst those tribes, and eventually they were moulded into one people under Cyrus the Great. From then on, they were known as Persians. Under him and his successors Persia expanded its territories towards Egypt in the west, India to the east, and even northwards into the Caucasus. The area prospered and knew relative peace for 200 years from then on, until Alexander the Macedonian got an itch to conquer. Eventually, he disappeared into history too, but that was not the end of covetous eyes.

The tribes that made up Persia mixed-and-matched several different religious beliefs until a major change occurred in the seventh century. The Islamic faith was a late starter, not blossoming until around 620 AD, and although based on Judean and Christian principles of peace and humility, some interpreted it as a command to spread the word. Arabic armies went on the march, along with its missionaries, and Persia was one of the first countries to be invaded.

For the next two centuries, Islam did its best to subdue Persia, but the Islam's main opponent was the Holy Roman Empire, particularly when it moved east and became the Byzantine Empire. Persia's conversion stayed mainly on the back burner, so Mongols and Turks also had a go leading up towards medieval times.

In 1501, the Safavid Dynasty created an Islamic State that stopped the speculation. Sunni and Shia Muslims had been, and still are, sworn enemies however, and it was the Shia sect that came out on top. And a fundamental belief was that Emperors ruled a Monarchy, and that Dynasty managed to keep a lid on things until well into the eighteenth century. But even that was too early for it to be about oil. Fats and oils from animals had been used as fuel for lamps and as lubricants for centuries, but speculating that a vast ocean of oil languished under the earth's surface would have attracted derision, if not death. And a means to extract it did not exist anyway.

Persia did straddle the 'Silk' route to Northern China, and by then a vast source of exotic spices had been discovered by the Dutch in what is now Indonesia. And Britain was also busily exploiting the fabrics and wonders of India, when a vessel with its holds crammed with such wonders could bring untold wealth to European owners.

But pirates from the African and Persia sea-boards on the Indian Ocean threatened this vastly lucrative trade, so Persia had to be kept sweet. Ambassadors from the west fell over themselves to manipulate safe passage, and they used any means possible to do it. So began Europe's long intervention in Persian internal affairs, and from then on it was European interests that governed much of what happened in Persia.

Russia did recover its Caucasus territories with little fuss in the early eighteen hundreds, but it was the discovery of oil later that awoke the area once more.

Innovation and a throbbing, whirling Industrial Revolution was the catalyst. From the late 1700s almost all aspects of industry and development were performed much more efficiently by machines. But machines needed fuel to operate and lubricate moving parts, so the need for oil escalated almost overnight. It is also said that 'war is the mother of invention,' and Britain had fought several in Africa around that time. Invention piled on invention, and uses for the black gold escalated almost overnight, so when oil was discovered in Persia, Britain was quick to monopolize it. An attempt by Iran to nationalize its oil in the second decade of the twentieth century gave her a reason for the control.

Persia's rag-tag army was no opposition for Britain's professional troops, and in 1925 she marched into Persia, quickly quelled any opposition, and established Resa Shah Pahlavi on the throne. Britain thought that he was their bloke, but once he had tasted power, he began to rock the boat.

Resa Shah was both authoritarian, reformist, and militaristic, and quickly raised a secret organisation to enforce his views. But he was also secular by nature, and no champion of Moslems or communists either. So initially Britain bit the bullet, and even accepted the change of Persia's name to Iran without major political comment.

But all that changed after the start of WW2. Resa Shah had convinced himself that Britain would lose the war with Germany, and started to court Hitler instead. And that was un-acceptable. A beleaguered Britain saw Iran as the back door into India, and a free India the key to victory. With Russia's aid, she marched again, deposed Resa Shah, and established his son Mohammad Shah Pahlavi on the throne instead.

Mohammad Pahlavi was neither as egotistic as his father, nor as ruthless, but did follow most of his sire's direction. His Savak, or secret police, made up for any ruthlessness he lacked, but he was not a strong leader, and riot and insurrection from the Islamic community escalated daily. It had grown to such proportions after the war that in 1954 he was deposed.

Still haemorrhaging financially from that devastating world war, this time Britain lacked the resources to intervene, but America didn't. The CIA pulled a few fast ones and spread some dollars around, and Mohammad Resa was back in power again. But this time with a powerful ally and access to modern armaments. Not surprisingly, he was ecstatic and eager to please. An influx of modern weaponry and special training for his troops would keep his head above water. For a time he was back on top, and even managed to suppress much of his opposition.

The beginning of the end came when the Shah exiled the Shia's spiritual leader, the Ayatollah Khomeini, to France in 1964. Unfortunately, it didn't stop the random killings and torture, so riots and unrest flared up again.

If anything, the civil disobedience worsened over the next few years, and an aging, sickly Shah began to wilt. The savagery of the Savak was meant to discourage dissention, but didn't, and after a disastrous Vietnam war, the USA was reluctant to intervene again. When Jimmy Carter got sworn in as the thirty-ninth President of The United States in 1977 on a strong civil rights platform, it was over.

Months later, Mohammad Pahlavi handed over government of Iran to the Islamic clergy, gathered his entourage, and headed for Egypt. In turn, the remaining Shias invited Khomeini back to Iran to form a government. The torture and executions didn't abate, of course, but this time it was payback and the perpetrators were on the other side.

Chapter Seven
Southwest Iran

Nick Evans had never been into history much and the years spent isolated in a sparsely populated 'Top End' hadn't provided much opportunity. He'd read up about Iran before he packed, but things had changed, hadn't they? The Shah was gone, and the country was stable again. Things were back to normal. Unfortunately, there was nobody in his circle to tell him anything different.

Even then, over 6000 miles to the northwest, three people sat silently in a dusty black and white Buick tearing up vortexes of dust on its way north from Abadan. Two were there by choice—one wasn't.

The vehicle was one of twenty delivered to Iran several years before as part of a job lot from America, and it really was a police car. A sturdy wire mesh separated the front from the back, the doors locked from the dash, and red and blue strip lights hung from a bar on the roof. There was a weapon's rack in the trunk.

The driver's dark shirt held a few badges but didn't show any rank tapes, and its rough cloth was already saturated with dark, wet sweat patches. Cold, pitiless eyes seemed to protect him from whatever he saw, but his brutal, vague look said he was a follower not a leader.

In the back, an elderly local sniffled noisily, his sallow face both anxious and intimidated. Dried blood streaked a dirty, worn countenance and he was working hard at the string of beads in his hand. He didn't know why he was there, nor why it was late afternoon when they set off north.

But it was the third male in the passenger seat who looked totally different. Tarek Achmed was loosely labelled a Mutawain, or religious interrogator, and went out of his way to look it.

He habitually wore several shades of black that added a sinister twist, and an ebony leather jacket was pulled over a black T-shirt. Even his jeans were black. And if that wasn't bad enough, the whole was emphasised by a closely shaved bluish skull. But it was his piercing eyes that chilled. Somehow they managed to look as if compassion had taken a holiday some time before. He'd chosen not to speak until they were well on their way.

Achmed pointed to a depression not far ahead. "Pull onto that track over there." The driver nodded but didn't stop before he was a hundred metres along it. He slithered from the passenger's seat and opened a rear door. The man inside shrunk even further into himself as Achmed stared at him for several long seconds.

"Out and stretch your legs, Aref, and pee if you want to. The next stretch is a long one."

Aref wheedled. "Where are we going, Mister Ahmed? Achmed Why are you doing this to me?"

"You are a Christian leader who disparaged our beloved Allah, Aref. That's why Tehran wants you. I told the mullah that if I find you, I'll bring you up myself."

Aref picked up on the tone. "Does Tehran know I'm coming?"

"The phones weren't working, but they will know when we get there."

It was a slim chance, but he had to take it. "This is all a mistake, Mister Achmed, nothing like that happened really. Is there any way we can straighten this out?'

Tarek Achmed tried hard not to smile. It worked every time. He let the tension build.

"Nobody really knows about your arrest yet, Aref. You could buy yourself out, I suppose, but you told me that you have no funds."

"I could get my hands on some, Mister Achmed, but it would be back in Abadan."

"Not good enough, I'm afraid. It's too risky. Get back in the car."

"No, no—I have some savings, quite a lot really. Take me back and I'll give them to you."

"It doesn't work that way. If I'm convinced, you can buy your freedom and disappear. If you are lying, I'll kill you, your wife and your son. What's it to be?"

There was no other way out of it. How much was his life worth anyway.

"There is a small shrine to the Virgin Mary in my garden, Mister Achmed. It has a loose stone behind the altar. There are diamonds in there."

"Fine, Aref, you should be able to disappear in a couple of hours then. Hop in the car and we'll be on our way."

The Christian elder stood taller as he turned towards it. He didn't hear Achmed draw a weapon, and barely the shot that took the top of his skull off. Achmed ordered the driver to help with the burial. His face was bland.

Chapter Eight
Tehran – Later

Nick got a big surprise when the Emirates air liner deposited him in Tehran late in the northern autumn. He had his illusions, and desert sands and the Middle East conjured up pictures of excessive heat, unfriendly camels and dry, musty air. He hadn't expected Iran to be as wickedly gelid, nor most of the land he'd flown over so empty and desolate. He'd been relaxed and comfortable in business class, but once outside the heated aluminum tube, an unexpectedly cold breeze whipped fiercely at his trouser legs. It dragged up memories of wisps of steam coursing around his feet on Cardiff station many years before.

And when he got there, the jostling, animated hordes in arrivals weren't his thing either. He steered towards baggage to collect his only suitcase, and was first to push into the cacophony of the crowded terminal. And that hub-bub unsettled him, made him jittery. He wasn't used to bustling crowds dressed almost anonymously in a multitude of robes and headscarves. The sinister posters of local clergymen draping any spare wall-space didn't turn him on either, with digitally altered pictures of Ayatollah Khomeini particularly intimidating. And on top of all that, he could smell the raw aroma of sweating bodies and acrid taste of scorched, dry sands. Nick sneezed as if he had an allergy. He felt uncomfortable, bordering on claustrophobic.

He stretched to peer over the bobbing heads and registered a local in an anorak holding up an ink-stained cardboard sign over his head. Nick's name was on it. He attracted the man's attention and from then on it was easy. The driver took him to the grandiose Persian Evin Hotel to register and dump his bags, and then to a down-town high-rise. Nick rode the elevator to the third floor.

A company honcho with an iron-grey crew cut was waiting inside the full glass doors. He introduced himself as the inevitable 'Chuck,' and shook hands as if it was a contest. The company also expected a Canadian geologist two days later. Chuck mentioned that he would be taking them both south to the small base in the Kavir desert. Until then Nick would get the grand tour. An hour after the meet and greet, he was taken back to his hotel.

Nick turned up for the inevitable company's 'boots and all' brief first up the next morning. He was told it would answer any superfluous questions, but it seemed a bit vague. A visit to the American Embassy after eased it out of his mind, and that evening Chuck and a company publicist joined him at the hotel for dinner. Nick didn't exactly learn much then either, but at the time he was too jet-lagged to notice. It was next morning when he realized he knew nothing about the company's politics. Nick felt the first prickling of apprehension.

He had seen his share of barren, green mountains in Wales and Scotland, and had operated around bigger ones in Norway on the odd detachment. The word conjured up pictures of large, stony bumps on treeless, wind-swept moorland. When the car crested a hillock well to the north of town, his gaze fixated. The Elburzs were in a different league all together. Those leviathans were still young and feisty, nowhere near as eroded as other mountain ranges he'd seen, and they completely swamped his senses. Jagged rocks, as sharp as shark's teeth, punched high into the pristine layers of cooling atmosphere, and the ragged crags easily disappeared into the horizon on each side. The higher reaches were already draped in a cold blanket of shimmering snow. Nick felt as if somehow he'd been dwarfed.

But it was the almost perfect volcanic cone of Mount Damavand itself that truly impressed. At over 18,000 feet high, Nick knew it was the highest peak in Iran, but what that meant hadn't meant much. He hadn't realized how central the mountain was to Tehran's north either, nor how Damavand over-awed, nay, dominated the shimmering city. It resembled Mount Fuji in Japan, only set amongst other mountains. Tehran itself was a conglomeration of glass and concrete, regally reminiscent of many a county's capital, but it was the glacial, impossibly high mountains that the eye was drawn to.

Only the cocktail party at the British Embassy later surprised him more. But that was for other reasons.

Chuck, his wife and Nick arrived at the glass and sandstone edifice of the British Embassy promptly at six. As a business concern of an ally, the company always got a couple of tickets and as a national Nick was a natural. He'd been made aware of the importance of cementing good relations with the embassy staff, and he was happy to be included.

And although they were spot on time, the party was already in full swing, with the ambassador and his wife still greeting guests when they arrived. They got his obligatory few words before a steward presented a silver tray. Others circulated with more booze and minor mountain of canapés and finger food. Talk and laughter had already climbed high up the decibel scale.

Glass in hand, Nick circulated through a colourful cross-section of people who chatted and laughed in small animated groups. Some were locals, while others were the staff of resident Embassies, so the dress was varied too. Generally, males favoured lounge suits, or even national costume, while most women were draped in elegant, expensive dresses and were as bright as butterflies. There was a sprinkling of pristine military uniforms, bedecked with vivid awards and medals to elevate the tone.

Chuck looked around and pointed with his chin.

"That dude over there is Gerry Hawkins. He's the real wheeler-dealer. He handles ex-pats, visits and social events. It will pay you to get to know him."

Chuck embedded his wife in a diplomatic circle and led off toward a small group from the embassy. A tall civilian in his late thirties turned as they approached, almost as if he sensed them. Chuck did the introductions.

"Hi, Nick. I was hoping you'd make it. There's some stuff I need to fill you in on before you head south. Give me a half an hour while I do the circulation thing, I'll look you up after." The voice was pure foreign office, but the twinkle in the pale-blue eyes suggested it was more about the right schools than affected sentiment. It could have been diplomatic evasion of course, but Nick didn't think so. A bit later, a hand gripped his shoulder.

Gerry Hawkins raised his voice over the laughter. "You're a British citizen, Nick, so I just wanted a quick word in private before you head off south. Fear not. You've only been here for five minutes, so I won't swamp you with too much." He canted his head and led off towards a passage on their right. They slipped into a small, empty office, where he indicated a chair.

"Your engineer can fill you in on the nuts and bolts when you get down there, and I'll give you anything you want expanded on when you pop up again. Do you know much about what's going on?"

"Not as much as I thought, mate. I do know that a high-profile cleric exiled by the shah has been let back into the country, and the shah shot through to Egypt. I don't know much about the politics of it."

"That's it essentially, but it goes a lot deeper. The shah was pretty liberal and pro-western, whereas Ayatollah Khomeini, the Shia Muslim's top dog, is a rabid fundamentalist. Bottom line, it's about direction and power." Hawkins put his drink on the desk.

"Riots and street fighting were big time here recently, but eventually it was going against the shah, and he saw the writing on the wall. He hopped it while he could. After that, the Shia clergy brought the Ayatollah back and he was voted into political power by playing the religious card. It's still dangerous out there, especially at night, but we think the recent stuff is more about payback."

"Jesus! I thought I'd left all that religious bullshit behind me."

Hawkins grimaced. "You and Jock are British subjects, but your company is American, so none of us are sure where this is leading yet. Both the Brits and the Americans propped the shah up, so neither is all that popular here either. I'd use the embassy for duty-free grog, and also it'll be safer to use us as a mail drop. Jock Sinclair pops in every month to do that stuff, so if there is anything a bit controversial, save it until you come up. I'll keep you up to date."

"I'll be honest, Gerry, I had no frigging idea that things had deteriorated this much. I was looking for somewhere a bit more peaceful."

"That's life, Nick, I guess. Jock can fill you in on most of it, but what I'm saying is watch your six o'clock. That's it for now, so if you're happy, we'll re-join the punters."

Nick nodded. Gerry Hawkins handed him on to a group of Embassy military staff when they returned. And that's where the second surprise came from.

A British commander on the defense staff introduced him around as an ex-navy flier. A lieutenant commander in Iran naval uniform turned towards him. Both started when their eyes met. Nick struggled with a name initially. "Farhad Amini, isn't it—Fred? I didn't expect to see you again."

Amini smiled. "Nick—the Evans bit gave it away." He turned to the others. "Nick and I were teammates at Dartmouth many eons ago."

They were into old times almost instantly, but Chuck hunted Nick down shortly after. Amini and Nick exchanged cards as they parted. It was the first card that Nick had presented from a stack the company had given him. In fact, it was the first card Nick Evans had ever exchanged.

Chapter Nine

At seven sharp the next morning, Nick Evans rocked up for breakfast. Three Caucasians were eating in the sparsely populated restaurant. One looked up, the other two he'd seen at breakfast before. He ambled towards his table and the redhead half rose.

"Hi, I'm Nick Evans. You must be Floyd Webster." The man shot out a hand.

"Arrived yesterday evening and got a quick rundown then. I believe we're off south this morning."

Nick nodded. "Mind if I join you?"

"Fill your boots. The stuff I was told seemed a bit vague. So perhaps you can fill in a few gaps."

Nick nodded again. He went to the buffet before he sat. He ordered a pot of coffee before he waded in.

Chuck was waiting when they descended to the foyer in the same lift. He waved towards an SRV drawn up at the main entrance.

"The company's taken care of the hotel, guys. Throw your stuff in and we'll be on our way."

The drive south was fascinating. Like other capitols, Tehran had its modern glass and concrete edifices, and groaned with sprawling suburbs. Only the mosques were brightly coloured, and generally crafted from hard, sun-baked mud. They all looked medieval and had a distinctly Arabic look about them. All were guarded by stands of straggling palms.

Once out of the city, the tiny villages and hamlets were built almost exclusively from what looked like adobe, but this time crumbling boundary walls leaned drunkenly against rough, uneven oblongs, set along roads that haphazardly varied in width. The tattered, emaciated palms in them drooped more than grew, and pastel streaks of wind-blown sand piled high around moth-eaten boles and rough-caste walls.

When they reached Qom, it was something else again. Sure there were some tall concrete structures, but also a myriad of narrow, dark lanes that were packed so tight the people had to take turns breathing. Chuck passed through Qom without stopping.

It was twenty minutes later before they rolled onto a gateless airfield. Chuck aimed towards a semi-circular hangar and long, prefabricated building in the distance, pulling up alongside a similar 'Cherokee" SRV. All three climbed out, and Nick Evans kneaded an aching back with balled knuckles as he looked around. An ill-defined sun glittered through vaguely distorting alto cirrus, but it was still blistering for all that. He pivoted slowly, the heavy silence hurting his ears.

"Nobody's out here, Chuck. I don't suppose they can do much without a pilot and surveyor anyway."

"They wouldn't leave a truck here and the hangar half open if they'd left, Nick. There'd be nothing left inside an hour. I didn't tell them what time we'd arrive so they're probably in the hangar. Jock's got a team of four mechanics here to do the heavy stuff, but that's the lot. They're pretty thin on the ground. His name is Alistair, by the way, but if you call him that he'll probably thump you."

Nick smiled. He swung up the two steps onto the building's veranda and slowly he spun again. A pair of single-storey buildings to the north squatted close to large fuel tanks on concrete bases that were distorted by a mild autumn mirage. About thirty metres further, a windsock sagged immobile and dejected in the wavering heat. The buildings had the fuzzy outline that advertised adobe bricks and untrimmed straw binders, with flat roofs that were almost certainly made of bitumen-covered ply. And apart from a single, sealed runway, that was it. The company's buildings were located as far away from them as the airport allowed, as if they would contaminate native Iranians if they got any closer.

Perhaps it was the pair of Bell 206 Jet Rangers that were seen as a threat. Nick smiled. The Allison 250 C20J engines or the main and tail rotors could bite when they were turning, but casual observers weren't likely to get that close anyway.

Nick panned the horizon and saw the higher rise buildings of Qom shimmering further to the north. He didn't want them any closer than that. As he swung down again, a rattle of chains came from the hangar.

Two figures took their time strolling towards them. The taller of the two was dressed in a loose, light robe and pantaloons, with the mahogany skin and finely chiseled features of someone from the north of the Indian sub-continent. The other was European.

Jock Sinclair could have been somewhere in his mid-fifties to early sixties. Everything about him looked lived in, especially his creviced face. It was if he'd fallen into a tumble drier and not been rescued soon enough. Nick had expected the baseball cap, and knew most Scots were vertically challenged, but Sinclair was also wide and muscular. Nick looked at Chuck. It seemed to beg a question.

"Jock's feisty, Nick, but he's about the best flight engineer we've got. If he fixes it, it stays fixed."

When he got close, Sinclair scanned them with wary eyes and then tossed a bunch of keys to his mechanic. "Stick the kettle on Imran. I need a pee."

The chat was casual until they'd drunk their coffee, after that Sinclair took charge.

"I've finished what maintenance there is, Chuck. I'll show Nick and Floyd around here and then take them home myself. We left the boys back home so there's plenty of room in the truck, and I brought their keys."

The American nodded.

"Okay. Give me a minute for a quick chat with Nick and I'll be long gone." Chuck took Nick's elbow and steered him outside. He almost whispered.

"I'll give you the short version, and Jock can give you the rest. He's been here a couple of years already and can answer any questions you might come up with."

"Sounds okay to me, mate. It's my first time in the Middle East."

"Okay then. No bullshit. It's all about oil and minerals and who controls them really, and the company wants to be part of it. Unfortunately, with the shah booted out and the ayatollah in charge, we just don't know where we stand right now."

"Jesus, so how do we play it then?"

"Low key and by ear, Nick, that's all we can do. You're the nominal leader down here, and the others will look to you for guidance, so try not to piss anybody off until we're better informed. It's all I can think of right now. The company and the embassy are always on the end of the phone if you need them, and as far as we know, it's only Tehran involved. If you keep your head down, it could be all over before you know it."

Nick could think of nothing to say. He nodded.

Chuck was on his way back to the capital fifteen minutes later. Nick watched him go. He went back in the block deep in thought.

Chapter Ten

Nick Evans refilled his coffee mug before Jock Sinclair grabbed their attention again.

"I've got some paperwork to finish before I give you a heads-up on what we do and what we've got to do it with. After that I'll give Floyd a quick run around before we go home. I'll do the other stuff tomorrow if that's okay with you, laddie?" It didn't sound belligerent, but Nick detected a hint of a challenge. 'Bugger—a pissing contest and I've only been here five minutes.'

Jock Sinclair wrote up the maintenance he'd just carried out in the aircraft documentation. It was an inviolate ritual that came first and the dregs of his coffee were cold when he got to them. He drained his cup, and his mouth puckered distastefully. He rinsed his mug and turned back into the room. The others waited for him to speak.

"Right, guys, Apart from here, the company's got seven operations in country. Three small ones like this near the mountains, and another four involved with oil exploration in the gulf and sandy stuff. If you ask me, we've got the best of it. We're pretty much left alone down here."

"I thought we looked for oil as well."

"We don't explore for it, Nick. Our job is to find mineral deposits in the mountains, but any seepages we do see in the shale, we report. The company doesn't want to miss anything, but they don't make that obvious."

Webster jumped in. "I was told to give you an update on minerals, Nick. Copper shows up as pale-green smears, iron ore as dirty grey smudges, and chromate and manganese deposits glitter like mica chips in those softer rocks. Gold, tin and tungsten deposits sometimes show up as well, but they're rarer than Vestal Virgins at a bikie conference. I'll give you a proper brief before we go looking." Webster grinned before he continued.

"The thing is, mineral traces show up better from the air when the sun's low, so I'll give you a heads-up when we start flying." Nick nodded.

Jock Sinclair picked up the brief again. "Okay then. It sounds good if you say it quickly, but in fact we do things pretty much on a shoe string around here. I've got the degree in aircraft engineering, while one of you does the looking and the other takes him where he wants to look. Apart from that, I've got four mechanics to help with the repairs and maintenance." He half-turned to the Pakistani who sat slightly apart.

"Imran over there is the senior guy. Ignore the ugly bugger's hooked beak and flashing eyes, all of them are like that in the Punjab where he comes from." There was nothing subservient about Imran. He smiled lightly and raised a vertical index finger.

Sinclair grinned. "Okay, I'll take Floyd around the maps and reports while you look around up here, Nick. We can do the hangar when we come out next."

"Okay."

The cluttered room took up half the prefabricated unit and a thick glass window at one end took up most of the width. A sliding glass door opened onto a small veranda alongside that. On the side walls two small aluminum-framed windows let in muted light, but that was about all. The outside ledges were festooned with a tangle of dusty cobwebs with the glass smeared and badly in need of a clean, but no-one seemed to notice. Then again it was all males out there anyway.

But it was the number of things to sit on that had Nick Evans smiling. The several over-stuffed, un-matched armchairs sagging haphazardly around the room had probably been scavenged separately from the local markets, while two aluminum and plastic tables, with chairs that did match, filled the centre of the room. A wood and felt card table and stainless chairs occupied one corner.

The only other furniture was a utility steel cabinet propping up an outer wall, thick with dog-eared magazines strewn on its shelves. Colourful booklets boasting garish pictures of motor-cycles, cars or aero planes on the covers also spilled randomly over the plastic tables, but there was nothing solicitous or even vaguely pornographic in the room. Not even a spicy calendar. A two-year-old copy of *Flight* was the youngest magazine available.

Internal doors set into a painted ply wall blocked off the whole of the inboard end of the room. One led to a small locker room with slim metal cabinets for flight gear, and the other larger cubicle held a desk and a mandatory drawing board. There was another small desk set under a standard window for the pilot, but Nick couldn't see himself using it much. The floor was chip-board squares which had been varnished once, but now only glistened where no-one could walk.

After a look through the map library, Jock Sinclair led Webster into the surveyor's office and rifled through the large, oblong desk. Nick could see that it would take time, so he made himself another coffee before moving on. Like most pilots, he practically main-lined the stuff, and it didn't take long to finish. Minutes later, he descended the small veranda and turned down the side of the building.

A gloomy, grease-streaked workshop abutted the office area with entry through its own battered door. Inside, shrink-wrapped spare parts for the choppers and large, intricate tools were stacked on metal shelving around the grimy walls, the hand-tools highlighted in white on composite boards. There was a heavy vice bolted to one corner of a stained workbench. Obviously it was where Jock and his boys got their hands dirty, as self-respecting engineers were expected to.

The last few feet of the weathered, pre-fabricated building were given over to a toilet, but labelling it a toilet was bordering on the posh side. Two deep holes had been bored in the sand, and crowned with a smooth wooden box. Nick surmised it would hum both literally and figuratively in the high summer months. Slight discolouration in the nearby desert sands suggested they saw more urine than the holes ever did.

By the time Jock was finished with the surveyor, Nick was sprawled in an armchair. The afternoon had only run half its course by then, but Sinclair pointedly swept up the key ring and went out to lock the rest of the building. When he returned, Nick waggled his coffee mug to let the Scot know he wasn't above making coffee for anyone, but Sinclair declined. He clapped his hands for attention.

"I'll make do with whisky later, Nick. The sun's over the yard-arm somewhere on this frigging planet. We'll get on home soon, but before we go, I'll clue you in on domestics."

Nick frowned. "Doesn't the company take care of that?"

"It does indeed, mate, but some political stuff happens there as well. You need to know about that, too."

"Jesus. It's bloody complicated for this one-horse operation here." Nick smiled lazily to take the sting from his words, but it didn't reach his eyes. Webster scraped his chair around to face Sinclair more directly.

"Okay. Shahabad is about ten klicks from here and it's a bit over twenty-eight from Qom. The Qom River and a secondary road to Golpayegan run past the town, but its main importance is that it's a gateway into the Zagros foothills. The people are semi-nomadic herders of an ancient Bakhtaran faith and can trace their ancestry back to the ancient Persians. Families run their sheep and goat herds together and take turns up in the high pastures in the warmer weather, but they all own some lower pastures to take the pressure off when the weather turns shitty. They don't have a lot in common with other Iranians either, so they don't even try to integrate. There are lots of them in the Zagros Mountains, but they've never really united, so it puts them pretty low on the food chain."

He paused. "If anybody's got questions, I'll answer them, but it's best if you see it all first." There were no takers.

"Okay. The company rents two adjacent houses in Shahabad which are a sort of collective asset for the town. You and Floyd share one and me and the lads the other. I like my food spicy, the way the boys cook it, so the rent is taken out of my pay, while they do some domestic stuff as their share. That allows them to send a bit more money home to their families." He drained the dregs of his cold coffee before he continued.

"An older lass called Sarah and something I can't pronounce is your official housekeeper, and her husband Mohammed is the odd-job man for both of us. Sarah's a town elder and administers the houses, so her English isn't bad, but Mohammed doesn't speak English at all. If you're happy, let's go."

They were on their way within fifteen minutes and not long after took a left at a painted-on roundabout at the bottom of an incline. Only a few houses were visible from the river. Nick had envisaged mud Beau Geste type castles set in shifting, beige sands. When they got there, it was short on legionnaires, but it did have a distinctly Arabic look about it.

Shahabad sprawled along a valley covered in ankle-deep, mobile dust, with the only healthy flora growing along the moist banks of the river. Houses in the small town were mostly single storey, L-shaped boxes with flat, castellated roofs, and a high courtyard wall enclosed each building into a rectangle. A single door breeched the outer courtyard walls, sporting an oversized iron keyhole. Nick couldn't see any other outer doors at all.

By now it was no surprise to him that all the houses were built from adobe, but here they were coated with white-washed animal dung, spread thick and liberally for durability. Other building materials were scarce away from the cities. He knew that costs put them a long way down the wish list. "Is there any power out here, Jock? I can't see any pylons."

Sinclair pointed to a rise on the northern edge of town.

"A single spur runs out from Qom to these few blocks. The rest of the town makes do with kerosene. To be honest, we use the stuff for some things too, but ours comes from fuel for the choppers. There aren't too many other resources out here either, no post office or garage for instance, and even the cop shop uses a radio to talk to Qom. The company did spend some dough on decent phones out to the airfield though."

"So what religion do Bakhtarans go for?"

"Most of them are Baha'i. It's peculiar to Iran, fairly progressive, and fairly casual. They don't even pretend to be Islamic. Some to the north and west are even Christian, and a few down south Zoroastrians. I had a job in Sri Lanka once and it's the only other place I've been where the religions mix so freely. The mosques and churches over there even have got places set aside for other religions to worship at. Here they celebrate each other's holidays quite happily."

Nick Evans must have looked sceptical.

"Trust me, mate, would this face lie?" Jock's smile was almost cherubic. "Obviously they have quite a few celebrations and holy days, whoever's doesn't matter, and they slurp large quantities of a particularly vicious homemade hooch when they're doing it. None of the women wear chadors either, and not many of them even bother with headscarves. If you've got to live in Iran, mate, it's the place to be."

Sinclair stopped outside the end house of a block of eight. A buxom older woman jerked the door open and approached with open arms even before they'd climbed out. She slopped a kiss on Jock's craggy cheek and then ignored Nick's proffered hand and hugged him tightly. He heard his ribs creak. She did the same to Webster, but

Imran obviously knew what was coming. He headed for next door with an airy wave.

"Nick and Floyd, this is Sarah." That was it. Sinclair dragged the baggage from the rear of the vehicle and helped move it towards the house. Nick stopped and looked around the small paved court-yard.

Somehow desert areas weren't meant to look snow-blown and frigid, but already he knew better. The construction made sense. A seven-foot high, adobe wall squared up the "L' of the house with the one next door, and formed the small paved patio he stood in. Unpaved areas within it allowed hardy cacti and dark-green, animated date palms to grow, and bare bushes nestling amongst them were worked around two rustic wooden benches anchored firmly to the stout outer wall. Although denuded for the winter, Nick could see they were roses and had read somewhere that the rose was Iran's national flower. They were bound to be there somewhere. He nodded unconsciously. The courtyards would be cool in summer and sheltered from blasts of icy wind in winter, and the exuberant flowers would get some protection too.

The only other fixture was a battered, galvanised tank on a timber plinth leaning against the outer wall in one corner. The top was not completely parallel with the base. Sinclair saw where he was looking and grinned.

"That's the real bit of luxury, Nick. Water gets pumped up from one of the wells into the tank in the few houses with power, and it's plumbed into the houses. Running water is real up-market around here."

Nick followed the others inside, dropped his bags and waited for his pupils to widen. Webster had already dumped his bag into a bedroom pointed out by Sarah.

"We'll want a drink first up, laddie, so what's your poison? The guy you relieved left some bottles, but there's only whisky, brandy or some wine until we run up to the embassy."

Nick opted for whisky, Webster a brandy. Sarah declined on her way to the kitchen.

"Sarah's cooked up stew for us, Nick, but it won't be ready for a while. I'll give you some more stuff until then. You might want an early night."

"Sounds good to me, mate, I'm knackered. But why don't I have a look around first? It might save some nattering."

"Okay, laddie, it'll give me more time with the bottle." Sinclair's face creased and Nick smiled too, but he already suspected that booze compensated for something else in the Scot's life. Nick sipped from his drink before putting down his glass.

The inside of the house looked more familiar to him. Comfortable furniture and light, highly polished woodwork demonstrated a significant European influence, with armchairs, a settee, a cabinet and a television filling the sitting area. A kitchen squatted in the short 'L' at the end of the room, while a wooden table and chairs showed where they ate. An elderly oven and stainless-steel sink unit were pressed against two walls in the kitchen, and fridges propped up a third. One was electric, but the other obviously ran on kerosene. A medium-sized chest freezer butted up against that. Nick strolled back into the sitting area and took another sip before drifting towards the passageway.

Here the floors were also compacted earth as hard as concrete, and the bedrooms sported portiere not doors. He ran the heavy, woollen curtains through his fingers. They were as thick and heavy as carpets, and dyed in vivid primary colours of red, blue and yellow. Several similar squares adorned the sitting room walls. Obviously it was a local craft. And at first he thought the bedrooms would also be indigenous, but when he moved the curtains aside, Europe was in there too. The rooms were on the gloomy side and the windows narrow and high. He snapped on a light.

All three bedrooms looked the same, with a double bed, a wardrobe and a dresser pushed hard against the walls. There were no drapes on any of the small windows while in the truncated bathroom an exhaust fan compensated for no windows at all. It was comfortable enough without being flashy.

Nick wandered out to the lounge area again and nodded to Sinclair. "I'm happy enough, Jock, but why are the windows so small, and what's the rent like?" Sinclair squirmed more upright.

"Glass is bloody expensive out here, Nick, so you don't see much outside cities, but the rent's dead cheap. We pay a bigger duty-free booze bill than we do rent."

Nick was content and nodded his satisfaction.

Chapter Eleven

It didn't take Nick long to organise a simple routine, but then again it could hardly be called challenging. He'd flown Jet Rangers in Australia so he only needed a flight test before he left for Iran, and was flying on his second day at Qom. The company brief hadn't specified a flight schedule either. It had been left up to him. He had a get–together with the others and they elected for a flight at eight thirty in the morning and another at three in the afternoon. That gave them most of the daylight hours for shopping and servicing, and an early or late sunlight was better for surveying.That was fine on paper, but as the weeks slipped by, Nick realized that Jock had his maintenance to keep abreast of and Floyd his maps and reports to fiddle with. Only he was bored.

It was the Kavir that got his interest at first. The mobile bands of red, white, and yellow sands shimmered and wrestled incessantly to dominate each other, and rounded, puce mountains of weather-blasted rocks to the west provided relief from the gritty expanses. Often they were distorted by mirages, or lost all together in streaks of hazy azure, while sometimes he had to get airborne before they came into focus at all. It was bland, very bland, and it wasn't long before he yearned for the lush greenery he was used to.

Verdant, fertile fields ran along the river banks to be sure, getting browner and drier as they got higher, and larger, more majestic trees struggled in the lower gullies of the foothills, but the open desert supported little more than a few gnarled and stunted bushes. Colossi they weren't, and so sparse that they could be counted on one hand to the square mile. Momentary relief was provided by the antics of myriads of tiny desert finches inhabiting them thickly enough to snap off dry branches with loud cracks.

Most days were hot and dry and crowned by endless metallic-blue skies, the nights as clear as crystal and bitterly cold. But huge stars, flashing like diamonds tossed haphazardly on black velvet, did make up for those frigid, dangerous temperatures. Artificial light wasn't much of a competitor out in those lonely dust bowls, so there wasn't a lot else to look at anyway. It was not a place for city dwellers.

Nick had long ago landed from the early morning flight when spiraling dust devils started dancing half-heartedly before a strengthening breeze. He collapsed his five-foot-ten frame into a battered armchair in front of the plate glass window. Nick had spent a lot of his adult life wearing uniforms and suits, so jeans and a short-sleeve shirt were now as formal as it got.

He rested his scuffed desert suedes on the sill, retrieved his coffee from the floor, and scanned the hills idly, sipping from a mug that had been a laconic present from his engineer. It said something about FIG JAM. After a few gulps, he replaced the coffee mug with Zeiss 10 x 10's.

Nick already looked as if he belonged there. By then his skin was dark from the inevitable tan, and savage suns and high winds had etched a few more creases that thirty-six years might not have done on their own. He was the epitome of the Celtic Welsh really, but the normal sing-song lilt of the Welsh voice had largely been bred out of him. Rugby had re-shaped his nose slightly too, but he did smile easily enough, even though it tended towards the whimsical. He was more ruggedly manly than he was pretty.

Both choppers had needed some time-based maintenance that morning, so Jock Sinclair had designated it a non-flying day. The water was on the boil when Sinclair led his boys up from the hangar and signaled for coffees all round. Nick complied with a slight smile, suspecting it was another test, but made them anyway. Sinclair was about to comment but was distracted by a troop carrier pulling up in a cloud of fine sand and squealing brake pads.

His voice vibrated in a harsh whisper. "Careful, Nick, the bastards never came out here before."

Some sort of policeman climbed down as Sinclair and Nick moved to the entrance veranda. He wore a black shirt with a few gaudily colourful badges sewn on it and light-blue jeans with a handgun strapped to his belt. He hadn't shaved in days. Nick stepped down the steps and held out his hand.

"Nick Evans," he offered warily. The policeman would have looked menacing enough without the squint and the armed trooper who backed him up. He ignored the proffered hand.

"I know who you are, Evans. All foreign companies have been instructed to report any staff changes." His English was fractured but understandable.

Nick let his hand drop. "Fine, so you know what we do. How can I help?"

"My name is Mohammed Arak, but you can call me Mister Arak." He was deadly serious. "The revolutionary government is taking a greater interest in what happens in our country, so I wanted to see what went on out here." His voice raised an octave. "We need more control, Evans. From now, you will fly only one flight a day and report to the blue mosque in Qom if you want more. Also you will drive, not fly to Tehran, and in future, you are not to overfly any Iranian cities or establishments. Your flying is restricted to the Zagros only."

Nicks eyes half closed. He turned towards Sinclair, but the Scot gave nothing away.

Nick nodded. "That's not a major problem, mate. If the company wants to make an issue of it, they can. The less flying we do, the less we're likely to find, Mister Arak."

Arak sneered. "We can up the rate or nationalise everything if we want to, Evans. We'll let you know." The askew eyes bored into Nick's uncomfortably before Arak turned his back. Minutes later, they were heading back to Qom.

Nick called the office in Tehran as soon as he was back inside, but the company was non-committal. "Comply, don't rock the boat, Nick. There's some agro towards the company that's new. Tread carefully." Nick was infuriated and slammed down the phone. Sinclair beetled his brows.

"They haven't got any answers and told me to do what the pricks want. I'm sure they've got more clout than that, mate. They're a bunch of fucking pussies."

Sinclair nodded slightly, his eyes slitted.

"Well, we need some accurate info: first, so let's give them some time. We can't plan until we know what's really going down, but maybe we should start protecting ourselves just in case."

"I'll buy that, and our best source of info is the Brit Embassy. We'll nip up north and talk to Gerry. We could do with some duty-free and Floyd can nose around HQ."

"Sounds like a plan, mate. Gerry will know what's going on, and we'll go around the bloody twist speculating. You tell Floyd while I finish up here, but I'm driving. I know how to get there."

Nick didn't argue.

They set off at eight in the morning. To Nick, it seemed like a holiday, like a day release from prison. He kept Sinclair busy with his questions and Webster contributed his share. They dropped the Canadian at the company and were headed for Ferdowsi Avenue in what seemed like no time at all.

Hawkins was expecting them. Nick had let him know the day before and the diplomat descended the stairs two at a time. He thrust out a hand and shepherded them to a side-room.

Hawkins had swotted up on the politics of his posting some time before, and since then had learned a lot more. It was a tight situation with an uncertain outcome and he'd been told to play it close to his chest. And Hawkins was a game player. He was sympathetic but let their questions dictate how deep he went.

"So what's happening, Nick, how can we help?"

"We've just had a visit from some bloke in Qom who I'm sure does the mullah's dirty work. He's already restricted our flying and made a few veiled threats about our operation, but the company seems coy about doing anything. I want to know where we stand."

Hawkins nodded and unconsciously brushed his trousers while he thought.

"You know that the population is pretty diverse here, and it goes back a long way, but there is some recent stuff too. If you add separatist Kurds in the high country to that, and some unwelcome meddling by the west, it makes for quite a disjointed history. Coups have been two-a-penny around here for decades, five in this century alone, and we're hoping this will blow over soon, too."

Nick nodded. "I know the shah got ousted and replaced by a Muslim sect, but I'm not sure how that affects us."

"Okay. The Americans are copping it because they propped the shah up, and helped de-stabilise the Shia Arabs. The Arabs have played the religious card this time, and it looks like a winner. It's always been about religion, really, and nothing has changed." He shifted uncomfortably. "The Sunni Muslims down south are a bit more relaxed, and they and the minority religions hate the Shia, but obviously a lot of people don't. The election Khomeini won seemed a bit dodgy to us, but the world saw it as democracy in action, so they haven't kicked up much of a fuss."

72

"Jesus, so it's still a huge bloody mess and our biggest problem is we work for an American company."

Hawkins nodded. "You two are British subjects though, and that counts for something."

"So are things improving?"

"Not from what we can see, Jock. To be honest, we reckon the new regime would have done the shah in if they could have, but they knew the United Nations would go ape and didn't want to risk it. They may not be so lenient with other Persians they're looking for though."

"So what's your best guess?"

"We don't see any need for drastic action right away. Most of this is internal, so carry on doing what you do, but keep your heads down. Now that you've expressed concerns formally, we can put you on an official list, and your names will be filed as being protected by the embassy. I suggest you phone us once a week from now on so we can keep you updated. If things look really dodgy, we'll bring you in."

"Right, Gerry, we'll do that, and we'll need a top up from duty-free before we go. The only other thing is how do I get a gun license?"

"Christ, you aren't planning a stand-off, are you?" From his face, Nick couldn't say whether Hawkins was serious or not. Nick smiled.

"Course not, but all I've had to eat since I got here are stews. There's nothing wrong with them, but I fancy something a bit different sometimes. I've seen gazelle and wild goat amongst other things in the hills, and my housekeeper says that the locals knock them over when they can."

Hawkins grinned. "Okay, Nick. There isn't anything hard and fast about owning guns, other than licences for hand guns in cities. Half the frigging country is armed anyway, and a lot of hunting goes on around the Caspian. There's a big sports shop on the other side of Ferdowsi, about 200 yards south. I'll give you a certificate for a rifle

73

and they'll log it to the embassy. Is there anything else before I fill it in?"

"No thanks, mate. We'll pick up the Canadian and be on our way home after a top-up."

Chapter Twelve

Lank moth-eaten camels and pale, fast donkeys had often crossed Nick's path on flights in the hills, but they weren't practical for the pot. Nimble desert gazelle or incredibly agile ibex were something else again. With that in mind, he selected an expensive Tikka .222 hunting rifle of Finnish origin, with a powerful scope. And the bug had bitten, so he treated himself to a pair of spinning rods and a box of tackle to fish the high mountain streams with. An hour after getting home, the rifle was cleaned, the small magazine was loaded, and both rods were rigged with lures.

Jock had returned to his own pad by the time Nick stowed them. Sarah was making coffee.

"What's the difference between Shi'ites, Sunnis and Baha'i, Sarah?"

She brought the brews to the dining table and sat down before she spoke.

"Sharia law becoming most popular for Iran and countries nearby now, Nickie. It old Islam. Four wives for men, no teach or working for women, nobody allowed strong drink and men say who women can marry. City men like it, more jobs and learning for them, and if wives don't do as told, tell her to go with words, or even punish her bad. Not work in the country though." She paused to sip her drink.

"More Sunni in Iraq, Jordan and Saudi, but not much in Iran. Still not supposed to drink alcohol, but some women can go school and work in some areas, and have vote and not so ugly dresses. Still too strict for us though." This time she smiled.

"Okay, I'll buy that, but I don't understand Baha'i at all."

Sarah smiled again. "It mostly in Iran among my people, Nickie. Baha'i like taught today only in use about 150 years ago, but Bakhtaran peoples been worshipping pretty much same way, how you say—since time of stone. We make changes to suit us over many years."

Nick Evans pondered before his eyes cleared. "You mean it's been with you since the Neolithic, a long time ago, but it's changed with the centuries. The last time was about 150 years ago."

Sarah nodded. "Baha'i believe only one god, but different religions worship him in own way. Also, men have only one wife, and she work with him all the time. Children do too when older. Girls go to school as well as boys, and dance and singing and some bright clothes part of Bakhtaran way. Mullahs want us to stop drink and cover up more, but it part of celebrations. None of my people will change anything. Government tried before, but not many mullahs come into hills though."

"How about what other people believe?"

"In south of country, some Jewish people, some Sunni and some Zoroastrian people, and not all Bakhtaran people Baha'i neither. Us and other religions not close together enough to tell government that Sharia stuff not suit them though."

"Thanks, Sarah. You've given me something to think about." His own family couldn't get it right either and they were of the same bloody religion too.

There was another eighteen months to run on his contract, but he couldn't see it happening now.

Chapter Thirteen

He saw it before he heard it. "Shit! What was that?" The fluted legs of Nick's chair screeched loudly as he scrambled to his feet. He grabbed for the well-used 10 X 10's. It was around lunch time and Sinclair and three of his lads were playing cards at the small table. They froze as if waiting for a command to continue, watching closely as the pilot squeezed onto the tiny, paint-chipped veranda.

Outside, the blistering noonday heat hit Nick in waves. With the humidity close to zero, the hot, musty smell of dry sand wafted strongly on the light breeze, and wavering mirages blurred the distant horizon. Between the sand and sky there was a pale demarcation which jumped and slid randomly, as if separated by a thin sheet of turgid water. Nick tweaked the binoculars and saw what had grabbed his attention.

A smear of russet billowed rapidly above the shimmering horizon, supporting bruised purple clouds that raced angrily skywards. Jagged forks of blinding light jumped spasmodically as clouds muscled aggressively over the top of each other, causing the matte-red vortex to bulge even more prominently. Distant rumbles of thunder reached him every few seconds.

At first it reminded Nick of Uluru, that great, red monolith in the central Australian outback. He soon realized, however, that its rolling front was preceded by a soft, distinct hiss that growled menacingly between the grumble of angry crashes. Nick knew exactly what it must be. He dashed back into the crew-room.

"There's a bugger of a sand-storm on its way and it's not far off, Jock. Get the hangar shut down."

Questions would have been superfluous and Sinclair didn't waste time on them. He and his boys raced outside to the corrugated-iron shed while Nick wrenched the door to the survey office open. He yelled at a disconcerted Webster to get the windows closed.

Nick shut the air-conditioners down before racing to the small workshop for canvas sheets and cord, and in a mad dash around the demountable, tied them around the louvered metal boxes. By then Jock and his Pakistanis were breathing hard and ragged as they tumbled through the sliding door.

"I guess more flying is out of the question then, laddie." Sinclair gasped. "It's a pity we don't keep a few bottles out here." For any self-respecting Scottish engineer, a bottle of whisky was the first tool when there was a problem to solve. Nick smiled.

Only a few minutes later the first restless gust buffeted the building savagely, driving a red cloud of choking sand that obliterated the blazing sun in seconds. Dust filtered under the front door at first, but Jock quickly sealed the gap with an old, worn table cloth. It wasn't long before abrasive grit and howling winds were battering the building with an abandoned fury. The neon strips could barely cope with the gloom, and only yells got through the shrieks and bangs from the blistering storm. It didn't blow out until early evening.

The visibility was still low when they motored home that evening, with little more than the defused lights of Qom showing. It was the first time Nick had driven back in the dark and the brooding emptiness was eerie. He turned to Sinclair, who was driving.

"I didn't notice how little there is out here during the day, Jock."

"Aye it's a real surprise, laddie. Just Qom and a few farms and villages lit with kerosene lamps. We fly night circuits every couple of months to keep your night-hours up and we haven't done that yet. You'll see a bit more then."

Nick Evans realized he'd have to do that soon. "Is Qom the biggest city around here?"

"It is, lad, but it's not that big really, it just spreads a bit. Ayatollah Khomeini did his training there when he was a young clergyman, so now it's considered the country's holiest city. All inland towns are communication centres in Iran anyway, but that makes Qom seem more important than it really is. That's good though. It's too bloody holy for riots, but there isn't any entertainment for us either."

Nick nodded. Sinclair had been there over two years already and knew the local area. It got Nick thinking.

"Right, we'll get some night flying in next Wednesday and have our first look at the game tomorrow."

"Suits me, Nick, but I'm not into trophy hunting. I've done some shooting for the pot before, but if you want to get the heads mounted, go with someone else."

"That suits me too, Jock. Sarah's stews are great, but it's always a bloody stew no matter what's in it. Sometimes I fancy a roast or stir-fry, but I'd like to know where the meat comes from. What about a couple of quid on a one-shot one-carcass policy?"

"Aye, but we'll be doing it from the chopper. You'll have to land to get your shot in so I don't have to shoot on the move either." They were both grinning when they shook hands.

Chapter Fourteen

The recent coup hadn't exactly improved the company's prospects in Iran, but up to then it hadn't affected it much either. There was little point in an early morning rush though, so lounging in front of a biased, scratchy news service took precedence over an early morning flight.

Although TV wasn't exactly an art form on the high desert plains, two snowy channels did beam in from Qom, but not only was the sound quality poor, they were also in Farsi. Nick had picked up some of the language from news and foreign documentaries by then, so he and Jock made reading between the lines something of a competition. They confined it to bulletins and the odd history programs. It was about all they could stomach.

Nick had been in Iran virtually a year when his world started to change ominously. He was sprawled in an armchair half-watching the early news bulletin, but that morning it was different.

The news normally started with the same wavering, snowy static before a ten-minute religious harangue. This time the atmosphere crackled with tension, and a fuzzy picture hardened to where a wobbling camera panning over an angry, gesticulating crowd. Nick couldn't place the venue, but the dowdy chadors and scarves definitely looked Iranian. The excitement driving the jostling masses transcended what they were wearing anyway.

Nick sat bolt upright. He'd never seen a crowd as animated as they were. A procession of hyped-up talking heads added to the excitement as they blustered through similar broadcasts, all fighting for their fifteen minutes of glory. Nick Evans dragged his chair closer.

The wavering backdrop flicked and jumped erratically at first, but then it swung to a focused, wide-angle camera showing a gaggle of youngsters waving and yelling outside the tall, red-brick outer walls of a dazzling white façade. The males were easy to identify, but most of the girls were hidden inside acres of flowing material billowing like collapsed tents dragged in from the desert. Many of the youngsters held rough cardboard placards daubed in an untidy Arabic scrawl, but the picture of the US president on them was un-mistakable. Although glimpses of the building looked familiar, he couldn't place it, but the city was definitely Tehran. It got his attention. He yelled for the surveyor and his housekeeper.

Sarah bustled in from the kitchen, wiping plump hands on a muslin cloth. The surveyor appeared from his bedroom. Nick trusted her English much more then he trusted his Farsi.

"Something heavy is happening guys. Can we pick the bones out of it?" The surveyor nodded absently and pulled up a chair. Sarah didn't sit, instead moving behind Nick and unconsciously putting a light hand on his shoulder.

A different, animated babble now boomed from a local announcer. The snowy screen scanned to a horde milling aimlessly through lush green gardens bordered by concrete pavers and ornate cast iron lamp-posts.

"Boharesta Square," Sarah offered.

Other fuzzy landmarks swam into view, the atmosphere in each dark and excitable. All contained quotas of Iranians shouting angrily to each other, and Sarah recognised most of the sites. It was as if the whole population was on the move, as if people were filling up every open space that Tehran had to offer. Then the large building that had first caught Nick's attention swam back into view.

"American Embassy." There was no hesitation.

By then a camera had fought through to the gates which allowed the crowded courtyard to be photographed. It showed sullen, un-armed Marines in khaki and white, surrounded by dozens of animated people in robes. Bewildered Caucasians were kept apart from the Marines on the concrete steps of the entrance, while friends or relatives dragged local staff through the milling crowds, their Western garb dishevelled, askew and torn.

And the noise and excitement was growing not diminishing. A camera panned to an anonymous woman in a blue chador, down to the rusty bolt cutters she held in both hands, and then to the Embassy gates. A thick chain was still draped through the heavy steel bars on one side, but it had obviously been cut through and now swung gently as more rioters nudged through the yawning entrance. It didn't take a brain surgeon to explain the method of entry. Nick couldn't believe what he was seeing.

"Christ, they've taken over the American Embassy. That's part of a country's home territory, you can't do that." He looked around wildly, but the Canadian just shrugged.

"They say it not government, it done by students."

"Well, some of the bastards don't look like students to me."

It was mesmerising, horribly addictive, but the channel was soon recycling the same stories over and over, with the same howling crowd shots being repeated endlessly. Khomeini and his clergy remained ominously silent.

Sarah had chores to do and left Nick and the surveyor to toss around the implications, but it left them going round in circles. Nick jumped to his feet.

"I'll try the phones at the airfield, mate. Jock can come with me and we'll try to raise someone in Tehran. Keep watching, and if anything new pops up, let me know."

He hurried next door to collect Jock.

That morning Laleh Amini had fronted up to the American Embassy quite early. She had one report to finish and another she'd barely started, dealing with emigration trends linked to religious affiliations. It was already becoming a hot topic and there was a deadline.

Laleh skipped up the entrance steps and was let in through the heavy front doors by a young Marine guard she'd known for some time. Even so she flashed her ID. Marines were like that. The banal pleasantries they swapped brought a smile to both faces, and only moments later she was letting herself into her small, first floor office.

She flicked the kettle on before opening up a battered filling cabinet, and by the time she'd rooted out the reports the kettle was singing. Laleh made herself a jasmine tea and settled down with the paperwork.

She remained absorbed for the next hour, barely registering the vehicles crunching the gravel of the car park below. Minor demos and even the odd flag burning had been going on for some time, but usually they were over by mid-morning. But on that morning there was something menacing about the yells. The loud, almost musical hub-bub cut into her subconscious and she looked up. Mystified, she moved to the window.

It wasn't all that chaotic out front yet but already leaning that way. Two gesticulating Marines stood inside the perimeter walls against the large, wrought-iron gates while an angry, swirling mob rattled the stout ironwork from the outside. As she watched, someone cut through a chain on the gates with bolt cutters and the horde poured into the car park. The two navy infantrymen were quickly overwhelmed.

Several other Marines saw it happen and fired off tear gas canisters before flying down the embassy steps to help. Laleh realized they wouldn't use lethal weapons against an unarmed home crowd though, and moments later they were also surrounded by chanting youngsters. A number of embassy staff was dragged out to the car park with them. She looked around and realised that some of her files were sensitive. Laleh dashed back to her desk and began stacking them back in the cabinet.

A more insistent racket in the large working space outside the offices now virtually drowned out the muted sounds from outside. Looking through the half-glass walls, she saw dozens of robed locals racing through the large outer office in noisy excitement, tossing machines and papers towards the floor as they passed. She rushed to lock the door but stopped a few paces short.

Two older males in jeans and black shirts peered in, one whippet thin, the other bordering on obese. They reminded her of a Laurel and Hardy film. Laleh almost smiled until she saw their eyes.

The way the thin one opened her door and slowly edged in was creepy enough, but it was terrifying when the obese one slowly closed off the venetian slats. Involuntarily, she took a step backwards. The thin one continued his slow advance until she was hard up against her desk then unexpectedly slapped her across the face. Laleh ducked as her head snapped sideways, her eyes instantly leaking, only to see him already loosening his belt as she faced him again. She knew what was coming and her fury was mindless in its intensity. She launched herself at him, leading with her longish nails, and raked his sweating face and neck.

This time he cursed and hit her hard in the solar plexus with a balled fist. Laleh went sprawling backwards across her desk and hadn't even gasped properly before her arms were pinned savagely above her head by the other one. Her assailant yanked her mini-skirt hard up around her waist and she felt a cold draft as her nylon panties were torn from her. All she could think of through her sobs was that the bastards had done this before.

Laleh screamed and struggled as she felt herself pulled half off the desk surface, but with her legs unsupported and torso pinned hard onto the desktop, there was nothing much she could do. She caught a whiff of foul breath as her legs were spread, and groaned deeply when he penetrated her roughly. Time stood still for her after that, but really it was quick. She barely noticed when they changed places.

The obese one finished quickly too, but she only became aware of being dumped on the carpet when the thin one delivered a final casual kick to her abdomen.

Nick Evans opened up the Cherokee along the sandy road to the airfield, beige grit arcing high from the racing rear wheels. Small, heavier pebbles spat viscously sideways as he drifted through the flat, dusty corners, and the potholes on the road edges threw Sinclair around the confines of his seat. The Scot cursed bitterly and yelled to Nick to slow down. The airfield was only a few kilometres away, and the pilot wasn't committed to such a destructive speed, but he just couldn't help himself.

Within minutes, they were rolling into the ominously quiet drome. The squat company complex still looked isolated, lifeless and forlorn, and there were no fresh wheel tracks around their buildings. There were no signs of life around the domestic terminus either, just a pair of vehicles parked in its hazy morning shade. Nick left it late, screeching the SRV to a sliding halt outside the pre-fabricated crew-room. It would always be the crew-room to him, a hangover from his navy days.

Two handsets, one in the survey office the other in the communal centre, worked better than most. Instant communication with HQ in Tehran and decent air traffic and weather info were essential to flight operations, so the system had absorbed a fair bit of company money. Nick headed for a phone while Jock checked out the hangar.

He tried head office in Tehran first, but the phone on the other end rang endlessly. Repeating the call got the same result. Phoning the American Embassy obviously wouldn't help much either, so he tried a number for the British Embassy, and was patched through to Hawkins almost immediately. "Gerry, Nick Evans at Qom, what the hell is going on?

"You may well ask, old son. We're still trying to get a handle on it ourselves."

"Have they really taken over the American Embassy?"

"That's what it looks like, and we're afraid it might happen here as well. The boss sent the local staff home just in case. That's why I'm doing a stint on the phones."

"But that's bloody illegal. It just can't happen." Nick Evans knew he was stating the obvious but didn't know what else to say.

"You're right about that, Nick. It's a real international cock-up. The government was quick to blame the students, said it had nothing to do with them, but our guess is that the mullahs are behind it. Khomeini's pretty shrewd though and could be waiting to see what Carter does before he moves again. If there's a violent America reaction, the Ayatollah can quickly defuse it, but if there's not, he'll milk it for all its worth. Our SIS bloke thinks that Carter will wimp out, so it's anybody's guess."

"What about companies like mine?"

"The party line is that they've been closed temporarily to protect the staff, but I reckon that's bullshit. I don't think the Americans are ever likely to open up again."

"So how the hell do we get out?"

"Well, you're better placed than most. I said that you and Jock are British subjects, but working for an American company doesn't exactly help you much. You're on the Embassy social list though, and you've helped us with visiting dignitaries, so I reckon you're pretty flame proof." Hawkins sucked in a ragged breath, almost reluctant to go further.

"Take my advice, and back off for the moment, Nick. A lot of people have been shot and others have been lynched and left hanging on building site scaffolding up here, but no foreigners that we know about. It's still a bit hazy, but it looks as if some sort of payback is going on. It seems to be restricted to a few bigger cities so far, and most of the attention is on Tehran. Keep your head down and ring me in a week. It should be a lot clearer by then."

Nick's voice speeded up a notch, the sing-song Welsh tone now more audible. "We've got enough stuff to survive that okay, Gerry, but a week sounds like a bloody long time before we get more information. After that we'll start running out of things and none of us fancy tromping around Qom right now. I'll give it a go, but if things do change I'll be yelling immediately."

"At-a-boy, Nick." Hawkins sounded relieved. "If you get a girl on the switch ask for extension twenty-three, you'll get straight through to me."

Nick Evans looked thoughtful when he put the phone down. He briefed Sinclair when he got back to the crew-room.

Chapter Fifteen

The next day Nick took Jock on a short sortie more to observe the game's reaction to the chopper than to actually hunt. He ignored a bunch of camels breaking ahead of the helo, their winter coats streaming raggedly in the wind, and then surprised a flock of mountaineering ibex leaping up a steep rock face. The chopper could slide up and down the crags with them and that was all they needed to know right then.

They went looking for gazelle after that and ran a small herd down just as they were about to quit. They could easily out distance them and follow where they went, but the big surprise happened when they flared to a hover to let them go. The herd stopped too, nervously watching it. That was too much of a temptation. Sinclair dropped a fine doe. They were flush with success when they returned with the carcass and overly flamboyant when they shared it out.

Two days later, Nick took the Canadian on a meandering, low-key flight into the lower ranges, more for something to do than the chance of finding the big one.

There wasn't a lot on the lower slopes, just acres of beige, dried grass being tugged at by herds of shaggy sheep or multi-coloured goats, attended by thickly-clad locals on small, hairy ponies. Higher up, rustic animal enclosures and adobe dwellings dotted the more sheltered valleys, already looking abandoned for the winter. Those huts often acted as refuges from savage autumn storms in the cold months, but most of the people had already moved lower for the winter. For Nick, it had been more about escaping the soul-crushing boredom, about escaping into a pristine, cool atmosphere as clear as the best Dartford crystal.

The chopper was back on the ground by ten and Webster disappeared into his office with coffee, maps and forms. Nick leafed through a flight magazine for the twentieth time, but really he was watching the surveyor.

He couldn't work out what all the writing was about, what Webster was so absorbed in. The flight had been short on possibilities, a busted flush, but the surveyor scribbled furiously for thirty minutes before rolling up what he was working on. Nick looked up when the Canadian left the office.

"It's still quite early, Nick. I think I'll run this up to Tehran and try to find out what's going on from my embassy."

Nick's eyes narrowed perceptibly. "Is that necessary, Floyd? We didn't find any minerals and the British Embassy said to give it a few more days yet."

"I know, but I'd rather get a handle on things sooner than later. My lot might have something the Brits haven't got."

"Well, it's your choice, mate, but I don't think I'd want to be driving around Tehran this week. You know the company office is closed down, don't you?"

"I do, buddy, but it's only a few hours round trip. I'll nip home for some stuff in the second Jeep first." He forestalled any more chit-chat by walking out. Nick followed his hurried movements, but the penny had dropped. There wasn't much he could do about it.

They all knew better than to bank in-country and none had many possessions with them. The fewer ties in Iran, the better. Each received just enough at a local bank for their purchases and daily expenses, while the company payed for fuel, housing and airfield rental through the American Foreign Office. They had the odd knick-knack and a battered case or two for clothing, but that was about all. It wasn't desperate yet, the pressure hadn't built up all that high, so drastic remedies weren't called for.

Nick guessed what Webster was going home to collect. The reports and the rolled up maps were window dressing, his motivation for the trip if he was questioned. Nick watched him take off in a cloud of choking dust as Sinclair wiped greasy hands on a rag.

"Where's Floyd off to?"

"He said Tehran for a chin-wag with his Embassy, but I don't think we'll see him again. Canada's a bit remote from all this so I reckon he's hoping they can get him out while things are a bit confused." Nick was conciliatory. "Can't blame him, I suppose. It'll get worse before it gets better."

"Aye, you're right, laddie, but where the hell does that leave us?"

"All I can suggest is that we look as if we're doing what we're paid to do. You keep both birds filled up and ready and I'll go through the paperwork in case there's anything a bit iffy. We're still okay for food and other stuff, and the fuel and rent are still being paid, so we can relax. I'll phone the Brits the day after tomorrow and see if anything new has turned up."

"I'm okay with that, laddie, but if the whisky runs out, I start getting cranky."

Nick Evans grinned. The Scot wasn't joking.

He shredded some of the more doubtful reports and surveys that were stacked in the map drawers while Jock Sinclair finished up. With only one Cherokee out front, he had to ferry the rest back home anyway.

There wasn't much that was controversial. Some of the jottings in the margins could be taken two ways and there were results only the company knew about, but within a half hour, he was looking for something else to do, and swept the silent acres with the 10 x 10's. He was becoming fascinated with the lonely landscapes he was in the middle of. Waning rays of sun glanced off rocks from a profusion of different angles, and delicate pastels and darker purple shadows flitted and jumped endlessly with the sun's steady passage. He was refocusing when the phone shrilled loud and insistently. Puzzled, he turned. It couldn't be the company or the American Embassy, so who the hell was phoning him out there?

"Nick Evans, can I help you?" There was a long pause.

"Nick, do you recognise my voice? We played rugby at Dartmouth together in the good old days, and met briefly in Tehran about a year ago." The English was impeccable with hardly a trace of an accent.

He thought hard before the puzzlement cleared. "Fred, is that you?"

"Close enough, Nick, that'll do. I think I'm in deep shit friend, so I'm phoning from a hotel. I need to get away, but I can't trust the office phones, and driving from here would be too risky. There are only two pretty long roads out, so they're easy to block, and I thought maybe you could do something. I know it's a big ask, but you know what's happening and where I come from. It's not about getting the sack, mate, it's about being topped, about disappearing all together." Farhad Amini sounded edgy and desperate. "Think about it, Nick. I can't plan much else until I know one way or the other, but it's got to be soon if you can."

Nick hissed. Right then he felt completely out of his depth. He had enough problems of his own and this was outside anything he could have dreamed about.

"Where are you, Fred, and what the fuck do you want me to do?"

"I don't trust the bloody phones at your end either, Nick. If nobody is listening in now, they soon will be. Give me a bell from some hotel in town at nine tomorrow morning if you'll help. I'll wait for thirty minutes. If I don't hear from you, I'll try something else."

"Give me the number and I'll think about it, Fred. That's all I can promise."

"Fair enough. Can you remember my personal score on the day we played against Sandhurst together?" Nick Evans thought and then grunted a yes. "Okay. Add that number to any different digits." Amini rattled off a string of numbers.

Fred's tally had been three points. It was the match-saving try. "Okay, Fred, nine o'clock tomorrow." There was little else he could say right then no matter what his choice might be.

"Thanks, Nick. I wouldn't have asked unless I was desperate."

Sinclair secured the hangar with a rusted chain and brass padlock and strolled back to the prefab with his laughing, jostling team. Nick was deep in thought on the veranda when they arrived, and pre-occupation oozed from him in waves. The Scot sensed it before he even got close to the grimy sliding doors. Nick ran his fingers through longish, dark hair.

"Imran, would you give me ten minutes with Jock before I drive you home?"

"No problems, Mister Evans, we'll get a coffee." The Pakistanis were still laughing when they bundled into the communal area. He'd never been able to get them to call him by his first name.

Sinclair paused short of the veranda. Nick negotiated down the warped steps.

"So, what's all the secrecy about, laddie?"

Nick wasn't sure where to begin.

"I've just had a weird phone call. Someone I knew a long time ago." He stopped, still unsure.

"And?"

"He wants some sort of help," the pilot blurted.

"So, Will you do it or not?"

"I don't know what he wants yet, but it sounds a bit complicated. I've got to phone from a hotel in Qom tomorrow. He'll tell me then."

"How well do you know the guy; do you trust him?"

"We were quite friendly once, but that was at Dartmouth fourteen years ago. I've only seen him at an Embassy cocktail party in Tehran since. He was at their defence HQ then. That's the only other time we've met."

"Time isn't the issue here, though, laddie, it's about something else. Would he help you if you needed it?"

"I suppose so, but I don't know really. I can't imagine me asking anybody for help anyway."

"That's self-deluding bullshit, Nick. You're already leaning on the Embassy and you know I'd be there for you." Sinclair sounded angry, maybe even a little sad.

"Our job attracts either weirdos or loners, laddie, and you're not an odd-ball. You've been in combat and you've got a bravery medal, and anyone who flies those bloody things for a living isn't a wimp. How about the weather you went up in looking for those two lost kids this year. They would have died in those mountains if you hadn't persisted. No boyo, it's not courage you lack, it's a commitment to people. You've got a lot of acquaintances but not many friends, and you've deliberately kept it that way."

Nick Evans exploded. "What are you, a fucking philosopher or psychiatrist or something? I don't see you inundated with too many friends either."

"I've been at this game a lot longer than you, sonny, and I've got a lot of mates in the shit-holes we work in. That's where they are though, not in some cosy headquarters somewhere. I'd help them and they'd help me if it was necessary, and we wouldn't have to think about it. Maybe that's the difference between you and me."

"Well, thanks for the bloody lesson, Jock, but it doesn't exactly help. I still don't know what to do."

"Aye, well if it's my advice you're after, it can't hurt to find out what he wants. We know what's going on here, and only the shah's people would have got overseas officer training fifteen years ago. No points for guessing why he wants to disappear. This regime will be feeding people like him their own bollocks before long."

Nick was still angry and defensive, but Jock made sense. The ego had taken yet another battering, but he stifled a heated retort. It wasn't the time or place and he knew it.

"Okay, I'll make the phone call and you ride shotgun. We'll take Sarah along and it'll look like a shopping trip."

"Aye, that sounds more like it, laddie. The choppers are both serviceable and topped up, and I've filled two fifteen-gallon plastic containers. It might be difficult to get a fuel bowser over before too long. If you're okay with that, we'll be on our way home."

Chapter Sixteen

Sleep hadn't been easy to come by throughout that long, stuffy night, and Nick was too agitated to stay in bed. He paced the empty house and courtyard before the dawn's infancy. He wouldn't have thought it possible, but even the earth floors echoed eerily with Webster gone. Sarah wasn't due for another two hours either, so he brewed up.

Back in the day, his class found a different frustrating challenge in every flying lesson, but he hadn't felt this nervous and insecure since then. And that got him thinking.

What the hell was he getting himself into; how risky would it be, really? And if dangerous ears and eyes were already monitoring them, who the hell did they belong to?

What Jock had come up with the day before sounded reasonable, leaving him with some options, but somehow it didn't feel quite the same today. Nick had a sneaking suspicion that once he heard Amini's voice again he'd feel compelled to try whatever he wanted anyway. That cranky, enigmatic Scot had got under his guard and pricked his conscience again. Sinclair was forever an amateur philosopher and some of his jibes wriggled into areas that were supposed to be hidden and safe.

Then another disquieting thought hit him. Did he have any friends, or were they just acquaintances? Did he get along with people, or did he merely use them? He'd never married, hadn't even had a relationship that lasted more than a few weeks, and he'd certainly never met a woman he could consider a soul mate. He'd had no answers then so he'd quickly buried those fragmented, disturbing images, but it seemed to get harder each time. He'd begun to suspect he was emotional driftwood.

Nick Evans tried switching off. Qom was less than thirty minutes by road and it was some time yet before he had to go. He brewed another coffee and took a tentative, uninterested bite from a sandwich before picking up an old *National Geographic*. But he couldn't concentrate, and his maps didn't help much either. He dumped them in frustration, dragged on shorts and T-shirt, and went for a run.

A spruced-up Sinclair wandered in with forty minutes to spare, looking cool, casual and unconcerned. Nick was back to pacing by then.

"Relax, laddie, we'll have a better handle on it shortly."

"Fuck you and the horse you rode in on. We could have enough problems of our own before this lot's over."

"Take the long view then, Nick. A few more won't make much bloody difference."

"I knew you'd say that, you prick, but I've been thinking about it. If we do pick him up, what happens after that? We're restricted to Qom and Tehran and he'll still be smack in the middle of a huge unfriendly country. His bloody problems won't be over by a long way."

"Aye, but we don't know that, laddie. He might have it all planned from here on in."

Nick shook his head. "I doubt it. He doesn't even know how he's starting out yet, and if he stays here for a while, we'll have to be really careful. If we're caught harbouring him, we'll be as popular as a pork chop in a synagogue.

"Aye, well we better not get caught then, eh."

Nick threw his hands towards the heavens.

Those with warrior genes can get a bit hyperactive at time. They need something concrete to settle them down. Nick Evans needed to be on the move. He gave Sarah a call.

"Bugger it, Jock, let's do it. I'm fed up with going around in circles."

"Right, sunshine, but I'm driving. You're so wound up we'd be bloody lucky to get there in one piece."

Nick knew better than to protest. What the hell, it was less than thirty kilometres anyway. Then he remembered he needed coins. In his haste, he wrenched a top drawer out completely and left it on the dresser, but felt himself calm down as soon as they moved toward the vehicle. Sinclair could sense it too and smiled.

It took Jock Sinclair twenty-five minutes before he edged through the outskirts of the small city. The crowds still seemed indifferent to the Europeans, but then again Qom had benefited from the odd company project over the years, and the people were used to seeing company vehicles on shopping trips. The explicit logos on the Cherokee attracted only a few casual side glances and that could end up being a bonus.

Sinclair slid into a parking spot near the busy, odorous market in the shadow of a blue, high-domed temple. Nick helped Sarah wrestle her straw shopping bags free before he headed towards the town centre. Sarah went for the pungent, colourful stalls.

Nick looked around carefully before sliding into one of the smaller, less pretentious hotels. He'd deliberately avoided the few high-rises that dominated close to the markets, but even that hotel was owned by an American chain. He knew the phones would work in there, and five minutes to nine was close enough.

Nick dialed. The phone at the other end was picked up instantly.

"It's me, Fred."

"Thanks for calling, Nick. I really mean that."

"So, how do you think I can help?"

Amini had already thought about what to say. "I'm stationed at Abadan, a small city in the Shatt-Al-Arab delta, close to Iraq. I'm a commander now and CO of a flotilla of six patrol boats that run from a small naval base on the Karun River. The Iraqis are building up a big army position just across the river from us, but nobody knows what for yet, so we're building one north of the city ourselves. I need to disappear before something solidifies, mate." He caught his breath.

"Right now the whole area is pretty hot politically. It's probably why I haven't been picked up, but I hear it's happening in town."

hit, Fred, Abadan and back, that's a long way! The things I fly haven't got anything like the legs for that. There are heaps of people at your end too, so it would be difficult to scrounge fuel as well."

"I know, Nick. I've been hammering the maps too. The Karun is navigable to Vey where it joins the Dez, and I'm pretty sure the Dez is okay, but there's a hydroelectric dam being built where it leaves the mountains. Are you familiar with Do Rud on your side of the mountains? It's a Bakhtaran town with a few mullahs but nothing high-brow."

Nick thought about it. "I've flown around north of there for sure, but not down the river."

"Okay. The patrol boats have got a fairly shallow draft, so I know I can get one that far, and most of the people in that area are Bakhtaran. I should be able to pay for a vehicle to get us beyond the dam site and we can hire a motorboat above the dam site to get to Do Rud. My boats normally carry twelve blokes, but I'm working on a smaller crew to do a maintenance run with me. They're all Bakhtaran. Not everybody here follows the radical clergy and they want to get out too.

"Can you get as far as Do Rud?"

"I haven't got a map handy, Fred, but isn't Do Rud hundreds of miles from Abadan?" Seamen and airmen think in nautical miles.

"It's slightly under 300. The boats can do twenty-five knots, with a range of over a 1000 miles at economical cruising. Distance isn't a problem, but I do have to get through both Ahvaz and Dezful at night for obvious reasons. That's about 200 miles in the first fifteen hours, but that's my problem, not yours."

"If I remember rightly, Do Rud is less than a 300 mile round trip from here, and I've got long-range tanks. I could do that okay. There isn't much in the way of roads on the higher slopes either, and the few people up there are related to the people in our town. Above that it's a water-shed and that isn't populated at all. As long as I avoid a couple of bigger towns, I'll be okay."

"You're making it sound feasible, Nick. I'd be eternally grateful."

"Cut the crap, Fred, we're not there yet. When's this all supposed to happen?"

"Towards the end of next week. The Sabbath is pretty strictly enforced amongst the civilians down here now, so I'll book the boat out for a test on Thursday afternoon. I'll tell the staff I'll chug around up river until we get it fixed. The base would be pretty much shut down for Friday's Sabbath by the time we'd be expected back, so we probably won't be missed until Saturday or even Sunday."

"So where do you want to meet me and when?"

"How about twenty-five klicks south of Do Rud at 1400 on the Saturday? I can do that and it's still pretty isolated and mountainous in there."

"Okay, but anything could happen in the next week. I'll phone this number next Wednesday at the same time and have a look around tomorrow to bowl out any problems. We'll have to be honest with each other though, Fred. I work for an American company and things are a bit unsettled at this end too."

"Thanks, Nick, and honestly I won't drop you in it."

Nick Evans was deep in thought when he replaced the receiver. It was a good ten minutes before he climbed into the Jeep. He studiously ignored an inquisitive glance from Sinclair. Sarah had returned with brimming baskets as he arrived, so he didn't open up on the trip back south either.

Chapter Seventeen

They dropped Sarah off before heading back to an ominously quiet airfield. Sinclair made coffee while Nick laid large-scale topographical maps on a table. The Scot had mugs in his hand when he sat.

"I've held my peace for some time now, laddie, but if you don't say something soon I'm going to smack you in the bloody eye."

Nick waved at the map. "I'm sorry, Jock. I needed this in front of me to make some sense out of it."

"So what does your navy mate want?"

Nick opened and smoothed out a plastic-covered small scale. He pointed out Abadan.

"That's where he is." He pointed south of Do Rud. "And that's where he wants to be picked up."

Sinclair contemplated the vast acres of beige and purple, only studded with strips of green around the coast and rivers. "Well, you're the one who knows about distances and payloads. Can it be done?"

"He runs a squadron of patrol boats and reckons he can get as far as Do Rud. I've done a few surveys around there and the birds can make that okay."

"Sounds like a piece of piss then, laddie."

"Hang on though, Jock. Something is already going on down there. People are disappearing and someone is enforcing some pretty harsh rules, and it's only the military that haven't been affected so far. Iraq is building a big army base across the border from Abadan and nobody's worked out what it's for. The military haven't been shaken down yet, but it will happen."

"So what have you agreed to?"

"I'll do the planning at this end, and he'll fix up what he needs to at his. I'll give him a quick phone call a week from now to confirm."

"Right-o, laddie. We'd better lay a few smoke-screens then."

Jock Sinclair and his boys dragged a machine onto the oil-stained pad and plugged in a chipped yellow battery starter. Low, thin vortexes of sand whirled and cavorted around the company buildings, scouring the flaked paint further, but nothing else stirred. The civil terminal flickered in the distance, seemingly liquid and distorted, more a kid's drawing than a set of buildings.

Nick climbed the steps onto the veranda and checked towards Qom. From higher up, he could make out minarets and high-rises dancing randomly in the afternoon heat, but no army vehicles drove the dusty bitumen strip that ran to Kashan.

Nick was carrying two lightweight headsets and a map when he strode out. There were two heads in the cockpit when they surveyed, so Sinclair had been elected to keep up appearances. The Scot didn't know much about minerals, but he had a firm grip on the Tikka.

They were ready to go in minutes. Although it was a courtesy, Nick did radio airport ops. for flight clearance, but he wasn't surprised when it was ignored. He tried again before giving Imran a thumbs up. Nick kept low as he accelerated past the mud-brick terminal building, but it was impossible to see through the reflective film on the windows. Nobody came out to watch him whistle by.

They buzzed up a slow, placid Qom river, and only started to climb after the chopper passed Shahabad. Thin carpets of green along the river's edge were dotted with herd animals browsing amongst stands of healthy walnut and fig, while most of the lower ravines sprouted oak, poplar and willow. Above that, flattened, pied tussock covered the flats between the rocky tors, and the higher he went, the more the rustling grasses were burnt to a uniform straw by uncaring elements. The bare, stunted bushes that linked them were as twisted as varicose veins. Battered coastal mangrove looked healthier.

But it wasn't surprising, really. Up there it was frigid almost all year round with the rolling mountains seeing more precipitation than the inland plateaus ever did. As they climbed, shallow trickles threaded haphazardly around the rocks and yellowed grass, the tumbling, icy water flashing silver rays as it merged and widened into meandering streams. But flora needed something more than just water to flourish up there. It didn't seem to worry the few ibex they saw.

The temperature plummeted noticeably as they climbed, and now eroded, snow-covered peaks filled the Perspex windscreen. Sinclair called them braes, and couldn't break the habit. They didn't look much like the misty green Scottish high-lands to Nick.

And he needed this recce. The pick-up would be over territory he hadn't flown before, with the isolated hamlets and small villages connected by a network of dusty, rural roads. He needed to know exactly where they led.

The mountain people were Bakhtaran themselves, he wasn't worried about them. They were descended from the earlier Persians and it was unlikely they'd even seen an ayatollah, let alone tried to appease one. Some of the larger towns and small cities, he was less sure about. There could be other than Bakhtaran eyes up there, particularly on the lower slopes.

High in the hills, Nick followed meandering streamlets that dodged through the lonely beige valleys carved into the lilac mountains eons before. Streaks of thin radiation fog mottled the saturated, boggy ground, while the few tracks were little more than narrow, potholed wheel-ruts. The chopper did run down some ram-shackled, temporary dwellings on the lower, less barren slopes, but they were far apart and he was lucky if he saw them before he thundered passed.

And as he got in deeper still, the snow-dusted hills became as under populated as the Antarctic on a bad day. There were no herds or people up there at all. The land was useless to build on, far too difficult to drag materials up to anyway, and there was nothing around to heat the dwellings with either. Even the yellowed pickings the herds might scavenge were short and sparse. A prickling apprehension that had been with him since the phone call began to abate. It was cold, stark and unfriendly, just what Nick wanted.

Neither were there any surprises up there. He could see that the vast Zagros chain was composed of old, soft rock by the way it had been battered and broken by unforgiving elements. It was as if a celestial giant had lashed around with a huge blunt axe. Bands of granite were studded with darkened areas of grey shale, but erosion had far out-reached any growth from tectonic plate movement. The rounded, rolling range was definitely on the decline.

They'd mostly been muttering in mono-syllables up to then, but the next stretch was over virgin territory that the trip could hinge on. Nick handed the map to the Scot and pointed with a finger.

"The Dez is about ten klicks ahead and loops back to Do Rud about twenty klicks north. Got it?"

"Aye, I can see that. What do you want to do?"

"Keep us at least fifteen klicks south east of Do Rud but I want to see what it looks like down river. Take us southwest to avoid the bigger towns. The people are mostly herders around here, but some could be a bit iffy."

"Okay, your first heading is 210."

Nick descended as he skirted a small, indistinct township before turning towards the gloomy, steep ravine that the river had channelled for itself. This was new ground. The hills were steeper and more barren.

Nick had never flown south of Do Rud, so he didn't know what to expect. The single railway track running along the river wasn't part of it. That could be a real danger if knowledgeable eyes saw him parse. The synapses sparked instantly, fuelled by a tidal wave of adrenalin. Once in the river valley, he'd figured it would be a cake-walk, but all that changed in just thirty seconds.

Nick knew that the rail line from Tehran ran to Do Rud , but he hadn't known it carried on through the mountains. And the steel track sparkled and glittered where it was hit by the rays of morning sunshine. It obviously got some use.

"Shit, I thought there was only a dirt road in there, not a bloody railway as well?" His voice was a notch higher.

"I can't see a railway on this map, Nick, but it's small scale and a 1938 edition. The track could be newer. Did your mate mention it?"

"No way. Perhaps he didn't want to spook me. Right-o, mate, get us out of here before some tosser wonders what we're up to."

They returned low level, landing fifty minutes later.
A dented fuel truck rumbled up when they called for it and the driver joked in his fractured English as he helped them refuel. Things were still normal, but Sinclair knew that the small airfield got half its annual revenue from the company alone, so he wasn't surprised. Amen. He after-flighted the machine before his boys helped him put it away.

Intestinal butterflies were still with Nick when he sketched a route on his topographical. The railway had him worried, although a later, large-scale map of the area did show tracks all the way to Abadan. He'd never used that map and had rarely spotted a train using the tracks north of Do Rud either, but 'Murphy's Law' didn't apply just in Ireland. It could be a problem, but he had to get philosophical about it. Down there was Amini's problem. He just needed to amend the pickup.

Nick poured over a brand new Do Rud 1 in 25 scale map he'd bought locally. A tiny, isolated village called Lenjabad hugged the rail line several kilometres into the river gorge, but the dusty road wasn't marked beyond it. No other villages showed on the line either, none even got close, and there were no junctions of road or rail until the track crossed through to the Euphrates Plains. A poorly maintained dirt track at the start shouldn't matter all that much.

Getting that flight in early had been the right thing to do. Now he had answers to many of his questions, and many potentials weren't problems any more. He'd go for another flight in the high country, but he didn't need to visit Do Rud again. Nick scribbled a few things to jog his memory as the maintenance team straggled into the building.

"Got the escape all sorted out then, laddie?" Jock looked serious.

Nick flashed Sinclair a warning glance.

"Relax, Nick, we can't do this without help from these lads. They're Pathans, real tough bastards. I'd trust them with my life, mate. They're going to see him when we get back anyway." Sinclair pulled out a chair and sat opposite the pilot.

"The chopper ride isn't the end of it either. He's going to spend time in your shack and he's hardly going to prance around in a fancy bloody uniform while he does it. Baggy Pakistani clobber and a headdress sound's okay though, and where do you think we'll get that from? If you've got it sorted, include them. They'll appreciate the confidence."

Nick inclined his head. He could see through the reasoning. "You're right, Jock, but I've been regimented all my bloody life. I've had to live with all that need-to-know crap for donkey's years. This is all a bit new to me. I didn't think about the implications of most of the things I did before, but now it's different."

"Aye, but we're out on the end of a swaying branch this time, so we're going to need someone watching our six o'clock."

"I know, but it's a funny feeling. Nobody's relied on me for quite some time."

"Well I never, laddie, welcome back to the human race."

The Jeep snarled its way towards Qom again on the Wednesday morning, Nick in the passenger seat and Sarah behind with her basket. Sinclair parked in almost exactly the same spot, and while the housekeeper attacked the markets, the pilot strolled casually to the entrance of a different hotel. He and Jock had refined some more on another flight and it was a goer. He got through again without any problems.

"Fred; Nick, I'm happy to give it a go from this end."

"That's really great, Nick, because things are hotting up around here."

"Okay. There's a village on the river called Lenjabad thirty odd klicks southwest of Do Rud. I'll pick you up five klicks south of that. Did you know that a single track railway line runs from Do Rud to where you are?"

"I did, Nick. Two trains run in either direction each week. It figured in the plan originally, but there are a hell of a lot of long isolated stretches on route. We can't afford to be trapped if the train is searched, and you can bet your sweet ass it will be if someone notices we're gone."

"Well, if you're happy with it, it won't affect me much."

"It won't, Nick. My engines chief and four sailors will be with me. They're all Bakhtaran and it's only a few kilometres' walk to the roads and a railway station from there. They could be anywhere a few hours after we arrive, and they'll be amongst their own people anyway."

"Wouldn't it be easier for you to catch a train as well?"

"It's not so easy for me. My genes go back to Aryan Russians and Alexander the Great. It's why the skin's a lot lighter, and the nose can be a bit prominent on us males. I'd stick out like a sore thumb." Amini laughed.

106

"Former shahs used to hunt with hawks, Nick. They got to look like their birds in the end."

Nick smiled. "Okay, Fred, I'll be there at 1400 on Saturday. Is there anything else I can do?"

"That's it, Nick, I'll do the rest."

"Okay then, mate. Keep your head down."

Chapter Eighteen
Abadan

The light ivory skin and prominent aquiline nose did mark the tall, slim commander's genetic line. Farhad Amini lounged behind a solid wooden desk, with scratched black plastic in and out trays guarding one corner, and buff files stacked meticulously in and beside them. It bordered on neat to immaculate. He wasn't normally so fastidious or nervous, but today was the big one. There were a few hours still to go.

Amini picked up a replica Kris paper knife and dragged a pile of official and private mail to the centre of his white blotter. Although not full sized, it sported a sharp, five-inch wavy steel blade, a leaving present from the Malaysian navy's staff course. A couple of pewter tankards graced a shelf behind him, and there were tokens from other places he'd been assigned to. The frosted-glass office door shuddered before he'd opened any envelopes.

"Come," he grunted.

A short, squat chief petty officer entered, his stomach straining against a broad leather belt. He closed the door carefully behind him.

"How's it going, Chief?"

"I broke off a couple of plug electrodes on the starboard engine and widened the gaps, sir. It's running rough, but it won't take a minute to put in new plugs when the time comes. I've been revving it up a bit. Everybody knows it's sick."

"Any problems fixing a test run?"

"None. I do the rosters anyway so we got the crew we wanted. I told them just one bag with personal stuff. Nothing obvious."

"Fine. I've ordered three of the boats to patrol beyond the mouth of the delta to see what the Iraqis are up to. They'll take off south shortly. With another officer on duty at the gate and one crew on leave, it'll be pretty quiet when we do go."

"Still set for 1400 hours, sir?"

Amini nodded. "It'll be at least 1700 when the other boats get back, and blokes not on duty will take off for the Sabbath when they do. The gate staff changes over at 1800 as well, so we shouldn't be missed in all that turmoil. We'll be half-way to Ahvaz by then, and with no moon, it'll be pretty dark when we do."

"Right, sir. I'd better go on playing with a sick motor then."

"I'll go with you, Chief. I need to stretch my legs."

Tarek Achmed sprawled casually on a divan in the mullah's office at the back of the main mosque in Abadan. A strong smell of jasmine wafted into the small but richly ornamented room from the body of the mosque and two hard-line clerics sat primly in the office with him. Achmed operated through them but worked directly for Tehran, heading a small but vicious team that covered the Abadan area. He expected its size and power to grow with the revolution now underway. Even the clerics were wary around him, maybe even a little scared. If Abadan was the backside of Iran, Achmed was several miles up it.

Changes had been inevitable after the revolution, but the takeover of the American Embassy had accelerated them out of all proportion. And Amini was right. Several family heads amongst the town's elite had disappeared and Achmed was behind it. The warrants he issued said they'd gone north for questioning, although none had made it further than a hundred kilometres out of Abadan, but the rapid military build-up over the border had confused the issue. That was what they were discussing.

All three knew that Iran's Officer Corp was made up largely from the shah's nominees, all of whom had been trained overseas. That was where the military expertise lay, and Iran was suspicious of Iraq's intensions in the Shatt-Al-Arab. The honchos in Iraq were Sunnis, and Iran knew Iraq wanted a deep-water port in the Gulf. Would they invade Iran?

It was possible. Turkey was closely allied with the Americans, so piping oil through there was risky, and Sunni and Shi'a Muslims had always been at each other's throats. It was time to tread carefully. Achmed was looking for direction, but held the dithering clergy in withering contempt.

"Do I start on the military or not?"

A cleric with bottle-top glasses slouching in a high-backed chair, shifted un-comfortably. "We must wait until we know what Iraq is planning. We may need the military expertise in the elite."

The other cleric butted in. "If it does come down to some sort of war, who will do the planning and lead the fighting? If casualties are heavy, maybe half your job will be done anyway."

Achmed could barely keep the sneer from his face. "And if it doesn't happen, we give them more time to disappear, Imam."

"Perhaps you are being too zealous though, Tarek Achmed. Your job will still be necessary six years from now."

"That is being timid though, gentlemen. The revolution has started and cannot continue properly until we have purged Iran of Western influences. A lot of them are in the officer corp."

"Perhaps you have another motive though, Tarek. You've got rid of people, but you've not turned up much of their personal wealth yet." The senior mullah peered at him through his heavy horn-rimmed glasses.

This was dangerous ground. Achmed didn't want to go there. He had to defuse this right away.

"I left others to track their assets, Imam. That isn't my job, but I could let the military know they will be next."

"Visit the military then, Tarek, but don't make any arrests. You can confiscate their parse-ports, though."

"May Allah protect you, gentlemen. Thank you."

It had gone way past just being restless for Farhad Amini. He strode to the rugged concrete wharf with his chief and paused while the engines were flashed up. The port motor rumbled instantly, but a reluctant starboard motor groaned and laboured before it caught spasmodically, coughing and spluttering thick clouds of black, unburnt diesel from the exhaust. Satisfied, he waved to his chief. The four sailors going with them were already on board and gave him conspiratorial nods. They were ready too. Amini looked at his watch as he headed back to his office.

'God, still four bloody hours to go.' He nearly despaired, but couldn't let his doubts show. He was the boss. He was supposed to ooze confidence.

Amini distracted himself with the mail when he got back and was just about finished when his phone shrilled loudly. He jumped.

"Commander Amini."

"Duty officer main gate, sir. Someone's here with some sort of warrant card who wants to see you urgently. Won't take no for an answer."

Amini's heart skipped. "Is he on his own?"

"There's no-one else in the car, sir. He said it won't take long."

"Right, you'd better tell him where to come then."

He looked around his office. It looked too damned tidy, especially his desk. Amini scattered the files and mail around before moving to the large picture window.

He saw that three sleek patrol craft were easing from their berths, the turning props causing muddy white water to churn violently. A crested green, white and red Iranian flag stirred limply on each metal mast. Somewhere nearby, the ragged throb of labouring engine bubbled in the background, and as if on cue, a dusty black and white disgorged a swarthy Arab outside. He adjusted his black leather jacket before heading for the ground floor doors. There was no point in delaying this, so Amini moved into the empty outer office. His supply officer and the clerk were part of a boat's crew, so they weren't there. Heavy steps echoed on the wooden stairs.

"Commander Amini." He thrust out a hand to the sinister-looking policeman, or whatever he was.

"Come into my office."

Achmed took his time, deliberately looking around before following. Amini's backside was propped on the edge of his desk with his hands lightly curled around the edge when the interrogator entered.

"How can I help you?" Farhad Amini withheld a title. He had a fair idea who this joker was.

Achmed's stare was as hostile as his words. "We are concerned about some things that happen at this base that we have no control over, Commander. We want to be more closely involved."

Amini had guessed right. "Who is we, and what the hell do they know about naval operations?"

Achmed's hatred wasn't far under the surface. He'd grown used to fear, followed by instant capitulation, but this time it wasn't happening. The commander was even starting to bristle. Arrogant pigs. His younger years had been difficult and it was time to exercise his new authority.

"Who doesn't matter, Commander, either you'll do it, or someone will do it for you." The spittle was beginning to spray, but Amini looked calm and unfazed. Achmed decided to rattle him. His eyes slitted. Deliberately unclipping his holster flap, he moved towards Amini.

The Persian knew that an armed threat or maybe something worse was coming and he fumbled behind him before he eased to his feet. This couldn't be happening with the departure so close. But this man wasn't a normal policeman either—ergo he had to be someone who did the ayatollah's dirty work. He knew what that meant, and it wasn't just about him now either. Others were linked to him, at least in the short term. Their last-ditch chance would be gone along with his.

Achmed was a pace or so away, with his revolver half clear of its holster by then. And that was close enough. Amini stepped forward suddenly. His left hand trapped the half drawn pistol against the inquisitor's body, while his right, gripping the Kris, was not far behind. It went in low, angled upwards, under the sternum. The commander knew where the heart was.

At first Achmed's eyes registered shocked disbelief, but then quickly started to glaze. Amini held Achmed upright as he wiggled the vicious knife and felt it grate against something solid. He knew better than to withdraw it. He didn't need hot, glutinous gushers of blood splattering him and everything around him. He helped the body sag slowly to the floor.

Farhad Amini was awash with the genes of many an ancient warrior, and killing this animal was necessary. It didn't bother him. It did alter everything the moment he struck though.

His chief was alone in the boat's maintenance office when he phoned.

"No questions now, Chief. Get the lads to prepare the boat for sea right away and I need you up here now. We've got a few things to tidy up."

"Right away, sir." There was no hesitation.

Amini ignored the limp body and turned towards a tall wooden wardrobe in one corner of his office. A fresh pair of coveralls he wore on his boat hung alongside a dress uniform and sword. A black holdall lay collapsed on the floor. He fingered his uniform and then smiled. One way or the other, he wouldn't be wearing that again.

Amini stuffed photographs, papers and his passport into the zippered pockets of the bag. He slipped into the coveralls before going next door.

A large, green safe that held the cash to pay contractors and his troops was anchored to an external brick wall, and he and the supply officer had the combination. It was open in seconds. The stacked bundles of gaudy, large denomination notes looked healthy enough, but in reality, rabid inflation had dented its worth. Farhad Amini stuffed as many of the coloured wads as he could into his bag and was back in his office when his chief arrived.

Much like his boss, the senior sailor was now garbed in coveralls, with rank epaulettes on the shoulders and a round, gaudy flotilla badge on the right arm. He glanced at the grotesquely crumbled body and then back to the commander. Not a shadow crossed his face.

"The clergy's revolutionary police, he was about to spoil our day."

"What do you want done with it, sir?" It was already an it.

"No-one will miss him yet, so he can go in my wardrobe. If we're caught later, it won't matter much what we say, and we'd probably be seen if we dumped him in the river in daylight."

The chief nodded.

Several sturdy clothes hooks lined the back of the cupboard, and after a struggle, they lifted Achmed's body and draped his jacket collar firmly over two of them. Amini kicked the feet in, locked the door and pocketed the key. "Right, chief, his car's out front. Can you get rid of it somewhere?"

"There's a compound for marker buoys and caissons at the far end of the jetty, Commander. I'll stick it in there."

"Good lad. Take my bag with you while I return the office keys to the main gate." The chief was probably ten years older than the commander, but that was how officers address their favourites. He'd learnt that in Britain.

Chapter Nineteen

Nick touched down from a survey at about the same time that Amini's patrol boat wheezed and coughed its way out into the torpid river. It hadn't been about minerals. Sinclair tossed him his headset.

"Bring the boys in when you've done the after flight, Jock. I'll put them in the picture." Sinclair nodded as Nick headed to the crew-room.

He still wasn't sure what to say and felt edgy when he unfolded and flattened his map. Then he shrugged. What the hell would they know about maps anyway, and when would they have ever used one? But that was immediately followed by a deep frown. God, that was a bloody racist thought, and he didn't think he had a biased bone in his body. And that got him thinking at a tangent. His relationships hadn't gone all that well either, and neither did he think he was chauvinistic. But maybe he was, maybe it had been him that stopped anything going too far. He could have been his own worst enemy, could have been looking to blame anything as long as it wasn't himself. That bloody Scotsman must be getting through.

Nick looked up as the door screeched.

The maintenance team wasn't normally so quiet when they arrived. Jock must have said something. Nick gestured for them to drag up chairs, but Sinclair remained standing behind them. Nick knew that Imran was the leader, and would do most of the talking, so he twisted the map towards him. He wasn't sure where to begin, before realising that if he needed their help, they needed it all.

Nick cleared his throat and the four Pakistanis focused on him with deep concentration. They weren't all fluent in English, and they didn't intend to miss anything.

He kept to what was happening in country and to the company at first, and then let them mull over what he'd said. The highlanders spoke rapidly in Urdu, bouncing questions off Imran, but it didn't last long.

"We're happy so far, Mister Evans. Our embassy will get us back by train if they have to, but Jock said something about an escape as well."

Nick hesitated then nodded.

"There's an Iranian navy bloke down south who was my friend at the British naval college. This new regime could arrest him and maybe even execute him, Imran. He's asked if I can spirit him away somewhere."

Then another thought hit Nick. None of this was an issue in their country and Pakistan was Islamic too. They might not want to help.

"Imran, I'm sorry. This isn't your problem and I'm assuming too much. If you don't want to get involved, say so now. I'd certainly understand and won't say any more."

Imran looked at the others and caught the slight nods.

"This man is your friend, Nick, and we are all friends here. If one of us needed help, we would do what we could. That is how it works with us. You intend to rescue him with a helicopter, yes?"

Nick had caught his Christian name in amongst that and could see they were all with him. He nodded with a sigh of relief.

"Okay then. Jock and I will take off at 1230 tomorrow and it's close to a three-hour round trip. We don't know what he's going to do after he gets here, but I suspect he'll want to stay for a while. Webster's gone, so it will be with me."

"Is Floyd coming back?"

"I don't think we'll see him again, mate."

Imran nodded. "So what can we do?"

116

"Well, the first thing is a decent disguise. We thought that the loose gear you guys wear and one of those shemagh things would do the trick. None of the ayatollah's mob will risk wandering into a Bakhtaran town uninvited with most of the townsfolk armed to the bloody teeth, so if he keeps out of the lime-light, he should be okay. If you bring some gear out with you, we can kit him up from the word go."

"How long will he stay in Shahabad with us?"

"Who knows, Imran. It depends on where he wants to end up. We might even have to look at a few places we can take him in a chopper."

The Pakistani nodded. "Bring us out early tomorrow and we'll see what we can do around here too. Is there anything more we can provide?"

"No, mate. If we can get him into our town, we're home and hosed."

Amini cast off. There were no other people around, but with two patrol boats still tethered to the chipped jetty it had a warlike look about it. The torpid river mouth was a good fifty kilometres from the base and Amini had given orders for a survey of the Iraqi coast beyond that. The boats wouldn't be a problem either.

Amini limped his patrol boat up-river, keeping close to the naval base and a small civilian jetty further inland. Occasional revving kept the engine spluttering, but it was superfluous. A small, rusted freighter nuzzled the oil-streaked stone blocks north of the base, but the crew were disinterested. Only a few fishing feluccas ruffled the oily, placid surface.

Farhad Amini shut down the labouring starboard engine some thirty minutes later, and his chief and a helper changed the spark plugs. It roared healthily when Amini hit the starter again. The chief raised his thumb. Amini smiled. A raised thumb in Iran meant exactly the opposite to what it did in Britain. Perhaps the chief was inviting the navy to sit on it.

That vast but shallow valley they travelled through was probably the greenest part of Iran this side of the Elburz. It was also wet and marshy, and that was no surprise. The Karun and the Karkheh Rivers emptied into the Persian Gulf around there, but so did the mighty Euphrates and Tigris in Iraq. A myriad of smaller rivers and streams also tumbled down from the Zagros ranges. Amini had read somewhere that rudimentary farming began there over 6000 years before, and it wasn't hard to believe.

Apart from Abadan, only rustic subsistence towns and villages nuzzled the inland waterway, and the people along the river were tied to those arable acres. Amini felt free to push the shallow draft boat hard. The isolated population was used to sleek patrol craft venturing up river, with powerful propellers carving a white frothy path in the sluggish, green waters. He was twelve kilometres short of Ahvaz by evening.

Amini needed full darkness for what had to happen next. The darker the better. The boat was moored to the bank under a healthy stand of pistachios, and after his sailors ransacked it for anything they could carry while, they waited.

Nick gave the British Embassy a bell before they headed for home.

"Gerry Hawkins, can I help you?"

"Nick Evans, mate. What's the score?"

"I'm glad you called, Nick. Things are a bit clearer here now. How about your end?"

"Nothing much is happening yet, but we're getting low on a few things."

"Okay, here's what I have got. Only the Americans seem affected so far, everything else is virtually back to normal. We aren't expecting any more problems for the time being either, but we've taken a few precautions like getting the Swedes to provide our security. I'm only on the switch because the local staff was stood down."

There was a pause while Hawkins dragged up a chair.

"The party line is that America allowed the shah to travel to the US for cancer treatment at the Mayo Clinic, but the hard-liners reckoned he should have been left in Egypt to rot. It's all about that the government says."

"Jesus, that sounds a bit harsh."

"It's not really that simple either, Nick. America froze a lot of Iran's financial assets in world banks during the revolution, and now she wants them back. Our intelligence bloke here predicted that Carter would do bugger all about the takeover, and he was spot on, so Khomeini is using the hostages to make it happen. They let a few with health problems go, but they're still holding about sixty of them. No doubt they'll keep them until they get what they want."

"How about people like me and Jock?"

"A couple of foreign companies operate under fairly strict supervision, Nick, but none of them are American. The clergy have impounded all their files but still bill the Yanks for fuel and rents, and the American State Department still pays. The companies have got to protect their people, I suppose, so it could be all part of the negotiations. Carry on as you are for now, but drop in at the embassy sometime soon." The diplomat gave himself time to think.

"We're holding our Christmas party on Thursday week and you guys should get your invitation soon. We can top you up and give you an update at the same time, so let me know if you can make it. We've also started negotiations to get British subjects out, but it's still a no-go if they worked for the Yanks. We've got a few real innocents out so far, but you won't be on that list."

"Okay, thanks, Gerry. I'll keep in touch and give you a bell soon on the Christmas thing."

"Right, Nick. Take care."

Nick was thinking hard when he motored back toShahabad. Tomorrow was the big day and the embassy couldn't do much about it if they were caught. He updated Sinclair over a Teachers when he got home.

It was dark and sticky on the river, with no moon at all. A light, eerie mist blotted out the stars, but a dim yellow glow reached skyward from Ahvaz. It made the city look almost holy, as if it was surrounded by a smoky biblical halo. Amini eased his boat away from the river bank to avoid the few lanterns where houses existed. There was no hurry, but the poor visibility didn't help much. The engines barely ticked over.

When he got closer to the town lights, Amini could see that a savage revolution hadn't been all bad for him. Any garish touches were long gone, no flashing electronic advertising anything, and only a few dim street lights flared spasmodically. The early to bed ethic on the eve of the Sabbath helped too.

There was no-one was fishing and no amblers along the river banks with waterside cafés already shut. The riverbanks were as dark and silent as a graveyard at midnight. Amini knew that expensive houses spilled out onto the western bank, but there was hardly a glow from those either. What light there was only washed the right-hand river bank. He eased to port.

The downtown business area was also steeped in deep black shadow, with only a few apartment windows reflecting dully off the ebony waters. That scared him. If the boat was the only thing moving, it would be the centre of attraction. But he needn't have worried.

Amini couldn't see the bulk of the channel buoys at all, only the ghostly green or red lights flashing at their peaks. His confidence climbed as he reached the northern outskirts.

Dezful was about the same distance they'd already motored as the crow flies, but patrol boats were short on wings. The first thirty kilometres weren't a problem with sparse housing and a wide river, but it didn't last. The Karun had been dredged as far as a small town called Vey, but that was where the dredging ended.

Four tributaries emptied into Karun waters at Vey, but the river banks were low and vague, and the gaping river mouths difficult to identify. Amini knew that small villages and towns on the main river were supplied by shallow barges, but which one was the Dez? Roads weren't all that plentiful either, but decent surfaces were probably not even stable in that swampy runoff. He had to rely on logic. A lot of water gurgled from the Dez. The boat only drew five feet, and the main river had to be marked. He wasn't worried about grounding, but navigation from here on could be a nightmare.

But almost instantly the first part was solved. His boat over-ran an unlit buoy marking the river's mouth when it was barely moving. The waters closed in quickly after that and soon he could see both banks in a strengthening silver moonlight. Large, sturdy trees hugged the lazy water, adding to their cover, but several huge branches had cracked and tumbled into the river's shallows, and those irregular barriers cut down further on its useable width. Amini had little choice. He opened up the taps.

Shahabad had been sleeping for hours, but not Nick Evans. He was prowling again before six. Re-heated ibex stew and flat bread left over from the night before did for breakfast, and he was less tense now he was on his feet. He'd made his decisions and fed on the enthusiasm of the others. He was ready to go.

Minutes dragged like hours, and the hours seemed like days, but it was far too early yet. He scanned a month-old magazine over a second cup of coffee and then blitzed a bedroom and dresser for Amini. Even so, Sinclair was early when he appeared with his team.

"Imran wants to sort out a few things at the airfield, Nick. It's gone nine so we might as well go now."

A relieved Nick tried not to show it. He tried to look cool and collected.

"Okay, I'll get my sun-glasses."

It didn't take long for the Cherokee to glide out to the airfield. Jock dismounted on the run, and he and his team pre-flighted a helicopter while Nick gave the maps a final hammering. Twenty minutes later, Sinclair sauntered into the crew-room alone.

"The boys are sorting out a few things in the hangar, Nick."

Nick nodded and went back to his maps while the engineer made himself a brew. The Scot had barely sat before the phone trilled. Both jumped in surprise. Nick answered it.

"Nick, it's Farhad. Thank the gods you're there."

Nick's pulse rate headed north. "The team are sorting out a few things before we go Fred. What's the problem?"

"I'm not going to be anywhere near where I said. I'm phoning from Andimesht, the last big town before the mountains, and it's nearly ten already. Luckily I brought your card."

"Jesus, Fred, I haven't got the legs to get anywhere near there and back. What the hell happened?"

"We got through Ahvaz okay and then started up the Dez, but the river was a bloody nightmare. Big trees overhung the water everywhere and all of it was a lot tighter than I expected. But that's not the real problem. It twists and turns like a bloody corkscrew with rickets. We were constantly changing direction so I couldn't open up the taps, and we didn't get near the dam. I swear the distance to Dezful by river is over twice the distance by land, and by the time it was getting light, we'd only made it to a place called Safar. It's about fifty klicks south of where I am now."

"So what are you going to do?"

"Well, we got lucky there. The village was Bakhtaran, the same tribe that my sailors come from. Their dress is different, easy to distinguish, and the lads twigged it right away. I lifted a fair bit of money from the safe at Abadan when we left, so we paid one of the farmers to bring us on in his wagon. It's one of the bigger Japanese four-wheel drive jobs, so there was plenty of room."

"So how much further can he get you?"

"That's it, Nick. The road from here parallels the mountain folds heading for Khorramabad. It doesn't cross them. The rail line we talked about meets the road where it turns hard north, about fifty klicks from here. Several villages run along a dirt road running beside the railway, so he's happy to take me a further forty-seven klicks to a village called Toveh, but that's at the head of the dam waters and as far as the road goes. They've got some feluccas in Toveh but unfortunately no motor boats. We'd never reach anywhere near Do Rud on time."

"How many people are we talking about, Fred? I can only carry five and there'll be two of us already."

"That's not a problem. Several villages have sprouted up around the junction and my sailors prefer to be let off there anyway. It's easier for them to scatter from the main road."

"I'd better have another look at the maps then."

"I've done the calculations, Nick. If you straighten out a few corners on the river, it's an extra seventy-odd klicks all up."

Nick exploded. "That puts me right on the bones of my ass for fuel, Fred. Christ, depending on winds, I might not even get back!" You could smell the growing tension. Wisely Amini said nothing. It was Sinclair who jumped to his feet.

"Nick, listen."

"Stand by, Fred, Jock wants to say something." He cradled the phone against his shoulder.

"I filled two twenty-gallon containers a few flights ago, about 160 pounds in each. If we take them, we'll piss it."

"It's Fred's stuff-up, though, Jock, and it all adds to the risk of us being seen. I'm beginning to feel uncomfortable about this one. You got a frigging death wish or something?"

"Not at all, laddie, but if you don't do this, you'll remember you didn't for the rest of your bloody life."

Jock knew Nick would; he just needed to believe he could.

Nick mused with the phone still on his shoulder. Bugger it! Why not?

"Fred, you'd better make it or I'll kick your skinny ass all the way to Tehran myself. Get going now and I'll pick you up on the railway line north of Toveh. It'll be about thirty minutes later than we talked about. And shit, will you owe me."

"I'm sorry, Nick, and I know what I'm asking. With the distance I've got to go, and you getting there at about 1430, I should have walked about eight klicks up the track by then."

"Right-o, Fred. We'll see you this afternoon."

Chapter Twenty
Home Run

Amini eased from the battered call box in the dusty town centre into a swarming mob of chattering, animated people. Nobody seemed interested in him at all. He'd been offered a multi-coloured woollen shawl to drape over the upper half of his coveralls and a vivid woollen beanie for his head, but he'd declined. The smell of half processed wool and animal fat nauseated him, but he had got rid of his epaulettes and unpicked the squadron badge. Three of his sailors waiting nearby looked local.

The vehicle needed fuel, so he'd watched the chief and the driver go before he phoned. Now he felt exposed and apprehensive as he scanned around nervously, but the vehicle lumbered into sight before anxiety became concern. Amini and his sailors piled in and the chief raised his eyebrows. The commander gave him a quick rundown.

Their driver didn't race the Toyota along the main arterial link to Khorramabad, but it ate the distance rapidly even with a steepening gradient. Within forty-five minutes, they'd reached a junction with the railway and gritty, potholed side road. Amini knuckled his aching back when he stepped down. He knew he wouldn't see this area again.

Tortured steel rails lumbered in from the south and disappeared quickly to the northeast, flashing brightly in the dazzling sunlight. Wooden sleepers that supported them were weathered and splintered, and once pristine pebble ballast was now streaked by generations of scalding steam and dripping black oil.

Nearby, huge stone crags thrust reluctantly towards an intimidating steely sky, while rolling foothills effectively hid their vehicle from the main road. The peaks were domed rather than jagged, the upper reaches relentlessly beaten down by un-sympathetic elements. A dusting of snow said it was cold up there.

The pastures nearby were more battered and tangled than those on the southern tracts, and although still a vibrant green, they were neither as dense or tall. Vast acres were reduced to spongy pockets the size of handkerchiefs and sparsely covered with short, pale strips of forage. Dozens of daggy sheep did their best to crop them down further still.

Occasionally shallow streams forced a passage through the uneven tussocks, and small silver ponds supported the darker green of reeds and sedges. The steeper slope forced the rivulets to run faster and angrier up there, and tumbling waters broiled into mini cascades as they fought around pale, washed rocks.

Small islets of bulging ground did support leafy trees and bushes, but a high water-table stopped them getting too feisty. The adobe villages on the periphery were harder to see, their positions marked only by the hazy spirals of smoke writhing slowly above them. It looked bleaker and lonelier than it did scenic, more a place to struggle with, than to enjoy. Amini sighed. He rummaged through his battered black grip while his sailors dragged their gear from the Toyota.

The patrol boats carried a Bofors up front and fifty cal: on the bridge wings. There was also a steel armaments cabinet on the bridge itself. That held three automatic rifles, two handguns and a heavier rifle/grenade launcher combination, all of American origin. All were in pristine condition. But the cabinet on their boat didn't have weapons anymore. Those with Bakhtaran genes are born with guns in their hands and it would have been impossible for them to leave any behind.

The unmistakable clatter of rifles being loaded got the commander's attention. The weapons he'd expected, but not the smaller pots, pans and utensils from the galley they were stuffing into their bags.

Amini turned back to his chief with bundles of gaudily colourful notes in his hand and gave each of his troops one. They weren't huge amounts, topping at about 500 American dollars apiece, but it was a small fortune to them.

"There you go, lads. Something to get you started in a new life."

The sailors looked at him soberly, his chief's eyes a little moist even then. It appeared as if he wanted to do or say something, maybe even get physical, but rigid naval discipline prevented it. It was their final farewell, and Amini guessed what they were thinking. They weren't in anyone's navy anymore.

Amini dragged the chief into his arms before hugging each of his sailors in turn. The moisture in the chief's eyes overflowed and the eyes on the others sparkled too.

"Thank you for all you did, lads. May your gods smile on you." Amini could think of nothing else to say. He was finding it hard to speak himself.

The old farmer in the background nodded his approval.

"Thank you for our lives, Commander. We left you the grenade launcher, a pistol and distress flares, just in case. The other guns suit us better. Your plans are in the hands of your God, sir, but remember that news travels fast in these hills. If you need us, let someone know. We will find you."

Amini nodded gratefully and thrust out a hand. Each shook it before turning towards the nearest village.

"Okay, Grandfather, let's go. There's more money for you if the villagers at Toveh haven't heard or seen anything."

"We'll have to do what we called a hot refuel when we do the pick-up, Jock. I won't chance shutting down. There won't be any hoses either, but kerosene's pretty docile, and we've got some metal nozzles in the hangar. The containers are heavy though. Get Fred to help you before he climbs in, and I suggest you only use one. Keep the other handy just in case."

Nick was back on top, beginning to think ahead again.

"You sound as if you're really enjoying this, Nick. Could be it's a bit of action that's been missing from your life." Sinclair grinned, but Nick looked startled.

"Knock it off, mate. I just wasn't enchanted with all that military bullshit in the end."

"It might have been the nonsense of Ulster, though, laddie, not the military itself. You were never posted to any other combat theatres, were you?"

"Up yours, you bloody Scottish heathen! It's just been a bit boring around here lately. It's nice to have something to do again, that's all."

"Aye, well you be careful, laddie. Remember you've got my heathen Scottish ass in there with you."

Nick Evans snorted, but Jock was right, he did feel alive again. His tail was definitely in the vertical.

Amini said his farewells to the wrinkled, perpetually grinning farmer, but maybe it was the elder's lack of teeth that made him look like that. The villagers at Toveh quietly circled them with serious faces, but any explanations he'd left to the Bakhtaran. They were his people, and his attitudes were their attitudes. He'd know what to say. Amini picked up his bag and the ugly weapon, waved his farewells, and headed for the tracks.

He'd never tried this before, but then again why would he have. The distance between sleepers was about as awkward as it could get. Missing one didn't work, the stride was too long for human legs, and stepping on each one didn't help either. It forced him to mince. He hadn't gone far before his legs began to ache severely. Eventually, Amini tried walking on the sliding pebbles beside the track, but that didn't work either. It was like wading through an unstable, rattling sand dune. The commander prayed that the helicopter wouldn't be late.

In the end, they set off ten minutes early. Nick couldn't hold himself in any longer. He'd studied the map 100 times, identified Toveh 100 times more, and poured over the extra distance minutely. The land was higher in there, even more isolated and thinly populated, and any indiscrete inhabitants would take a week to reach civilisation over that heavy, torturous terrain. And following the river made it easy. A handful of swift waterways tumbled into the Dez from the hills, and the slope itself also helped the navigation. The shortish stretch overland near the end saved him twenty kilometres, and it was wild and woolly up there so no-one should clock him anyway. He felt good, and he was ready to go.

"Right-o, Jock, let's get this over with."

"I'm ready if you are, laddie, and if we're a bit early, he won't have so far to walk. There's one fuel container in the luggage compartment, and one on the deck in the cabin. I remembered to throw in a nozzle as well." There was a hint of sarcasm in it.

Nick snorted. The Scot had crewed many helicopters over the years so the basics weren't a mystery to him. They were airborne within ten minutes of walking out to the hangar.

The chopper winged down the river past Shahabad at its maximum recommended of 120 knots. It wasn't exuberance. Nick had factored the speed in, knowing that the faster a turbo-jet flies, the more distance it covered per pound of fuel. Aircraft fuel loads were measured in pounds not litres. It was what he did for a living.

Although sometime in the past the Zagros had been majestic and angry, savage erosion over the millennia made it easier to pick a route. Gigantic cliff faces were eroded into Titanic boulders, and once jagged slopes were now gentle and friendlier. Nick zoom climbed towards the Dez rarely having to sacrifice speed for height.

The air was pristine, and the visibility a hazy endlessness, so it was easy to keep away from anything bigger than a village. He flew barely fifty feet above the burnt pastures as the chopper twisted around the rolling, rocky tors, and although they didn't see much, not much saw them either. The mark one eyeball was the only detection device up there, and Nick wasn't worried much about that.

He'd thrown the map onto the instrument panel hood when they started off, but after Do Rud it was virgin territory. He handed it to the Scotsman.

"Follow the Dez to a place called Espirizi, Jock. Can you see it?"

Sinclair paused. "Aye, I've got that."

"We'll leave the river to the right there, go cross-country and re-join the river again at Tang Panj. The heading's 190. I've written it down."

Sinclair smiled. "That's right, laddie, and Toveh is about twenty klicks passed that."

"Okay. We'll come out the same way we go in, but keep us away from Tang Panj itself, there's some sort of highway running through it. Fifty miles and we can go home again, mate. Thirty minutes or so."

Chapter Twenty-One

It was still early afternoon. The mallet of a fierce but ill-defined sun hung stationary in a pale metallic sky, making the deep river valley an anvil wilting under the hammer blows of blistering heat. Lines of winking steel disappeared into watery mirages not far ahead, and Amini was struggling rather than striding along the railway track beside them. His coveralls were unzipped to the waist and his once white T-shirt was saturated and stained a dirty yellow. Blood-shot eyes stung from the rivulets of salty sweat trickling down his brow. He had forgotten about something to drink in the turmoil of the moment, so heat exhaustion wasn't all that far away either.

But although a scramble to the river was getting closer, he fought it. The water had to be polluted down there after passing through several townships. He still clung to his bag and the ugly black weapon.

A couple of hundred metres further on, Amini had to rest. He doubled at the waist, dragging in as much of the hot, thin air as he could. And it was as his breathing quietened that he heard a muffled, mechanical clatter peaking above the silence. It had to be his baked, addled brain playing games. It had to be an illusion. He was in the middle of nowhere, for God's sake.

At first, Amini dismissed the clatter, but it grew louder and more insistent, the thump of rotor blades now compelling and distinct. Something klicked, and along with the return of reason came frantic action. He tore open the zip of his bag and rummaged for a signal tube.

One end was a bright magnesium flame for night use, but that would be pointless in the harsh sunlight. What he needed was smoke, but he had to hold the flare close to his face to work out which end to use. The operating ring separated with a loud pop and he watched the thick orange tendrils swirl loosely around his legs.

The mechanical clatter changed slowly at first, getting slightly louder and more insistent, but then through eyes too dry to lubricate themselves properly, he saw a hazy white shape materialise on the tracks ahead. It was like the second coming. Amini raced towards it.

The distance between the rails was about the same as the distance between his aircrafts skids, and Nick knew when to be careful. He biased his landing with the right skid over a rail, but still on the end of the sleepers, before lowering the machine gingerly. He put more room on the left where the refuelling point was, and as soon as the skids touched, Sinclair hopped onto the unstable, rolling pebbles. The Scot shuffled in a crouch to where Amini had slid to a halt and grasped his grimy, damp hand.

"I'm Jock and you must be Fred." It wasn't the most imaginative of greetings.

"That's right, and boy am I glad to see you." Both grinned as they yelled over the noise of the whistling engine.

Sinclair shouted a warning about the rotors to Amini, pointing as he did, and then grabbed the bag and led off in a crouch. He stuffed both the weapon and bag under the back seat before raising a hand to stop Amini climbing in. The Scot wrestled the squat, white fuel container and the nozzle free and motioned to the Iranian to help lift the jet fuel. When the container was empty, it joined the bag and gun.

Sinclair was strapping Amini into the cabin bench seat when he froze. A long whistle, fluting mournfully in the distance, peaked faintly above the sound of the idling chopper. The Scot squinted towards the source. Wavering layers of heat hid the engine, but he could see a column of billowing, greasy smoke twisting and bubbling above the quivering mirage. It was behind Nick who wouldn't be able to hear in the noisy cabin either. Sinclair speeded up dramatically.

It didn't take long to buckle Amini in. The lap strap was laid across the rear bench seat, and a lightweight headset lolling beside it went on quickly too. Sinclair slammed and locked the rear cabin door. He plugged in his own headset as he scrambled in.

"Move it, Nick, there's a fucking train a couple of miles behind you."

Nick had looked relaxed and complacent watching the two embark, but that rapidly turned to startled. He lifted quickly and dumped the nose while barely glancing at his instruments, accelerating so hard the power flickered in the red. The light helicopter rapidly ran down the lake's headwaters and the small sepia village of Toveh beyond. Before he reached the village, Nick zoomed steeply and then turned for the high, neutral mountains. Jock Sinclair was still fiddling with his harness as the lake disappeared swiftly behind.

It was safe up there ducking through the isolated, lonely valleys. Nick trimmed the speed back and adjusted his flight path before glancing over his shoulder with a grin. It faded quickly. Amini had tears in his eyes and an embarrassed pilot turned forward again. It was several more minutes before the Iranian broke the silence.

"Thanks so much for this, Nick, I'm really grateful. I didn't know what else to do." Amini choked over the last few words. It sounded as if he had something stuck in his throat.

"That's okay, mate, we needed something to relieve the boredom anyway. Sorry about the frigging train though, we must have missed it when we went cross-country." Nick didn't look behind, but continued talking casually.

"If you push that small circle of plastic in the window outwards and turn the open bit forward, you'll get a good blast of cool air. I've got to concentrate on what I'm doing now, so we'll natter about your trip over a beer tonight."

Farhad Amini would need time to collect himself again. Sinclair knew it, and he'd seen Fred's reaction too, but was surprised that Nick realized it. He threw a shrewd glance.

"Did you guys bring anything to drink? I forgot. The inside of my mouth is like the bottom of a bird cage."

Both Nick and Sinclair carried a bottle of mineral water. Both were still half filled. Both passed them over. On the way back, a dirty beige haze hid most of Do Rud, but minarets and high-rises pushing aggressively into a clearer sky marked precisely where it huddled. The helicopter was well south of the town, however, skating low through barren hills, and wouldn't be heard or seen out there. It had been easy, almost completely un-eventful, and the build-up of tension evaporated like a warm ether bath. Nick kept the natter casual and light for the rest of the trip, keeping it about the treeless landscapes, the rolling frosted hills, and the vast empty stretches they were thundering through. He dropped the speed when they were in Shahabad's humid river valley, pointed out their house and then Qom looming some twenty kilometres beyond.

Nick turned the machine directly towards the isolated, dusty airfield, but as the ground around them dropped even lower, Sinclair shot bolt upright.

"Shit Nick, there's a couple of troop carrier things in convoy on the road from Qom. They could be going to Kashan, but I bet the bastards are bound for the airfield." Three pulse rates climbed towards the roof simultaneously.

Nick pushed the nose further earthwards, taking the speed over the top. The machine was low and smoking when the company buildings obscured him from the north, making the troop carriers look as if they were parked. His flare was harsh with a 100 metres to go, and his collective lever danced to some demonic aria as he juggled to stop the chopper from ballooning. The only other time he'd flared that seriously flitted through the memory banks. He didn't have time to smile.

The machine stopped abruptly in front of the hangar. Imran gave him the unmistakable, whirling hand above his head to keep the helicopter turning. Nick obliged as two of the maintenance team dragged Farhad Amini and his luggage out of the cabin and fled into the hangar.

Nick was faced into wind, away from the aircraft shed, but could see the tension drain from an agitated Imran almost instantly. The Pakistani gave the order to cut with a casual index finger slashed across the throat.

By the time the troop carriers braked in a whirlwind of swirling sand, the rotors had almost stopped. The adrenalin high now merely bubbled. Mohamed Arak climbed down from one, two armed soldiers from the other. They stayed well back, covering him. Nick and Sinclair scrambled to the concrete warily.

"So we meet again, Mister Evans. We saw you were airborne. Where have you just been?" He didn't offer his hand and ignored the others.

Nick wasn't about to show he was apprehensive, and he'd read somewhere that attack was a good defensive move. He gave that a go. "A survey in the hills like we're supposed to, mate. The fuel and rents are still being paid so we'll keep on doing our job."

"Very commendable, Mister Evans" Arak continued in his fractured English. "Where will you submit your reports?"

"We haven't found anything yet, mate, so I haven't got a clue, but I was sure someone like you would be out to tell me before long."

"That's what I'm here for, Mister Evans. The government wants any positive reports immediately and a summary of negative reports every two weeks. You are aware of the golden mosque in the centre of Qom? We have an office there."

Arak had been straining to see into the gloomy hangar and deliberately walked towards it. Nick looked alarmed. The Scot inclined his head slightly. Nick hurried to catch Arak up.

"What do you keep in those big boxes, Evans?"

Nick thought quickly. He tried sounding casual.

"A spare engine in one, and a main gearbox in the other. It's dusty and sandy out here, and they're hermetically sealed in thick plastic until we need them. Both items costs over a half a million bucks, Mister Arak. I'd hate that on my slop chit if we opened 'em before we needed too.

Arak looked at Nick and then the large ply boxes. He wasn't sure where he stood himself. He shrugged and walked outside again. Nick kept the pressure on.

"I presume there are no further restrictions on our activities, Mister Arak?"

"Only one, Mister Evans. I've been requested to hold your passports for safe keeping at our office. Can I have them please?"

Nick frowned. He could see Sinclair fiddling with the machine while trying to keep himself within earshot, and saw him shrug. Nick knew they wouldn't be catching any flights out soon. He was being deliberately wound up and began to boil. His fingers twitched. He was about to lose it.

"They can have mine, Nick. We'll get them back when they let us move on."

Nick listened. It was hard, but he held back.

"Fine, Mister Arak. They're in a safe in our office."

Nick led off without looking back with Arak running to catch up. Sinclair tagged along at a more leisurely pace. There was a mottled gun-metal safe bolted to a wall in the survey office and Nick screened the door with his body while he twirled the combination.

He handed Arak a well-used red booklet, and a near pristine dark-blue one with a kangaroo and emu crest that belonged to him. Arak looked surprised.

"I didn't know you were an Australian citizen, Mister Evans."

"Well, you do now, Mister Arak. Perhaps you could somehow get a message back to your government. Their current actions are going to piss off a lot more countries than just America."

Arak paused. He looked less sure of himself. "There are three Westerners here, where is the other one?"

"Mister Webster went to Tehran a few days ago. He's a Canadian, and I suspect you'll have to ring their Embassy to find out what he's up to. As I said before, you've involved a lot more powerful countries than just Americans in this already."

Arak felt further confused and could think of nothing to say. Minutes later, the troop carriers disappeared in a billow of dirty sand towards a disembodied Qom in the mid distance. The pair watched through the plate glass window.

"The Australian passport, Nick. Nice touch."

Nick turned. "It struck home when I was walking in, Jock. Ours is an American company and there are only seven of us out here, but with your team as well that's five big countries that will be pissed off about what's happening. I bet nobody has really thought about the full consequences yet, so I felt like giving them something to think about. Make them a bit more cautious."

"Aye, well, it should keep 'em off our backs for sure. I'll find out what the boys did with Fred."

But they had to wait. The bowser motored up billowing clouds of black diesel as two of the team fitted small rubber ground handling wheels to the skids. Nick and Sinclair watched with hands in pockets as it was refuelled. The bowser was on its way back again before Imran walked to the stack of boxed spares in the corrugated shed. He opened four quick-release screws from an empty engine container and helped a bedraggled, sweaty Amini climb out.

Within minutes, Amini was rigged up in a loose pair of baggy trews, an open-necked cream shirt and a light sleeveless jacket over it. All pre-used, but all cleaned and pressed. Amini really looked the part after the Pakistani wound a loose shamagh around his head, with the frayed end of the headdress draped loosely across his lower face.

While the maintainers dragged the helicopter away, Nick took Amini to the crew-room and put the kettle on. He went outside to throw Amini's coveralls down a thunderbox, and when he returned Amini, was effusive, if not gushing. An embarrassed Nick brushed it off.

"I don't think anybody will go looking down there for them, Fred, but drink your coffee and we'll chat about the rest of it tonight." He pointed to the small changing room. "Take your bag with you but stash the gun behind the lockers. We couldn't explain it away in Shahabad, but we could deny all knowledge of it out here."

Jock and his team bundled into the crew-room shortly after. Nick locked up and drove them home.

Mohammed Arak phoned Tehran as soon as he got to Qom, asking for the Imam who controlled the religious police. It took several minutes before he got an answer.

"Holiness, I have confiscated the passports as you instructed. They seem to be operating normally out there from what I could see."

"Let them continue for now then, Mohammed. We do not have the expertise to do what they do, and the minerals will be ours in future anyway."

"There is one small problem, Mullah. It's an American company, but there are several other nationalities working out there. Four are from Pakistan, one from Britain, and one from Australia. A Canadian was with them, but now he's at his embassy in Tehran. I thought this was about our problems with the great Satan America Mullah. The Australian pilot pointed out that we were already inconveniencing a large group of other countries, and I didn't quite know what to say."

There was silence at the other end. Arak waited impatiently.

"What should we do about this, Mullah?"

"I must talk to others, Mohammed. This was not thought out fully, so give them a long rope for now. They can do little other than shop in Qom or visit their embassy, and we don't want any more international incidents for the time being. If America and the West put an embargo on food and we can't sell our oil, we will be in real trouble. As long as they submit their reports, keep out of their way."

"It will be as you wish, Mullah."

The Pakistanis stayed next door playing cards, but Nick, Sinclair and Amini shared a pot of thick lamb stew over bottles of light beer. The Iranian was effervescent, stumbling through his story while they ate, but he knew he had to be careful. He'd already done some thinking about that one.

Sure, they'd gone out on a limb for him, but how well did he know them, really? And they were Westerners and British at that. They might not think the same way as he did, might have scruples about getting one in first. It might not go with their national ethic of fair play.

The uncertainty, tension and unpleasantness at Abadan was like 'Boys Own' stuff and easy to accept, so he gave them that, but skirted around Achmed's death. He did allude to him having something to do with the disappearances, and that was controversial enough for now. Amini let that play out first.

Nick sipped until Amini stopped for a draught himself, and then took a few minutes to describe what they'd seen on television and with what the British Embassy had come up with. Much of it was news to Amini. He hadn't heard much in Abadan, and only vaguely knew about the students' revolt. But Nick knew how to read people. He suspected that Amini was holding back.

"Do you know what you'll do next, Fred?"

139

"I haven't got a bloody clue, Nick. Getting out of Abadan before it was too late was all I could think about. Would it be okay if I stay here until I've sorted something out?"

"Feel free, mate, but we'll keep an eye on what develops." Nick didn't hesitate. Sinclair's craggy face crinkled slightly.

"How about relatives? Are there any still around?"

"My father worked directly for the shah's internal office and got exiled along with the entourage, but he was quite elderly and already sick, so he may not even be alive. I certainly haven't been able to track him down, and my mother died years ago from some kind of fever. I've only got a younger sister besides that, and I believe she's still in Tehran. She was when I met you at your embassy anyway. Apart from that, there are a couple of aunts somewhere, but I haven't seen them in years."

"Can you get in touch with her?"

"I'd better put you in the picture, Nick, because Laleh is fairly liberated, even by our standards. She got a degree in Sociology and Human Studies at the University of Tehran on Kargar Street and then completed her Master's at Cambridge. She's only been back in Iran for two years. Compared to now, the shah's regime was pretty progressive, but some of our ideas are still like the rest of the Middle East. Her years in Britain changed what she considers acceptable about a lot of that. Mine too, I suppose, but I'm a male so it's easier for me."

"You aren't in touch then? That's a bit odd if there's only the two of you left."

Sinclair broke in before Amini could answer.

"Easy, Nick. I don't think either of us is qualified to suggest how families should behave. Keep going, Fred."

"Our father didn't object to Laleh getting a degree, but he did arrange for her to marry a fairly powerful man in his office after she'd finished. From what we could see, it would have been a good marriage for all concerned, but she refused to do it."

"Arranged marriages are a bit archaic in this day and age though, Fred. It was bound to piss her off."

"She was pretty direct about it, Nick. She told my father she'd never marry the fat old pig, even if he was the last man on Earth. He was about twice her age. They argued some more, other things were said in the heat of the moment, and my father knew she meant it. We'd both been left some money by our mother, so Laleh took off to England and they never spoke again"

Amini obviously took it seriously. Nick's eyes sparkled and the Scotsman had a job not to chuckle too. "So why aren't you two closer? It must have been a few years ago now."

"I'll admit our society is patriarchal, Nick, so with our father out of it, I did the male thing when she got back from the UK. I tried to talk her into mending bridges with him, to let him fix something up if we could get in touch. He was old school and she'd disgraced him, so he would need that."

"And she wouldn't do it?"

"She actually told me to fuck off, Jock. She said that she'd had a couple of affairs in England and was no longer a virgin, so it didn't matter anymore. The way she put it shocked me and I sort of blew up too. We haven't spoken since then either."

"So you've no idea where she is really?" Nick was pensive.

"She was flatting with friends of my father in Tehran when I last saw her. He's a Professor of Surgery and also heads up a small teaching facility at Shahid Beheshti University. Their kids had already left home so there was plenty of room."

"Is she still there?"

"She may be, Nick, but that's not the real problem. She was working for the American Embassy when it was taken over. I don't even know if she's still alive."

Both Europeans sat up as if they'd been stung. "Do you have his phone number? Can we get in touch with them?"

"I haven't got his home number, Jock, and I'd be careful about dropping him in it right now. He's pretty high profile and even this regime needs top-class surgeons. I'm pretty sure he won't have any problems as long as he keeps his nose clean. He'll be watched though, and if he's caught helping people like us, anything could happen."

"Shit, this all seems like a bloody great mess to me, Farhad. It's not just about religion or even money, is it?"

Amini paused to collect his thoughts. Persians had always been proud of their history, particularly prior to the Arab invasion. It had even been a compulsory subject in schools until recently. He enjoyed Persian history.

Amini learned that Iran sat strategically across the ancient silk route and that led to many relentless conflicts over the centuries. Different blood lines with diverse attitudes melded into what was now modern Iran. But differences still bubbled just under the surface, and resentment and jealousy between the bloodlines were still active. This was something else he had to be careful about.

"More about religion than money, for sure. My genes go back to long before the Arabs got here, and that's part of the problem. We feel different, no, to be honest we are different. We resent the Arabs being here. It's caused a lot of the conflict." He paused to sip again.

142

"A lot of people have wanted their go at the top, Nick. And this time it was the Pahlavi's turn and my family are distantly related to the shah through my father. I didn't really notice that the rest of the country wasn't doing as well as we were. I was pretty young though, and I went overseas for several years, and missed most of it. I do know that the religious leaders exiled the shah when they got back on top, and know that the United Nations wouldn't let them get away with anything too nasty, but those of us left won't be anywhere near as lucky. We're for the chop if the regime catches us, mate."

"Jesus, that's pretty heavy, Fred. Why can't they let people they don't want just take off?"

"Outsiders don't understand, Nick, but a lot of Iranians aren't Arabic, and Sharia laws are harsher than any other form of Islam. Even my religion is different, with some Judaism and Christianity thrown in with some Islamic and Zoroastrian stuff. It's all about history and power, mate, and whose turn it is next." Amini drew a ragged breath and lifted his glass.

"It's not a criticism, but a few hundred years ago the Scots, Irish and English were all at each other's throats in your country too."

Nick took his time answering. "Well, quite honestly I'm glad that I was born when it was all over then, Fred."

"It's all about fate, not democracy here, Nick. Whoever is strongest at the time rules, and that's in the lap of the gods."

Chapter Twenty-Two

The stress had been flicking on and off like it was connected to a faulty light switch and Fred's revelations hadn't helped. They felt drained and out of their depth. It was already deep and murky, and quickly getting beyond their collective experiences. Nick Evans and Sinclair needed to think. Jock yawned.

"Well, guys, I'm totally knackered and I need to sleep on this. What say we continue after breakfast tomorrow?"

Dark rings circled Amini's eyes and his shoulders slumped even though he was sitting. Nick felt pretty ordinary himself. It didn't take a lot to agree.

Nick showed Amini what had been Webster's room and then the bathroom. There was a blue towel thrown on his bed and Nick tossed him a spare toothbrush and disposable razor. The commander had little except underwear to unpack. Shopping for Amini would be a major priority.

"Jot down a few things you need with your sizes and I'll nip into Qom tomorrow. All the shops will be open on a Sunday, but I think you should keep out of there for a while, Fred."

Amini nodded, his eyelids already drooping. "Thanks again, Nick. I'll get out of your hair as soon as I can, mate."

"Don't worry about that now, Farhad, just get some sleep." Even though dead tired and safe, the commander took a long time to settle. Adrenalin had been washing through his system for a long time. He was coming down, but he wasn't there yet. Nick was asleep as soon as his head hit the pillow.

It was already late when Nick emerged, but Amini was still asleep when Sinclair rocked up for morning coffee. They stuffed meat slices into pocket bread and sipped from steaming mugs in silence. The Scot was taciturn in the mornings. It gave Nick time to mull over what to say.

A lot of time had passed since he'd taken charge of his fellow man, years since he'd juggled with life and death decisions, but he soon realised the basics were still there. In the end, it was about priorities. When Amini finally stumbled in, yawning sleepily, it was the motivation that Nick needed.

"We'll have to be logical about this, Fred, so the first thing is get your sister out of Tehran. For her sake, but also for your friend's from the way I see it."

Amini still looked tired but already more relaxed. His ready grin was infectious. "Laleh, Nick, Laleh. It means tulip in Farsi. When she was in the UK, everybody called her Lily. At least that was another flower. I think you British have a need to reduce foreign names to something you can recognise and handle easily. She was happy with that one. Call her Lily."

Both Nick and Sinclair grinned. "Lily it is for now then, but from what you said last night, I might wait until I know her better before calling her that to her face."

"She's been called worse, Nick. Rottweiler was a word I used."

Nick smiled again. "Whatever. But the thing is, will she come with us or want to stay in Tehran?"

"Maybe I gave you the wrong impression last night. Laleh's headstrong, but she's pretty smart. She'd know that she's at risk up there, and would know she's putting others in danger too. I'm just not sure if she'd trust two Western strangers."

"Have you been to the house she's staying at?"

"Yes, I have. I went around there a couple of times when she returned, but I don't remember the phone number. I buzzed Abdul at the university when I was dropping around."

Nick absorbed that first. "Okay, Fred, this is what we'll do. The British Embassy is having a Christmas lunch next Thursday. I'll let them know that Jock and I will be coming and we can top up with a few things while we're there. They're both good reasons to travel and we've done it heaps of times before. It's only about an hour and three-quarters drive to northern Tehran, so we'll drop you at your friend's house first, then pick you up a few hours later. The embassy is on Ferdousi Avenue, in the city centre. I don't want you in there if we can help it."

"It's okay if I come then?"

"We don't have much choice, Fred. Directory enquiries are probably already monitored, so it could be a dead giveaway if we phoned them. She'll be okay about coming if you're there."

Sinclair was thinking too. "Get Sarah to buy one of those old-fashioned chador things for Laleh when she goes shopping next. One with just a slot for the eyes. It's called a Niquab, I think. With Fred in his Pakistan gear and Laleh in that, they could be a man and wife on the way back home."

"Good idea. We'll top up with fuel in Tehran as well. It's best not to take Fred through the centre of Qom for the time being."

In the end, Nick Evans saved the shopping trip until early Monday morning because Sinclair's comments about a chador had opened up another, different box. Laleh would only have time to pack a bag or case because she wouldn't know they were coming, and her needs had to be part of the equation too. The men went into a huddle, using the spare time to beef up their list.

When they got to cosmetics and the more delicate stuff the girl might think essential, they hit a blank wall. Only the obvious sprang to mind. Sarah let them mutter uneasily amongst themselves before she drew up a chair.

She rattled off a list of basics, and then told them she would attend to it herself. All the men knew to keep out of that one, and when Nick sighed audibly and the other two looked guilty, she realized it had been a set-up.

That morning, Nick drove them all to the airfield, leaving Amini and the Engineer out there while he drove on to Qom. Farhad would be okay. He was a commander, for God's sake, and didn't have to spend the day alone. Fetching and carrying for Sinclair would keep them both happy.

Nick knew they'd be in Qom longer than usual this time, so he let Sarah finish with the markets and dump her purchases at the vehicle first. A regiment hadn't arrived, only Amini, but the housekeeper had filled two baskets as if she was feeding the whole of Shahabad. And even then she wasn't finished. Next she dragged Nick to a nearby neighborhood that sold Bakhtaran fashions.

Nick and Sarah squeezed passed the tiny shops and jostling crowds that cluttered the dark, twisting alley-ways, made narrower still by a line of temporary, crude stalls. Brass work glittered brightly, precarious stacks of earthenware looked close to toppling and the booths were all aflutter with bright, fabric knick-knacks. Sarah ignored them all. Instead, she steered him towards the airy arcades off the back lanes. That was where the serious clothing shops were, and that was where she was in her element. Even better, Nick was doing the paying.

Any flamboyant, warm colours or anything that approached the exotic seemed largely absent even in the bigger shops, but Sarah wasn't deterred by what showed in windows, nor what didn't show either. There was some older, more colourful stock still around and Sarah had a nose for it. Most of what was on offer approached the underwhelming at first, but not for long.

Letting Sarah have her head was the right thing to do. After just two sorties into department stores, Nick was glad she was there. Sure, he'd shopped for himself, clutching a grubby, well-worked list before, but nothing like this. Somewhere he'd heard that serious shopping was a gender thing, and that confirmed it.

She crammed skirts and matching blouses into plastic bags along with and a couple of coloured headscarves, but still wasn't finished. Next, she dragged his red face, through shops for underwear and cosmetics. She wasn't so successful with that. The 'lines' she did find were less than exotic, and certainly unlikely to inflame a rampant desire. Amen. She picked up a few changes and a nightshirt or two for Amini, but his were almost an afterthought.

Sarah was smiling contentedly when Nick dropped her and the shopping off. He returning to the airfield for the others, but phoned the embassy before returning them home.

Tehran was still a few days off, but the hype climbed steadily as it got closer. Nick ambled through long walks and impromptu fishing trips with Amini, but nothing seemed to settle them, nor tire them out either. He, Amini and Sinclair even tried sight-seeing and a hunting trip in the chopper. Nick was almost screaming by then.

But that Thursday finally did arrive with a brilliant blue sky and the promise of another warm, arid day. About par for the course out there. The Canadian's skin had been too delicate to let much sun hit it, so there was a large tube of tanning cream in the bathroom cabinet. Nick tossed it to Amini and it darkened him up nicely. With a shemagh covering most of his face, and loose clothing hanging to his feet, there was little of him visible. A final touch was a loan of Imran's passport. With darker skin, the resemblance was fairly close. Amini looked more a wandering Tuareg than a resident of Iran.

The function they were headed for was semi-formal, so Nick and Sinclair pulled on smart casual clothes and real shoes. The Scot even scrapped off three days' growth. They were ready to roll.

Nick was at the wheel when they headed through the western suburbs, deliberately avoiding the busy centre of

Qom. He was working hard to avoid a ticket, so he kept his speed down while he headed for the four-lane highway north to Tehran. Only a few vehicles travelled fast enough to throw off-white nomadic sand from the bitumen, and Nick wasn't one of them.

A bit over forty minutes later, they saw the Elburz Range playing a game of hide and seek with towering cumulus in the far distance. Nick knew the upper slopes were perpetually covered in snow, but that far out, the whole mountain range was a steely blue-grey against the lighter azure of the sky. Ragged wisps of white cloud straggled downwind from the sharp peaks, and several vivid streamers flirted with nearby frigid mountain peaks, but even below the snow line the huge range threw back the same hazy colours. It took another twenty minutes to reach the outskirts of Tehran.

The traffic thickened and the roads widened to six lanes as they neared the city centre. It should have made driving easier but it didn't. Accumulating driving skills wasn't high on the list of things to do in Tehran, with some residents ignoring traffic lights altogether, while others expecting blinkers to help them turn corners, not let someone know they were about to. By the time they reached the eastern ring-road, Nick was damp with sweat. They dropped off Amini and headed for the centre of town.

Although it was elegantly understated, the warm yellow sandstone and light tinted glass gave the British Embassy an exotic and ancient look. Somehow it resembled a desert castle, complete with battlements and slitted windows, with a pseudo keep at its centre. Pristine, sheltered lawns dotted around its edges, and the sealed car park out front was already half filled with expensive-looking sedans. Crazed marble steps rose from its ornamented centre towards a pair of finely etched glass main doors. Inevitably, they were etched with the English lion and unicorn coat of arms.

149

Nick and Sinclair leaned on the wide, high desk while an insistent pager summoned Gerry Hawkins. It took only minutes for him to arrive and apart from a swift handshake, there was no preamble. Hawkins grilled them in a side room before passing on an update that had recently come in, but nothing had changed. It was almost impossible to get people out, and those two wouldn't be amongst them.

Hawkins fixed up day passes for the Christmas party and then made his excuses and dashed off to change. Nick and Sinclair loaded cases of booze and several cans of specialty foods before drifting out to the gardens.

The extensive, exotic grounds were elegant too. It was Nick's first time out back and he noted the whitewashed perimeter walls screened by stands of stately willow and plane trees. And although they were bare for the winter, that year's growth did show up as thin, lighter shades of grey sprigs. Older, contorted limbs spiraled upwards, reminiscent of out-of-control fishing line, while healthy stands of native bushes hemmed in the thickened trunks. Disciplined clumps of reeds had been allowed to cluster around several of the impressive water features. The pale, washy sky and exuberant vegetation reflected starkly in the still, dark ponds strategically sunk around the gardens.

The garden party was already underway. It had been set up on a cool, friendly grassed area, cleverly shaded by taller evergreens, and was already half filled with laughing, colourful women, and slightly more serious males. It was also getting noisy and frivolous as people sipped enthusiastically from mock crystal glasses.

As parties went, it was more resplendent and refined than most, though like so many such functions, it was also stereo-typical. Acres of finger food got washed down by a copious variety of colourful drinks, and as the booze flowed, the English voices got plumier and the laughter grew louder. It didn't happen that often and people were there to relax, but on that day, the conversation drifted from the banal to the more serious without much prompting.

Nick and Jock circulated casually, saying a few hellos, offering a few opinions, and cracking a few jokes, but neither heart was in it. Both couldn't stop looking at their watches as if they had a train to catch, and a couple of hours were all they could take. Their goodbyes were brief.

Chapter Twenty-Three

Sinclair was at the wheel when they cruised into Ewin twenty minutes later. Nick punched the doorbell inside a bricked porch-way while Jock parked around the side of the house. The solid, carved door was swung open by a strikingly handsome woman even before the second ring had stopped echoing. Finely chiseled features, a hint of grey in her shining midnight hair and soft, flawless skin put her anywhere between forty and sixty. She cracked a light smile and held out a beautifully manicured hand.

"Hi, I'm Minu."

She knew who they were, and used their names freely as she ushered them through the arched red-brick portal, and offered a glass of tea. The professor made a sweeping gesture towards chairs around a solid wood dining table while Amini did the introductions.

"The news isn't all that great, Nick. I'd better let Abdul explain."

"Welcome, Nick. It's a bit complicated, but maybe not as bad as it could be. We'll have to do something while things are still chaotic though if we can." Abdul dragged up a chair. "Farhad told me that you know what I do."

Nick nodded.

"Okay. First of all the campus is huge. It's got a teaching university, a large hospital, laboratories, a medical research centre and even a school of medical law. I'm on the board and operate three days a week at the hospital, but I'm also in charge of a small specialised facility in the research centre. In there, we teach highly specialised surgery to qualified surgeons, using cadavers from the city morgue before they get cremated. Also, we use the ward to study patients with unusual conditions, or when they've got something we're not sure about. It's not advertised, but it's quite a normal set-up for teaching hospitals. Several days ago the government took over the facility so that some of the people from the American Embassy could be treated quietly. As head of the faculty, I had to do the arranging."

Nick wasn't slow on the uptake. "So that's where Laleh is now?"

Abdul nodded. "Currently there's a male Iranian and three females in the ward, along with an American administrator with a broken leg, and a Marine corporal in an induced coma. The Marine got clobbered with a tyre lever when he was tossing tear-gas grenades around, while the administrator fell or was pushed down an outer staircase, The locals are all ambulatory but ended up with some dislocations or cuts and abrasions that needed stitching and antibiotics. No-one is considered dangerous, so there's only one guard on per shift."

"You think we might be able to lift her then, Professor?"

"Abdul, please, Nick, Abdul. And it may be easier than you think. The faculty complex is on the ground floor along one side of the medical research building, and the floors above it are used for accommodation. The block joins onto the uni at one end of the main building, but it's totally autonomous and isolated. We do need to get on with it though."

"So we're looking at night-time and fairly soon. What staff can we expect?"

"That's why I think we can pull it off, Nick. Another reason for the government using it is the small numbers involved. Even with me doing a shift, there are only three doctors and a half a dozen nurses staffing it. Occasionally we get in a few nurses from the main hospital, but only if the ward is full. Minu picked up Laleh from the embassy

153

and took her home before I was told to open the facility. Let's say she needed some woman stuff sorted out, and I could do it better there. I volunteered to do a stint so that I could keep an eye on her, not because of any misplaced loyalty. We've been careful, and very few know she was actually staying with us, but with the way things are going, it's best if she disappears from Tehran completely."

Nick didn't comment. Amini leapt to his feet, unable to contain himself. This was his sister they were talking about.

"Abdul volunteered to do the overnight shift because he's tied up with some departmental stuff in the uni during the day, Nick. There isn't much actual doctoring going on in there, and there's a small room in the hospital with a cot for doctors to put their heads down if they aren't busy. He's using that."

"Okay, but how the hell do we go about it? You know the place, Abdul. Any ideas?"

Abdul leaned forward, single-minded intensity flashing from his dark eyes. "I've been thinking about that ever since Farhad arrived."

He ripped a sheet of paper from a notebook lying on the table and drew for several minutes.

"Okay. This is the basic layout." He turned the sheet towards Nick and pointed with a pencil.

"The main entrance is a sliding glass door that opens onto a lounge area with a divan, armchairs and a table and magazine rack. A reception area and a room for files and records takes up the other side." He pointed to the rear of the block. "The only other entrance is a fire exit door at the rear here, which we also bring stores through. It's kept shut, but it's got a crash bar on the inside like a cinema door. There isn't any access to the accommodation above us."

Abdul used his pencil again. "The corridor is quite wide with a medical store on one side and the cleaner's room opposite, and towards the front there's a locker room and staff toilet with a patient's toilet beside it. The ward is opposite that, and between the ward and lounge, there's the doctors' bunk room and a ready room for the staff. The theatre is on the other side, and the entrance lounge is about four metres beyond that." He stopped while Nick picked the sheet up and studied it.

Amini was impatient. "What do you think, Nick, can we do it?"

Nick ignored him. Farhad reluctantly gave him space.

"Well, I've done a commando course and operated with the Marines, and you were in the navy, Farhad, but that's a long way from us being assault troops. It might be possible with only one guard, but it's one hell of a risk if Laleh isn't in any real danger."

Abdul stretched a hand to cover Nick's forearm "I might have given you the wrong impression, Nick. We're pretty sure the regime is behind some executions still going on up here, and they all seem to be the former shah's people. It's a bit confusing right now, but if payback really gets underway, Laleh would be better off out of Tehran."

"Shit. So what you're saying is we need to do it now?"

Abdul nodded. Farhad's eyes glittered without blinking.

Nick looked pensive. "Okay guys, first things first. Where will everybody be at say three in the morning?"

Abdul looked skywards, thinking. "One nurse will be in a small office in the ward, the other at the reception desk. I'd be in the small bunk room and the guard would be on a settee in the lounge with the lights turned down. Change over isn't until eight the next morning, so everyone would probably be dozing by then."

"How would he be armed?"

"I've only ever seen him with one of those banana rifle things in the week we've been doing this."

"That's an AK47 semi-automatic assault rifle, Abdul. What about side-arms?"

"He wears a belt with a bayonet scabbard, but no holster or jacket, so I don't think so."

"If he's armed, it's still a problem though. We haven't got any weapons ourselves."

Amini cleared his throat, a bit embarrassed. "I'm sorry, Nick, but I didn't know what to expect up here. I brought the automatic with me."

Nick's face initially flooded with anger, but almost immediately he backed off.

"Not the wisest thing you've done, Fred, but I would have talked you out of it if I had known, so maybe it's not a bad thing. Have you got anything else we can use as a weapon, Abdul?"

"Sorry, Nick, I haven't got any guns, I'm in the healing game. We've got some large kitchen knives if that would help though."

Nick shook his head, smiling slightly. "Knife fighting's a bit of an art form, Abdul. Someone once said never to take a knife to a gun fight."

Just then Minu came swishing towards the table with glasses of tea on a tray. She had heard the last exchange and put the tray down before sitting beside her husband. "Would a lead club be any use, Nick?" she asked. Abdul looked at her in amazement, and Nick looked surprised. "That would be much better than a knife if we could get hold of one, Minu."

"We changed over some old lead water pipes for copper ones in the garden and we've got some lead pipe in the shed we could cut up." Minu smiled at her husband. "Abdul never throws anything away."

Jock Sinclair spoke up. "What about coordinating it, Nick? Without radios, that could be a problem and we don't want Abdul or the nurses to look as if they were part of it."

"I've been thinking about that too, Jock. We can't do anything for the Americans anyway, so we need it to look like a local thing. You'll have to do the talking, Farhad. You're the only one who speaks Farsi. It mustn't look as if Americans are involved at all. We'll have to rough you up a bit as well, Abdul."

"You get Laleh away and that's the least of my worries."

Nick looked through the notes he'd scribbled alongside the diagram again. "Right, I reckon we're nearly there, guys. What about the car park itself, Abdul? Any evening traffic, and is it wide open or landscaped?"

"The complexes are huge, Nick. There are cars and taxis coming and going most of the night, and a lot of students' cars will be parked there. There's also a narrow car park along the rear of the block because there's a back entrance to the accommodation about eighty metres up from our fire exit. All those sections are planted with trees and bushes for summer shade, and that includes the car park out back. There's a standard road between it and the fire exit, but that's all."

"Any random security patrols?"

"A bloke from college security checks the front door at about midnight if we're using it, then nothing until between six and seven the next morning. The campus is vast, so he'll be mostly roving in a vehicle."

"Right. Well, the only other thing I can think of is a local disguise. You'd be okay in your Paki gear, Fred, but Jock and I need something too."

Minu interrupted again. "I've got some dish-dashas in a cupboard upstairs that our boys used to wear, Nick."

"What on earth is that, Minu?"

"Men's full-length white robes. We haven't got any turbans, but I've got several beanies we use when we go skiing. I can roll down the rims and cut eye holes in them, or I've got some nylon stockings. When do you want them by?"

Nick took his time thinking. "Well, it doesn't sound too complicated, guys, and it could all change suddenly. Stuff it. We'll do it tonight and be back home by dawn.

A fine, persistent drizzle ahead of a slow-moving warm front drifted over the Ellsbergs from the Caspian that night. They had to expect that. It was winter. And even though it was close to midnight, Daneshjou Boulevard was still awash with car headlights that flared unexpectedly when the bright beams were distorted by water droplets. The soft squeal of wipers was mesmerizing, but the males in the Cherokee weren't even close to drowsy.

As they approached the northwestern outskirts, the area opened into big car parks studded with tall buildings, the stretches of tarmac illuminated by pinprick glows from lampposts, their shimmering cones distorted by gently waving branches. The buildings soared high enough to pierce the low cloud base, and neon tubes shone from a number of curtained windows. Several of the entrances were marked with defused lights. Sinclair's attention re-focused as the left winker on the Mercedes just forty yards ahead blinked insistently. He slowed automatically and flicked on his own.

"I'm bloody glad Abdul led us here, Nick. It would have been a pain in the ass to pick the right building on a night like this."

"Roger that, Jock, but we've still got to leave it until after two before we do it. It'll mean an hour in the truck at least."

Amini picked up on the concern. He was embarrassed at the risks he was pushing his mate into and tried to atone. "The weather should help though, Nick, and there should be plenty of cars in the car park."

Nick smiled, but it was ironic. "We'll know soon enough, Fred. The sign says Kudakyar Street, so we're nearly there."

The Mercedes slowed but didn't stop in front of the dark, glass-fronted edifice ahead, turning into an access road that looped around the southern confine. Light blazed from a number of the windows on that wing, and both cars were forced to stop at a pedestrian crossing. A group of giggling students, their heads bowed against the rain, disappeared through glass doors into the accommodation. A shaken Abdul took off slowly, pointing vigorously left only 100 yards further on. The Cherokee was close enough for the occupants to see his frantic gestures in their headlights. There were no windows on the ground floor here, only what looked like a double steel door embedded in pale brick-work. Jock flashed his lights and took the next right turn into the car park. Abdul disappeared around the corner opposite.

And the car park Jock turned into wasn't all that small either. Two double rows of parking slots joined both the big car park out front and ran into another behind the research centre's buildings. Like the larger parks, it sported its share of vegetation. The Scot pulled into a slot almost opposite the emergency exit, comfortably shielded by healthy flora. Now he was just another one of several cars parked in nearby billets. He switched off with a relieved sigh.

Nick turned to Amini in the back seat, his voice tight. "Put the balaclavas and Laleh's chador on the back seat, Fred, and hand me the roll of duct tape. I'll go over it all again because I've just thought of a couple of small extras." He cut off several strips of tape with a pen-knife.

"Okay, guys. Abdul will open the crash bars when he does his ward rounds, but we've got to give everybody time to settle down again before we move, so we're still going to wait until after two. What we can do now though is put some duct tape over the car door micro-switches. We don't want internal lights coming on every time a bloody door is opened. Pull the doors half closed after, don't slam them either. Okay. Do that first."

Amini jumped down before Nick had finished. It didn't take long before they were out of the rain again.

"When Fred and I go for the back door I want you out of the Jeep, Jock. Stay on this side of the road amongst the bushes, but if anything does happen, that extra couple of seconds might make a difference. Start us up as soon as we come through the exit later. You okay with that?"

Sinclair nodded.

"Right, this one's for you, Fred. When we get to the ward, you slip in and tape up the nurse. She'll probably be dozing too. After that, show your face carefully to Laleh and tell her to get dressed. She can tell the locals to grab any taxi that pulls up to the accommodation blocks, so don't forget to give them some money just in case." Both the Scot and Amini nodded this time.

Nick paused to think.

"I should have clobbered the guard by the time you're done, Fred, so don't hang around. You can subdue the other nurse while I'm taping the copper and then we'll lock them in the medical store. One of the nurses is sure to have the key, or at least know where it is, and Abdul knows to stay in his room until we go for him."

"Sounds simple enough to me, laddie. We should be on our way fifteen minutes after that."

The last hour went slowly enough, but the final ten minutes were like drawing teeth without Novocain. By then they'd slipped into whispering, and Amini was actually fidgeting. Nick looked at his watch for the umpteenth time and saw it was five to two. Close enough.

"Hand me my club and the sock, Fred, then cock your piece." The snick of the sliding breech sounded like thunder in the quiet car.

"Okay. Take the tape. You'll need it to tie up the nurse in the ward, and don't forget to tape the exit doors together again after we're in. Use a fresh bit of tape, not the bit Abdul used. We don't want them blowing open. Here, take my pocket knife as well." He passed one of the smaller Swiss Army knives across. "Okay, guys, let's do it."

All three got out. Farhad Amini, distracted, shut his car-door firmly and then hissed a quiet 'sorry.' The other two closed theirs gently. Jock Sinclair followed them to the bushes but then crouched. He watched as they crossed the road and eased the exit open. Seconds later, it was if nothing had happened. He climbed back into the driver's seat but left his car door partly open. They'd want twenty minutes before he needed to move.

The lights in the corridor had been switched to just one bulb out of three, but it was enough for them to see what they were doing. Both the medical store and cleaning cupboard were marked by brass plates, but what they said was conjecture to Nick. They were in Farsi.

A few metres further on, a dim night light struggled to illuminate the corridor outside the ward, and here Amini touched Nick's arm and took the lead. He peered carefully though the glass top of the swing-door and then turned and put his lips near Nick's ear.

"Piece of cake, mate. She's actually got her head on her hands on the desk."

Nick whispered too. "I'll give you five to sort her out and talk to Laleh, before I go for the guard."

The pilot continued slowly towards the lounge area on the balls of his feet. Amini eased open the ward door. The night lights were dim, bordering on gloomy, and no-one moved in the beds that were occupied.

The nurse didn't stir when Amini opened the small office door, and merely grunted when he unrolled a couple of feet of tape. She lifted bleary eyes only when he wrapped her wrists with tape. She had barely started to open her mouth when he closed it again with another strip. Amini put his lips alongside her ear and whispered in Farsi.

"Complete silence and you won't get hurt. This is nothing to do with you." She turned terrified eyes towards him, and he wriggled his automatic before returning it to a pocket. The eyes behind the slit in the shemagh looked cold and intense, but nothing else showed. She nodded, still terrified. "Okay. I'm going to tape your feet and we'll be gone in ten minutes. She swung her lower legs towards him almost eagerly.

In the ward, Amini saw that the men were ranged on one side, the three women opposite them, with the flowing screens around the occupied beds partially deployed. Up to then, it had been pretty quiet but now several of the patients twisted and muttered close to consciousness. It must be a thing of the senses. He located the bed that Laleh occupied, opened his headdress and clamped her mouth gently with his hand.

She woke instantly, her eyes wide and fearful, but fortunately recognised him even with an upright finger to his lips. He nodded and she nodded too. The fear drained instantly from her eyes. Amini dropped his hand from around her mouth. She struggled to a sitting position.

"No questions now, Laleh," it was breathed more than whispered. "Get dressed and ready to travel, speak in Farsi only, and don't identify me at all. Okay about that?"

His sister nodded.

"Okay, I've got to help some friends who are with me, so you get the other Iranians up and dressed, and then wait for us. No matter what you hear, wait until we come for you." Amini's five minutes were about up. He hurried from the ward.

Nick took his time easing along the corridor wall, the eighteen inches of covered lead pipe hanging in his right hand. Occasionally, he flicked his eyes down to see where he was walking, before cupping an ear just short of the corner of the lounge. He tightened his grip. Craning forward, he could see that the other nurse was also dozing, but this one slouched upright in her chair. He took another step to locate the guard, and then another.

The Kalashnikov was leant casually against the coffee table, but there was no sign of the guard. Nick straightened in confusion and stepped further forward to clear his vision.

Already hyped, Nick didn't register the click of the toilet door opening. The guard was almost on him before the self-closing arm on the door slammed it shut. He spun, but the hand holding the cosh was still by his side.

With his face already streaked with mobile sweat, the heavier guard propelled Nick backwards over the sofa, his hands groping for the pilot's eyes. They bounced onto the floor with the Iranian still on top, but his hands had either been dislodged, or he'd used them to protect himself. Nick saw a chance and dropped the lead pipe. It was too cumbersome to manoeuvre from underneath. Instead, he drove his palm into the savagely distorted face above. It wasn't as forceful as he'd hoped, and his position was wrong for that, but the heel of his palm did hit under the bridge of the nose. The guard reared backwards, his eyes streaming, allowing Nick to get his left hand between them as well. This time, in shear desperation, he went for the eyes and mouth. It was then that the Iranian remembered he had a bayonet.

The guard twisted to his left to get at the steel, and for a second Nick thought he had him. When the Iranian rolled back and the point nicked the left side of his neck, he knew he didn't. He struggled even more fiercely, getting his hands around the guard's wrist, and with a super-human effort forced the sharp blade several inches from his throat. The guard's face distorted with an even greater effort, and he had gravity on his side. The vicious blade crept closer again, and Nick could feel his arm muscles burning.

When he had been operational, Nick's personal weapon was a Browning nine mil, and that sound was totally different from the strange metallic slap he now heard. For a micro second it didn't register, and then the straining face above him distorted further, followed by a cone of brains and gore spraying above and to his left. Most of the dead weight followed the spray. Nick struggled to sit, his dilated eyes coursing rapidly. He saw the nurse now standing and petrified with whitened knuckles to her lips, and a yard or so to his right Amini still leant into his shot with the weapon in a two-handed grip. Nick's first disjointed thoughts were for the repercussions.

"Jesus, you should have just whacked the bastard on the head!"

Farhad didn't look remorseful. "No time. It was you or him. He was a revolutionary guard anyway. Fuck him."

Nick Evans' senses returned rapidly. "You're right, mate, I'm being stupid. If you hadn't, I'd be toast by now." He stood and picked up his club. The nurse was still blubbering, but more quietly by then.

Nick whispered. "You bind her, Fred, and I'll drag Abdul out. He must be wondering what the hell happened. And just in case, we'd better leg it soon."

Sinclair took a quick squint at his watch before sliding down to the tarmac again. He grabbed his lead pipe but left the driver's door half open as he moved to the edge of the road. He'd barely squeezed into a bush, put off by the still wet foliage, when headlights tracked around the corner from the front car park. He pushed further into the vegetation.

Initially, Sinclair wasn't alarmed that much. He guessed it was another batch of students getting back late when the vehicle stopped in front of the accommodation doors. The driver got out of a van and wore some sort of uniform. Sinclair cursed. It was campus security. The Scot glanced quickly at the fire exit. Thankfully it looked shut.

Although the concrete still glistened, it had stopped drizzling some time before, so security didn't hurry. He watched his footing as he strolled to the half-glass doors, and gave the handles a jiggle. He seemed satisfied, so Sinclair surmised that residents must have their own keys. Unhurriedly, the security guard turned and ambled back to his van, but paused when a muted slap filtered through the waterlogged atmosphere. His looked more curious than alarmed when he stared in Sinclair's direction, and then mounted his van. Sinclair ignored the wet vegetation and eased around the bush as the van stopped again. The Scot eyed the double door, and from his new position he could see a thin sliver of light at its centre joint. He cursed.

Security looked at the exit uncertainly. He knew the theatre had been requisitioned by the government, so maybe it had something to do with that. He dreaded making a mistake. His job was important to him.

The vehicle was parked only feet from where the Scot crouched, and the guard was unarmed. The body of the van was between them, and Sinclair used its cover to get closer until Sinclair was only yards from the man's back. The road was lit by the lights from the building, and Sinclair was sure he hadn't seen the guard radio in. He gripped his water pipe tighter and launched himself towards the guard's back.

Maybe the man sensed him in the last micro-second. His head certainly started to turn, but it was too late. The lead pipe was on its way by then and bent around his skull with a dull thud. The guard dropped without a moan. Sinclair bent over, gasping and trembling, but then he realized that the van and the prostrate body were exposed. He was still shaking when he bundled the guard into his van and drove it into the car park.

Amini bound the nurse's hands, stuck tape around her mouth and marched her down the corridor. Nick opened the cubicle door and found Abdul sat on the cot with a worried expression. His face flooded with relief.

"That had me sweating, I didn't have a clue about what was happening."

Nick still looked serious. "A cock-up is what was happening, Abdul. The guard was having a pee, not crashed out, and nearly had me. Farhad was forced to shoot him. We'll have to wrap this up right away and get out of here."

"Is there anything I can do to help?"

Nick thought. "Farhad is locking the nurses in the drugs room. We'll nip Laleh back with us after to say goodbye. You hunt out any files on the locals and we'll get rid of them. Make your farewells with Laleh quick, mate, and we'll head on south right after. I'll keep our embassy up to date from there. A bloke called Gerry Hawkins is my contact, so give him a safe number to call, not your home number. He's on extension twenty-three at the embassy"

"Okay, Nick, I've got that. I'll sort out the files."

Nick waited outside with the ward with the foyer nurse while Farhad collected the ward nurse. Both were locked in the drug's store, and when he entered the ward, all four locals were dressed. Three of them looking bewildered. Amini addressed the man in Farsi.

"Grab anything here that could identify any of you. We've got your medical files and we'll destroy them later. We'll be on our way in two or three minutes, so be ready to go." Amini took Laleh by the arm with no hint of recognition.

"We need to talk to you separately. You come with me, and we'll let you go after."

The others looked puzzled as Amini led his sister towards the corridor. She played her role straightfaced. When they trooped into the passageway, Amini didn't introduce Nick right then, and with him in a dish-dasha with a balaclava pulled over his face, she had no idea who or even what he was.

Amini and Nick hurried back to the lounge where Abdul was rifling through a metal cabinet in the records room. He held out four thin, blue folders.

"This is all there is. Get rid of them well away from here."

Nick, up front, pointed. It was only then that Laleh saw the gruesome, blood-spattered corpse behind the settee. Surprisingly, there were no histrionics. She gazed for a few seconds but made no comment, although her face was on the sad side. She opened her arms when she was close to Abdul. Nick didn't understand the Farsi, but the farewells were swift. He took charge again.

"Okay, guys, we'd better hit the road. You okay, Abdul?"

"You'd better really clobber me, Nick. With the guard dead, it's got to look good. Thank you for what you've done for us and our friends, and don't expect too much from Laleh right now. She's been severely traumatised and might be quiet for a while." He looked at Amini when he said that.

Nick acknowledged. "Okay, let's get on with this."

Abdul pointed to the curve of his skull above and behind the right ear. "Hit me there, Nick. It's the strongest part of the skull, with plenty of blood vessels." He held out a hand to Amini, and Nick struck as he turned. Nick avoided the blood when he went for the carotid pulse and nodded. Amini led off with Laleh hurrying between them. They picked up the other Iranians on their way out.

Jock Sinclair was standing opposite the fire exit door when one side opened tentatively and Nick peered out. The Scot hurried to the Cherokee but was fumbling so much he stuffed up the first start. He breathed deeply, deliberately slowing himself down, and it fired with a roar on the second attempt. Amini had pulled a rear door fully open by then, while Nick reached to help Laleh in. She recoiled at his touch, and levered herself in with the help of the grab rail. Amini followed her with a sad shake of his head, and indicated the chador on the back seat.

"Just put the top bit on, Laleh. We won't be stopping again."

There was little chat while Sinclair motored the eighteen kilometres west on to Bagh-E-Feyz. When they passed Mehrabad International, Nick expected to see airliners, but the skies above were empty. The Scot turned into Qazum Street, then down Shahid Raja, and from there they were on the road south to Qom. Sinclair kept rigidly to the middle lane after that, and when the suburbs were behind them, clamped mandibles loosened amongst the men.

The night turned slowly from a dark grey to a strengthening pale yellow as they motored south. The trip had been incident free, and the Scot was chatting as animatedly as the others when they breasted a small hillock a few kilometres north of Qom. On the other side a black and white was drawn up on the side of the road.

It didn't register until they were quite close, and then Sinclair saw who was relieving himself. The last time he'd seen the tosser was in a troop carrier at the airfield.

Instinctively Jock's foot stabbed for the brake, but there was nowhere to go and he was on top of the vehicle before the pedal had even started to bite. Just as quickly, Nick hissed harshly to keep driving. The men stared rigidly ahead, Laleh glanced side-ways and then ahead again.

But it was an anti-climax. Arak half turned, but continued what he was doing, although he couldn't miss the company logo on a rear side panel. There was a local couple in there too, so they had obviously done an embassy run. But Arak had been summoned and that was his priority. He could always use it to rattle them when he next saw them.

Chapter Twenty-Four

Sarah knew what they had gone to do and was at Nick's house before six. When they hadn't returned the night before, she'd guessed it would be early the next morning. She heard the vehicle arrive, so switched on the kettle before bustling out to open the courtyard door. She didn't have to think about whether they'd want coffee or not.

The men were emptying the back of the Jeep of boxes and crates, but a chador-clad woman, her eyes downcast, reared back when the housekeeper opened the door. And it couldn't be body language, it had to be instinct. Sarah grasped the covered arm, guided the girl into the third bedroom, and then drew the heavy portiere.

Sarah tossed the girl's colourful beaded bag on the bed before leading her to the wardrobe. She showed her the Bakhtaran outfits and some purely girlie things on the dresser, and then helped lift the heavy robe over Laleh's head. It came free in a rush. Sarah could then see that tears washed the dark, soulful eyes, while a wayward trickle meandered down one cheek. Again it was instinctive. Sarah dragged Laleh to her and enfolded her in plump strong arms.

The women were still busy in the bedroom when the males collapsed untidily into the furniture, sipping coffee laced with Jameson's. It was a bit early for booze, but the tension had been strong, more insidious than any of them would ever admit. They were dealing with it the way men do. They laughed easily, made funny comments and derogatory observations, and were noisier and more animated than normal. And Amini even led the conversation at times, something he hadn't done before. His sister was safe though, and it made a difference. The adrenalin was still on the high side, but the conversation got less noisy as the implications sank in.

Sarah came out of the bedroom twenty minutes later and began dicing vegetables. As she finished, Amini climbed to his feet to refill his mug. Then he stopped.

The large brass rings on the bedroom curtain screeched harshly as Laleh eased into the room, and stunning didn't do her a lot of justice. She'd been gifted with all the best features of the diverse peoples of her vast, sandy nation. Amini moved towards her with arms out-stretched while Sinclair and Nick scrambled to their feet. Both where a little over-awed.

A darkish brown skirt hid bare feet, while a bronze flowery blouse, buttoned to the neck, covered the upper half. Proud, high breasts pushed provocatively against the constraints of the thin sateen blouse material, and mutton chop sleeves tumbled half way down her arms. Glistening blue/black hair framed the almost perfect ovoid features, and her complexion was certainly no darker than Nick's. The whole was emphasised by a delicate plum lipstick.

But it was the eyes that compelled. Dark brown and penetrating, they were framed by eyelashes brushed with a dark mascara and highlighted by a medium blue eye shadow. They seemed to skewer you. And she looked sad as well, although a stubborn tilt to her neck said a fighter dwelt in there somewhere. Amini was hugging her before they could see any more. Jock came forward with a proffered hand, but Nick was still shell shocked and lingered behind.

"Laleh, you haven't really been introduced to Nick and Jock properly. Nick's the one with his mouth still open. They've taken quite a few risks for us." Amini grinned.

Jock Sinclair took her hand in both his, raised it, and kissed it gallantly. He wasn't just an extrovert, he was a romantic extrovert, and it gave Nick time to clamp his jaw. He thrust out his own hand.

"I should thank you, gentlemen. These are difficult times." Her English was formal and only fractionally accented. Her voice was like chocolate dripping over expensive toffee. "Until Farhad appeared I had no idea how this would end for me."

"Welcome, Laleh, I'm glad that we could help." He was still floundering, and it all sounded a bit inane.

It was Sarah who would mostly control the rest of that day. She sat the girl next to her brother on the divan before she brought her coffee. She was a woman, and knew that after her traumatic week, Laleh wouldn't talk until she was ready. She needed to come down first.

"I show Laleh around town. Be back this afternoon. You boys drive to the airfield and tidy up." It was said with authority. There wasn't room for argument.

Nick strung it out as long as he could, but by early afternoon he'd had enough. "Bugger it. Lock up the hangar, Jock. We're going home." The Scot looked up from the aircraft documents. "No resistance from me, laddie." He swooped up the hangar key-ring. "Give me a couple of minutes."

Nick rinsed the coffee mugs and two minutes later signaled to Amini. The women had beaten them home, and there was a pot of stew already prepared.

That evening the meal was on the table before six. A shrewd Sarah broke the sombre mood. "It been long two days, time you all eat."

Nick had cracked a good Merlot to honour it, but the wine glasses barely got sipped from. They looked exhausted. After they'd eaten, Sarah shoveled what was left in a container to take with her, and stacked the dishes to wash in the morning. She took off home, and Sinclair was not slow in following her. The other three scanned magazines as they drooped further. Within the hour, Nick raised his head.

"Do you guys want a nightcap?"

"England introduced me to a taste for alcohol, Nick. A final one wouldn't do any harm." Both Iranians smiled.

"If you have soda, Nick, I would like to join you in a whisky."

"We can get any of the mixes at the Embassy or in Qom, Laleh. There's ginger ale, Seven Up or Coke if you prefer it?"

"Soda will be fine, Nick. Not too much whisky." She was beginning to unwind herself.

They sipped their drinks slowly and in silence. It was a time to meditate not natter. When the drinks were finished, they trooped off to their beds.

Chapter Twenty-Five

Sinclair arrived early the next morning, but coffee was flowing for a second time before Laleh emerged. Her clothing was subdued this time, like Bakhtaran matrons wore on ordinary days, but somehow she added a flair that was more elegant than her country cousins would ever achieve. All three males stood. Nick asked how she took her coffee and moved to the kitchen area to make it. As he poured, he pondered.

This was all new to him, and he felt uncomfortable. His instincts were to play the gentleman, to appear protective and in control, but he couldn't stop feeling uneasy around her either. This was somewhere he hadn't been before, nor something he intended or even understood.

Sarah was washing crockery and saw his bemused expression. She looked passed him to the girl.

"You treat her good, Nickie, she hurting," Sarah whispered.

Nick threw his housekeeper a startled look, wondering what the hell she could see. He hadn't worked a lot out for himself yet. He did realise he wasn't reacting defensively though, the way he usually did. He frowned.

It had been the long time between drinks for him. Was testosterone the culprit, were rampant pheromones trickling into his crystal atmosphere? He didn't know for sure, but he did know he was fumbling like an adolescent. He took her coffee. It seemed safer than thinking right then.

Laleh thanked him, and Sarah followed up with some sliced fruit. Nick let her eat while Sinclair fixed a coffee for himself, not sure how to begin. He still felt tongue tied, but being around her was already some sort of catalyst. Somehow he felt responsible for them both, and already it was important to come up with a plan. They seemed to accept that it would be him who safe-guarded them. Nick thought about it while the girl finished her coffee. The others looked at him when he cleared his throat.

"A hell of a lot has happened in the last few days, but the basics haven't changed, guys, so let's not get carried away. And right now I'm looking for answers, so jump in if you think of something. We've got to get some priorities sorted out right away. Jock and I should be okay for a while for instance, but you two may need to get out as soon as you can."

Farhad and Laleh Amini were lounging on the sofa. He moved his hand to cover hers.

"There's no point in pretending that Laleh and I have any future here anymore, Nick, but we're slap in the middle of a big country, and being surrounded by other Islamic states could be a problem. They've all got elites who aren't too popular with ordinary people either, and that bit of Russia to the north doesn't exactly help much. Probably the only safe thing would be to get out through Turkey. It's an Islamic country, but more Westernized and pro-American than most."

"Did Abdul suggest how it could be done?"

"It's all too new, Nick. He didn't have any answers. I took down several phone numbers of people who might help, but I'll have to be careful. We don't know which way they may have to jump to save their own skins. There's another option, though. The sailors I escaped with come from the Zagros Mountains northwest of here. They said to put the word out with the elders if I needed help. They'd find me."

"It's winter, though, Fred and the Zagros stretch over a thousand kilometres from here to Turkey, and it's bloody freezing up there too. I doubt Lily would make it over that distance in those temperatures."

Laleh broke in, sounding peeved. "Stop treating me as if I wasn't here, Nick. Not all women in patriarchal societies are content to wear gags, and I've lived with that macho bullshit all my life. You come up with something, and I'll tell you whether I can do it or not. I'm stronger than I look, and getting killed if I can't is a pretty strong incentive."

Amini glanced at his sister but not with anger. Nick guessed he'd overstepped some line on the ground and blustered as he tried to qualify.

"I'm really sorry, Laleh. It wasn't intentional. It's because I've mostly done the planning for the things I've been involved in. It's a pilot thing. This is a bit different, but really it's just another problem to solve."

"I know that, Nick, and I wouldn't pretend to know how we can do it, but ask me if I'm prepared to try what you come up with. Don't assume I can't." Her eyes were glistening again as she stood and headed for the courtyard. "If you'll excuse me, I'll get some fresh air while you guys hammer a few things out."

Sarah gave Nick a blistering look that would have melted rock and followed her.

"Shit, I really blew that." He could think of nothing else to say.

Sinclair's smile had a laconic touch. "You're obviously not very good around the ladies, Nick, me boy. Maybe that's why you're still a bachelor." He wasn't one to let the pilot off the hook.

"Up yours, Jock. It wasn't what I said. She's pretty wound up about something and I was in the firing line, that's all."

Amini stood and paced, battling with rampaging thoughts. He made up his mind and turned to the other two. "Nick, Jock, this is my fault. We're all pretty much tied up with each other out here so it's only fair that we start on the same page. We come from different cultures, and that could cause problems enough, so things that affect us all should be shared by all."

"When it comes to saving our asses, I suspect we're all pretty much the same, Fred, but Jesus H Christ, Lily sure is touchy."

"Well, you guys will have to decide how you handle this, but it's got to do with sacking the American Embassy. As you said Nick, there were more than just students there, and Laleh was caught in her office by two of the so-called religious police. She was knocked around and raped, and pretty traumatised when Minu got there to pick her up."

Sinclair whistled, but Nick went further. "Jesus. That must be horrible for any woman, let alone in this country, Fred. She might never get over something like that. No wonder she's a bit anti."

"I'm not making excuses for anyone, I'm stating the facts, so don't take it the wrong way, but knowing Laleh, she was in a mini skirt and obviously one of us. Our lighter skin colour and features are fairly distinctive, even though the women's noses aren't as big." Amini smiled. "Fundamentally it was a power-play, a way to get back at us." The smile was wry.

"I'm ashamed to admit it, but I can see now that Iranian women have always been chattels and this was about putting a brand on her, about making her unacceptable in her own country. I'm sure you've heard of arranged marriages, honour killings and using rape as a punishment in other Islamic countries? Well, it happens here too. She's strong and highly intelligent though, and her degrees included a fair bit of psychology. It all helps. If she's treated the right way, I think she'll get over this fairly quickly."

"How should we play it then, Fred? She wouldn't want us to know about something like that, would she?"

"I told you she was pretty tough, Nick. On the way to bed last night she told me to tell you when the time was appropriate. I think it's now, before we go any further. She won't be pregnant because Abdul did a dilatation and curettage procedure, a D and C, you English people shorten it to. It's why she was in the hospital and why she is going to need some understanding for a while."

"Is there anything we can do now then, Fred?"

Sinclair jumped in. "A brother would try to restore her fractured ego and self-esteem, Nick, but it's different when another male does it. You pissed her off, so it's up to you to start building her back up again." The Scot flicked his head. "I suggest that you get your ass out there and start doing it."

Amini nodded but said nothing. Nick looked startled.

Women had always been a bit of a mystery, but now he realized that Sinclair was too. It just hadn't been obvious with no eligible women around. He clambered to his feet and headed for the courtyard.

Laleh sat with a hand in Sarah's when Nick approached the bench. Intoxicated butterflies rioted around his insides, and he needed guidance, any sort of guidance. He expected Sarah's look to be venomous, but somehow it wasn't.

Sarah rose with a small smile as he got nearer. Something else he couldn't fathom. She held her head high as she walked passed him, so Nick sat but kept his mouth shut. He didn't want to put his foot in it again so he thought carefully before he spoke.

"Laleh, I'm really sorry I ignored you. It wasn't intentional, but it wasn't very clever either."

"I assume that Farhad has told you why I'm edgy right now." That was a statement not a question. "The last few weeks have been horrible for me. Not just what happened in the embassy, but that it could have happened at all. It seems that the comfortable, safe world I was used to vanished overnight. I know it was a power thing, done by people who've never had any before, but I feel dirty and I

177

want to feel clean and whole again." She paused to dab at a few tears.

"Right now, I need to know that I'm still appreciated as a person, that my opinions are at least considered, and that I might even be desired by someone in the future. I just can't see any of that at present, but I am sorry I overreacted and you were there to cop it. I lived in England for several years, and I know it's completely different over there."

There was nothing to follow that up with, so Nick didn't try. He looked at her and then the hand Sarah had been holding. He hesitated, but then he thought 'what the hell'.

Nick anticipated a fierce withdrawal when he did move to hold it, but it didn't happen. Her slim fingers curled around his slightly although she continued looking straight ahead. He was happy for it to stay that way. He sat with her without a need for words, and sensed her growing calmer.

"Laleh, let's have another cup of coffee and I'll try again. I'd really like your opinion on some of the stuff we need to talk about. The priority is to get you and Farhad out of the country safely, but we have to be careful. You're both okay here for a while, so let's concentrate on that first."

The girl half turned towards him, maybe looking for guile or cynicism, but whatever she saw, she seemed satisfied. She nodded briefly before standing, and moved back to the house. She kept his hand hold until she floated through the door.

Arak made the mullah's office in Tehran within thirty minutes of seeing the company vehicle on the Qom road. He'd been told what to look for by telephone before he flew to Abadan, but it was some five days later when he'd phoned his findings in. The mullah had insisted on a personal rundown in the capital. Arak was ushered in as soon as he arrived.

"Welcome, Mohammed." The mullah seemed distracted. "This breach could become more serious than we expected and we must contain it right away. I sent you because you were the only active detective before you joined our group. I need to know everything you know."

Arak cleared his throat. "Ah, now I understand, Mullah, but there was not that much to find out."

"Were his team of any use?"

"Not much, Holiness. They had no idea where he was. He didn't confide in them, but they did put me in touch with some Imams he spent time with. I found his body from what they said."

"So he was definitely murdered?"

"When I found him, he still had a knife in his chest, but the smell would have given it away before long anyway."

"Do you know who did it?"

"Almost certainly a naval commander called Farhad Amini. The local mullahs agreed that Achmed should shake up military officers because they were mostly the shah's men, and the naval base was the second place I visited. It was Tuesday morning before I got there, though, and the idiot officer on duty told me that the CO had been absent since Thursday. Amini was the CO so he was unlikely to confide in his juniors if it was personal. They were waiting for him to appear again."

"Do you know where Amini is now?"

"Unfortunately, not Mullah. The body was in a wardrobe in his office, but no-one knows where Amini is now. He said he needed a small crew with him to test the engine on a boat, but that was obviously a trick. The Dezful police reported finding it near the city later, but the crew hadn't set it on fire so it wasn't discovered immediately. They were long gone by then. Amini took a large sum of money from the establishment safe as well."

"What's your best guess?"

Arak was careful. "I think he was going on the run anyway and Achmed got in the way, Mullah. Some of

Achmed's dealings were a bit suspect, so I think it was personal. The crew Amini took with him was all Bakhtaran, and from where the boat was found, I'd say they've taken off to be with their own people. It will be impossible to find them in there."

The mullah nodded thoughtfully. "So it's a simple escape not the start of resistance. Thank you, Mohammed. You may return to Qom."

Chapter Twenty-Six

They had some ground rules to establish and it was a non-flying day, so they huddled. Christmas was just over a week away and everything would stop for it. They needed a plan.

Sinclair filled the Aminis in on Baha'i first, letting them know about their religion, and the Bakhtaran appetite for a good party, no matter whose religious ceremony it was. This Christmas week would be 'different' for the them.

The concept was alien to them. Their beliefs had been set when they were much younger, but neither professed to much religious affiliation anyway. They wouldn't have a problem with the week ahead.

"And neither would the Bakhtaran," Jock said. He told them about the uninhibited music and abandoned dancing that went with it, and warned them about the home-brew. It didn't seem to matter if it was made from bran, vegetable peelings or fruit either. It tasted close to paint thinner, with pretty much the same effect on the brain. Even the kids got in on the act.

It was still a few days before Christmas when Nick called for any last-minute thoughts, as the town would virtually close for business until after the New Year street parade. Sinclair got in first.

"We'd better put in some sort of report to Qom soon, Nick. Another flight wouldn't go amiss either. They know what happens out here around this time of the year and it'll stop them wondering about what we're up to. They'd need a company of soldiers if they wanted to move in, so if everything looks normal, they aren't going to bother."

Nick nodded. "You're right, Jock. We'll do a trip this afternoon and I'll fake up a couple of reports after it." He turned to Farhad. "You come out with us in your gear and help with any humping and shifting, Fred, but it would be best if you stayed here for a little while yet. Lil, I know Sarah is dying to drag you into town again and you can dress casually around here. Some women wear headscarves, but not everyone even bothers with that."

Laleh nodded. Nick thought of something else.

"Are there any other things you need when we go shopping, Lil? You know, ladies' things?" He looked embarrassed. She smiled gently.

"Not yet, Nick, but will I be able to go into Qom before the Christmas thing? I need a few cosmetics and I could do with something to sleep in. I'd enjoy a look around as well. It's a girl thing."

He was learning quickly, but military aircrew live in an insensitive, dangerous world.

"You'll have to wear your chador, but you can come in when we submit the reports on Christmas Eve. Sarah will need to do some last-minute shopping then as well. There isn't a great selection of cosmetics anymore, but you might get most of what you want if you tell them it's to please your husband." He was mortified when he realized that there was implied chauvinism in there somewhere. Lily's eyes crinkled.

"If I buy a fair bit, I could say that I'm shopping for all my husband's wives to share. That's even more politically correct."

Amini grinned, but Sinclair couldn't let that pass. "Well done, Nick. We'll have to send you to your bedroom and only let you out when it's dark and there's no-one around."

Nick Evans turned his eyes to the heavens. It was agony, not theatrics.

It had happened again. He felt physically sick. He had to make amends. He had to climb out of the cess pit he'd dug for himself. But what would do it? The answer leapt at him almost as quickly. Everybody enjoyed a ride around the local area in a helicopter. Some said it was the most fun thing you can do without sweating.

"To compensate for my big mouth, can I fly you around the local ranges, Laleh? I'll wear a gag, I promise. You'd like that for a change."

She smiled brightly. I've wanted to do that ever since I knew what you did, Nick, but you and Jock have done so much for us already. I was a bit too shy to ask."

This time, he thought about his response, already getting less defensive. "I would be honoured if you would accompany me, Laleh. It would be the most enjoyable flight I've had for a long time." He missed the nod and smile of approval from Sarah in the kitchen. The Scot didn't.

Chapter Twenty-Seven

It upped the ante to have a plan roughed out. Nick flew a pseudo survey over the ancient, icy hills and sketched in an imaginative negative report, and the next day he took Jock and Farhad into the hills with the Tikka. They pulled down both a fast gazelle and a nimble ibex on that one. The ibex would be roasted over a spit for the New Year celebrations. The gazelle would be shared with those around them.

A spitted carcass was tradition, and Jock had cut a forty-four-gallon drum lengthwise to use as a bar-be-cue. They would use it for the New Year. A lot of people dropped in to eat after the main street parade and nobody was turned away hungry. It was a big goat and barely fitted into the chest freezer. Nick hoped it would be cooked before the fire-water started to take its toll.

The next day was Laleh's time in the sky. hough it was still early, the day was already crystal clear when Nick dragged himself vertical. He tried to look wind swept and debonair but hadn't felt this anxious for years. Why he did eluded him. What was wrong now? He'd taken people flying before, often playing the high income taxi driver for VIPs, but somehow today it felt different. Also, both Jock and Sarah had warned him to think about some of his comments, and they'd hardly been covert. Some things he had said did seem to sting, but they were automatic responses, not deliberate. Perhaps that was it. Perhaps he'd become a cynic. That one would take more thinking about.

Laleh was probably sleeping better than she had in weeks when Sinclair and his boys trooped in. They all knew what day it was and didn't hold back on some mild joshing. Nick tried not to rise to the bait, tried not let them get through, but everyone seemed to be at it, and Sarah didn't help much either.

"I make lunch for you and Laleh, so you show her round up there. Where your flask thing?" She'd said that loud enough for them all to hear and the boys made appropriate noises. Sarah was smiling quietly as she sliced meat, but Amini couldn't stop himself snorting out loud. Life had been tough for weeks, and his rank as a CO had forced him to stay aloof. Now he was enjoying a close, family atmosphere for the first time in his life. Before, others' expectations had always taken precedence over his own needs, but what really got to him was that it happened among such varied religions and social backgrounds.

The friendly, pointed hassle didn't fade until Nick escaped into the courtyard with a brew. He didn't hear his housekeeper curb the exuberance. "That enough. You all be quiet now. They both in need this so don't spoil it." All of them knew better than to buck her. Jock Sinclair followed Nick out.

"No more of your bloody wise-cracks, you Scottish asshole. I've had enough for one day. I made a few stuff-ups and now everyone wants to jump on the bandwagon. I haven't been around an aggressive woman before and I didn't know what to say."

Sinclair's look was shrewd. "Do you see Lily as aggressive or strong?"

"Aggressive or strong, what's the frigging difference? Every time I open my mouth I put my foot in it."

"There's a huge difference, Nick. Do you remember that bit of soul searching we did when we were blubbering in our cups this time last year? You told me a bit about your growing up and your family. How your mum had an answer for everything, even if it was wrong, but everyone was her enemy if they didn't agree with her. Even you recognised that when you were not much more than a bairn." He let that hover.

"People with low self-esteem are often like that, Nick. That's aggression. Not having enough confidence to be wrong. Hiding away from other people's viewpoints even though they're true. You've been there before, laddie. You know what that's like."

Nick frowned and tried to quantify. "I didn't mean Lily was like that. I just say the wrong things when she's around, and she reacts."

"Well, you may be protecting your own iffy ego because of your childhood, mate. Maybe you chose the women you've known, not because you wanted them, but because they didn't challenge you. It could be why nothing lasted very long, but Lily isn't like that. We already know she'll stand up for herself if she needs to, but she can see when she's wrong as well. She's comfortable with admitting it too, and appreciates other opinions if it's something she doesn't know much about. I can see now that she'd fight just as hard for her bloke as for herself, mate. She's trying to tell you she may be a woman, but she's not a bloody wimp. That's where the difference is."

Nick was still truculent, still a bit edgy. "So when did you suddenly learn so much about women?"

A dark shadow dulled Sinclair's eyes. He sighed deeply before he opened up. "Nobody knows much about this, laddie, and I'll no be repeating it, so you'd better listen good. I was married to a bonnie lass from Stirling once, doing pretty much what I do now, and she was always going to travel with me. She got pregnant early though and before the first wee girl was out of nappies, she got pregnant again. In the end, it was the babies, nappies and kids schooling for her, and I sent the pay-cheques and occasional letters home. We never got to travel together." Sinclair contemplated before he went on.

"Jesus, half the time she didn't even know where I was operating from, and those times I did get home were few and far between." Jock reflected before he continued.

"One year I turned up after fourteen months overseas, and found the house was rented to someone else. The girls would have been in their late teens by then, and I had no idea where they might be, and their nan certainly wasn't about to tell me. My wife had developed an aggressive cancer just after I left and died three months before I got home again. I didn't know, and I wasn't there to bury her." Sinclair blinked rapidly.

"That was ten years ago and the girls would have bairns of their own by now. I've never seen them again and I've never seen my grandchildren at all. I didn't know much about women then, laddie, but I sure as hell do now."

By then his eyes were glistening.

Nick put an arm around Sinclair's shoulder and pulled him close. "I'm so sorry, mate, but you've never said any of this before."

"Well, I have now so take your bloody hand off my shoulder. You two are a bit like the kids I never knew, Nickie. Both me and Sarah can see there's something different about you two. Something about the way you look at each other. I fucked up big time, and I'll no let you do the same. Now, away with you, and I'll be in shortly. And you respond to that wee lassie a bit different in future."

Amini, Imran and Laleh stood near the kitchen talking animatedly when Nick went back inside. She was eating from a bowl of sliced fruit, and glanced over her shoulder and smiled. Nick felt more abashed than amused when he returned it. It seemed the more he had to think about, the more he needed to. Sinclair had rattled his cage again, but he tried to shrug it off.

"Jock's almost ready, guys, so we'll go after I've had another coffee."

"Sarah and her husband offered to take me around the stock yards, Nick. Can you look after Laleh if I go with them?" Amini asked.

No smart-ass replies came even close to the surface this time. "I can't think of anything I'd enjoy more, Fred." Laleh was obviously expecting a different response. She blushed a delicate pink. Sarah switched on the kettle with a faint smile.

Nick nodded absently. He manoeuvred past the group to make his coffee and was forced to hold on to the girl's shoulders as a fulcrum. She was dressed in jeans, a duck egg-blue T-shirt and brown leather moccasins that must have been under the chador when they brought her down. It was a light touch, totally asexual, more a need to pivot.

Laleh didn't move away, involuntarily she swayed towards him, but the slight movement was enough. There was no cringe, not even a flinch, and the warm play of muscles in her vibrant body although minute, was still noticeable. Nick wanted to hang on, to prolong it a second longer, but he was almost through already. Reluctantly, he released her.

"Nickie, give me rest of water for flask thing after you make coffee."

He poured and complied, and then turned with his mug. This time the girl was facing him just two paces away. Her T-shirt was tight and the brassiere marks showed prominently, but that's not what got his attention. Her breasts looked larger, more up-lifted in the T-shirt, the smaller swell of her nipples were now more proud and obvious. He looked up in confusion, hoping nobody had seen his reaction.

The men hadn't, they were facing away, but Laleh had. She didn't appear concerned, although she looked at him steadily. He didn't dare brush past again.

The boys climbed into the back of the Cherokee while Sinclair opened the front passenger door for the girl.

"You sit up here, Lily, or you won't be able to see a damn thing in that bloody chador. I'll hop in the back with my team."

Nick hovered too, holding out a tentative hand to help her in. He half expected a refusal with the others now present, but Laleh took it without hesitation and levered herself up with it. She dragged the rest of the long skirts in with her before smiling her thanks. He could see the expressive eyes crinkle.

Only minutes later, they reached the galvanised hangar and the maintainers piled out. Nick drove the short distance on to the office and started the flying ritual.

"A cup of instant, Lily?"

"Yes, please, Nick. Are the things I'm wearing under the chador okay for the flight?"

"They'll be fine, love, and you can get rid of that now. The terminus people aren't likely to wander over here."

"You're sure you won't get too excited?" She was grinning playfully when she said that, remembering his earlier embarrassment.

"I think I can cope if you don't wriggle around too much." He grinned back at what he could see of her. Then he realized he wasn't uncomfortable.

Laleh dragged off the slate-grey robes while Nick rummaged through the basket. He took out some long-life. Instant and sugar were in twist top jars beside the kettle.

"White with one isn't it, Lily?"

"Yes, please." Her response was muffled as she dragged the heavy under skirts over her head.

"Phew. I'm glad to be out of that bloody thing."

"I've got to admit that I much prefer you without it myself. I'd never make it as a Muslim." He grinned again. It was another automatic response, but he was getting a lot happier with where they were going.

Nick spread his topographical map over the table and pulled out chairs before he collected the coffees. The faint but heady musk she wore was more noticeable now their bodies actually brushed against each other, and both were

189

conscious of how close they were. Nick concentrated hard to get going.

"Do you prefer Laleh to Lily, or aren't you worried? I can remember if you kick me hard enough."

"I'll answer to either, Nick. It really doesn't bother me as long as it's not Rottweiler. I wasn't too keen on that one." They both grinned, and Nick shuffled even closer. "Right, we'll keep within this area for this trip." He put his left arm around the back of her chair and traced with his right index finger, pointing out Shahabad and Khomeyn.

"It's fairly high country that far in. The Bakhtarans have built some summer huts along the mountain streams, but no permanent villages." He pointed out a nearby peak almost in the centre of the area. "That one's the highest, with a great view and a couple of small flat meadows on it. Sarah packed us a picnic hamper, so we'll stop there for lunch. We can always look at other places on the next trip."

"It's not a problem then, parking it?"

The terminology had Nick smiling. "It's not a thing we did much in the navy. We flew bigger, long-range choppers with different missions, but I worked with the Army Air Corps for a while and they fly smaller things like this. They're air cavalry, and treat helicopters like horses, and when I started flying surveys, I found that we did too. We were forever stopping to chip out chunks of stuff for assaying. Jock will stick a spare battery in the cabin because we're shutting down, but if I know that bloody Scotsman, he'll take the other chopper and come looking for us if we don't get back on time."

"Okay Nick, I'm in your hands, but I didn't know Jock could fly."

"The silly bugger can't, Lily, but it wouldn't stop him from trying."

Nick knew it wasn't unusual for military pilots to get a bit blasé after years of flying, even with the exciting stuff. They can get jaded repeating the most adventurous things, but showing a novice the ropes swings the pendulum back again. Nick's interest had climbed back up a notch. Laleh's astute questions were breathing new life into it for him.

She must have spent most of her life in cities, and wanted to know lot about her country's flora and fauna. The questions she asked about cheetahs, and panthers, about wolves and camels were pointed and relevant, but she already suspected they would be too far south for most of the carnivores.

"Mostly that's right, Laleh. Jackals and hyenas live on the desert fringes as well, with maybe the odd tiger up north, but that's around the Caspian and the northern Zagros Mountains. We've only ever hunted ibex and gazelles in our mountains, but we've seen wild donkeys and small herds of camels here. We've never shot them, we only shoot for the pot, but we have had a go at the odd pig. In a country that's so anti-pork, I'm surprised there are any still up there."

Laleh giggled. "When I was in England, bacon, eggs and tomatoes were a breakfast tradition on Sundays. I loved it."

Nick grinned. "Okay then. We've got a couple of roasts and a side of bacon in the freezer. Only Jock and I eat pork, but we could have that for a change."

"Farhad won't touch it so it can be our little secret."

"The higher streams have got some beautiful trout in them as well. We can always do a fishing trip if you want?"

"I love trout. I'd really look forward to that, and all of us eat fish."

"Okay, we'll give that a go too. Having the chopper helps, but we'll do it later. There'll be enough to do on this flight."

Sinclair barged through the door as Nick was finishing up, pausing dramatically when he saw them hunched over the map. "You're ready to go, laddie." They both looked up.

"I don't remember you getting that close when you were showing me where we were going." He grinned. "Should I fetch a lever or a bucket of water or something?"

Nick picked up the grubby rag he'd used to clean the plastic map covering and threw it. "I wouldn't dare you, ruffian. You'd think I was trying to crack onto you." Lily grinned at their banter. She was female. She could already sense the deep bond between them.

"Well, at least your taste is improving boyo." He left that one hanging in the air and went to make a coffee.

"Okay, Jock. When you've finished, we might as well go.

"Aye, and if you're stopping up there for a while, Lily better take an anorak with her."

They all had warm jackets stuffed with soft down for working in the high country, issued by a grateful company. The best. Webster's was still in a locker. Nick had already thought about it, but let Sinclair do his gallantry thing. He collected two anoraks from the locker room and handed one to Laleh.

"There's a heater in the cockpit a bit like a car blower Lil, so I'd save the jacket until we climb out. It's pretty cold higher up, and there's plenty of snow around at this time of year." She nodded and folded it over her arm.

Nick picked up the basket. "Okay, let's get on with it."

Jock and Nick fussed over the girl in the front passenger seat, snugging her straps down tight and balancing the light-weight headset carefully over her ears. Nick secured the hamper and jackets on the back seat. As he walked around to the right front door, Sinclair touched his arm.

"She's pretty impressed already, Nick so none of that fancy airy-fairy crap. You two just enjoy it up there."

Nick showed his surprised. "Honestly, Jock, it never crossed my mind. She's not the sort to be impressed with stunts and I'm really looking forward to this myself."

192

"Aye. Well you get her back here with a gleam in her eye, not a spew bag in her hand. I don't want to have to kick your ass."

"You old bastard, you've got a crush on her."

"It's nothing like that, Nick, but I do feel a bit protective. Now fire the fucking thing up and be on your way." Sinclair strolled to the crew-room with his head high and hands thrust deep in his pockets. He didn't look back as Imran controlled the start-up.

Chapter Twenty-Eight

The engine spooled quickly with the characteristic high-pitched whine of its kind. Nick's hands and eyes flashed over a myriad of light grey switches and gauges before checking his control movements. He settled himself a little more before looking across at the girl. "Ready, Laleh?" Her eyes were wide, but she was fascinated with what he was doing. She didn't look apprehensive at all when she nodded. That was unusual for a first timer.

"What do you say, Nick, let's get on with it?" She grinned.

Nick flashed a thumbs up at Imran. When he got the same response, he lifted up a few feet and swiveled left and right to clear behind him. The helicopter's vicious downdraft whipped up a swirling sand storm. It was standard for helicopter pilots to clear behind, but right then he would have given birth if another aircraft had been there. It was clear as he knew it would be. He lowered the nose gently and let the machine accelerate towards the west, aiming for where the River Qom entered the foothills.

Nick kept fifty feet above the dark, lazy waters, cruising rather than speeding, but even so they were on top of Shahabad in minutes. It was market day, with hordes of colourfully-clad people thronging through the narrow, shadowed streets. A lot more than there were houses for them to fit into.

"Farhad's down there somewhere, Lil. Give him a wave."

Laleh held one hand above her brow like a visor as she squinted at the sun-drenched town and waved the other through the open window. Many waved back vigorously, her presence amongst them not a state secret. Nick saw her shade her eyes so he tugged off his Polaroids and passed them to her.

"It's all right, Nick, I can get by. You'll need them."

"Take them, Lily. I'm fine for the time being. If the snow gets glary at the top, you can give them back." She thanked him, and Shahabad was gone before they had finished the exchange.

"There were some houses in the higher ravines I've never seen before, weren't there?"

"They're shacks, really. They're only occupied in the worst of the weather when the herders are pushed down from the lower hills. It's a pretty hard life, love, and it totally depends on the seasons. I can't imagine any religious leaders getting much support for their ideas around here either, so you guys are okay for a while."

"So where was the house we're staying at?"

"There's a hill above the river on the northern edge of town. We're in the second row of houses and it's the only part of town with electricity. I'll show you on the way back."

Nick jammed the collective with his left knee and pointed at some boats ahead with his left hand. "We're coming up to Khelajabad, and that's were those boats come from. Sometimes people get good catches up here."

Several fast, lean feluccas heeled hard over by wind resistance on their rust, triangular sails tacked towards a mud brick village a few kilometres ahead. The houses were buried in a grove of leafless willow trees, surrounded by narrow strips of pale-green fields leaking along the river banks. Flocks of sheep and goats floated through them like mobile blobs of cotton wool, tended by young boys riding slowly through their ranks.

"A couple of roads and the river meet at a place called Neyzar, about twenty-five klicks further on, Lily. We'll turn right and climb into the mountains before we get there."

"What's a klick, Nickie?"

"Sorry, Lil, it's service speak for a kilometre. Most maps are calibrated in kilometres now, but the navy works in nautical and statute miles on some maps and charts, so we use either. There's just under two kilometres to a nautical mile. I figured you'd be more used to them."

The girl smiled. "You know a lot about this area, don't you?"

"It's more like being familiar with it, really. It's a pilot thing. We brought Farhad this way so I had to study the maps more than I normally would, but it all seems a bit new again with you on board."

He was going to leave it there. Anything more would get personal, and he wasn't sure he wanted to go there yet. He felt Laleh's eyes on him though and felt compelled to look at her. It was like examining his own soul. He quickly looked ahead again. She said nothing, knowing he would continue, but not sure how far he would go.

'Bugger.' Uncomfortable or not, he did feel more, and this was the sort of woman who would expect him to say it.

"I've been flogging around this same bit of dirt now for about eighteen months, Lil. Initially, it was all new and exciting, but it got pretty familiar in the end. I've only seen discolouration in rocks that might be minerals for a long time."

She turned her head towards him as Nick looked at her again. She was smiling gently, and the dark liquid eyes were telling him to continue. He struggled at first.

"It's happened before, that's all. When you take people for a flip, you often see things a bit differently again."

Sod his ego, he'd let her decide. He'd go where it might lead. Right then he felt as insecure and out of his depth as he had as a child.

"It was different from the start with you, Laleh. I enjoyed being around you, but I was a bit nervous too. You seemed so tough from the word go, grappling pretty well with things that must be horrible for you, and I was afraid I would come across like an immature jerk. I realize now I tried to stay aloof from it, to fend you off with smart-ass remarks that I hadn't thought much about. Maybe I was putting up walls before you did."

"You didn't have to look after me or do some of the nice things you did, or even bring me up here if you didn't really want me around."

Nick had killed most relationships almost as soon as they started, and didn't know why. This time he wanted desperately for it to take off, and he didn't understand that either.

"God, how wrong can you be, woman. When I thought up this trip, I couldn't wait for it to happen. I was like a bloody school boy dreading that something would stop it happening. I wanted to show you that I had some talents as well, I suppose."

"But you're being very unkind to yourself, Nickie. Do you really know what it took to do what you did for Farhad? You've hardly seen him since Dartmouth, and getting me out of Tehran was pretty risky." She stopped to cover the hand he had on the collective with her own.

"Even down here you're sheltering us in your home, and that's taken the pressure off some very dear friends of ours. I'd say that was a pretty brave thing to do when you've still got no idea what will happen to you. We're locals and it's not your country, so what you've already done is extraordinary. I'm quite in awe of you, Nick. It might seem a bit early for me to say something like this, maybe even a bit silly, but remember I'm an educated and travelled Iranian." She paused.

"I know what I went through was pretty unpleasant, but I think I know what it was really about now. Old Islam is dying, Nick. It can't adjust to a modern world and a lot of insecure males are desperately hanging on to archaic religious rules because they couldn't attract a woman or a decent job if they had to rely on their personalities or qualifications. They don't want women educated either because their egos couldn't stand losing jobs or arguments to them. The change will still be bloody in the short term, but I think it's inevitable. You can see that the hordes of moderate Muslims will win out in the end. It's why I was drawn to you from the beginning. You seem so different from any males I've met before. I just thought you didn't like me all that much."

"Jesus, Laleh, didn't we stuff that up then?" He looked ahead. "Oh shit! We've almost reached Neyzar. I'm going straight up and then hard right. Hang on to your seat."

Chapter Twenty-Nine

Nick pitched the nose up sharply and added a fistful of collective. The machine screamed skywards like a demented nightingale. The speed bled off quickly, but as it reached sixty-five knots, he lowered the nose again and turned tightly right, heading for a major crease in the rock. The chopper was already 1000 feet above the river when they slid into the rolling lilac hills. He looked at Laleh, but she didn't look scared. She was more into enjoying herself.

"I'm sorry, Laleh. Jock threatened to kick my backside if I pulled any stunts while you were in here."

"Oh, was that a stunt? I thought that was the way we went up." She was grinning shyly, but he wasn't fooled.

"Right, we'll be okay up here and everything's back to normal. Enjoy."

Rounded, mottled tors, the lilac tops covered in crystalline snow and eroded skirts more the gold of blasted sandstone pushed up through wind-burnt grass plateaus. Crumbling boulders as big as houses littered their bases and they were linked together by more sickly beige pasture. Laleh could see the silver glint of water dribbling around the tussocks, and dark-green fingers spread randomly from the liquid tracks. Stretches of pristine snow covered at least half those areas, the edges rounded and tortured by a cool sun. Lonely beige stalks poked high through the flat snowy patches, and water dripped wherever the questing sun caressed.

"Do any animals live this high up?"

"I've only seen a few wild goats up here for a couple of months in high summer. Most of the game is at least 500 feet below all year round. The villagers can't get up this high with their herds either."

She pointed to a col between two tall, rugged tors. "That's back towards where we came from, isn't it?"

"Well done, Lil. I'm not patronizing you, but most people haven't got a clue where they are after a few twists and turns in the hills. They hardly even know if we're the right way up."

"I didn't see it that way, Nick. I've thought a lot about it already and I can see it now for what it was. I'll be okay. You don't have to tip-toe around me anymore." He flicked another quick glance at her, but she continued at a tangent.

"So this hasn't been seen by a lot of people?"

"Quite honestly you may be the only woman who ever has, Lil. You'd have to be in a helicopter. There's no other way up, and only company ones fly around here."

Her hand flew to her mouth as she looked around her. Nick felt good. He was sharing his world with someone he really wanted to. They headed for the col at a sedate sixty knots.

"That tall peak I mentioned is just around this corner. We'll find somewhere to stop and have lunch.

Nick slowed over a larger, wind-burnt paddock and flew a slow clover leaf to assess the drift. Laleh was busy watching and didn't look up at all. He landed into a breeze off the desert and only then did she notice what was in front of her. She gasped involuntarily.

Ahead, the Zagros dropped dramatically. Just one rounded peak towered high in lonely isolation on her left. Others got quickly smaller as they dipped towards the featureless plateau. Up there it was too exposed for deep snow to cling to the caps, but a cold white blanket piled high around the bases. It took her breath away. Distances seemed endless in the gin-clear atmosphere, and she hadn't even climbed out yet.

Nick Evans cut the engine and stopped the rotor but was still around to her door before she'd figured out how to undo her seatbelt. He helped her disembark, dragged out the basket and jackets, and held one for her to wriggle into. Getting into his took seconds and he even had a couple of beanies in a pocket.

He picked up the basket and started towards the escarpment with Laleh skipping as she waded through the icy slush. She hesitated when she caught him, and then thrust a hand into his spare one. They parked their lunch basket on a pile of flat rocks that overhung the yawning edge, and he covered her chilled fingers with his. The panorama was vast, defying description, and although they looked, there was little to say.

Megalithic lumps tumbled ever lower for kilometres, diving hard for the desert plains. From there the bland landscape stretched endlessly until insipid sand and a pale, lonely sky merged hazily on a far horizon. Qom itself wasn't that hard to pick out, defined by a pillar of mottled grey steam thrusting vertical from a resting engine, but which of the tracks it would use was a mystery. There were three to choose from. Closer to them tiny, dark villages stood out only because the sand was so pale, and railway lines or roads connecting them looked as if they'd been slashed on the landscape with a careless pencil.

To the north, Laleh pointed out what she was sure were the Elburz Range, a long way off. Certainly towering, bone-yellow cumulus with bruised, swollen anvils half-filled the horizon where they ought to be.

"Okay miss, park you bottom and we'll see what Sarah has packed."

Laleh selected a large flat rock, leaving half for him, but Nick stayed standing while he opened the gingham cloth the food was wrapped in. The housekeeper had excelled herself, had even got carried away. Thin slices of gazelle steak were wrapped alongside onions and tomatoes, with the inevitable floppy naan, but small parcels in a filo pasty nestled underneath. Peaches, apples, pistachio nuts and a whole honeydew melon separated them from a kitchen knife and coffee flask. She had even remembered a spare mug.

Nick stared. "Good God, how long did she think we were going to stay up here for? We could have brought the other two and still had stuff left over."

"Perhaps she thought we were going to."

He was still rummaging. "No way. I made it pretty obvious that this trip was for us two." That slipped out and he reddened when he realized what he'd said.

Laleh rested a hand on his forearm with a grin. "Perhaps she thought we'd want to keep our strength up then." There was a double meaning hidden in there somewhere. He knew it, and he was meant to.

Laleh bit into a filo packet while Nick poured coffees. He gave her the pottery mug, and took several noisy sips from the flask lid before picking up some of the food. Coffee was like a blood transfusion to flyers, and he was no exception. He sighed with satisfaction.

"Do you know, Lily, I've just realized that I haven't taken in this view for over a year, let alone appreciated it. You'll make a poet out of me yet."

"Being a poet is a tradition in Iran, Nick. They are very highly regarded. Have there been many other places like this for you?"

"A few now I think about it. Norway, Australia and even Scotland have got their share of spectacular mountain country, but I'm trying not to sound soppy. It's having you here that makes it really special. I've never noticed it that much before."

What the hell was this? What was wrong with him? What was he saying? His supposedly rock-hard values had been stood on their heads in the last few weeks and he felt totally out of control.

"It isn't a weakness when strong men have a softer side, Nickie. In fact, only really strong men are comfortable enough with themselves to let it happen.

Don't mind me, though, it's probably the sociologist talking."

She smiled herself, knowing that many conflicts between the sexes were fermented because people could handle stereo-types better than individuals. She'd lived with that for most of her life and now suspected that he pushed a macho barrow for much the same reason.

They nattered slow and idly as they worked through the sandwiches and fruit, but couldn't finish it. The pilot repacked what was left before draining the coffee flask. Already it seemed natural to drape a casual arm around her shoulders while they finished their drinks.

"How are you, Lily; not too cold?"

"My bum's getting a bit numb."

"Well, it is bloody freezing up here, love. Finish your coffee and we'll be on our way."

As they strolled back to the waiting chopper his arm was still draped lightly around her shoulders.

This time Nick Evans strapped Laleh into the right-hand seat before flashing up. She looked puzzled.

"Have you ever flown a helicopter before, Lil?"

"Flown one? I've never even been in one before. The closest I ever got was economy in an air liner. You don't get too close to the cockpit in that."

Nick smiled. "Okay then, let's do it. How they fly is a bit complicated, so we won't bother with that yet. We'll do it a bit at a time. First of all grip that stick thing between your knees with your right hand. It's called a cyclic and the helicopter goes in whatever direction you push it. I'm holding onto mine too, so just move it gently and watch what the rotor disc does."

Laleh moved the cyclic in a small circle. Even minute movements altered the sound of rotors thrashing through the air, and the direction the cone tilted in.

"You won't get that noise when we're in the air. Now, hold onto that lever on the left side."

It was at the level of her seat pan and she had to look down to find it.

"You have to be pretty gentle with this one. An old instructor of mine told me to handle it like a virgin on her wedding night. I think it put me off getting married."

He smiled and she smiled too. He didn't see her wrapped in egg shell so much.

"It's called the collective lever. Raising or lowering it alters the lift on each blade at the same time, so it makes us go up or down. We can't raise it much yet or we'll take off, but just follow me through."

Nick raised the collective a few inches. The noise level changed dramatically as the machine got light on its skids. It tried to turn and dance.

"Did you notice anything else when it got lighter, Lily?"

"It wanted to spin."

"Well, those two levers in front of your feet are called pedals. Can you reach them, or do they need adjusting?" She stretched her jean-clad legs forward.

"No Nick, they're all right."

"So when we increase power, we push the left one, if we decrease power, we push the right one. We need some when we turn as well."

"I can remember that."

"Okay, love. Now there's a thing under the compass that looks like a curved spirit level. Can you see it?" He pointed.

"That one with a white marble inside?"

"That's it. Don't worry about it too much, but if your pedals are okay for either the power you're pulling or the turn you're making, that will be in the middle. Just glance at it sometimes."

"It's not as easy as that, though, is it Nick?"

"Someone once said that learning to fly a chopper is like being a one-armed paper hangar, but it does get easier. Concentrate, Lil, you're about to become a pilot.

"Okay, let's get on with it." She beamed this time.

"Hovering the beast with the wind gusting around buildings and hills can be a bit tricky, Laleh, and you aren't ready for that yet. I'll get us going, but keep your hands on the controls and you can take charge in a minute. Right-o, here we go."

Nick lifted the machine gently, and checked the flickering needles on his side of the flight panel. They were all where they should have been. He lowered the nose and increased power to compensate, and the chopper started to accelerate quickly. He'd only done a cursory look-out. It didn't get much remoter than where he was right then, and he wanted to keep it simple. He was conscious of the slight friction applied by Laleh.

At the escarpment's edge, the ground under them dropped suddenly from a few feet to a few hundred instantly. It caused her to squeak and then whoop with delight. Nick smiled and continued to accelerate to eighty knots.

"Okay, Lily. That red button on top of your cyclic like a Chinaman's hat is called a trim. Operate it with your thumb. When you move the cyclic forward or back, take the pressure off it with the springs that it controls. Don't trim into turns though. Are you ready to take over the speed only?"

Laleh couldn't believe how far they had already travelled. "Okay, Nickie, I can do this. I have control."

Nick gave her a couple of minutes. "Beautiful. Now move the cyclic a bit to the right, you'll turn that way."

"It's turning, but is anything else happening, Lil?"

"We're crabbing a bit and I think we're going down too."

"Absolutely right. So when we turn we need to push the pedals in the direction we're turning and we need a bit of power as well."

"Got it."

"Okay then. Change speed and direction when you feel like it, but remember where the power and rudder positions should be. I'll move them, but you tell me when to."

Nick moved his right hand into his lap to let her see that she was controlling speed and direction. By then she was concentrating hard, but looked ecstatic too.

"Right. The only other thing with attitude is to use the horizon rather than the instruments. React to the position of the aircraft's nose on it, and only look at the instruments to check."

He let her wander where she wanted, keeping an eye on where they were. The time flew as well.

"Right, Laleh, I have it. Relax and shake the wrinkles out."

The girl sat back with a ragged exhalation of breath. "I think that was the most exciting thing I've ever done, Nick." She was bubbling.

"You haven't finished yet, woman. That'll be when you control everything at the same time."

She looked apprehensive immediately. "Oh, I didn't think I'd have to do it all."

"You're a natural, Lil. You've got a nice light touch, and it gets easier with practice. Put your feet on the pedals and hold the collective. Good. Now look at the gauge on the top right of your panel." He moved the lever up and down gently, adjusting the pedals as he did. The machine changed height as the needle rose and fell.

"Okay then. No big movements and don't go into the red bit at the top. You're in charge of the power and pedals."

Laleh made tentative movements at first, then larger ones as she got bolder. Time ceased for her, but Nick was keeping an eye on it.

"Okay, love, this is what it's all about. Bring your right hand onto the cyclic as well." The girl complied. "Right. Remember, if you change one, you've got to change the others to compensate. You have it." He held the controls lightly himself. She wasn't coordinating the movements much, but she was doing them positively. Nick was impressed.

Laleh was so busy making larger changes that it was a while before she realized he'd let go of everything. He pointed to an obvious ravine on his right. "The Qom river is in there, Lily. Fly us down to it please."

He lifted the map off the instrument hood and held it with both hands.

The helicopter's glide path wasn't a smooth, linear descent, more like it was on a giant staircase, and it wobbled and seesawed too, but it descended safely to just above the river. Nick took back control as he turned t and grinned.

"That was really good, Lily. Sit back and relax. It's not far to home now." Nick glanced at her as Shahabad slid by. Her head was back on the seat cushion. She couldn't stop smiling.

"Our house is on top of that greener hill there." He pointed, but whether she looked at it or not, he didn't know. Her head was back and her eyes were still closed when he glanced again.

As the machine roared out of the foothills, the pilot flicked a nervous glance at the road from Qom. A few cars travelled in either direction, but none were convoys or Hum-vees. He headed directly for the oil-stained concrete pad with the white circle and gigantic 'H.' Imran was waiting on the pad to direct him, and Jock ambled out from the crew-room as Nick got the cut signal. When the rotors stopped, the girl released her seatbelt and opened her door. Nick was still knocking off switches and radios when Sinclair reached the machine. Laleh threw her arms around him so rigorously that he had to step backwards to keep his balance.

"I flew it, Jock. I really flew it!"

Sinclair hugged her. "Aye, I bet you put that reprobate to shame in five minutes flat." He was grinning too.

Nick also had a grin on his face when he climbed out. Laleh ran around the chopper and launched herself with a metre to go. Her arms wrapped around his neck, her legs around his upper thighs, and her exuberance was catching.

Everyone was smiling by then. Imran broke the buoyant, noisy frivolity.

"You'd better get Laleh, back in the crew-room before we phone for the Bowser, Nick." The mood toned down instantly. Sinclair and Nick walked back to the offices with Laleh in the middle, her arms linked though each of theirs. The yellow bowser turned up again when requested.

Eating dinner that evening was noisy and boisterous, and went on for hours. The stew, pocket bread, fruit and cheeses were revisited several times, and the bottles got passed casually and often. Sinclair escaped to his own house eventually, but by then Laleh had repeated her day several times over. It was all about the same events really, just told in a different way.

And they'd already massacred two bottles of decent red while they ate, but the two males only just kept ahead of her with the whisky bottle too. Lil talked incessantly, but not surprisingly, they all began to wilt as the evening lengthened.

In the end Amini had to bring Laleh down, to let her know she was becoming a bore, but she was still animated when he finally shooed her into her room. She didn't go willingly, and was still calling through her curtained doorway while they cleared away. Farhad flashed a smile as they worked.

"Now I know how you pilots do it, Nick. It's a pity there wasn't an Iranian Fleet-Air-Arm. I obviously chose the wrong profession."

"I've only taken squadron people and the odd VIP flying before, Fred, but I really enjoyed being up there with someone who seemed so keen. It really got to her."

"Get her up there again and I reckon you've got a slave for life, mate."

That one really sobered the pilot up. He smiled reflectively. "One thing I've learnt in a very short time is that Laleh is unlikely to be anybody's slave, Fred."

Amini nodded soberly. "I was older, Nick, never really knew her all that well, but I'm pretty impressed with my little sister right now. She's become a real tiger. Joking aside, I reckon she'd make somebody who wasn't an over-bearing dick-head a pretty good partner given half the chance." He deliberately looked at Nick when he said that and then grinned. "Mind you, I think I'd stick to just one wife with her around."

Nick didn't deny it, but he did redden. He'd never been prone to self-analysis and found the thought uncomfortable. He was still not sure what he felt nor where this was going, but he didn't want it to stop either.

"Well, she's certainly not like any woman I've ever met before, Fred. Perhaps that's what scared me off at first."

Farhad didn't say anything, but his English was impeccable. He was certainly aware of the nuances of the past and present tense. He nodded. There hadn't been any comments flying from the other room once they started talking either. Nick missed that.

Chapter Thirty

The week flew by and soon it was time to shop in Qom again. It wasn't an imposition for Nick to do the driving, and it wasn't too obvious that the Scot and Amini chose to try their luck in the local streams with the rods instead. Ordinary days started early in Iran. Schools, businesses, factories, everything, so Nick and the women were on their way by eight. Sarah dressed as she always dressed while Laleh wore her chador. The comments were ripe as she pulled the thick robes over her head.

Struggling with the gentleman thing, he opened the passenger door for the girls with a flourish.

"Wrong, Nick. Good Muslim women walk behind, not alongside the blokes, and ride in the back with the goats." He could see little more than the expressive dark eyes but knew her face was creased with laughter. Sarah nearly choked as she climbed into the back. Nick's grin had some suppressed anger in it. "In that case, it'll be a bloody good job when we're living somewhere a bit more civilised."

Laleh stopped smiling instantly, her eyes riveted on his face. Did he realize what he'd just said?

He knew.

Nick returned her gaze lazily and unexpectedly stuck his tongue out. She couldn't stop herself grinning again.

"Right woman, climb in and shut the bloody door yourself."

Sarah was still chuckling as she poked Laleh with a gentle elbow.

The golden mosque, close to the pungent souk, was a replica of the big one in Jerusalem. Pricier, more up-market shops sprawled in a nearby suburb, and the women wanted to start with dress shops. Nick pulled up a few blocks away.

There were no directions anywhere in the mosque grounds, no obvious signage anywhere, and the few people around seemed to be deliberately ignoring him. It took fifteen minutes to find the office he was looking for.

Two men looked up when he entered the office, only their dark shirts resembling any form of uniform. One was Arak, but surprisingly the atmosphere was not hostile.

"How have you done, Mister Evans?"

"Not too good so far, but this can be a slow business. We found a couple of sites where the green of copper is showing, but they're pretty high up and don't look big enough to be commercial. After the Christian New Year break we'll look further south. We haven't been down there much yet."

"If you do find anything worthwhile we need an instant report—yes?"

"You'll be the first to know, Mister Arak."

Nick ambled back into the fierce sunlight. Arak opened an adjacent door where a man was stacking files.

"Follow him. See what he's up to."

It would be a while before the women re-appeared so Nick browsed the shop windows on his way back to the vehicle. He'd guessed that any goods on offer would be dull and colourless, infinitely less than exciting, and he was right. Nothing grabbed his attention. Chadors and even burqas in black, grey or slate-blue seemed the only choice for women, with the addition of ankle-length white dish-dashas for the men. Any hint of the exotic or even the fine didn't exist. Nick suspected that the women would be out of luck.

There was no hurry. He was wasting time and showed only casual interest in the goods, so a reflection in a shadowed shop window riveted his attention after it had happened twice. The black shirt and badges were distinctive, as they were meant to be, and now he was alerted, it happen again. It was no coincidence. His blood pressure climbed high.

Nick's first instinct was to evade, but then he dismissed it. He was on a shopping trip with two women and there was nothing sinister about that. He continued browsing as he returned to the vehicle.

Nick saw the women approaching from fifty yards away and gaped. They were bowed under several large plastic bags just like girls shopping in any city anywhere. He checked for the tail and saw he wasn't that close before stepping around to open the rear doors. He kept his back to the women so they wouldn't be tempted to wave and hissed that they were being watched when they reached him. They caught on right away. He climbed back behind the wheel while they lodged their parcels. They were restrained and demure like dominated women anywhere.

Nick kept his voice low and didn't turn. "We'll do exactly what we planned to do so it's the markets next, girls, but make it quick. I'll be disinterested and stay in the car while you guys get what you want. I mentioned to Arak that we've got a week's break coming up so he'd expect you to buy extra. If anyone asks, Laleh, you're Sarah's daughter-in-law down for the holidays. Everybody happy?

It was Laleh who spoke.

"Don't do anything that will get you into trouble, Nick. You've done a lot for us already."

"Bugger them, Laleh! I said before that I'm not Iranian and I'm not Islamic. I'll obey the laws of the country, but they can sit on their archaic rules. It's not how I think, so it's not going to be the way I act either. We'll do what's needed to protect you and Fred, but stuff the rest of it."

She sensed his underlying anger again and slid her hand over the seat back to squeeze his shoulder.

The markets were less than two miles away. They didn't hang around. The baskets got filled quickly and Nick was driving back to Shahabad within thirty minutes. As he turned off to the town, he relaxed. He might still be under observation, but he couldn't spot anyone following.

Meanwhile the religious copper returned to the mosque.

"Anything to report Qalat?"

"Nothing. He let two women off to go shopping before coming here and took them to the markets later. After that he drove home. I followed him out of Qom, but he turned off to Shahabad. They didn't go anywhere else."

Arak nodded thoughtfully.

The others were still fishing when Nick and the women got back to a dusty Shahabad, but then again even noon was some way off yet. The tension had eased, but the trip bothered Nick. He was deep in thought.

Most of the shopping bags had cloths for Laleh, and she decided on a fashion show to distract him. Nick draped himself over the settee with a coffee while the girl paraded.

The styles and colours the women had found were certainly more vibrant than the garments he had bought earlier, but even so, they were more subtle than stunning. There was nothing there to put the cat-walks in Paris or New York under any pressure, but even so, Sarah nodded approval with each outfit.

Laleh had found jeans and two tops that fit, and twirled in front of them in sateen blouse and skirt outfits, but what did get his attention were two sheer sleeping shirts amongst her purchases. One was in a deep purple, the other a diaphanous pink, and both had swirling patterns that extended to loose balloon sleeves. Some simple tailoring softened the shoulders and waist.

Nick tried blasé. He nodded with approval while seeming to ignore the faint outline of dark panties and brassiere showing vaguely through the sheer material. He wasn't hugely successful.

Chapter Thirty-One

It took Laleh several minutes to change back into jeans and a blouse. Sarah filled the mugs while she did, and Laleh put hers and Nick's on a small wooden side table beside the divan. She collapsed against him, and tucked bare feet under her in that elegant, loose limbed way that is so typically female. The chat was warm and lazy while she drank.

Although Laleh was folded into the crook of his arm, it was draped over the settee back and barely touched her shoulders. Their thighs touched lightly too, and it no longer seemed an issue that they did, but he was careful not to move his arm any closer. He was still unsure of how far she had come. Perhaps she was being braver than she actually felt. He would let her dictate the speed of her recovery, and he already suspected that it might well be worth it. He remained a little in awe of her.

They were still sprawled on the settee nattering when Sinclair and Amini got back home. Both glanced at the pair but neither commented. They gave Sarah some good-sized trout to conjure with.

"You guys will want a wee dram. And what about you ladies?"

The housekeeper shook her head.

"I'll help Sarah prepare the fish and something to go with it first." Laleh stood and looked down at Nick. She felt an almost overwhelming urge to kiss him but thought it might be a bit bold. She still wasn't sure if he would want her to do it anyway, but she deliberately levered herself up with a hand on his thigh.

"I won't have a whisky yet, just a cold beer." He rose and moved towards the fridge.

"Me too, Nick."

Nick tossed Jock a new bottle of Bowmore single malt from the cupboard before collecting beers from the kitchen fridge.

"The working week comes to a halt tomorrow, and I suggest we spend time in Shahabad. There won't be much happening in Tehran or Qom over Christmas, and there's plenty we can do around here."

Nick had already had a quiet word with Sinclair.

"I've got Mohammed to fix up a felucca for part of it, Nick. You two were sailors, so it should be like old times. That's fixed, isn't it, Sarah?"

She waved while she stirred.

Amini jumped in. "We had a couple at my base for recreation. They've only got one lateen sail, so they're pretty easy to manage."

"Okay. The village has got some nice trout in the streams, and we've got the New Year parade thing as well. That should fill the week up nicely." Nick turned his head and raised his voice. "You going anywhere, Sarah?"

"No, Nickie. My youngest son and family come down here this year and all kids bringing the herds down after holiday. I be around."

They had a late breakfast on Christmas Eve followed by a leisurely stroll around the dusty, brown streets. It was a slow start, and Imran and another of the boys went with them. There were a profusion of tools and trinkets on the noisy, colourful stalls, and even fledgling pot plants on offer with hints of buds straggling from bare, lifeless limbs. The group lost touch with each other as they made their small purchases. Nick and Laleh found themselves alone.

Laleh became more emboldened when they were on their own, and held his hand as they strolled amongst the heavy crowds. When they stopped for lunch, they shared a large kebab while sat on a mud-brick half wall overlooking the river. Nick didn't tear the thick meat sandwich into pieces. They nibbled at it alternatively. He was learning quickly about togetherness and discovered he liked it.

Laleh had planned to do the cooking, but when they got back, she found she'd been pre-empted by Sarah. There was a cauldron on the go already, and Muslim or not, Imran and the boys were hooking into whisky. Laleh protested mildly to Sarah.

"You have plenty time to cook for your husband later. Tonight I feed you all."

Laleh blushed. An indomitable Sarah wore a haughty smile.

The next two days were the real Christmas period. Christmas Day started with mid-morning coffee, heavily laced by Sinclair. He had a problem calling it Irish coffee, it was whisky not whiskey, although it did set the tone. It was a good start.

That year had already leaned towards the traumatic, but the real difference was obvious to Nick. They all got gifts, but Laleh was inundated, and everybody was in on the act. Colourful headscarves, trinkets of Bakhtaran jewellery, cosmetics and skin treatments, just about anything that was available was piled on her, and although Sarah was well looked after, it was Laleh who was definitely in the lime-light.

And Nick was totally indebted to the older couple himself that year. They must have been well aware of the risks they were taking. He asked Sarah to fetch her husband, and she bustled off to a few houses away to fetch him. Nick and Jock hurried next door to collect three young goats that had halters for easy handling, and locked them in the outside privy. Nick prayed that the couple wouldn't need to go when they arrived back. Neither would get over the shock.

Sarah and Mohammed were back within minutes, him hugging a large stone jar under his arm. There were at least two gallons of fire-water in there. Nick groaned.

"Okay guys, I just want to get this in while I still can." He nodded towards the jar, which caused a few hoots. "Mohammed and Sarah have been real helpful to us, and it could have got them into big trouble, so Jock and I wanted this year to be a bit special for them. Let's all go in the yard."

Nick, Jock and the boys knew, but the others were mystified when he walked towards the toilet. He opened the dunny door with a flourish. The goats trotted out with their heads held arrogantly high. It left the older couple gasping.

"Two young males and a female from a good stud, Sarah. The female is pregnant, but not by either of them. I hope that your entire herd benefits guys. Here are the papers."

Only Sarah of the two could express herself in English. "We know the ear-marks on them, Nickie. Do you really know what it mean to us?"

"I hope it means you end up with the best herd in the area, Sarah."

"Not only that. We improve our herd but start a stud of our own too."

By then everybody realized the significance to the pair. The older woman strode across the yard, quietly crying, and hugged them both. Nick thought she was trying to crush him and everyone was talking at the same time.

When he managed to escape, Nick walked Laleh inside the house and ducked into his bedroom. He gave Laleh two smallish parcels. The others crowded around as she opened them. Inside was a large Opium perfume and a cosmetics set from an Yves St Laurent collection. Laleh was speechless. She was well aware of what they were.

"How could you possibly get these in Iran now, Nickie?"

I asked the ambassador's wife about a present on my Christmas trip, and she'd just had a box of cosmetics shipped in. She suggested I buy some from her. She's quite fond of me, I think."

"This is so special here these days, though. I only wish I could have found something more appropriate for you."

"You'll get your chance, Lily." He took her face gently in both hands and kissed her, not caring who saw it. Not overly long but very thoroughly. It flashed through her mind that she'd thought about it earlier, but hadn't actually done it.

Roasted haunches, poultry ragouts, pared fruit and cheeses disappeared throughout that afternoon, and inevitably they drank. By mid-evening they were all suffering some collateral damage. The lads returned to their own house, smiling at Amini snoring lightly in an armchair as they passed, while Sarah stacked dishes. Not that expertly nor quietly either. Mohammed had staggered home leading the goats by their halters an age before.

By then Nick was sprawled on the floor with his back against the settee while Laleh was perched between his opened legs. Her head was on his upper chest, his right arm draped protectively across her chest. He cradled a half-filled glass but wasn't drinking. He wasn't smashed either, only in that maudlin, reflective state that says don't drink any more. Sarah finished what she was doing before peering at the others. Sinclair was the recipient of an expansive gesture.

"You help me put Farhad to bed then see you tomorrow."

Jock may have seemed unaffected, but he staggered when he rose. But Farhad didn't wake properly between chair and bed, nor when the Scot whipped his shoes, shirt and pants off.

"Okay, Jock. Nicki, help me with Laleh. His job to do this."

Sinclair smiled grimly, muttered something about surrogate mother-in-law's under his breath, said his good-byes, and headed for home. The bang of the door had

Nick jumping as if he'd been poked with a sharp stick. Laleh stirred sleepily before snuggling in tight once more.

"Sarah, you hold her upright while I get up. I'll carry her in."

The older woman grunted and complied, allowing him to wriggle free. He lifted Laleh bodily and deposited her on her bed before turning back towards the curtained door.

"Where you going, Nicki? I need some help here. I find her night thing, you take off pants and top." That one stopped him in his tracks.

"Perhaps you should do the rest now, Sarah."

She looked at him shrewdly. "I think you and her be together soon, so this not time to get shy. We make her comfortable for night. Now take off pants and top."

His fingers were all thumbs when he complied, but to say he did so reluctantly would not be true. The panties and brassiere were a deep navy-blue, gleaming seductively against the ivory of her skin. He could see no blemishes at all, not a mole nor a birthmark. The navel protruded slightly.

"Okay, Nickie, you lift her, I pull down bed-cloths."

Laleh groaned and held on tight.

"Okay, Nick, last thing. Take off other top thing and lift arms. I put this over her head."

Nick Evans struggled with the brassiere clasp, trying to ignore the taut cream breasts and provocative plum nipples. After laying her down again, he pulled the night gown to her thighs and stared. Sarah dug him in the back.

"You not viewing corpse, she still be here tomorrow. You go now, I do rest." She smiled as he left the room.

It was not surprising that they were a bit slow getting started on Boxing Day. Coffee, strong coffee, not a regular breakfast was a priority, and the plate of cold meat slices stayed in the fridge until much later. Nick looked in on Laleh, but she hadn't moved. He brought a new pack of Panadol from the bathroom and tossed it casually beside the kettle. Sarah was next, but forty minutes late. By then he'd sunk a couple of coffees.

"How you feel, Nick?"

"I'm all right. I got a bit cautious in the end. What about you?"

"Me too, I think. Won't rush around today though."

"Farhad and Laleh are still out of it. They tried some of Mohammed's brew, but I've been there before. I was a bit wiser this time."

Sarah smirked. "I finish dishes then wake them. Put bottles in separate bag. Can use them."

Nick collected the smoky-green empties and stacked them in the yard, before brushing goat pellets onto the rose beds. When he returned, he could hear strangled choking drifting from the bathroom. Farhad was tossing his cookies. He was a while before he joined them.

"There are times when I know why Muslims ban alcohol, Nick. I haven't done that since some of the blokes took me on a run ashore at Dartmouth."

Nick didn't respond. There was no need. He smiled as Amini collapsed into an armchair, and took him coffee and Panadol. Sarah was still in with Laleh, so Nick turned the screws a bit.

"Like a drop of whisky with that, Fred?" he asked innocently.

Amini groaned as Nick grinned. The housekeeper returned in time to catch the pilot's jibe. She smiled herself.

"I brush her hair, she be here now."

Sarah went off to the kitchen to start on the endless task of peeling. Nick again wondered how she remembered similar, yet different, recipes every day. He put a few chairs back into place and wiped off the table. Laleh appeared as he finished. Her hair shimmered, but she was devoid of make-up, and looked paler than his own normal skin tone.

"Coffee and a tablet, Lily?" He smiled when the girl just nodded with a grimace.

"I bring, Nickie. Coffee for you too. Sit with Laleh."

Nick looked up sharply. He had a feeling that Sarah was beginning to over-play the ambitious mother a bit, but good-naturedly sat anyway. Laleh collapsed against him before he'd even got comfortable. It remained that sort of day.

And the quiet day helped. They were all much livelier the day they went sailing. Mohammed had come up with a racy felucca, and although it wasn't new, it had been freshly painted in white and light-green. It was long but not wide, with fast aerodynamic lines, and a serious russet sail slapped noisily against the mast. The inevitable eye to ward off evil spirits was painted on the bows and it smelled vaguely of fish.

Laleh actually clapped when she saw it before helping load it with a basket and cooler bag of soft drinks.

"Can I drive it first, please? I've sailed lots of times in Iran and England." The two ex-mariners looked at each other and shrugged. Sinclair was more vocal.

"You'd better know what you're doing then, lassie. Real Scots don't take water in their whisky so I certainly don't want to end up in it."

That produced a chuckle as the felucca owner waved a fiercely animated hand for them to board. Nick deliberately positioned himself at the mast, ready to dip the spar when they gibed.

There was room next to the girl at the stern, but Nick avoided it. It was a thing of rebuilding confidence, and every win was one she wouldn't have to repeat. Initially, his sensitivity surprised him, but then he realized it was exactly what he had craved when he was younger. He'd wanted someone to build him up too, but for him, it hadn't happened.

Farhad and Jock shared a bench seat amidships, but sailing wasn't a thing the Scot had done much of. He was happy to leave it to the others while he appreciated the scenery. Amini fingered two ropes with quick release knots that reefed the sail to the spar. A jerk would free the canvas instantly.

"Ready everyone?" Laleh looked at the males intently. She was hyped. She caught their nods and gave the owner a wave. As they moved she yelled.

"Let go, Farhad!"

Laleh tightened the single rope sheet and the spritely boat leapt forward, heeling to a fresh wind coming up the ravine. She pulled harder and the felucca started to fly.

The opposite bank drew close quickly, but her timing was optimum when she prepared to go about. Laleh gave the command as she threw the helm and let the rope sheet fly. The boat swung rapidly through ninety degrees and Nick was smart in dipping the spar to the other side of the mast. He smiled grimly. She was wrapped in what she was doing, and he fully expected to be bollocked if he got it wrong. The felucca barely lost speed before it started to fly again. Laleh zigzagged up the river for nearly an hour.

Amini and Sinclair lunched on gazelle slices, naan and fruit before Amini relieved his sister. She handed over tiller and sheets with a ragged sigh before joining Nick amidships for her own. Amini stooged around while they ate. There was no rush, but they were still running against the river and it was beginning to narrow. When they'd finished, Amini called for Nick to take them back. He nodded, but then looked at the girl.

"How about you do it?"

Her eyes gleamed but then dulled. "No, Nickie, I've had my go. It's your turn."

Nick smiled indulgently and shooed her towards the stern with both hands. His ego didn't need the boost, but he knew he was getting better at rebuilding hers. She parked her shapely, jeans-clad bottom on the stern thwart, took the sheets and tiller, and he moved aft to join her. Laleh wriggled to make room for him and he stretched his legs casually with an arm around her shoulders. The sluggish river would be with them while a stiff breeze funnelled off their bow. If she headed it well, there would be no need to go about.

"Ready everyone?"

Only Sinclair looked surprised at the question. The two ex-mariners nodded as Laleh swung the boat directly down river and tightened the sail. It immediately began to point briskly against the breeze.

The fresh wind teased up the water into small white crests that tumbled south against a light northerly current. The felucca's sharp bow chased them down rapidly, tossing the foaming water impudently over its shoulders. Bubbling spray got thrown into squinting, animated faces, making the run home exciting and noisy.

Shahabad lay less than a mile ahead in hardly anytime at all. Laleh stayed in the centre of the river until she was almost level with the boats drawn up on the river bank, and then turned hard towards them.

She shook the sail out further. The boat heeled as the wind shifted abaft the beam, and with metres to go, she yelled at her brother to reef. Laleh let the sheet fly as he hauled rapidly, and the keel kissed the pebbly river bottom as it slowed. Two burly Bakhtarans continued its momentum until it tilted gently onto its port side. They clapped. Sinclair had been exhilarated by the ride himself but wasn't sure what they were doing. Nor why.

Fred and Jock disembarked with the bags while Nick and Laleh coiled and tidied the sheets and ropes. Nick climbed out next before lifting her onto the shingle, but as she slid down him, she tightened her grip, stared into his eyes for a moment, and then kissed him. It surprised even her.

"My turn," she whispered as their locked lips broke contact. She skipped up the beach towards their vehicle, tossing her hair as she cavorted. Inevitably, it was Sinclair who had to say something.

"When the time comes, you two had better find a non-Islamic country to live in. One with not too many bloody priests around either."

Nick pushed him. Hard.

Chapter Thirty-Two

It was the New Year on the following day so Nick and Sinclair dragged out the forty-four-gallon drum and gave it a clean. Fuel for the griller was just as difficult to find as domestic heating fuel had been, so with the help of a welding kit and his boys, Jock had engineered it into a bar-be-cue that ran on welding gas.

An ingenious perforated central shaft, one end sealed, the other with a connector from a blow torch fitting, provided the adjustable flame, while a length of fine steel mesh above it spread the heat. Metal 'V's, bolted at each end, cradled a hand turned rotisserie. A shop-bought one would have looked more elegant, but this one did the job.

Sarah and Laleh beat out and baked naan after naan before preparing corn cobs, pumpkin wedges and yams to slowly roast in the oven to roast. Basic hospitality was what the festival was all about, so there couldn't be too much food. The chances of there being anything left at the end of a long, frenzied day weren't that good.

While the women cooked, Amini threw his gear on then headed for Qom with Imran in tow. He chose a small, modern hotel to do his phoning from. Two of the Tehran numbers didn't answer, while the other two sounded scared and apprehensive, but neither was prepared to talk, let alone come up with something proactive. Both put the phones down when he pushed harder. Amini was depressed and didn't phone Abdul. On their way back, they dropped off at the airfield for the acetylene and oxygen bottles.

More jobs for the morrow took up the rest of that day. The plump ibex was lifted from the freezer to thaw, and later its surface was rubbed with garlic, pepper and salt. Naan went into baskets and metal trays got lined with half-cooked vegetables, while a few sharp kitchen knives were placed on the table for people to carve with. Anything else they'd eat with their fingers. Paper plates were unheard of out there and crockery was too valuable to be put in the hands of the almost certainly tipsy. A stack of tissues did for sticky fingers.

It was well into the afternoon before they gathered for a late snack. Amini picked rather than ate with his coffee, and didn't look all that happy while he did. The others noticed. Nick broke into the sounds of munching.

"Fred, you haven't said much since you got back from Qom. Is there a problem, mate?"

All eyes swung towards Amini. "Sorry, Nick, not really, but the phone numbers I had for Tehran were bloody useless. Nobody was even vaguely aware of how to get out or even interested in trying." He took a disgusted swig from his mug.

Nick looked conciliatory. "Well, it'll take some time to establish an escape route, and if we keep things normal, no-one is likely to bother us down here." He had to lighten this right away. "What's up anyway, you ungrateful prick. You fed up with our hospitality already?"

Amini smiled wryly. "Not at all, Nick. It's just that it's an internal Iranian matter that we're doing bugger all about. Only you guys from outside seem to be, and you've done so much already that I'm a bit scared that we might piss you off. I'll be honest though, I haven't got a bloody clue what to do next."

But it was a thing about service people, really. Nick knew why Amini was frustrated, and needed to do something about it. He'd been designated leader, so leadership had better be what he provided. Amen.

"Don't get the idea that you're not paying your way, Fred, because you are. You've thrown in financially and added a bit of zest to a somewhat boring existence, but more importantly, you're a mate who needed a hand. We'll only move you guys when it's safe to." He stopped to look at Sinclair and Amini deliberately. "I don't want you pricks giving me a hard time either, but there's something even more important to me. Without things playing out the way they have, Laleh and I would never have met. I'm not saying anything other than that, but I can't imagine a life where that didn't happen now." Laleh looked at him with surprise as he stood.

"I'm going out for some fresh air and a think. When I get back, we'll start nutting something out. You coming or staying, Lil?"

The girl slipped on her moccasins and stood. "I'm with you." He read that the way it was meant to be read.

Chapter Thirty-Three

They took the higher, rough track towards the river, staying well above the sluggish, twisting, waters. Nick was thinking and speculative, his shoulders hunched and hands shoved deep in his pockets. Laleh's arm poked through his, respecting his mood. She knew he would talk when he was ready now. They walked for a kilometre before the pilot pointed out a rock. His brow furrowed slightly when he sat beside her.

"First up, Laleh, I need you to say something to Farhad. I don't want him taking off or doing anything desperate because he believes he's overstayed his welcome. I think he's hard pushed to believe me. We're okay right now, and it could be a while before anything changes, so we've got plenty of time to work something out. Okay with that?"

She nodded. "I can see that, Nick. We shouldn't increase the risk to anybody if we don't really need to."

"Well, just to make it perfectly clear I'm not prepared for you to go with him either. You'd be exposing yourself to un-necessary danger. You're a big girl, and I know better than to tell you not to if you really want to, but I wouldn't be happy if you did. We'll work this out and I want us together when we do it. I wouldn't want it any other way."

Before, he was likely to have looked away when he said something like that, might have sounded capricious even, but this time he looked directly into her eyes. His gaze was riveting. Her liquid eyes sprinkled instantly, but her voice didn't crack. The right time had arrived.

"We've only known each other for a short time, Nickie, and I think we're heading somewhere important, so please indulge me. There are a few things I need to know if I'm to get over this completely." She dropped her eyes.

"The society I come from is much more restrictive than yours and looks at things in different ways. I want to know exactly how you feel about it." She still stared at her feet but held up a hand when she sensed he was going to speak.

"I had two short flings with students in England when I was getting my Master's, and both involved some fairly short-lived physical stuff. I can see now it was a backlash against how I was brought up, not really me at all, and you know I was raped by those animals a few months ago. I realize it was a deliberate power and humiliation thing, but I do still feel ashamed and dirty, as if I could have done something to stop it. In Iran, I would be finished as a respectable woman now, and that was the point."

This couldn't be rushed. The pain and horror would be the same for most women, but the implications were much more serious where she came from. Nick realized instantly that this was the crux. Was she damaged in some way? Instinctively, he knew what she needed. So far he'd been shooting from the hip, but now realized that it was a form of denial. This time he had to tap the emotional wells a lot deeper.

Laleh remained silent, her eyes misty, expecting a quick, maybe flippant response. She glanced at him through lowered lashes, thinking he might be horrified now she'd compelled him to think about it fully. She didn't see that.

He brought her around to sit on his knee. Now she was forced to look at him. A crooked index finger went under her chin, raising her head, and he kept it in place until he knew it would stay up.

"I've thought about this often lately, Lil, but never put it all together before. I'll try to give you the short version, but it's a pretty complicated subject so you'll have to bear with me. Also I know that this psychology stuff sounds like a generalisation, but it is true for most people."

She nodded.

"One-on-one teaching like I was involved in is a high-intensity environment, and as tough as it gets, so we got the basics when I was on instructor's course. The students ranged in age from eighteen to their mid-twenties and some of those were married with kids, so different things affected people in different ways almost daily. If you're okay with that, we'll look at the sex thing first." He shifted to make himself more comfortable.

"I'm older and wiser now, Lil, and one thing I've picked up on is that sex when you're young is mostly about ego, not commitment. Especially for blokes. Bodies are awash with hormones in our early adulthood, and that causes almost uncontrollable desires, but it's more about pandering to the Id right then, a desire for instant gratification much like babies. But for boys, it's also about looking macho to your peers, and the ego boost you get from others knowing about it. Unfortunately, youngsters don't have much of an idea about the responsibility and the consequences that go along with it at that age. But it isn't only about status either. Underneath there's also the vague knowledge that some supposedly rough and tough He-Men go completely to pieces when the shit hits the fan, so it's about insecurity too. Things like bonking any women who stays still long enough, or knocking those weaker than you around or even taking stupid, unnecessary risks are meant to show you aren't like that. Remember though, others have to see or be told about it, or it doesn't count."

She nodded unconsciously. He took a deeper breath.

"Some girls are getting a bit that way as well now, aren't they?

"They are, Laleh, and it's the wrong way for women to go. Girls mature earlier than blokes, sometime in their later teens, so they acted as a brake on young blokes, but now some women are actually doing the goading. Short version again, but in the earlier days, our roles were normally gender specific. Men hunted while women gathered and had babies, but now I think that it was the start of women using guile to make up for their lack of physical strength. And one subject was child birth. For a long time men thought there was something magical about it, but I'm sure that women knew exactly why it happened. They shrouded it in mystery, though, because it gave them an advantage. Now I honestly think that women are better at survival than men, but I don't mean in setting traps or making shelters, it's about women using flattery and mystic to get them and their children fed and protected better by the strongest male."

"But women are just as capable as men, in some things Nick. History is full of strong females, and many of them were recognised warriors."

"Too true, and it was the accidental mixing of copper and tin to make bronze nearly 5000 years ago that changed it all. Ornaments and god figures were made from soft metals like gold, silver and copper centuries before, but now they had a hardy metal that could be moulded into decent tools and weapons. Serious farming took off after that, and villages and towns quickly followed as the population stabilised. Men no longer hunted in groups just to feed the clan members, and farms couldn't expand with just one bloke tending to everything, so now women and children became important assets, a vital part of the economy. I think it was when the blokes first started to feel a bit insecure, because they didn't want some other bloke waltzing off with a valuable asset."

"Some women hunted or even fought alongside the men back in those days as well though, didn't they, Nick?

"Absolutely right, Lily. The British Celts had heaps of women who fought with their men. Even then they were recognised as superior archers, but they were also in the thick of it with swords and daggers too. By the time the Romans invaded Britain in AD 42, even the Royal line was passed down through the women, but being patriarchal, the Romans missed it. It led to Boudicca, a female Iceni leader, rebelling against the Romans. Her army killed heaps of them before she was subdued, and throughout history, other women like Joan of Arc and Elizabeth the First have led armies into battle. There are lots of stories about noted Asian female warriors as well, and even the American Indians, including the Apache, had female war chiefs amongst the tribes. History was written by the blokes though, so most of that is conveniently forgotten."

"I'd heard about the famous ones in history lessons, but didn't know about Asian and Red Indian female warriors."

"I've been a serious reader all my life, Lil, so I know stuff. It's why I look at things a bit differently than a lot of blokes. So here's another one that might really blow your mind. In the days of sail, even warships like *HMS Victory* at Trafalgar had a number of women on board. They weren't paid, but as the wives and girlfriends of sailors they earned their keep by doing jobs like powder monkeys, laundry or by helping the surgeons during battles. It's never been talked about officially, but you can forget about press-gangs pulling in enough competent sailors to man ships. The Navy would never have got enough experts like carpenters or sail-makers at sea if they didn't turn a blind eye to it."

Laleh looked surprised. "I didn't know that. So what the hell happened?"

"From what I can see, it was the Industrial Revolution towards the end of the eighteenth century that started it. Not everybody had farms, and any income was good income, so women and children worked in mines, factories and potteries, until machines were invented that did a lot of those jobs more efficiently. Suddenly there wasn't enough work to go around, so it was the blokes who got what there was. Over the next fifty years, women went back to their traditional home-keeping roles, and compulsory schooling was introduced for kids. Women have been fighting for equal rights ever since."

"That lines up with the stuff I learned in Sociology, but some cultures have never allowed women to work or be educated."

"Same basic principle from what I can see, no matter when it originated. In some societies, where there isn't a lot of education and skills amongst the men, the last thing they want is smart women coming along to bag the well-paid jobs. It's a fear based on insecurity that first world countries have largely got over. Generally, people now use what they've got educationally, emotionally and physically to improve any sort of relationship. We haven't got it completely right yet, but it's on its way. Experts now reckon that men and women evolved in different ways because of their differing circumstances, but time comes into it too. With the loss of hormones after menopause, most women's sex drive fades. Basically they evolved to produce children while it was safe for them to do it. A man's sex drive stays with him, because he was meant to produce replacements, because with no medical knowledge a lot of kids died early. We were still Stone Age only 5000 years ago remember, and that's too close yet for big, rapid changes. The best we've got at present is if it works, who the hell cares when it happened, and if it doesn't, at least we tried. It's not as if love and sex causes us physical injury like a gun or a knife would, love. It takes a lot of thought and effort to make even a good partnership work, and sex is only part of it. That's more the way educated societies see it now, Lil. Hardly anyone is a virgin when they get married. Quite a few get married more than once, and some don't get married at all."

"If that's true, Nickie, where does it come from? What made us that way?"

Nick gathered his thoughts again before continuing. This was pretty heady stuff, and he'd been down deeper and longer than he'd ever been before. He realized he's said more in the last ten minutes than in any other conversation he'd ever had, but instinctively he knew it was his only chance to destroy the remnants of an ingrained mind set. He had to keep going.

"It goes back to the Stone Age from what I can see. Each small clan had a leader, an Alpha male, and he got there because he was the best hunter and fighter, and probably the meanest bastard too. Naturally enough, the Alpha would get his pick of the food and females, so other males would have been sure to envy his power, but knew better than to piss him off. And life was too hard to carry passengers, so either you pulled your weight or you got the chop, and the Alpha was both judge and jury. Women already contributed in many ways, even fighting and hunting when they weren't pregnant, so it was the males with their more limited roles who were got rid of if they didn't perform."

He rubbed his chin while he thought more.

"Herds of animals and troops of primates still act that way today, Lil. If a younger, stronger male defeats the Alpha, the first thing he does is to kill all the small males the old Alpha sired or drive off those too big to kill. Competition is a no-no. It's ingrained in male DNA to get rid of likely challenges to show others they are in charge. It's why men from sixteen to sixty still need to be seen as the unemotional, macho type. It's in the genes. Men actually hate to compete, especially emotionally, but they see competition in everything they do. It's why they show off and do those inane, risky things, and why anger is the only emotion they can indulge in safely. What they're really saying is 'I haven't proved myself yet, but hey guys, I'm brave, I'm tough, you can't do without me,' And even if females didn't like the Alpha's personality, they'd still want to be under his protection and their kids to have his physical capabilities, so they'd play up to him to achieve that. That's where the bad boy syndrome that pisses males off even today comes from. Young, good-looking girls seem to be attracted to old, wealthy assholes, and ignore the nice guys. They don't mind being 'trophies' because it's about survival, and men and women see it differently."

Nick had talked so much he had to clear his throat, but he had to pull all this together.

"That pseudo bullshit isn't important to males once they know they can deal with danger and difficult problems, and I don't mean just in combat either. It might be rescuing drowning kids, or pulling someone from a fire, something like that. People can sense how tough and capable you are, so you don't need to lie to them. I've been there and done most of it in my time, Lil, so that sort of childish response isn't an issue for me. I've earned my spurs, and know how I react when the shit hits the fan. I'm happy with who I am, I suppose."

Nick wondered about any more self-disclosure, but could see the intense, dark eyes were following every word. Stuff it. She'd been pretty frank. He'd let her have it all.

"This started with us talking about the sex thing, which is totally different in our cultures, Laleh, and I've got fond memories of one affair that didn't quite make it myself. She was a bit older than me and taught me what should be important in a relationship, but we had different priorities and directions in the end. Quite honestly, I'm glad it happened, though, because it helped me to understand a lot of things. I never got anywhere close to it again, but she taught me that the past is history and can't be changed, so it shouldn't be a barrier to something good happening in the future. It's having a good partnership that really matters and sex should be a way of expressing it, not the end result of a relationship. Part of the enjoyment of it, not something you do to score points, or to get your own way."

It was like a light bulb flashing for him too. After he said it, he realized he believed it. It wasn't just empathy. Some of those people management lectures must have gotten through.

235

"I remained good friends with those students in England until I came back to Iran, Nick. Is that what you mean?"

"That's exactly what I mean. I've been tested a few times myself, and I've had to cope with my share of real danger, so life isn't a competition for me, and isn't it better to remember people with fondness not hatred if you can. We just have to accept that if something does die, it was probably going to anyway, but we're better for it having happened. Mind you, not everybody sees it that way. Things from your past or red-hot jealousies can get in the way, so really good relationships are still pretty rare. But the old saying that 'the truth will set you free' rings a bell for me, Lil. The gutless or under-confident often use lies to protect iffy egos, or hidden agendas, but eventually body language or poor memory catches them out. There isn't really any way back for them after that."

She smiled and flicked a wayward lock from his forehead. It prompted him to finish off.

"From what I've been told, relationships go through a so-called 'honeymoon period' that lasts about eighteen months to two years, and if there isn't anything there when the first flush off passion wears off, it's doomsday. There's got to be something more than just passion between people if it's going to last, especially when things like a decent home and car, or warm clothes and food for the baby become an issue. But that's life, Lil, that's what we've all got to come to terms with. Rape is totally different, Lil. Rape's a power and humiliation thing mostly done by males to make a point or maybe to get rid of tensions or fears they aren't really coping with. Their weapons become an extension of their dicks. They mean to intimidate people, to flaunt what they don't really have without them."

He had to be careful with the next bit. He paused.

"It's even worse in Islamic countries, as you know, Lil, because in those, rape is used specifically to punish you or your family. It's meant to humiliate and destroy your whole way of life forever, so really it's about power and dominance. What happened to you earlier was a normal part of growing up, and the rape later was not your fault. It didn't make you a lesser person. It happened purely because you were there. It wasn't about who you are, it was about what you represent."

She was looking at him intently now. "You've never said anything like this before, though, Nick. You're much deeper than I realized. I'm the one who's got a Master's in this sort of thinking, but you seem to see much more than I do."

"The navy's got a divisional system Lil, that is the envy of most military. Officers are taught to look after their sailors, particularly if they've got personal problems. I've also read a fair bit, and sat through lectures on this sort of stuff, but that bloody Scotsman knew there was a lot inside me as well. There hasn't been much else to talk about out here."

"You've been hurt as well, though. I think I can see that now."

"My childhood wasn't all that great, Laleh, but it did teach me what partnerships should be like, because I sure as hell know what they shouldn't be. Men and women talk a similar language but interpret the words differently, and I was afraid it would be almost impossible to meet someone who understood that." He looked at her again.

"Jock's been goading me ever since you came along because he thinks we would be right for each other. He's convinced that we can make it, but he knew you'd need to heal first, Now I think he knew I would as well. He's been deliberately dragging all this stuff to the surface to make me re-examine it, and it helps that we're with each other twenty-four-seven." Nick took her hand.

"Anyway, you know all this really, Lil, so we don't need to keep examining it. Your experiences just buried it for a while."

"I've always thought you were just being kind, and you'd drop the act when I'd mostly gotten over it. I needed you to be okay about touching me, though, and me happy about it happening. It's probably why I'm a bit physical, because it would never happen in Iran now. I didn't think you meant it that's all."

"It's not quite the time for us yet, Laleh, but I'm sure looking forward to when it is." Nick grinned wickedly. "I guarantee it won't be a brief exchange when the time does come either."

Chapter Thirty-Four

There was something different about them when they got back. Both Amini and Sinclair could sense it. He looked taller, she more self-assured, and they were still holding hands. Laleh peeled off to the kitchen and he to his bedroom for a local area map.

Laleh made coffee for them both, not asking how he wanted it, nor even if he wanted one at all. Nick took the charts to the settee where she joined him with the mugs, but this time, she sat at the opposite end of the settee. She removed her moccasins, hitched her skirt higher and swung her skirt-clad, flawless legs onto his lap. The pilot continued to study his map while at the same time kneading a shapely bare foot. She closed her eyes with a contented sigh.

Amini looked at the pair with fresh eyes. It had only been a few intense months, but they had been thrown together continually, and obviously already knew each other's preferences. He recognised instantly that he was no longer her first priority and sighed contently. He would always be her big brother, but she now had another strong man she cared for, someone who would also fight savagely for her if he had to. There was a lot still unresolved in Amini's life and the thought was gratifying. He felt Jock looking at him and shifted his gaze. They both grinned.

"Right, people, I'll toss around a few thoughts and you can let me have your opinions as we go."

Laleh opened her eyes at the sound of Nick's voice, but closed them again when he swapped one foot for the other.

"Okay, there's no defined threat yet and there may never be, but there are a few things we can do to hedge our bets. We can prepare, but we don't do anything risky unless we have to."

The males nodded.

"I was followed after I dropped off the reports the other day but nothing else happened, so I think it was more a spur of the moment thing, about the company ops out here, so we'll try to lower the odds a bit." He paused while he sipped from his mug.

"First up, I want you to take the vehicle into Qom and get that black film put on the windows, Jock. It'll be summer before long, so it'll seem the thing to do, but you can't see inside when that's in place. After that, Farhad and Laleh don't travel together unless it can't be helped."

Sinclair nodded.

"Secondly, Qom serves three railway lines, and that may be an option if we have to do a bunk. We need an updated schedule and information about checks or searches along the way."

"My boys would be ideal for some of that, Nick. They came here by train and went back to Pakistan on leave that way too. It would be perfectly natural for them to make enquiries."

"Fine, we can decide on routes later. We could always by-pass a few stations by using a chopper if we have too. You get that one rolling, Jock." The nod was enough.

"Next, we fly some surveys starting the day after tomorrow, and put in a few reports to avert any suspicion. We'll throw in a few positive sightings, but high in the hills, somewhere inaccessible. It'll keep them interested."

"Can I help with that one?"

Laleh got an indulgent smile and the others grinned too. "I thought more flying might appeal to you. Is everybody happy so far?" He barely waited for the nods.

"Okay. This is the controversial one. We'll need another trip to Tehran in the next couple of weeks."

"Is that bit necessary, laddie?" The Scot looked perplexed, whilst the others said nothing.

"Unfortunately, it is. First, we need the other Cherokee back for everyday stuff, but maybe for something else in the future as well. Webster would have left it at the Canadian Embassy and a top up from the Brit Embassy bond is a good excuse to get it, but really I'm going to try for some sort of official travel docs for Fred and Lily."

"The Brit Embassy isn't going to risk getting involved like that, is it?"

"Probably not, Fred, but they might have thought of something else. Right now, anything's worth a go."

"Would you contact Abdul while you're up there, Nickie?"

"I've thought about that one, Lil, and I think it's worth the risk. It was a no-no with Fred's Tehran numbers, but Abdul's pretty high profile and may have something worthwhile by now. I'll get Gerry to call the university on a sterile phone and arrange for Abdul and Minu to be at home at the right time. It won't be for long."

"God, I'd love to see them again." There was something wistful about it.

"You're bound to feel that way, Laleh, but think about it, because it would be incredibly selfish. You'd spend over six hours in a chador, make the embassy thing more risky, and you could compromise Abdul and Minu all for a couple of hugs."

"I know you're right Nick. It's a bit hard, that's all." Nick took her hand and squeezed. It refocused her.

"Hang on. I've got an idea."

He turned to Sinclair. "You've still got that Polaroid camera, Jock?"

"Bloody expensive, even in duty free, but it takes good pictures."

"That's the answer then, Laleh. Jock got it because we couldn't get other film developed around here all that easily. You can take several photos of what you want, and write Minu a letter. Farhad can pass them on when we get up there."

She smiled.

They tossed around a few more ideas, refined a few more facts, and then ate and went to bed. The morrow would be a very early start.

Chapter Thirty-Five
Shahabad

Amini helped Nick get the bar-be-cue flashed up early to allow the mesh to heat. A half an hour later Nick collected the seasoned ibex carcass, skewered it, and started it roasting. It would get turned by anyone who passed it after that. He had a final look-around and spotted Laleh leaning casually against the door jamb watching them.

She was still wrapped in her purple chiffon nightshirt, a very feminine gesture, she half raised an arm and wriggled her fingers. He smiled.

"Do you guys want coffee?"

Nick looked at Amini, who nodded. "Love one. Be there in five minutes."

Full light hadn't yet fully scattered the night's darker shadows, but Nick could already hear disjointed, shrill music drifting on the morning zephyr. It didn't sound much like a tune, more like instruments warming up. Or maybe cats fighting. When Nick and Amini got back inside there were two mugs on the table and Laleh was fetching a third. She looked over her shoulder.

"Yours is nearest the door, Nick."

He and Amini sat across from each other at the table, but when Laleh returned, she ignored a chair, and sat on one of Nick's knees. His left hand automatically went around her waist, and he found there was nothing under the crisp, dark rayon but flesh. It was innocent enough, not meant to be provocative at all, however Nick was acutely aware of dark nipples, barely discernible even up close, pushing delicately against the patterned chiffon. They were at lip level, and that wasn't helping all that much either. She was holding her mug with both hands, still half asleep, not yet up to conversation.

Amini was male and smiled to himself. He knew why Nick Evans was looking uncomfortable and expected the long, muffled 'Jesus' when the girl headed for her bedroom.

"Got a bit of a stomach cramp there, Nick?" A grinning Amini was getting less reserved by the day.

"She's still got a few yards to go yet, Fred, but if your sister keeps doing that sort of thing without thinking about it, I'm going to have a bloody accident."

"She feels safe with you, mate. Don't forget she lived in the UK for several years. She saw old couples walking down the street hand in hand, people kissing and hugging in the open, and youngsters crashed out on blankets in the parks and on the beaches. That sort of thing is totally different to anything she would ever see here. She's obviously got it worked out, Nick. She feels that partnerships should be like that. I can have a quiet word with her, if you like; she's still pretty naïve, really."

Nick's friend got a big grin. "I don't mean that, you asshole, and you know it. I'll put up with it, but don't smirk when you know what's happening."

Anything else was buried when Sarah and Sinclair came through the door laughing about something.

Sarah took charge. It was her people's celebration and she knew the ropes. She festooned a trestle table with baskets of bread and fruit and then layered the cooked vegetables on metal baking trays underneath the carcass. The ibex was already crackling by then and the vegetables would taste better with the juices dripping gently over them. She looked around critically and it seemed to be a sign.

It wasn't yet mid-morning when the sudden crash of cymbals and the mesmerizing thump of drums joined the high, twittering squeaks of whistles.

"We let this one go, be ready for next one, Nick. That much better."

Nick nodded. "Is there anything else we should do?"

"No, all done. Vegetables in drum and bread and fruit covered. Mohammed bring over jugs soon so we enjoy rest of day. You got plastic cup things somewhere?"

"I know where they are. I'll have a caffeine hit and then dig them out. Do you guys want a coffee?" Sarah and Amini declined, Sinclair nodded. Nick moved inside.

Laleh was exiting her bedroom as Nick pushed through the door. He stopped mesmerized. She was dressed festively in a skirt that flowed from waist to calf in broad pastel streaks, topped by a loose patterned matching blouse in a more subtle shade of purple. And although she wore little make-up, what she did enhanced every significant feature. Nick's stomach knotted. He didn't realize he'd frozen.

"Ta dah. You like?" The girl whirled. Nick stayed speechless as the others crowded in behind him. Sinclair was the nearest and whispered in his ear.

"You ever let that get away, laddie, and you need your fucking head examined."

Startled, Nick looked at him then back at her. "Laleh, you look absolutely stunning. I don't know what to say." But then something kicked in. "May I have the pleasure of the next dance ma'am?"

He guided her around the room for several animated, uninhibited whirls, and she was giggling as he guided her to the sofa. He had known how to react after all. That was exactly what she needed. Nick Evans totally forgot what he was meant to be doing. Jock got in the last word.

"That's okay, laddie, carry on gawping. I'll fix the coffee."

The festive hype grew on them like an approaching freight train. These things could be more about mood than alcohol. Even before the kettle had boiled, Mohammed turned up with two large stoneware jars. It was Sarah who suggested a shot with their brew. The others already knew the damage that would inflict, but Sinclair saved their livers.

"I've already put a wee dram in these, Sarah. It'll be a long day, so that's enough for now. What about you?"

"Not me for whisky, I have this with Mohammed."

The sighs of relief were barely audible, but they were tangible. Honour was satisfied. They were starting the parade correctly.

Nick claimed the settee again and Laleh was there with her legs doubled under her, but this time with linked hands resting over his shoulder. They were listening to Sinclair pulling funny stories from somewhere in his past. He was relating a fairly spicy one when interrupted by a loud clash of cymbals somewhere in the distance.

"This the best one," Sarah prophesised, "we go now."

Nick was last out and turned the sizzling carcass as he passed.

The lower streets throbbed with a disjointed cacophony as they strolled down to where the crowds were thick and tight. Many more than normally lived in the town were there again, and a lot of them were strangers. The locals were already animated and effervescent, with Sunday best the norm. And some had obviously been at the sauce from early in the morning, but here it was different. There were no arguments, no belligerence, just a lot of happy laughing people, and those who had lost a temporary battle with the local fire-water were smiling, even though slumped against house walls.

"They be up again soon." Sarah whispered within her running commentary. The drums, whistles and cymbals drew closer.

Most of the stalls and adjacent shops were still in business. Ragged children dashed everywhere, totally ignored by their elders, who lined the streets giggling themselves into jigs as the noisy procession drew nearer. They seemed unconcerned that half the musicians were playing different tunes. And a phalanx followed the band, several carrying large papier-mâché replicas of local vegetables, led by a wizened male of advanced though indeterminable years. He deviated in and out of the open shops and the parade dutifully followed.

Nick was amazed. He hadn't been this close the year before, but part of his flying training had been at a large naval air station in West Cornwall. He'd attended the Helston 'Furry Dance' at the beginning of the UK spring, and this was obviously a similar fertility ritual. Ten thousand miles shrank to just a few. As the band got closer Nick found his feet tapping to the rhythmic thump of the drum. That also was like many years before.

"Old man tell fortunes," Sarah whispered it as the music got closer.

The Europeans and Aminis were impossible to miss in that crowd and the old man cackled and pointed a talon-like finger as he pranced towards them. A shrill chant escaped through a wrinkled mouth, devoid of any discernible teeth, and he waved some sort of limp green twig towards them. When he was beside Laleh, he leaned forward and whispered in her ear. She blushed and he turned away still cackling.

Nick had an arm draped lightly around her shoulder and pulled her closer.

"What on earth did he say, Lil?"

Laleh paused for a few seconds looking at the ground. She was still red.

"He said that my man will give me fine sons. That I should treasure you."

They'd all caught that, and caught Nick's instant response too. "In that case, you should have told him that your man was certainly looking forward to the practice." He said that with a grin as he hugged her closer, but it went beyond the ribald for the rest of them. She thumped him.

As he turned and ducked in pretend fear, his eyes raked a nearby male who wasn't smiling. When he rose again, the man had disappeared.

247

The parade snaked through the cool but sunny streets for at least another half an hour. They joined in jigs with total strangers as the band passed, and then poked around the stalls before finally heading home. About half way back, Nick bumped into a tall, handsome Bakhtaran, who looked a few years younger than him. The man sported a couple of days' growth, and was inside a red anorak. He was accompanied by a striking young female in a loose blue headscarf who shepherded two young boys ahead of her. Nick and the Bakhtaran hugged.

"Baraz!"

"Nick!"

Sarah threw an aside over her shoulder to Farhad and Laleh. "This my younger son Baraz, and wife Nasrin. These boys my grandsons." You could cut her obvious pride with a knife. "They come down from hills for this and stay with me. We get back and carve meat. No more dancing now. People be hungry next." The enlarged group headed for home, with one happily squealing youngster on Nick's shoulders, the other on Jock's.

A rich aroma of roasted meat wafted enticingly through the almost motionless air a good block before they reached the courtyard. The carcass was crisp and roasted to perfection when they got there, and Nick lowered the youngster and turned the ibex for the last time. While he fiddled, the three women trooped into the house, returning with paper napkins and a roll of kitchen paper. Jock made do with a bottle, plastic containers and soda. By then, Nick had two halves of naan stuffed with crisp ibex and the boys were chomping happily.

Chairs got dragged out by Amini and Baraz while Nick prepared a pocket bread for Sarah and Nasrin. He then called Laleh over to point out the meat she wanted. The pilot knew the protocol. And before the males had prepared their own sandwiches, boisterous chattering people were pouring through the open courtyard door. The first few were neighbours, but after a while, Nick didn't know any of them. The almost endless succession of visitors declined the whisky but hammered the stoneware jars. And although Farsi wasn't a strong point for Jock or Nick, by then if they laughed loud and long, everybody understood anyway.

Without exception, the callers ate meat stuffed in bread, sampled the vegetables, threw down a small cup of fire-water and then moved on. Children included. It seemed so regimented, so organised and polite, but Nick thought about it some more. Perhaps it was prudence after all. It could depend on how many times you were going to do this in the next few hours. Sarah had always insisted they be a stop-off point, not festival nomads, and now he realized why. They could stage themselves. They could watch their intake.

And sometime later, when the visitors were thinning, Nick saw the face again. This time the man was filling a sandwich but kept within an animated, gesticulating crowd. Nick recognised his shifty, detached look instantly. Trying not to stare, he eased around to where Sarah was laughing with her family.

"Don't make it obvious, Sarah, but do you know that bloke with the pale-green anorak near the street door?"

His housekeeper started but only looked when she lifted and twirled a grandson.

Nick kept his face neutral.

"He with police force in Qom, Nickie. Father Arab but mother one of us."

"Is he religious police or an ordinary cop?"

"Ordinary police. Sometimes he work with police out here."

He nodded thoughtfully and was going to point him out to Jock, but the man had disappeared again.

By late afternoon there were little more than bones left on the carcass, no vegetables at all, and the second jar had been severely dented. It had been a remarkable day, but as the light died, so did the noise and festivities.

Sarah and her family were the first to leave. As she departed, she pointed.

"Leave carcass, Nickie. Bones for dogs. Mohammed pick up in the morning."

He nodded, and Imran and Jock took their leave after helping him clear up.

By the time they finished, it was already dark, but it wasn't that late when Farhad flopped into an armchair. Nick stretched on the settee with Laleh folded into him. She ignored her drink and was snoring delicately. They had staged themselves and kept clear of the fire-water, so they weren't under any serious pressure, but it had been a long, dusty day. Bone-crushing exhaustion was a by-product.

"What do you think, Nick, bed?"

"Sounds good to me."

"You okay with Laleh?" He wasn't being big brotherly or cute.

"I can hack it. Thanks, Fred." He gave her a nudge and she opened bleary eyes.

"Bed, Lil." She nodded as Farhad took off for the bathroom. Her eyes barely opened when Nick walked her into her bedroom and sat her on the bed. He turned down her doona, removed her moccasins, and then stood up to leave.

"You okay now, Lily?"

"I'm stuffed, Nick, you can help me."

"You sure that's wise?"

She opened her eyes. "I asked Sarah who put me to bed on Christmas Day and she said that you two did. You can help me again."

"Okay, but she's not here now, love."

Laleh wobbled but didn't topple as he scooped up her night-dress from under the quilt, and the blouse and skirt came off easily enough. The underwear was pink this time, and again he tried to ignore the proud breasts as he removed her brassiere. He held her tight while he slipped her arms and head through her night gown, and then laid her down gently. He contemplated the panties. Bugger it. They were virtually an item already, but obviously she

250

trusted him more than he trusted himself. He fingered the waist elastic and she drew her heels up and lifted her hips. Her eyes were still closed, but a lazy smile caressed her lips as he fumbled to remove them. Nick saw the shimmering, midnight triangle at the base of her pelvis for the first time.

But it was like an orchestra had hit all the high notes at once. If he did touch her, she would almost certainly be okay with it now, but this could be some sort of test. Although their time must be ever closer, he half suspected that she needed to be the instigator, at least for the first time. He cursed his newfound sensitivity under his breath. She smiled, but her eyes stayed shut.

Chapter Thirty-Six

Nick was up early the next day. It wasn't just another year, it was a new decade, and he knew something would have to be done about their future before long. That hadn't helped much with sleep, and when he heard Mohammed making noises disjointing the bones, he joined him with a mug. He muttered a brief greeting when he wandered out. Mohammed didn't need any help.

Shortly after the Iranian cackled his farewells, Nick re-stowed the drum. And both Farhad and Laleh Amini were up when he got back inside. Bleary eyed but up. They all exchanged grunts as Laleh hurried the kettle along.

Nick was sat across from Amini when Laleh brought the mugs. She skirted the table again, and he automatically thrust out his left knee. He was already familiar with her warmth under the nightgown, and now enjoying it, while Laleh felt more comfortable with his arm around her. Nick left it until they'd taken a few sips from their brews.

"It's the New Year, guys, and the silence has been deafening. It's time we got proactive. We'll get a flight in this morning and a couple early next week, then on Friday do the trip to Tehran. There'll be less people around on their Sabbath, so nobody should pay much attention to us. The embassies will be quieter too. You okay with that?

It was Farhad who spoke. "Mohammed and Baraz want to show me their stock in the upper paddocks later this morning, Nick. I don't know much about animals, but they seem to be pretty keen. That's not a problem, is it?"

"Not at all. They've both got reasonable utes but it'll still take most of the day to get up there and back. I'll set up a few things with the embassy this morning and then pop up myself."

Laleh was instantly awake. "Can I go?"

Nick grinned. "I wouldn't dream of trying to stop you. Farhad can do the trip after, and we'll try for a gazelle or ibex on that one."

"Oh good. Is it okay if I only wear the top piece of the chador. I hate the bloody thing."

"Nobody would notice, Lily. We'll go after I've phoned the embassy. We'll take a flask, but we won't stop this time."

"Do I get to drive too?"

He was getting better at this. "Of course. I wouldn't dream of going up there without a competent co-pilot." The girl leant back into him again, completely satisfied.

Sarah was spending a day with her daughter-in-law and grandchildren, and Amini was on his way long before Sinclair and his team bundled in. Nick let them know what was happening.

"Okay, take Papa Zulu. I've got some time-based maintenance on the other one. I'll keep them both up to date now, just in case, and you can fill in another furphy when you get back. We'll save the positive report for a day or so before we go into Qom again."

"Okay. Let's get on with it."

Laleh was up front when they piled into the Jeep. She was already distancing herself from the restrictions of her youth, and was effervescent and talkative during the twenty minutes to the airfield. Jock and his team opened up the hangar while she and Nick carried on to the offices. She was quick to whip the chador top off, revealing a black T-shirt with a cuddly teddy bear motive. Nick settled her down with the map. She quickly oriented it, and he traced where they would be going first, then the upper meadows where Mohammed's hut stood. After, he pointed to where fencing hemmed in their animals ran, and she knew exactly what she was looking at.

Nick made his phone call prior to getting airborne and got a male voice. The man asked a few questions before patching him through to extension twenty-three.

"How's it going, Nick?"

"Still no problems doing what we do, Gerry, but there's been a few personal complications since we last talked. I've got a couple of friends staying with me and I think someone in town is watching us."

Hawkins caught on right away. "Locals I presume."

"Sort of, but should I say they are unlikely to be welcome locals anymore."

"Jesus, mate, you're a sucker for punishment. How do you think I can help?"

"Jock and I need one more trip on Friday next week, and that may be the last for a while. I'll fill you in then if that's okay."

"Not a problem. Most of the Brit staff will be here but not many locals. What about the surveillance?"

"I don't think it's serious, Gerry. Nobody knows about our guests outside the village so it's probably because we're a Yank company. Can you call the professor of surgery at Shahid Beheshti University, a Doctor Rashid, and tell him we'll be dropping in? I'm not trying to teach you to suck eggs, mate, you'll know what to say, but let him know that two friends will pop in on the Friday morning. Call him Abdul and he's sure to know who it is. We'll be out of everybody's hair within the hour."

"I can do that. Nothing much has changed up here yet, but I'll try to find out who's interested in you. We've got a few contacts."

Nick thanked him and said his good-byes.

Laleh got strapped into the right-hand seat again, but it was Nick who got them going. Shahabad would be a distraction for her. He let that pass first.

"Do you remember what to do, Lil?"

"Definitely. I was awake half the bloody night thinking about it."

"Okay, come onto the controls." She did, but the expected wayward lurches didn't happen. He took his hands off completely. "That was really smooth, Lil. You'd think you'd been doing this all your life."

She giggled. "I remember that other thing your instructor told you. Handle the controls like you would a tramp's dick. I can't imagine ever doing such a thing, but I know what he meant."

He chuckled as they cruised down the river. The speed and height hardly varied at all, and he soon saw the valley he was looking for.

"Okay, Laleh, bring the speed back to seventy knots and climb up that valley on the left. Go back up to ninety again when you hit the top." The mix of instructions was deliberate.

Nick was so confident in her by then that he examined the strata casually, just pointing out where, and letting her get on with it. Laleh was ecstatic, but concentrated fiercely.

"Okay, Lil, I've got control."

She relinquished reluctantly.

"Which way back to the river valley?"

She didn't hesitate. "Behind us. Twenty degrees east of north would do it."

Nick shook his head briefly, impressed.

"Right. Pour me a coffee please, then take over and go for it."

Nick took his time with the coffee.

"Okay, Lily, head east along the ridge at sixty-five knots, and descend level with the hill tops as you do." The increasingly complex directions were now part of the learning curve.

Nick had a quick look at his map before taking control back. The Zagros shrank lower as they approached the desert. Only dusty mountain tracks crossed the arid flats, but the skids and wheel marks of countless vehicles stood out starkly in the light dirt surface. Laleh had finished her own coffee by then, but he kept control as he turned up a prominent valley. "We're nearly there so be ready to wave." She nodded, but looked more at what he was doing.

"Don't worry. We'll do this and then I've got a final treat for you."

A white utility slid into view almost as he'd said it, nestled alongside a small adobe shack. They were flying low and slow and could pick out the frost-ravished pastures between the tors, the wind-burnt, straw carpet more a mottled tan than a lively green, except where a mountain stream meandered. It looked arid, almost lifeless up there, but it wasn't. They'd already put up a small herd of camels that ran with an awkward, shambling gait that nonetheless ate up the ground, and startled several large, grey donkeys into a break-neck gallop. Nick knew that dull sparrows, soaring nightingales and melodic, twittering bulbuls also hid in the tussocks, while kestrels soared above the jagged crags around them. Also there were seventy varieties of snakes wriggling around up there somewhere, and tortoises and hares frequented the rocky outcrops. The hills sheltered a menagerie. It just wasn't an obvious one.

When they got there, Farhad, Mohammed and Baraz were easy to spot. They waved, and she waved back vigorously.

Nick Evans let her dodge through the mountains for another half hour before he took back control. He threaded through the hills and rough paddocks directly towards the airfield, and slowed with a flamboyant flare away from the runway. He used the windsock to line up precisely into wind and trimmed the beast at twice the height he would normally hover at.

"Look where the nose is on the horizon, Lil. If I yaw or I'm heavy on the cyclic, it changes, and if I do, we need a bit of power."

He demonstrated as he talked. "Okay, you have the cyclic."

She held it gingerly. His hands were fairly close. The helicopter wandered over the length of a football pitch. He'd expected that.

"Okay, I have it." She'd been trimming madly and there was a heavy force on the stick. He neutralized it. "Okay, try again, but keep your thumb away from the trim this time."

And it wasn't long before she could hold it within a small back yard. "Right, Lily, have a rest."

Nick split the controls again and this time gave her the collective and rudders. That was easier for her. He kept the machine steady, anticipating occasionally on heading with minute touches of the pedals.

"Right, woman, have another break, then you do it all." Laleh looked at him doubtfully, but he grinned at her. She wriggled her body more firmly into the seat and Nick reminded her about tiny movements. Initially his own hands and feet were close to all the levers.

Laleh wandered a bit, climbed and descended a bit, and yawed a bit too, but not by much. Within five minutes, she hardly deviated at all, and a quick glance told her that his hands were now completely clear. He deliberately scratched a shoulder and was casual about taking control back. Nick explained what and why as he taxied to the hangar and shut down.

This time, she didn't jump out while he knocked off the switches, but Nick didn't notice that she was still in her seat, her eyes closed, until after the shutdown. He hopped out and went around to un-buckle her. She hugged him tightly and started to cry when he helped her disembark.

"Easy, Lil, you did better than most of my students did after a half a dozen flights."

A belligerent, protective Sinclair was there at about the same time. "What the hell have you said, Nick? She's crying."

Laleh turned to Jock, the mascara running. "I'm fine, Jock. I'm just so happy, that's all."

"Aye, well that's all right then." He still sounded suspicious.

Nick dragged a handkerchief from a pocket and carefully dabbed the tears away.

"It didn't hit me until we were coming in. No woman in this country will ever get a chance to do what I've just done. There won't be any women scientists or engineers, and no lady pilots, police or doctors either. Nursing other women is about all they'll be able to do. I suddenly realized how lucky I am, that's all."

Chapter Thirty-Seven

They took some more leisurely flights into the rolling hills the following week. Nick had her fumbling through the start sequence and air taxiing on those, then some landings and take-offs. She proved to be pretty competent at that too. Farhad got a ride up to see the higher pastures on the second one, but Sinclair pleaded work and declined. The Pakistanis shook their heads in unison. Nick had expected that too. He'd never been able to get them airborne.

The Tehran trip was on them before they realized it. Imran would be going so he ate with them. Laleh wouldn't, but she sat close enough to Nick to be joined at the hip. Inevitably they all looked to him now to pull it together.

"Right. The Canadian Embassy is on Shahid Sarafraz, between the Brits' and Abdul's place, so we'll hit the British Embassy before we hit the Canadians. We'll need some official company documents for that bit too, Jock. There shouldn't be any trouble if we have them with us."

"Aye, well Abdul wouldn't want us to turn up with two vehicles either. Me and Imran will take off back here with it after he visits the railway station."

"I was going to suggest that. Just you and me to Abdul's Fred, and we'll see if we can park away from his house. We won't stay long, but with several different religious groups in Tehran, he may have something new. Have you got everything you need?"

Laleh answered first.

"I typed a letter to Minu at the airfield, but I'm still sorting a few photos out. I'll give them to Farhad after we've finished here."

Farhad nodded. "I've jotted down some questions for Abdul as well, Nick. I don't want to forget anything either. There's a small park less than a half kilometre from his house, so we can park there."

Nick looked up. "Can you occupy yourself, Lily?"

"Mohammed and Sarah are going up to help Baraz drench some sheep for worms and I'm going with them. I'll have plenty to do."

"Okay, guys." He raised his glass. "Let's hope the trip's worth it."

They got going early the next morning, with Amini carrying a passport belonging to one of Imran's men. Nick drove sedately, but they were still at a sun-washed British Embassy by 9.30. Imran stayed in the vehicle when the others piled through the glass doors.

Gerry Hawkins took only minutes to get to the lobby desk, and was just as quick ushering them into an empty conference room. A pristine, highly polished table and chairs took up most of the space, while an overhead projector was pushed into a corner. Thick drapes cut out any daylight. It was a place to work, not relax in.

Nick introduced the Iranian to the diplomat. "This is Commander Farhad Amini formerly of the Imperial Iranian Navy, Gerry." The full title was deliberate. It always impressed the Brits. Gerry Hawkins thrust out a hand.

"Farhad or Fred will do, Gerry."

Nick elaborated. "We were friends at Dartmouth some years ago, but if I say his middle name is Reza, you'll understand the problem."

Hawkins nodded towards the Persian.

"I'm sorry, Farhad, but you do realize there's nothing the Embassy can do in an official capacity."

"I realize that, Gerry. What about unofficially?"

260

Gerry Hawkins demurred, his level gaze raking each of them quickly. "We're still hoping the bans will be lifted soon, but we're not getting many of our own nationals out yet so let's say it's forced us to look at a few alternatives."

"Is it likely they'll lift the bans soon?"

"The Americans have kept up the financial squeeze so the hostages are still in the Embassy, Nick. It's anybody's guess. You've got some Pakistani lads on your crew, haven't you?"

Nick nodded. "Four came in by train straight from Pakistan."

"Okay, but if this ever gets out, we'll deny it. I'll give you some information about the rail system that isn't general knowledge, and you can do what you want with it. One of our SIS blokes did a bit of snooping a few weeks ago. He's a true blue British Arab, but also a Coptic Christian. It's still accurate as far as we know."

"Anything will help at this stage, Gerry. We're a bit stumped. We're in the middle of a bloody huge country with about 60 million hostile people in it, and we aren't sure how to go about this."

"Okay. Currently trains run from Tehran to the Turkish border three times a week and to Pakistan twice, with most of the pay-back crap happening in Tehran. There isn't much happening anywhere else, but paper checks are fairly stringent in Tehran and on the border. If you don't board the train in Tehran and walk the last few miles at the other end, you should be okay." Hawkins let them digest that before clearing his throat.

"Apart from the official exits into Turkey, the border is pretty porous. It isn't patrolled much, it's far too isolated, and the Pakistanis are mostly Muslim so the eastern border posts can be pretty casual as well. If tickets are bought by someone with a legitimate reason to do it, that's even better. I'll nip up in a minute and get more details for you."

"That's pretty useful stuff, and we can work on that. There's one more problem though, Gerry. Farhad has his sister with us."

"The same would apply, Nick. A shortish walk beats losing your frigging head."

"I'll put it different, mate. Laleh and I are together. It's not to get a flight out, Gerry, it's permanent. We really are together. If I go anywhere, she goes with me." He said that almost defiantly.

Surprisingly, Hawkins smiled. "Well it's about bloody time you got corralled like the rest of us. So what do you want? I certainly can't do anything about getting you both out yet."

"I know, but is there a way we can make this look official? Make people think. Give her some protection?"

Hawkins pursed his lips then his face cleared. "We anticipated ex-pats needing something like that, so we drew up some screeds on Embassy paper. They're all dutifully signed and stamped by the ambassador, and we type in an appropriate middle bit. I can produce something that says the Embassy recognises a de-facto relationship between you and that you've assisted with Embassy formal and social occasions as a couple. Is that what you mean?"

"That would be perfect if you can do it, Gerry."

"Okay, and if she always wears a chador or at least a headscarf when you are out and about, that could make it easier for you as well. We've noticed the regime's a bit funny like that. They brought in all these rules then got cagey about breaking them. If you obey the directives, they'll leave you alone. Is that it?"

"Sure is. We'll do a top up and get out of your hair."

"Okay, Nick, see George in the bond. I'll nip up and attend to the other stuff."

Nick Evans, Sinclair and Amini were fifteen minutes stocking their vehicle. Hawkins skipped down a central staircase only a few minutes after. He held two large envelopes.

"I'm handing these to, Nick, Farhad. He's a British subject and what he chooses to do with them after you leave here is entirely up to him." Hawkins was talking quietly because several people were transiting the large entrance foyer. He smiled when he passed the buff envelopes to the pilot.

"I've put the original of our letter on file, Nick. It will hold up anywhere, and Abdul knows you're coming. Fair winds and a following sea, my friend."

Nick thanked him profusely. They both suspected that they might never see each other again.

The Canadians had been expecting someone for weeks and the duty officer was relieved when Nick rocked up. He was with them in two minutes flat. Nick flashed his ID, and explained, and the Canadian confirmed that they'd got Webster out of the country weeks before. They'd been expecting a company representative for some time, so after Nick signed a formal release and got the bunch of keys.

"You probably saw the vehicle when you came in, Mister Evans. We disconnected the battery, and the tool kit is still open in the back. Have a safe trip, sir."

Nick nodded his thanks. The battery took two minutes to re-connect and the Cherokee fired on the third attempt.

"You take the one with the booze, Jock. I'll give this one a blow-though."

"Okay, laddie. Take care and we'll see you soon."

Chapter Thirty-Eight

Now he knew the way, it didn't take long to reach a leafy Sultanabad Road. Nick drew up in a small suburban recreational area that was like any city parkland area he'd ever seen. A few rough-wood tables and benches set apart from a couple of swings and a climbing frame, with a layer of wood chips on the deck. Some of the trees were evergreen and fecund, but some had shed their autumn foliage, looking naked, emaciated and forlorn. They waded west through the leaves and ducked into the drive.

It was Abdul who opened up to the chimes. He hugged Farhad and stuck out a hand to Nick. When they stepped into the large, comfortable lounge, Minu hugged them both. Farhad passed over Laleh's letter before she glided off to make tea while Amini and Abdul went into a huddle, quickly lapsing into Farsi. Nick perused the subtle, ornate room, admiring what were almost certainly genuine antiques.

Minu took a while before she re-appeared with a tray. She sat with Nick, who pumped her about the stylized pieces and the meanings of their embossed carvings. The other two barely noticed, nor that their tea was poured. They were still talking when a thick skin stained the rim of the delicate ceramics as it got cold. Minu shrugged and addressed the pilot.

"Come, Nick. Walk with me in the garden."

Nick lumbered to his feet and waited for her to open sliding glass doors.

The house was in the foothills, the garden watered by a heavy run-off from the Elburzes. It was luxuriously greener than was normal in winter, though still too early for flowers. Minu threaded her arm through his as they ambled the crushed brick paths.

"My little Laleh seems to be thriving down south, Nick."

"She's fantastic, Minu. Almost over her nightmare. I thought she'd need months of counselling, but I was happy to wait because I knew that couldn't happen until we got out of Iran." He felt a bit embarrassed. "I've never met anyone remotely like her before. She seems so free, yet in other ways so committed as well. She doesn't leave you wondering about much either. Certainly lets you know what she's thinking."

"According to her letter, it's all because of you. She said 'he carries me where I would never dare fly alone.' She's not talking about the helicopter, Nick, although she's obviously enjoying that too. That's pretty heady stuff. She seems to be very much smitten with you."

"If she is, I'm really glad, Minu. I haven't known many relationships that worked before, so I've been wary of getting my feet wet again, but with her it's not an issue. I've got a feeling we'll still be like this when we're in our seventies."

Minu inclined her head. "I know that Laleh feels that way, but I'm not sure she realizes you do yet. Did you see the photos she sent?"

"Not really. She and Jock were snapping away, but I was a bit preoccupied."

The older woman took the envelope from a skirt pocket and passed over four Polaroids.

The first was of Laleh grinning in the cockpit, and the second a semi-formal shot with her arm though his. There was nothing but white sand and purple hills anywhere else, but in the third they were wrestling playfully on what was obviously the settee. She was trying to pin his shoulders to the fabric, and both seemed to be laughing out loud.

265

But it was the fourth that was more than poignant. They were nibbling at each other while looking intently into each other's eyes, but neither seemed aware that the camera was aimed at them. Nick looked through them again before he handed them back.

"Those are how we are all the time, Minu. Any day, just different parts of it. I took the one of her in the cockpit, but I've never seen the others before."

"What is special to me is that she's fallen for someone outside her own culture, someone she can feel a woman with again, someone who she can respect and be respected by. It's what she needed, so please don't hurt her, Nick. She could never return to the inhibiting days of her youth."

"Well, I don't know what to say really. She's certainly much more physical than I expected an Iranian woman to be, so I do know that an arranged marriage would never have stood a chance with her. I reckon there can't be many like yours and Abdul's."

Minu smiled gently. "Ours wasn't arranged, Nick. Abdul was at Guys getting his Master's, and I was at the LSE getting a Nursing Management Degree. We met, fell in love and lived together in London for three years. We wanted our families with us when we did get married though, so we left that bit until we got back here." Her smile broadened. "The bump was fairly obvious when we did."

"I'm sorry, Minu. I just assumed that."

She smiled. "Both our fathers were old fashioned and thought they should have arranged it, so they had a few problems at first, but our mothers soon whipped them into line. If you'd seen the granddads bouncing their first grandson around later you'd have thought it was their idea anyway." Minu rubbed his arm.

"Okay, Nick, we'd better return, I need to write Laleh a short note."

The pair sped back, obeying signals when they could and protecting themselves when they couldn't. They cleared Tehran before they felt free to speak more than platitudes.

"I didn't think Tehran was all that smart initially, Nick, but it was great in the end. I feel better about a lot of things now."

"I've been a bit short on trusting people myself, Fred, my own experiences, I guess, but you guys have changed the way I think about a lot of things." He glanced at his friend. "As far as I'm concerned, we've got more information to work with, but that's all. There's nothing we need to act on yet and nobody who knows us would ever turn us in."

"You're right, mate, and I'm glad you put me in the picture the other day. I feel better about a lot of things, and friend to friend, I'm really chuffed about you and Laleh. In the end, I think you needed each other, and it's another load off my mind. Shit, you realize were virtually brothers now, don't you?"

Nick smiled. "Well, we'd better figure a way to get us all out of this dung hill then, brother. Was the Embassy any help?"

"I'm amazed at what they've got. Stuff about train schedules, safe cities and groups that may help along the way. There's even info: about getting up to the Caspian to hire or steal a boat. There are some places down south where we could try for Kuwait or Oman too. Their intelligence bloke must have earned his money."

"What about Abdul?"

"Pay dirt again. Things are slow in Tehran, but a Christian group is more active outside the capitol. They've got a few cells springing up, and believe it or not there's one in Qom. A member of his staff is the contact. I knew a couple of them were Christians, but he didn't say who. He told me to be extra careful but gave me an address and told me to go when the crowds are thickest. It'll still be quiet tomorrow so perhaps you can run me in on Sunday morning and pick me up on Monday? I don't want to risk being on the streets when there aren't many people around, or be seen dropped off in a company vehicle either."

"No problems, mate. So we got what we wanted."
Laleh hugged them both when they got back. The one for Nick was fiercer and longer, and it seemed quite natural to her by then. He handed her a hold-all of clothing that Minu had packed, and Sinclair ambled in shortly after with a glass in his hand. It called for a conference.

Sarah wasn't there, so Laleh beefed up the inevitable meaty stew with curry powder before putting it back on to heat. With some time to go before it would be ready, she swooped up the glass that Nick poured and settled against Nick. Amini started talking about his day.

Inevitably Nick Evans pulled it all together in the end, but he didn't mention his own official screed. He wasn't sure how Laleh would react to it, and he'd already learned not to double-guess her. Love him—obviously she did—but she wouldn't hold back if the presumption upset her.

"Okay guys. It's beginning to look good, but there's no need to get carried away. I'll drop Fred off in Qom on Sunday morning and you can pick him up on Monday, Jock. We'll try to avoid patterns, so we'll take the girls shopping with us, and if we need to make any decisions after, we'll have a lot more to work with. Any other ideas?" There were several solemn head shakes.

"Okay then, an easy Saturday all round."

Later, when Sinclair got up to leave, Laleh showed him out. She clung to his arm as they crossed the yard and when he opened the outer door, she leaned towards him.

"Sunday we roast a leg of pork with real potatoes." She grinned at his look of astonishment.
It was mid-morning before Nick Evans took off along the highway to Qom with Farhad in his standard rig, the shemagh ends pulled loosely across his face. He'd memorized a house number on Rostak Street near the southern edge of the open-air markets. The stalls were alive with jostling, vocal people by then, but there was no real belligerence, just a few dusky glances.

The elderly brick tenement they were after sported several chipped, eroded bricks trying to escape their binding mortar. It was just one more anonymous house in a row of them, and it wasn't hard to find. They agreed on ten the next morning when Nick dropped Farhad off, and Laleh was well into preparing dinner by the time he got back. Sarah knew they were roasting pork and had already gone home. It wasn't a criticism, it just wasn't her thing.

Nick raised expressive eyebrows, and Laleh nodded. While he was making the brews, Sinclair rolled in, and his 'me too' wasn't voiced either, but his eyebrows got the message through. Laleh smiled. God, these guys could be so predictable. She carried on with dinner and her coffee, humming a quiet tune while she knocked up lunch.

When she sat, this time Laleh occupied her own chair. At first the Scot thought they argued, but when he intercepted a look between them he realized he was wrong. They were secure with each other now, and no longer needed constant re-assurance. That was when he began to envy them.

"There's a sheep and goat sale at the other end of town this afternoon, do you two fancy it?" Nick automatically looked at Laleh.

"I've never seen one in all the time I've been here, but I've thought about it. You ever been, Jock?"

"Never.

"That settles it then, we'll give it a go."

Twenty minutes later they ambled down town. Laleh was between them with her arms linked in theirs again.

Both the Scot and Welshman had been on nodding terms with their neighbours before, but not with many others. It all seemed different now. Sure, friendly waves had happened since Laleh had arrived, but the New Year's parade had made a difference. Now the locals seemed to go out of their way to greet them, to insist on shaking their hands, and when they got to the yards, they were quickly hemmed in by animated crowds clamouring for their attention. What was going on was shrilled in badly fractured English or with Laleh translating.

The broiling dust came close to choking them as animals charged in every conceivable direction, chased by silent black and white collies. There were sheep underfoot almost everywhere, and bleats, barks and shrill voices competing constantly around them. It all seemed confusing, but really it was remarkably well ordered. Animals were sold hardly before they'd completed a circuit of the pen, and the next lot was auctioned as the others cleared. The experience was invigorating and exciting, but they hadn't a clue about the condition of the animals they were looking at.

After the market, they returned to the house, joking as if they'd always been friends, and it stayed relaxed and casual throughout dinner. Nick carved, they all fought over the crackling, and the pork got re-visited several times over. Jock Sinclair was close to groaning when he finally made his good-nights.

As usual in tropical latitudes, darkness fell as if it was in a contest, but it wasn't late at all. And with entertainment on the frugal side, Nick had built up an extensive library of books and magazines. With not a lot of stimulus in the evenings for her either, Laleh had also slipped back into perusing too. They read for a while, and then she suggested an early night.

Chapter Thirty-Nine

Nick hadn't been turned in for much more than ten minutes and certainly wasn't asleep when the curtain rings pulled along the door-rail. The bedroom windows weren't huge either, but it was near full moon and some light did struggle through the long, narrow panes. He turned and saw a shape hovering near his bed. It had to be Laleh.

"Are you awake, Nick?"

"I'm awake, Lil, can't you sleep?"

"I'm not stupid. I know this is very difficult for you, Nick, but I do so want to sleep with you holding me. Can we do that?"

It wasn't a queen, it was a double, but space wasn't the problem. "Maybe, Laleh, but you're a very beautiful and sensual woman. It won't be easy." Right then she needed reassurance not sex, but he felt he ought to warn her. It was himself he wasn't sure about. She half turned away. He could see that.

"I'm sorry, Nickie, this isn't a smart idea. I'll go back to my own room."

"Don't, love, I really want you here and I've been looking forward to when it did happen. If you're okay with it, hop in. I don't sleep in pyjamas though so you'd better keep that bloody nightshirt on." He held the bedding open. She slipped in.

His left arm was out flung and her head fitted into his shoulder as if they'd been whittled to do so, but his other arm flopped restlessly around his chest. Laleh solved that one. She pulled it onto a soft, warm stomach and hung onto it as if her life depended on it. She didn't realize how provocative that was either, nor when she nibbled, rather than kissed him. It was an exquisite agony he'd never known before and he couldn't stop himself swelling.

"Lily, this is difficult enough as it is. Do you think you could turn over and go to sleep now?"

"Sorry, Nick." She didn't sound it.

A smooth back and shapely buttocks thrusting hard into him was another, intense sort of agony, but she was asleep within minutes, still holding tightly onto his arm. He hardly slept at all, acutely conscious of the warm body touching him from chest to toe for the whole night.

It was early when Nick awoke, very early. He dozed as dawn slowly invaded through the small slit windows. Laleh slept on as innocently as a child, barely moving at all, and he was reluctant to rouse her. He didn't really care who knew where she'd slept, but he thought that she might, so finally he wriggled the arm she was lying on. She looked at him though bleary, half-closed eyes.

"What time is it?"

"Nearly seven. Sarah will be here within the hour."

"A few more minutes then." She closed her eyes again.

Nick accepted more punishment. When he shook her again, another half hour had passed.

"Time to get up, Lil."

"Okay." That was drawled sleepily. She sat up, and he used his reclaimed arm to help her before nuzzling her neck. "I don't think we'll try that again, Lil. How the hell I kept my hands off you, I'll never know. If I hadn't been knackered, you'd have been in deep trouble." He grinned to soften it. She didn't look up when she spoke.

"I know that, Nickie, and I could tell you were aroused, but I was sure you could do it." She paused. "Iran was always pretty progressive, but it's still an Islamic state, and women are still second-class citizens. In this country, it's always been about what men want, not what women might." Now she turned towards him. "I really needed to know that my feelings mattered to you,

272

that you could deny yours if what I needed was more urgent. I've been thinking a lot about it lately because I've never actually slept with anyone before." She pecked him. "I know now. It doesn't have to happen again."

"Jesus, woman, that's a bit profound for this time of the morning. I'll have to think about that one. Shift your bum and I'll make the coffee." They swung their legs in opposite directions. She wandered off to her room while he showered and got dressed.

They were drinking coffee and sharing a naan stuffed with pork slices when Sarah arrived. Jock Sinclair turned up not long after and couldn't resist a pork roll either. Fetching Farhad Amini was the only thing on the agenda and it was too early for that yet.

"Can the boys borrow the rods, Nick? They want to try the streams this morning."

Nick fetched them and the tackle box and stood them by the door.

"When you go in, park next to that small church on the south side of the market." Sinclair knew where Nick meant. "Don't cruise around looking for Fred either, he knows where you'll be, so let him find you. He won't make a move until he sees the girls return from shopping."

"Aye, laddie, relax, I've done this sort of thing before." Jock turned aloof eyes on Nick. "You just make sure you don't have a bloody heart attack before we get back again."

"I'm sorry, Jock, but it's your fault. A few months ago I doubt if I'd have given a stuff."

"Bullshit, it was always there, I just saved us a bit of time. You don't think about things before you're ready to, that's all. You'd got out of the habit. Is there anything you want while I'm in there?"

"There's a chemist thing right next to the church. Some safety razors and sunglasses for Lily would be nice."

While Laleh peeled and diced vegetables, Sarah cleared up the rooms, starting with Nick's. It was her day to dust and Laleh had virtually finished preparing the vegetables when she got out again. The housekeeper bustled into the girl's room next but wasn't in there all that long. Laleh blushed when she realized her bed was still made up.

When Sarah came out and moved towards the kitchen, Laleh's head automatically came up with the familiar, defiant tilt. She didn't know how the housekeeper would take it and wanted her to know she didn't really care much either, but as Sarah drew level she stretched out gentle fingers and stroked Laleh's face. The girl hadn't really known what she would see in Sarah's eyes, but encouragement and understanding probably weren't part of it. She touched the older woman's hand. Nick didn't notice and probably wouldn't have understood anyway.

Neither woman said anything, but for Laleh it was if lighting had struck. Many people were there for her, wanting what was happening to happen, and Nick had certainly made his views fairly clear. He didn't see her as diminished or soiled in any way, and he'd turned out to be just as strong mentally as she suspected. Who the hell was she to be demoralized anymore? She was humming quietly when she dragged on the chador.

Surveying had always been hours of mind-sapping boredom followed by a few moments of frantic activity. A bit like a day in combat without the adrenalin rushes. And Nick hadn't realized it before, but having Sarah and the Jock Sinclair around had somehow mellowed it. The days seemed shorter and more eventful, the nights cosier and easier, but with Farhad and Laleh Amini in his life, it had changed well beyond that. He'd experienced blank spots before, but never like this, never as if he was rattling around aimlessly in an empty tin drum. He finally understood what Jock meant about re-joining the human race.Nick told himself he hadn't been listening for its return when the vehicle ground to a halt outside. He pretended not to hurry when he went to meet them. He swung open the yard door nonchalantly just before Farhad got to it, barely recognising them at first. Sarah and Laleh followed humping baskets while Sinclair brought up the rear with another. To his complete surprise, his housekeeper planted a sloppy kiss on his cheek as she entered.

Nick waited impatiently while Farhad got rid of his gear and Laleh her chador. He kidded himself that he was only agitated because he needed to know what had happened, but even Sarah seemed slow in unpacking her bags, and the Amini's were closeted in their bedrooms for what seemed hours. When they did finally crowd around the table, Laleh hoisted herself onto his knee again. It calmed him almost instantly.

"Was it worthwhile, Fred?"

"Excellent, Nick, really good. I feel a lot better about getting out now."

"Seems strange that a Christian group are doing this."

"They can see they might be next unless some brakes are put on it, so their network seems fairly widespread already. Nothing much was said about that, but they did know I was coming, and they cover both the Turkish and Pakistani borders. I could go either way, depending."

Nick raised surprised eyebrows.

"There's a larger Christian population in the northern Zagros, so the Turkish border is monitored more closely, but that's mainly where roads and the railway run into Turkey. They said I should get on at Karaj, about sixty klicks from Tehran, and then run right through to a place called Khvoy, which is only fifty klicks from Turkey. They've got a large organization there to truck me close to the border."

"It would probably be better if you did go towards Europe, wouldn't it?"

"We'll have to see what happens, Nick. I can get on a train at Qom and get off at a place called Zahedan as well. It's less than sixty klicks from Pakistan, and there's a group to help me over the border in that city too. Either way, they can take care of tickets and extras."

"Did they say when you should do it, Farhad?" That came from Laleh.

Farhad looked at his sister. If he had ever doubted it, she had just confirmed that her destiny was now tied to the Welshman's. No matter what. The Persian was happy about that. Nick had a British passport and therefore a much better chance at a normal exit.

"They said the same as Nick did. If it's quiet, don't do anything. The more they use their routes, the more the chance of discovery. Things could still change so they'd rather wait until they have to. Is that a problem, Nick?"

Nick Evans shook his head. "You said the other day we've become pretty much like brothers, Farhad. I'm surprised you thought you had to ask it."

The girl twisted and touched his face gently.

Jock spoke for the first time. "Aye, well that's all settled then. We've got lots of options now so we can back off. It's been bloody morbid around here lately. What games have you got, Nick?"

"How about Scrabble? I've got that somewhere. I'll have a light beer as well. I don't want any whisky yet."

Sinclair poured himself a large one. "Welsh fairy," he pontificated loud enough to be heard. His wide grin belied his words.

The game started noisily and got steadily more riotous and they barely noticed when Sarah left. Some of the words the Aminis used were dubious to start with, and got more outrageous as the evening wore on, but it was all part of a plot. Both Aminis were quick to claim second-language status. Eventually Jock staggered home, burping involuntarily. The others had been much wiser.

Chapter Forty

Nick hadn't been in bed long before he heard the scrape of the curtain rings again. A groan wasn't far away. He guessed she needed more re-assurance, but he couldn't go through that again, couldn't cope with a repeat of the night before. He couldn't think of anything to say that she wouldn't take as a rejection either. He steeled himself.

"I'm here again, Nick." She sounded as if she were ten years old.

"I don't think I can keep my hands off you again, Lil. You'd better know that."

"I'm not worried about that anymore."

He threw back the bed cloths. It was later in the evening, with the moon's light more intense as it thrust through the small windows. This time he saw her tug the nightshirt over her head before she got in. Even so he was unprepared for the satin feel of her skin as she slid down the whole length of him. He was erect instantly.

She had little idea of the physical side of a relationship, and he hadn't been there for some time himself, but the testosterone had been waxing and waning for weeks. A clean, exotic taste of cinnamon went with a few deep kisses, before their tongues touched briefly. And a minor sortie around her honeyed breasts after was enough. She climbed on top of him before he realized what she was doing, and when she enveloped him, he couldn't stop himself letting go almost immediately.

A while later, Laleh nestled with her head on his left shoulder, happy but nowhere near sleep. She didn't know her inexperience had showed, but it did. A few adolescent fumbles and a vicious rape were obviously the only thing she knew about men and sex.

But what was important to her was that she had made it happen. She enjoyed being in his arms and when he'd penetrated her, she'd welcomed it, had felt no apprehension, had felt no shame. She had wanted it to happen and made sure it did as quickly as she could. Laleh felt content, but Nick was only glad that the initial pressure was gone.

They kissed and nuzzled without conscious thought after, wrapped deeply in their own private world. At first, Laleh was only vaguely aware of the delicious tingle of his fingers wandering lightly over her quivering, sensitive skin, but after a while, she realized the hand was becoming more insistent and was exploring every inch of her more boldly. And it was instinctive. She turned and kissed him deeply. He felt totally in control.

And there was nothing quick about it this time. Questing fingers ran down her soft inner arms, kisses ranged over her full lips, to her eyes, her throat, her neck and inner arms and armpits. Then the exquisite drag of his fingernails scraped gently over her hyper-sensitive breasts until she thought her engorged nipples would burst. He continued along her fluttering abdomen, skirted the swollen core and moved gently onto her outer thighs. He took his time before moving to the smooth, more sensitive skin nestled between her legs. When he retraced all the way back to her breasts and inner arms, she wasn't sure if she was moaning or only thought she was.

Nick paused for a few delectable seconds and then slowly retraced where his hand had gone with his lips. This time she knew she was groaning. She tried desperately to mount him again, but he anticipated that, and pinned her hands lightly above her head. Nick followed his original path, but this time deviated to where all the sensation seemed to be centred, and took an exquisitely long time there too. It was a massive relief when he did slide into her. She exploded in seconds, and he wasn't all that long after her.

Something was getting through the REM to the subconscious and Nick woke instantly, his eyes wide open. It was still early, and a hesitant daylight struggled half-heartedly with the deeper ebony of night. It was enough to see Laleh propped on an elbow studying his face intently. He became aware of her other hand. At first it circled his breast gently, twirling and combing the coarse hair on his chest. Then it moved lower. He could feel himself stir again, and she could have had no doubts about it. She kissed him.

"Can we do it again, Nickie?"

"I thought you'd never ask," he croaked. So they did.

Afterwards, Nick wandered out to the bathroom stifling a yawn. Laleh headed for her bedroom.

Chapter Forty-One

Nick Evans was first into the kitchen and dug out some elderly muesli for breakfast. It hadn't reached a used by date yet but was nudging it. He'd never been partial to sheep or goats milk, but the Scot had brought back cartons of thick, creamy cow's milk the day before, so the cereal got resurrected.

Shortly after Jock dropped in and helped himself to a bowl, and when Farhad emerged with wet hair from his shower, he did too. Laleh made do with fruit. They sat around the table while Sarah attacked the dishes, munching but not talking.

Although she stayed quiet, Sinclair noticed that Laleh took every opportunity to touch Nick while they ate. A flight was scheduled later, and Sinclair thought she was reminding the Welshman she was there, but the instant Farhad pushed his bowl away, she stood. It surprised them, and breathing remained on hold as she walked to the end of the table. She looked defiant yet apprehensive as she faced them with arms folded.

It was purely instinctive. The girl hadn't said anything, but Nick knew exactly what was coming. She shouldn't do this alone, and she deserved his support. He stood and moved behind her with fingers kneading tense, tight shoulders. Both the other males looked puzzled, but Laleh ignored Sinclair and looked at her brother intently.

"I don't want either of us creeping around in the dark, so I'll tell you all now. I'm moving in with Nick today." Her gaze stayed level, if still apprehensive.

Sarah carried on with what she was doing without looking around. Laleh's bed hadn't needed making for a couple of days now, so no surprises there, but there was for Jock. He'd seen it as inevitable, but it had come quicker than he expected. It was Farhad who stood and strode towards her, his face bland and hard to read.

Laleh felt Nick tense through every pore in her skin. His hands were no longer on her shoulders, but firmly on her hips. He was ready to get between them, but as Farhad got closer, he opened his arms and dragged her tight. Everyone had tensed when he moved, and now everyone relaxed. He hugged Nick too before whispering in his ear.

"Don't get used to it. We Persians don't do this very often." He didn't say anything more as he went for a refill, but then turned theatrically with the plunger still in his hand.

"So do you two think you can do whatever you're doing a bit quieter from now on? Some of us need our sleep."

Laleh's hand flew to her mouth, her eyes wide. Then she blushed. Nick looked at his feet with a smile on his face. They all heard the amused snort from Sarah.And suddenly it was a major anti-climax for all of them. Growing sexual tension, emotional trauma, apprehension and less than covert match-making dissipated almost instantly. There was no longer a need for any of it. And more doors had opened recently, so only in the background was the knowledge that they might have to use one eventually. Nothing much had changed in the big picture, but the realisation that they had all been hyped only came when they weren't any more. The pot had gone off the boil.

Mohammed Arak skipped up the wide flag-steps to Qom's central police station and headed for the office of the chief. Tehran thought that America's intransigence would end after the embassies takeover, but it hadn't. Arak had been told to turn up the heat, but not how, only to be careful about doing it. What the hell did that mean?

He suspected it was government speak for 'it's your ass in a sling, not ours.' He'd thought long and hard before heading for the main cop shop.

Arak was ushered into the captain's office as soon as he arrived, and knew he had to be careful. There wasn't much love lost between his organisation and the civil police force, who saw his team as illiterate thugs. The only saving grace for him was that he'd been a detective in the police once himself. The captain eyed Arak coolly.

"How can I help you, Mister Arak?" He knew they'd be looking for a favour.

"The Americans still haven't responded to the hostage situation, Captain, and Iran's assets are still frozen. Tehran has told me to harass American companies. I want some assistance."

"If they operate within the law, there's little I can do, Mister Arak. We can check their driving licences, and give them a hard time if they carry alcohol obviously in public, but I'm sure they'll know what is legal and what isn't."

"Isn't there anything else you can do?"

"Not legally, Mister Arak. The illegal we leave to you."

Arak caught his pointed stare. "I intend shaking down their houses in Shahabad soon, can you help with that?"

"I have a sergeant and three policemen in the town who are all Bakhtaran themselves. They get few problems with the residents, but I doubt I'd go in there with a small force if they did play up. I can get my police to back you, but only if you have a good reason for going in. When do you intend to do it?"

"We had a report that they are almost locals out there, and mix freely with others who do not normally live there. We don't know what that means, and we'll be going in mid-morning on Thursday to find out."

"I wish you luck, Mister Araki, but so what? They've just had their New Year celebrations and hundreds of outsiders come into town for that. If you find anything, let me know, but I can't do anything if you don't."

Arak mumbled his goodbyes and departed.

Qom hadn't bothered them since before the Christmas break and appearances had to be kept up, so Nick drew up a simple agenda. Another report would have to be filed soon, but his interest now was in progressing Laleh's skills. Certainly it was good to have her close, but something else scratched at the cortex. It helped that she was a natural as well, but the way the situation was stretching out bothered him. On that Wednesday he got her airborne in the morning and chanced another flight in the early afternoon, pushing her on even further. She continued to excel, and they were in high spirits when they got home. Sarah quickly destroyed that.

"Nephew of Mohammed call in home. He policeman in town. Religious people raid here tomorrow morning."

Nick felt as if he'd been gut shot.

"Jesus, I thought we were safe in here. What the hell do they know?"

"He say nothing. They just make it more difficult for Americans. We make it difficult for them instead. I talk to other elders and see what we can do."

Nick nodded but they all looked concerned.

The black and white pulled around the traffic island and started up the slope into Shahabad with Arak driving and a team of two in there with him. The trip out had been easy, but after he turned off to the town two Utes were stopped alongside each other on the brow of the hill ahead. The occupants chatted animatedly. He hooted, but they didn't budge. He was approaching the apex of the incline by then so he was forced to stop. Arak fumed as he strode the last of the slope to accost them. Up there he could hear a rumbling hub-bub beyond the brow.

It looked as if the whole town and all its vehicles were drawn up on the only decent route in. Arak roared and gesticulated to no effect and even when he strode down to the seething mass they ignored him. He felt impotent and humiliated, and then he made a bigger mistake. He drew his pistol and fired into the air.

Arak got all the attention he wanted after that, but it was angry and belligerent. A number of firearms were discharged into the air as if in answer, and he stepped back involuntarily as the crowd surged towards him. He was saved only by a police sergeant fighting his way through the angry crowd.

"It's illegal to discharge a weapon in a public place," he hissed.

"You know who I am. Get these people moved or I'll drive right through them."

The policeman wasn't a bit intimidated. "I know who you are, and I know what you want, Mister Arak, but I wouldn't fire your weapon again if I were you. There are enough guns in town to take on half the bloody army. I wouldn't try to drive through them either. I doubt you'd be alive after fifty metres. Go back to Qom and forget about this town. I'll get the information you want myself."

Arak was devastated, but it was a fait accompli. He climbed back in his vehicle, backed down the incline, and took off for Qom.

Sarah had lodged Farhad and Laleh in her own house and Nick and Jock had stayed at home just in case, but it was over all over before mid-morning. A smiling Sarah gave them the details when she returned with the Aminis, predicting there would be no more trouble in Shahabad. Nick nodded, but the escalating circumstances pushed him towards some deeper thinking. They all sat around the table while Sarah made sandwiches.

"Okay, guys, the way I see it, we use this to our advantage. I'll nip in with a report on Monday and tell them we were sorry they couldn't get out here. I'll offer up any info they want myself. Most of it will be bullshit, but they won't know that. Anything else you can think of?"

Jock spoke up first. "We'd better keep to the Cherokee with the window tint for trips to Qom, laddie, and Farhad only goes in if it's vital. Laleh would be okay in her chador, but I don't think we should push that too much either."

Sarah listened then called in from the kitchen. "Just you and me next for Qom, Nickie. You do report. I do shopping, Laleh stay here in case you followed again."

"That's good, what about you, Laleh?"

"As long as I get some flying in I'm happy to keep out of Qom altogether."

"And you, Fred?"

"I'm quite interested in what Baraz is up to with the stock, Nick. I can fill my days helping him. I'm sure it will ease off before long."

"Okay, guys, it's a done deal. Make it so."

Nick dropped Sarah at the Qom markets that Monday before driving to the golden mosque office. Arak seemed surprised to see him when he barged in. Nick's expression bordered on innocent.

"I'm sorry you didn't get to see us on Thursday, Mister Arak. My housekeeper said there was some sort of demonstration, but I couldn't tell you what it was about."

Mohammed Arak was caught completely flat footed. He blustered.

"It was nothing important, Mister Evans, just a social call really." He thought quickly. "Iran is known for its hospitality. I hoped you were making new friends, that's all."

"Not really, Mister Arak. Our housekeeper had a lot of her friends and family in town for the holidays and it was nice to meet them, but none of us speak Farsi, so it was hard going."

Arak's eyes slitted, but he could think of nothing to say. Nick was motoring south before he thought to have him followed.

Nick wasn't concerned with surveys anymore. The company no longer got the reports from exploration flights, and teaching Laleh to fly was something he wanted to do. He took her through more hovering, landing and take-offs, and half way through the second trip headed for the foothills. Nick took over in the river valley and ignored the tacit looks of longing she threw his way.

He knew that Fred was helping Baraz muster the last of the stock, and they were already up there with the Ute. Nick landed near the shack, climbed down and re-fastened the empty seatbelt tightly. He grasped his mic-tell lead.

"Okay, Lily. I need to talk to Baraz. Two left-hand circuits and landings while I do it, and then pick me up again." He unplugged and ambled casually to where the men waited. Laleh looked shocked at first, but she gritted her teeth and picked up into a hover. He watched without seeming to.

Nick had been there and done that on a number of occasions. He knew that the two big landmarks in a pilot's life were his first solo and the first time he entered a spin on a solo aerobatics sortie in a fixed wing. If Laleh was to progress any further, she had to know he trusted her on her own. He'd let both Jock and her brother know that. Her proficiency was growing daily and they understood the effect it would have on her self-confidence.

Laleh touched down once and then circuited again before picking him up. By then the determination had changed to ecstasy. As a treat, he got her to fly up to where they had initially picnicked, and when they stepped out to stretch their legs, she deliberately seduced him. It was cold, so it was quick, but they giggled a lot on their return to the airfield. Nick preferred their bed. He realized now he'd need other ways to distract her.

Nick thought about that over a glass when they got home. "Do you want to learn to shoot, Lil?"

Her eyes glistened. "I didn't ask because Jock and Farhad went when you took the rifle, but I was in the uni shooting team. I'm not too bad."

Nick didn't even look surprised. Her talents seemed endless and her interests universal, although he no longer felt threatened by them. "Now why did I expect that?"

Laleh grinned. "Sarah keeps stopping me, but I'm a pretty good cook as well. Not all that home-grown stuff either, I got a bit exotic at Cambridge. There were lots of international influences there."

"Okay then. Jock can clue you in when he's here for dinner next."

And that happened a couple of days later. After they'd eaten, Nick collected the rifle and a box of ammunition from his wardrobe.

"Jock's the main shooter, Laleh, so he'll do this bit. Listen up though—it's important."

Sinclair nodded. "Okay, Lily, what did you shoot in uni?"

Laleh thought. "Small calibre pistols at ten metres, and .22 rifles at fifty metres."

Sinclair nodded again. He removed a .222 round from the carton and passed it to her. "Tell me about that, lassie."

She turned it in her hand. "Well, the bullet is only slightly broader than those I used to fire, but it's over twice as long, and the charge is a lot bigger. It has to be more powerful."

Jock nodded and passed her the rifle next. In seconds, she'd worked the bolt, identified the safety and sighted along the scope before easing the bolt spring. Sinclair looked at Nick with a small nod of approval. She handed the rifle and ammunition back.

"That's right, Lily. The slug is a bit wider than the .22s you shot, but the round is a lot longer, and a small bullet with a large charge makes for a high-velocity projectile with a flat trajectory. It's an extremely accurate hunter's weapon, meant for medium game over long range. The small bullet hole doesn't cause much damage to the skins. You okay with that?"

Laleh nodded.

"Okay then. A Tikka is Finnish made and high performance, so it's quite expensive and highly lethal. It operates the same as most rifles, as you've obviously

287

realized, but I'll take you through stripping and cleaning it after we've fired it." He unconsciously sighted it himself

"At first, I'll pick some targets at about 200 yards for you, and when you're happy, we'll switch to game. Remember though, you don't cock the rifle until it's aimed out the helicopter window, and you never point it at one of us. Any questions?"

Laleh's eyes shone. "No, Jock, that's pretty clear. When can we shoot it?"

It was Nick's turn to smile. "Jock will come with us on the next couple of flights and we'll find something up there to shoot at. I hope you can live with that." There was a hint of sarcasm in his grin.

Sinclair went along on their next few sorties and usually chose a distinctive mark on a rock for her to fire at. Before long, she could group within an inch or so at 200 yards. Consistently.

And almost invariably now she flew them back after, knowing instinctively how to get there. From then on Nick left the air taxi and landing to her as well. At first the machine wobbled and the skids danced as she touched down, but before long it didn't happen at all. On the day she grouped four shots within an inch and then landed from a fairly harsh flare, they were pumped.

Nick couldn't keep the admiration off his face. She was grinning when they climbed out and he hugged her tightly. The Scot shook his head and waited until she was talking to Imran.

"Remember what I said before, laddie, because you'll need a bloody good psychiatrist if you do screw this up."
"We'll have to get another carcass on the flight tomorrow, Fred. You okay?"

"Stuff it. I told Baraz I'd help to mark some lambs and kids from the autumn drop. You and Jock can do that though, can't you?"

"Not a problem. We're getting a bit low, that's all."

Sinclair signaled to the pilot, put a finger to his lips, and then called to the girl.

288

"How about it, Laleh. You ready for a hunting trip?"

"Can I go, Jock? I'd love to."

"How do you feel about being the shooter? I'll do the gutting and skinning."

Her eyes gleamed. "I don't mind helping with that too. When I was getting my Master's we went to an abattoir as part of showing us the different attitudes between country and city people. We watched it all from the slaughter to hanging the quartered carcasses in the cool room. One or two seemed to think that a joint started out in the butcher's shop or in the freezer, but they soon learnt differently."

"Okay, but it's a lot different from shooting at targets. Sit with me on the settee and we'll talk about it."

Laleh virtually skipped when she joined him. They were talking for a long time.

Prior to the next flight, Jock held the long rifle while Nick took both her elbows in his hands and forced her to look at him. She did, intently.

"Remember, Lily, you're the shooter, so you won't be flying, at least until after. Sometimes we get out to shoot, and sometimes we do it from the chopper, but today we'll keep it fairly simple and do it from the machine. You'll sit in the left seat because only the front windows slide open, and you'll have the gun with you at least until it's done. You happy with that?"

"Yep. Jock told me about the deep breath and holding half of it when you shoot."

"That's shooting, Lil. I'm talking about aircraft safety."

"Oh."

"When you're settled, Jock will hand you the gun and it always points outwards through the window. Always. Remember there's another cyclic on your side as well. Don't get the rifle sling tangled up in it."

Laleh was looking at him soberly now. "And one other thing. Don't lever in a cartridge or put your finger through the trigger guard until you're ready to fire. Got all that?"

This was more serious than she realized, but she could see why when she thought about it. It wasn't a game. Laleh nodded, completely sobered, and accepted the weapon once she was seated. Sinclair climbed in the back and plugged in his headset.

"I'll pick your target and remind you of the sequence on this first one, Lily, and one accurate unrushed shot only. We don't want to be chasing down injured animals up there."

Nick got airborne with his characteristic. "Okay, let's get this done."

Nick bored down the river valley past Shahabad and then zoomed into the mountains to the north. There were still flocks grazing in the yellowed pastures that hugged the lower hills, so he went higher and to the north before they started to look. After thirty minutes, they'd seen nothing worth shooting, so Nick turned towards the southern ranges.

At first they didn't have much luck further south either. Nick ran down what was probably the same bunch of shaggy, moth-eaten camels they'd seen weeks before, but not a lot more. He was keen for her first hunt to be successful, so he turned back towards the Kavir, and ten minutes later pointed to a small herd of gazelle. Sinclair took charge as the animals started to run from the helicopter noise.

"Gun out the window and chamber a round, Laleh." They didn't hear it over the chopper noise, but Nick positioned them to the right of the herd. He could see when she was ready.

"I'll run them for a while before landing about a hundred yards behind them. They'll stop and look back. Now listen to Jock again."

"Right, Lily, your target is the doe running three back. She hasn't got a fawn so keep an eye on her. Don't go for the buck. Their meat is too stringy and rancid. Okay, if you're happy, safety catch off and finger the trigger."

Laleh settled herself, knocked off the safety, and tracked her target as Nick slowed to land. Predictably the herd stopped and looked at them nervously.

"Right, Lily, rest the rifle in your hands, not on the window frame. The machine vibrates. Aim a foot in from the shoulder and the same below the spine." The herd still shifted restlessly.

"Right. A deep breath then let out half. Squeeze, don't jerk the trigger."

Laleh squeezed. The gazelle's head arched backwards and it took two quick steps before dropping. Jock whooped as Nick closed the shivering target. Laleh was out as quickly as Sinclair. He shoved the Tikka under the back bench seat before drawing a sharp, wooden handled knife from under his anorak. It was a clean kill, with the huge, liquid eyes already starting to glaze. Sinclair cut the throat to bleed the carcass and then turned and hugged her. She half-heartedly hugged back.

"You can get back in now, Lily I'll do the rest."

"I'm all right, Jock. It's my kill. I'll give you a hand. It's a bit sad, that's all."

Gutting it took only minutes and the steaming grey mass was quickly discarded. Skinning took a lot longer. Laleh pulled while Sinclair parted the pelt from the fat, but she turned away when he decapitated it. Jock wrapped the carcass in the skin and bundled both in the cabin. As Laleh climbed back in, Nick looked at her astutely.

"You okay, Lil? The first time isn't all that easy, is it?" He covered her hand with his.

"I was wrong, Nick. Visiting an abattoir isn't like killing something yourself at all."

"The French call an orgasm 'le petit mort', Lil, the tiny death. I had no idea what that meant until the first time I shot a gazelle. That almost mystical joy mixed with sadness that something special has gone seemed exactly the same to me."

"I know exactly what you mean, Nick."

"Hey guys, a bit too much information, thank you. Can we head back now please?"

Chapter Forty-Two
Operation Iron Eagle

Several thousand miles to the west, the previous days hadn't been all that tranquil for President Jimmy Carter. Operation Iron Eagle had been on the drawing board for months by then, but nothing had changed for the embassy hostages. The President had to bite the bullet. Someone would have to go and get them.

It wasn't rocket science. A rescue operation was going to be big-time. Jimmy Carter knew there were over sixty hostages to pull out, so his advisers confirmed it would take a minimum of six RH 53D Sea Stallion Helicopters to pull it off. To be certain, he ordered eight on the US Nimitz be available just in case. Marine crews would fly them while the recently formed Delta Force would do the extraction. Delta was well aware that it was its first serious mission when it shipped out.

The objectives were clear, but the strategy was a nightmare. With Tehran so far north, even those huge choppers would need in-country refuelling, so the Americans had identified a vast, isolated desert tract west of Tabas for that. Even so, 'Desert One' was one hell of a long way north. Inevitably, the operation would run into a second day.

As most military brass tend towards optimism, it was assumed that the refuelling would go without a hitch. After, the helos would hole up in the mountains north of Tehran until early the next morning, when Delta planned to hit the embassy just after dawn. A C130 was scheduled to pick up Delta and the captives from a small civil strip on Tehran's southern outskirts after the raid, and the choppers could scram for Nimitz via another refuel at 'Desert One'. It was an operation planned by desperate people who didn't have to actually do it.

The logistics for the 'op' were just about as complicated as it gets. Three Air force C130s at Masirah Island, off Oman, were tasked to carry internal fuel bladders for 'Desert One' while more C130 gunships, bristling with mini-guns, were designated as their minders. And they would need an in-flight refuel, so other C130s would do that. Also a CAP (Combat Air Patrol) from Nimitz would lift sometime after the C130s and choppers, and be airborne around the clock until the helicopters got back. Airborne refuelling was required for the CAP as well.

To say that the rescue mission was complicated was an understatement, and even well-planned military operations rarely survive the first enemy contact. Operation Iron Eagle was no exception.

The Arabian Sea was as flat as glass as Nimitz ploughed into it at thirty knots. Her task force of destroyers and cruisers cut through the oily, swirling ripples around her like angry guard dogs, and like her, they were darkened. The only lights glimmering at all were low-energy blues and reds on Nimitz's flight deck. It was a friendly enough wind right then for sure, but a thick dust storm swirling in low from off the desert kept the visibility down to low and dirty. It wasn't expected to affect an op that was many miles inland. The helos didn't need a deck wind that strong, but the heavily loaded Tomcats would need every knot of it.

The fuel-rich C130s had further to go, so they rumbled NNE for their airborne, refuelling long before Nimitz launched. Even so, such a large op was impossible to keep completely secret, so the carrier's crew was as hyped as any combat crew ever could be. When her aircraft did finally flash up, the harsh roar of multiple engines bouncing off the flight deck and island would have caused deafness in anyone caught without earmuffs. The launch went well at first, but that didn't last.

The choppers coasted in low and fast near the Pakistan border where there weren't any Iranian surveillance radars, but unfortunately the haboob was still blowing south, and that was only the start. Almost immediately on crossing the coast, one of the choppers developed severe mechanical problems and had to land.

The remaining seven carried on towards the desert strip, but by then they were flying in mountains with appalling visibility and air as turbulent as a tumble drier. Their tight, stagger-trail formation rapidly degenerated.

And it was about to get worse still. While still in the mountains, another of the RH 53Ds developed a flight-inhibiting instrument failure and was forced to turn back to the ship. Suddenly the helos were down to the bones of their backsides, and they hadn't even reached the refuelling rendezvous.

A few days before the op, a clandestine air force light aircraft flew CIA operatives into the proposed refuelling strip for a quick surface inspection. Right then it looked good for landing, so they planted markers visible only through ultra-violet goggles, and gave the go ahead. But Murphy's Law is a world-wide phenomenon, and the Great Sandy Desert has some of its own.

By the time the C 130s landed on an isolated sealed road at 'Desert One', the helicopters were widely scattered in the mountainous terrain and abysmal visibility. It took another thirty minutes before they started dribbling into the rendezvous, and one suffered an hydraulics failure as it came in to land. Murphy had struck big time now, but he wasn't finished yet. The dice got rolled again when it was realized that the two choppers that had already aborted were the ones carrying the rapid-use spares.

And at almost exactly the same time, a bus filled with Iranian passengers appeared on the road being used as an airstrip. It was promptly stopped by troops from Delta, who off-loaded the passengers, but almost immediately after a fully laden fuel tanker also cruised by. This vehicle didn't stop, and one of the special forces soldiers with a rocket launcher was forced to fire. The tanker exploded savagely, lighting up the scene like daylight.

The agonising decision to abort was not easy to make, but there was little choice. There weren't enough helos to carry out the mission and by now it was almost certainly compromised anyway. Command in Washington cancelled the rescue via sat-phone, but the serviceable choppers still needed to refuel before they headed out.

And now the tired, stressed chopper pilots hit another snag. When it had ripped across the strip, the haboob had deposited tonnes of sand in its wake, and the surface was now almost shin deep in gritty sand. The first helo to refuel couldn't ground taxi through it with its small wheels and was forced to hover taxi to get close enough to a C 130 to refuel.

In loose snow, it was called a white out. The chopper's downdraft whips up the loose surface until the pilot lost all visual references close to the ground, and sand and dust had the same affect. The pilot was blinded by the huge clouds of sand his down-draft created, and his helo lurched into the fuel-laden Hercules.

The explosion was staggering in its intensity and sent a vivid red and yellow fire ball writhing high into the featureless night sky. It was accompanied by twisting tongues of black, oily smoke. To which the burning RH 53D added its share.

Deep, rolling thunder reverberated far and wide across the shifting sands, and razor-sharp shards of jagged aluminum, along with exploded ammunition, spread outwards at well over the speed of sound. The other choppers were peppered with holes much like nails wrapped around an IED would have done.

The shock lasted for several long seconds, but these were seasoned military, and there wasn't time for recriminations. And most troops have an ethic of bringing back its injured and dead, but in those circumstances, Delta could do little more than recover the wounded. It was that omission which pissed them off the most.

The injured got hustled into the surviving C130s and Delta and the helo crews boarded with them. Minutes later, the big transports screamed south for Masirah Island, leaving a burned-out C 130 with a Sea Stallion melted tightly into it, and a further five damaged RH 53Ds for the Iranian revolutionary guard to find. It was on the telly within hours.

Chapter Forty-Three

Nick had expected something big to happen after the Christmas break, but it was as if the world was holding its frigid breath. They made the most of it. They kept clear of Qom as much as they could and from Tehran completely. Now each day started with the morning news flash.

And even the 24th April 1980 started normally enough. Nick and Farhad were drinking coffee in front of the set while Laleh took her shower. The telly was throwing out more snow than normal and the sound was more a sibilant, grating rasp, Nick was barely watching, but a minute or two later the hash hardened into excitable, animated babbling much like some five months before. His stomach knotted.

A gesticulating crowd milled around the same Tehran landmarks while talking heads jostled to get noticed again, although the cause was vague until Ayatollah Khomeini himself was interviewed. He blustered about Allah's protection, alluded to some sort of divine intervention, and then a grainy camera traversed across a stretch of glittering sand. The foreground was smudged with large blackened fire stains and littered with military devastation. The pastel desert framed a jumble of burned-out, blistered metal spars, while out-of-focus choppers sagging dejectedly in the distance.

The badly burnt ribs and frames of the RH 53 and C130 were hard to distinguish until the camera zoomed in to black on grey American markings on a metallic slab of junk. Talking heads identified the featureless stretch of sand as the great salt desert near Tabas.

America had tried to rescue the hostages, but had abandoned the operation because of some sort of disaster. Deaths had occurred, though nobody knew how many, but enough clues survived to work out that a chopper had barged into a fueled up Hercules. The blast was elaborated on excitedly by the bus passengers.

Nick looked worried and Farhad looked devastated. Jock rushed in as they watched, while Laleh hurried from the bathroom with towels wrapped around her torso and hair. She caught the gist of it. Nick started thinking rapidly and out loud.

"Right guys, the shit is really going to hit the fan after that, so we'll have to think about another way of getting out. No heroic gestures though and we'll all stay away from Qom, okay?" He looked specifically at Farhad.

"There's bound to be a big clamp-down on any movements made by Americans now and the regime will be watching US allies like hawks, but any searches for you Persians should be on the back burner for the time being, Fred. I'll have to get in touch with Gerry Hawkins right away though, because this is bound to overturn anything he gave us We need an update before we do anything else, okay with that?"

They all nodded.

"Okay, Jock, you and me to the airport in twenty."

"Gerry, what the hell happened?"

"A gigantic bloody cock-up is what happened, mate. Our senior military attaché was with the SAS, and almost wet himself when the news came in."

"Have you got anything useful?"

"It's raw, hasn't been confirmed yet, but our senior SIS bloke has a number of contacts. Let's just say that they aren't necessarily all in Iran, okay?"

"Raw or not, Gerry—anything."

"Well, it seems that three Hercules stuffed with refuelling bladders, and eight Sea Stallions from Nimitz went in to rescue the hostages. The Iranians have got a fair few still, so the Yanks needed a minimum of six big choppers to do it. Two went unserviceable before they got to a refuelling point, and one went tits up at the refuelling point itself. That pretty much snookered them before they were half way into it." He drew a long, audible breath.

"Believe it or not, it got even worse after that. They'd briefed an isolated spot in the great salt desert for the refuel, but the chopper that went unserviceable there needed a hydraulics pump, and that's when they found that the ready-use stores were on the two that hadn't made it. Their HQ in Washington cancelled the mission."

"That explains some of the telly footage, Gerry, but it looks as if they abandoned all the bloody choppers."

"They did, Nick. Unfortunately, there was a violent sand storm in the area, that hadn't been expected, and one of the choppers hit a Hercules while it was trying to refuel. Five air force and three Marines were killed, and the pilot and co-pilot of the chopper were badly burned. They high-tailed it out of there as fast as they could. That's all I've got so far."

"Jesus! So what will happen now?"

"Well, the Yanks would have definitely got up some noses after that one, but the Iranians have got plenty of hostages so we don't see them picking up anyone else. The real downside is that anything American is sure to be impounded, and with only a few roads and two railway tracks out of the country, every city on those routes will be flooded with cops. If you haven't got the right papers, you'll be accommodated at the ayatollah's displeasure."

"Will friendly embassies be watched in case they try to help?"

"For sure, Nick, but not so much physically. There are too many for around-the-clock surveillance, but I bet every scrap of paper involving travel will get hammered to death. If it gets rough, I suggest you get your ass up here and shelter in the embassy. You and Jock are British subjects and Laleh is recognised as your de-facto now, so we can shelter her too. I can't do anything about Farhad, though. He's an Iranian citizen, and he might have been a

300

naughty boy in Abadan. Should I say that a rather nasty copper met with a fatal accident down there, and it would be big trouble if we harboured him."

"How about Abdul and Minu?"

"It hasn't affected them at all so far. He sends his thanks by the way."

"What on earth for?"

"The interrogation technique thing you talked about when you were up here last. He phoned a few days ago. Two uglies did visit him after getting Laleh's home address from her US Embassy files. He told them that he couldn't find her after the takeover, but didn't report it in case she was with another family. He admitted that Farhad had visited several times as well, but the last time was eighteen months ago when Amini was in Defence HQ. He hasn't heard from him since. Abdul thought they were going to get a bit mean, but it seemed his honesty took the wind out of their sails. One let slip that they found Farhad's patrol boat on the western side of the Zagros, so now they think he's in the mountains with his crew. They still want Farhad, but they've left Abdul alone since. What was it mate, ten per cent truth mixed in with ninety percent bullshit, as long as it can't be verified. Works every time. He said to tell you guys to keep away, though. He thinks he'll be watched for a while."

"Thanks for that, Gerry. It's given me a hell of a lot to think about. Will the vehicles be impounded as well?"

"Maybe, Nick. Only one vehicle anywhere obvious at any time from now on, and the US company logo doesn't help, so be careful. Air travel is totally out, of course."

They said their good-byes and Nick put the phone down thoughtfully. He saw the familiar troop carriers stopping outside the crew-room when he looked up.

The hangar was shut, so the pilot and engineer must be in the demountable. The trucks made directly for administration, skidding to a halt in a swirl of billowing sand. Arak climbed out of one, two armed troopers from the other. Their ill-fitting khaki uniforms looked creased and grubby, but not so the guns they carried. Arak stepped up onto the wooden entrance veranda while the soldiers covered the building. Nick and Jock had already climbed to their feet when he entered, but he took in the patchy paintwork and scattered magazines before he spoke. There were no preliminaries.

"No doubt you've heard the news, Mister Evans."

"Vaguely. Some rescue attempt that went wrong as I see it."

"Correct, Mister Evans, so we can no longer be so lenient with American companies. There will be some changes."

"You've come to arrest us then?" Jock threw that in.

"That won't be necessary, Mister Sinclair. You've nowhere to go, so this is as good a prison as any, and we don't have to feed you out here. I'll be putting our own locks on your hangar though, and taking one of your vehicles."

Nick bristled. "I couldn't care less about the choppers, mate, any surveys were for your lot anyway, but we need the Cherokee for shopping."

"You have two, Mister Evans. You can hang on to the other one. There will be no more flying, and you won't have much else to do, so one vehicle is enough."

Nick was getting really angry, already white around the lips. "And how do we exist out here if the company stops paying the bills?"

Arak's eyes slitted and his nostrils flared. "That will be your problem, Evans, but I don't think it will happen. The American State Department knows that there are still dozens of their citizens and overseas employees in the same position as you. They won't want that sort of diplomatic pressure, so they'll keep paying."

"Will you drop us off in Shahabad then, Mister Arak?"

"No, I won't Evans. We won't be going in there again so you'll have to walk."

Nick was ready to blow. Sinclair laid a restraining hand on his arm.

"It's not far, Nick. Leave it."

"Keys please, Mister Evans, and we'll be on our way."

"They're in the ignition."

Arak inclined his head and left. He gestured to a trooper and the vehicle, and then stopped at the hangar. Nick and Sinclair watched through the plate window as chains were wound through the door handles and padlocked. Arak didn't miss the small access door on the side either.

"I could willingly kill that bastard," he muttered as they watched Arak's small convoy take off for Qom. Startled, Sinclair glanced at the pilot. He meant it. It was in his eyes.

Nick and the Scot got lucky walking home. They were picked up by a battered blue Ute five kilometres from town.

As it was only midday when they got back, Nick called for a revamp. It was Sinclair who put a dampener on it.

"International flights are out, we've only got one vehicle, and an escape by train seems pretty bloody impossible now. And with only one decent road and railway at each end of a 2000 kilometre-long stretch, they can block those easily. We're pretty much fucked, Nick. None of us have travel papers, and we don't know how to get forgeries either."

"Could Gerry suggest anything?"

"He only had one idea, Fred. Jock and I could hole up in the embassy and Laleh is recognised as my de-facto now, so she could as well. He can't do much for you, though, and I didn't even ask what might happen to Imran and his boys."

"Would Sarah be okay?"

"For sure, Laleh. She wouldn't be expected to know anything considering how they think about women They

303

wouldn't have a clue how things really are out here either, and there are a lot of Bakhtarans around. I can't see them over-turning that apple cart willingly. They probably wouldn't even question her."

"If you two and Laleh can hole up in the embassy, I'll put the word out. I can take off into the Zagros and join up with my crewmates."

"That's pretty risky though, Fred, and God knows how long we'd be in the embassy anyway. Shit! the way things are going, they may even sack that place next. I wouldn't let Laleh go through that again."

Nick started thinking outside the box, and it wasn't long before the germ of an idea sparked around the receptor centres. He needed a few more facts before he decided. "Farhad and I are going out to the yard, guys, so indulge us for a moment." Amini looked surprised but followed the pilot out.

"No bullshit, Fred, what happened in Abadan?"

Amini looked steadily at Nick. It was several long seconds before he spoke. "A particularly nasty religious policeman dropped in just a few hours before I was going to take off. I know he was responsible for what happened to some of my friends in Abadan and he threatened me personally. I pissed him off and he was drawing his revolver to emphasis his point, but I got one in first. That's all. Me and my chief hung the prick's body in my uniform wardrobe and took off." The commander didn't sound contrite.

"I'm not criticizing, Fred, but they obviously want you a bit more than most, so I needed to know. Quite honestly, if I met the two that got to Laleh, the bastards would be joining him. Okay, let's go inside."

Nick remained standing when he did. "I've got some ideas, but I need an hour in the fresh air to nut things out. Can you guys round up Sarah and Imran while I'm gone?" He looked at Laleh. "You coming, Lil?"

She didn't answer but grabbed her moccasins. They took the high track again but didn't go as far along it before he stopped.

"Do you want to hang around hoping things will change, or do you want to try getting out, Lil?"

"If you mean the Embassy, I'm a bit doubtful about that. We can't take Farhad and there aren't any guarantees for me either, and even you and Jock could have problems. If you've got another plan, I'd like to hear it."

"Okay. All the normal means of transport are locked out, but there's one they haven't thought of yet. What about we use a chopper and run for Turkey."

Laleh looked startled. "The bloody thing won't go that far though, will it?"

"It's a bit under a 1000 Klicks. We can fly over 600 on full tanks, and we've got 300 pounds in containers. That's good for 200 more. Even if we can't refuel, we'll only have about 120 klicks to walk at the other end. It will be in the mountains, so we'll have some cover, but it will be bloody cold."

Laleh thought about it. She knew Nick didn't want gut reactions, but her mind was soon made up. "I can walk that if we have to. Where do you think we might get fuel?"

"Several small airfields en route support survey ops and probably only American firms will be closed up, so some might still be operating. We won't need much either. I'll look at the maps, but we have to go soon. We need to be the first."

"At least that will give all four of us a chance. I think we should try it."

Nick gave her a hug. "Okay, let's get back."
The others were talking urgently but quietly when they appeared, the atmosphere serious and intense. Nick made the inevitable mugs before reversing a chair to sit on.

"Okay, guys, here's how I see it. It's looking dodgy for us as well now, Jock, and other means of transport are a no-no, so we'll nick a chopper and all four of us will go for it. It will have to be soon though, before someone else gets the same idea, because aircraft will be off the menu after that. I reckon we go on Friday. Use their Sabbath against them again."

A noisy hub-bub followed the startled looks. Nick let it die naturally before he continued.

"How about your guys, Imran?"

"Don't worry about us, Nick. We're from a big Islamic nation right on their bloody doorstep, and we're small fry anyway. They won't want to piss off Pakistan over us. We'll let our consulate get us home."

"Okay. So early on Friday you lads take us out to the airfield at first light and then take off for Tehran. I'll lift off from inside the hangar, so we won't need you guys for that, and make it around 7.30 when you should just about be at your Embassy. I'll need full daylight if I'm going low level through the hills anyway. What about you, Sarah?"

"Not a problem for me neither, Nick. Police in town our people too. I show rooms with things still in, say you told me nothing and only know when I find you all gone."

"I'm sorry about the rent, though."

"No problem neither. French, German or Russian be doing same thing in few months. We rent to them." She smiled. "I not report so maybe Americans keep paying for while anyway."

"Okay. Are the new chains and padlocks a problem, Jock?"

Imran butted in. "I shouldn't hear any more, Nick. If someone did question us a bit heavily, we don't know a thing. I'll be off now and see you tomorrow."

"Same for me, Nick. Dinner prepared and naan in oven for later. Laleh, start cooking stew in one hour." Both Imran and the housekeeper left.

"I've got a universal key for the locks and chains, laddie. Some people call them bolt cutters."

Nick couldn't help a smile. "I'll plot a route shortly, but there are a few other things we can do as well. Even with the two fuel containers, we'll be about a hundred klicks short of the border, so we'll have to find some fuel or we'll have to hike it. The good thing is that we'll be doing it only a few hours after we leave here, and we won't have far to go. Depending on how quick they react, we may keep ahead of them."

Farhad shuffled in his seat. "Will we take the weapons, Nick?"

"I thought about that, and I think we should. Heaven forbid we do go down, but we might need the Tikka to get food, and if they chase us, they could use anything to get at us. We'll take your cannon as well. We can always ditch it if we need to."

"There won't be room to take much else though, will there, Nick?"

"There won't, Lily, so choose carefully. We can squeeze the fuel containers and a spout into the luggage compartment, but everything else goes in the cabin. The guns go under the bench seat, along with one bag each, but we can seat three in the back, so with only two, there'll be a bit of extra room. I want you up front as well. It'll be a long flight at low level and I'm going to need you to spell me. You'll have to keep us roughly on track if we have to deviate as well."

She nodded.

"Right, Lil, there'll be some heavy stuff to hump at the last minute, but us boys can do that. You think about catering. We'll never remember all that on the day."

"Okay. First thing, I'll need your flasks. I can't imagine you without coffee." She grinned.

"I'll make some fresh bread for sandwiches as well, and see what we can take from the larder."

"Good, we've got a couple of army water bottles somewhere we can dig out too. The only other thing is what to wear. We'll need sturdy boots, and it'll be bloody cold if we have to walk out, so we'll need something warm on top as well. We've only got the three flight anorak, Farhad. What about you?"

"Your surveyor left some things in his wardrobe. There's a reasonable parka that fits me and I can wear a jumper underneath. I came away in boots, so footwear isn't a problem."

"Okay. If anybody thinks of something else, bring it up right away. We'll have a break then I'll sort out a route."

Vividly coloured topographical maps, some large scale and some not so large, lay scattered over the table. Nick and Laleh poured over them alongside the inevitable mugs, their chairs and heads almost touching. He had a navigational computer, dividers, a rule and grease pencil to do the pilot thing with, and had already sketched in a few preliminary tracks.

"I'll throw up some facts and you remember what I've said, Lil. If I forget anything important, you can let me know. We won't be able to change much once we're on our way either, so we've got to get it right from the word go."

"Hang on. I'll get a piece of paper to write it all down then."

He waited.

"Right. First, we could try for Kuwait. It's a bit shorter, but most of Iran's radars and military assets are on the Gulf and it's heavily populated. There's nowhere to hide for a long track across the sea either, and we'd still end up in the middle of several Islamic states. I don't fancy it much, but put it down as a diversion."

"Some are fairly friendly though, aren't they?"

"They are, but it's almost a war zone down with Iraq and the Sunnis. Anybody might take a shot at an unidentified chopper over the sea."

Laleh nodded and marked down a few notes.

"Pakistan is getting more radical in the border areas these days as well, so I'm inclined to put that lower on the list too. I reckon our best bet is Orenburc in Turkey. It's less than twenty klicks over the border, making the trip a fraction under 1000 all up. Also it's on the main route out of Iran. We can bus to the nearest Turkish rail head from there and get a sleeper to Istanbul. After that, the world's our oyster. Ankara's the capital, but it's out of our way, and Istanbul has got a big British consulate. Turkey's vast though. We'll have another 150 klicks by road to do, then 1200 on the train."

"I didn't realize it was that far."

"It won't matter, Laleh, we'll be free. I've got some mates in the Consulate at Istanbul as well. We can fix up a few things there before we move on."

"Let's hope we can get some fuel then."

"That's next. Put down Hamadan, Sanandaj, Urmia, Naqadeh and Tabriz. They've all got large commercial airfields, so we've got to avoid them, but we can use them as decoys. We'll hide the route we're actually taking, but I'll work that out properly later. Where we will refuel is at a place called Azar Shahr."

"I've never heard of it."

"It's a small, isolated airfield like this one near the eastern shore of Lake Urmia. It was developed because a good road and a railway run passed it, and it's close to the mountains. It's only thirty klicks from Mount Sahand as well, and that's a good landmark."

Nick pointed out the mountain and then the small airport to Laleh.

"I went there on a company famil: flight when I first got here, so I know the basic layout, but what's really important is that a Norwegian company runs the heliport side so they probably weren't closed down. We don't need much fuel either. A few hundred pounds and we can make it."

"Isn't somebody going to be looking for us by then?"

"That's the rub, Lil. Write down Ardabil. It's northwest of Tabriz and there's a big air-force base and army camp there. Unfortunately, they've always got an F14–Tomcat on ten-minute standby and that includes their Sabbath. The Shah bought most of Iran's military equipment from the Yanks as well. It garages Hercules,

Sea Stallions and Kiowas, and Kiowas are the military version of what we're flying. They'll have a pretty good idea of our capabilities."

"Oh."

"It's not all bad. Ardabil is over 250 klicks from Azar Shahr, so Tomcats could take thirty minutes to get there even with a scramble, and one of their big helicopters would take well over an hour to even get to the lake. We should be okay in the mountains. It's just the last 200 klicks that will be tight."

"We don't have a choice though really, do we?"

"Well, there are a few things in our favour. The bigger survey companies always have some spare fuel containers and as far as the regime knows, we may not need to refuel anyway. America put an embargo on spare parts and aviation fuel after the revolution as well, so Iran may not have all that many aircraft left that can fly. They certainly won't waste what aviation fuel they have got unless there's something to go on. They'll guess we're going for Turkey after a while, but it's mountainous and the border is over 200 miles long. We could be going for any bit of it." He took a sip while she wrote.

"Searching for people isn't all that easy either, Lily. I've done it a few times and often we couldn't see survivors at a half a mile even over fairly flat sea or land. It would take a Tomcat thirty minutes to get to where we were, and by then we could be anywhere within 300 square miles. It's a hell of a lot harder than you think, and we won't be making ourselves obvious. We'll try to convince them we're going south of the lake. It's a bit shorter, and with Tabriz and Ardabil to the north, it'll seem logical."

"Well, we could be in Iran for a long time and not get out in the end anyway. I want us to get on with our lives now, Nickie. I vote we go."

"I knew you would. We'll work out some decoys and I'll update Jock and Farhad."

Laleh excused herself when Nick called the two men to the table. She already knew what odds they faced. She went to the kitchen to get dinner under way, but before she started to heat and stir, she looked back at Nick with a grin.

"The first thing you do when we settle somewhere is to cook me something special."

He couldn't keep the warmth and affection out of his response. She probably didn't realize how much of an optimist she was, how tough but flexible. How she kept carrying them to a better place.

"It might surprise you to know that I'm quite an accomplished cook, young lady. I've ended up in some pretty ordinary places and I'm not all that keen on baked beans on toast."

Laleh was still smiling when she turned back to what she was doing. Nick got back to the maps.

"Before I start, guys, I'd better tell you that the first 800 klicks should be a doddle with what they know, but the last 200 could bring tears to your eyes. There are some things on our side though, so we think the odds are worth it."

Nick got some serious nods before he skimmed over the departure. He took his time over the end game, highlighting the positives and elaborating on the dangers. Then he pointed out a small tarn, high in the mountains, just north of a place called Saqqez.

"That's where we'll refuel from the containers, Jock. I'll stop the rotors but keep the engine idling, and we won't be in any hurry, so it can be a pee and a stretch the legs break. It's pretty isolated and heavily forested, with a few low-grade roads around the northern end. Saqqez itself is over thirty klicks south of the lake and only rough dirt tracks run up to the lake from there. We'll cross it in the middle where it's the most rugged."

Jock Sinclair jotted down a few notes.

Nick pointed out Sandandaj next, a large yellow dot wallowing in a sea of green and beige.

"The airfield is fairly large and it's got an approach radar on a hill. We'll let it sweep us a couple of time while we're heading south of our real destination, and won't change direction until we're back on the deck again. They may think we're heading for south of Lake Urmia if they spot us. I'll refine it, but that's about it unless anybody can think of something else?"

"There's a big chance of me getting caught the longer I stay here, Nick, and harbouring me isn't going to endear you two either. Let's do it, mate, I'm all for it."

"Me too, laddie. Life's been a bit boring lately and it's time we stirred the pot a bit."

Chapter Forty-Four

That last, mournful evening was on top of them before they expected it. Irritable snapping and long empty silences were part of the growing stress. Shrill chatter turned to unnatural laughter at the drop of a hat, and the best two bottles of red disappeared swiftly with Sarah's stew. This time Sarah ate with them and cleared away while Nick and the Aminis sorted out what they would take. Sinclair had already done this and sat reflecting over a large single malt.

Packing a few essentials didn't take long, and the hype and the enforced jollity slowly died with it. Faces got longer and sentences got terminated abruptly as if they were at a funeral. Obviously they needed an early night and someone to make it happen.

"Okay, guys, early start tomorrow, so let's hit the sack." Nick walked towards the housekeeper with his arms spread. "Sarah, I'm really going to miss you." He hugged her tightly and both their eyes glistened. She swayed her shoulders away and looked at him intently before kissing both cheeks.

"You're the mother I never really knew, Sarah. Thank you for everything." It was all he could get out before he choked up completely.

"Go with your god, my son." It was all she could get out too.

Sinclair and then Farhad did the hugging bit next. The Scot tried to hide what he felt behind a cough. The commander tried stoic and in control, but didn't do a very good job either.

And when it got to Laleh and Sarah's goodbyes they both ended up crying openly. It wasn't good for Nick and Sinclair either. They wiped moist lids quickly with soggy sleeves, but then again, big boys didn't cry, did they? It had been a long time for some, for others not that long at all, but it didn't seem to matter much either way.

It was unnecessary, but Nick set the alarm clock as they climbed into bed. Right then he was happy just to hang on to Laleh, but she had other ideas. She was as ardent as ever and a few hours later roused him from a light doze for a repeat performance. He didn't sleep at all after that and rolled out before the alarm's shrill buzz. His light movements were enough to get the others going.

Nick suggested a big breakfast. He didn't want them running on empty, but none were that hungry. However, the plunger did take a hammering before Laleh packed cloth bags with any food that would travel. In the end, Nick had to remind her about space. She muttered a sorry before concentrating on the flasks, while the males put the baggage in the yard. They were ready to roll before six.

Imran and his boys were stacking the vehicle when Nick unlocked the courtyard door, and shortly after Sarah and Mohammed wandered up. Rib-crushing hugs did the rounds again before they clambered into the vehicle, and although there wasn't that much room left, somehow eight people and a heap of bags fitted in somewhere.

It was knocking on May on that chilly spring morning and rampant green flora already fought to break from its restricting buds. And although it didn't look like rain, dawn did see the eastern horizon wreathed in thick bands of multi-coloured clouds, with the Zagros peaks dominated by thin stratus writhing energetically in the moist cool air. It took time before a juvenile sun sent broad javelins of yellow and orange westwards, and that was just when their vehicle reached the squat aircraft buildings. The sky had an intimidating look about it, almost an omen if you believed in such things.

Imran squealed to a halt beside the hangar side door, away from the terminal's hostile front. Sinclair, Farhad and the boys started unloading the vehicle, while Nick led Laleh to the crew-room. She made a brew while he opened up the workshop and took the bolt cutters to the hanger.

"The boys can stack the chopper any time they like, Jock. No lights and remind them not to show themselves."

Sinclair grimaced. There was no humour in it.

"Relax, Nick. Everything's in hand. I'll crack both roller doors for some light, and open 'em properly later."

The Scot and his maintenance team manhandled one of the machines just behind the hangar entrance. They left the machines doors pinned open, and in seconds the luggage was stacked inside it.

Sinclair edged out front to the tall hangar access doors after. He looked carefully around the hangar wall before snipping the chains from the big rollers. The cutters joined the chains in the sand. He opened the sliding doors a crack before slipping back through the side door. WZ was ready for a start by then and the boys milled around the Bell in a tight bunch, concern etched deeply into each mahogany face.

"Do you need a hand with anything, Jock?"

"Nothing more, Imran. I'll open the hangar doors fully later and we'll go from in here.

"You sure?" It was as if he needed something to do.

Sinclair looked at him with something more than affection. "Piss off, you ugly bastard, before I do think of something."

A large grin lit the Pakistani's face. He turned towards Nick and dragged an amulet threaded on strong black twine from around his neck. He fitted the replica of his nation's crescent and star emblem around Nick's neck. The pilot fingered it and realized it was gold. He protested.

"Hush, Nick, it has always brought me luck and I'd rather you had all that is going around right now."

315

Nick muttered an embarrassed 'thanks'.

"Get going, Imran, and name your next son Nicholas."

That started another round of goodbyes before the car took off in a knee-high swathe of whirling sand, with disembodied hands waving from open windows. Nick knew he was being a pain in the ass, but couldn't stop himself either.

"You sure there's nothing I can do down here, Jock?"

"Shit, not you as well, Nick. Me and Fred can do anything else and you and Lily get to do what you do shortly. If you want to help drag out the cannon and put the kettle on, we'll be up there shortly."

Nick grinned and left for the demountable.

It was the waiting that was the hard part. Nick was restless, almost fidgeting as he shredded a bin-load of papers with the company logo that Laleh had stacked. He needed action of some sort, and needed it soon. He noted a sheen on Laleh's brow when they finished, and when he ran a hand over his own it came away damp too.

Nick dreaded bad weather in the mountains right then, and like aviators everywhere, he had a healthy respect for 'Murphy's Law.' He couldn't exactly phone for a met update anyway, and he'd learned that expecting the unexpected made for octogenarian pilots. He grabbed the map again, folded it into a concertina to make it easier for Laleh to handle, and then called her to the table.

"Your watch accurate, Lil?"

"It's okay, but I'll set it exactly to yours." She adjusted by a minute.

He applied an estimate of the wind from the fluttering wind-sock.

"That's the last thing I can think of except to dig out Farhad's cannon."

"Okay. I'll do Jock and Farhad a coffee when they get here, but the water's boiled if you want one now?"

"Any time, Lily, any time."

Laleh grinned.

The Scot and Amini bundled in as Nick dragged the cannon out, so Laleh filled more mugs while Farhad checked over the weapon. He loaded four ugly explosive cartridges into the grenade reservoir, a magazine into the rifle, and chambered both parts before he applied the safeties.

"That's it then, laddie. We're all packed and ready to go."

The dawn had gained some authority by then. Sinclair and Nick looked like mirror images sipping coffee at the picture window, each with a hand in a trouser pocket. Both drew back when two Utes pulled up to the rear of the civil terminal, and three figures climbed out. The nonchalance didn't seem to alter much, but their pulse rates climbed immediately. Nick tried to appear casual when he turned.

"Ten minutes and we'll do it guys. Imran must almost be in Tehran by now." Even waiting that short length of time wasn't great for the nerves.

They kept the grey demountable and the terminal between them when they slipped towards the hangar access door. The blue and white chopper crouching menacingly near the hangar egress was fully loaded, with all four cabin doors pinned wide open. Nick placed Laleh on the right and Amini pushed his weapon under the rear cabin seat before helping strap his sister in. Sinclair did the same for Nick on the left. When she was ready, Nick got Laleh to spool up while Jock waited for her thumbs up before moving with Amini to open the roller doors. Nick took control and gave the girl the map to orient. She could follow it easily now, no matter which way it was held.

Nick had mentioned it was largely a thing of gender and mathematical orientation, but it takes a lot of practice to read a map aligned in the direction of travel. She'd smiled at first, thinking it was still about reconstructing her self-confidence, but he'd known what she was thinking and shook his head. He'd only had one instructional tour, but no student had picked up on things as quickly as she had, and some of those guys had become competent instructors themselves. He let her know that too. It primed her for a long day.

Nick decided to get them going from inside the hangar, and hunched expectantly as the huge corrugated steel doors lumbered open. Jock had remembered to keep the steel tracks greased so there with no screeches of tortured steel, but there was nothing he could do about the roar of the engine in the confined space. As the two raced back to the vibrating helicopter, Sinclair caught the pilot's urgent gestures. Both he and Farhad looked back.

A white Ute was racing towards them in a flurry of choking sand only a few hundred yards away, and could easily block the machine's passage out of the hangar. Amini didn't hesitate. He yelled at Sinclair to board, and wrenched the ugly weapon from the cabin floor, before racing back the few paces to the doors.

Everything seemed to slow to a crawl when he skidded to a halt. Amini half turned the weapon to locate the safety, aligned it briefly, and then shot from the hip. A disconcerted Nick Evans didn't hear him fire, but seconds later a plume of sand, dirt, smoke and pebbles erupted skywards a few yards right and ahead of the utility. Braking hard, the vehicle snaked viciously as loose sand hurtled skywards, totally obscuring its frantically sliding passage. When it became vaguely clear again the vehicle was fish-tailing hastily back to the terminal. Amini threw himself in the chopper and dragged at the door behind him.

"Go Nick, we're okay."

Nick Evans was low enough to be trailing an arrow of tumbling sand in his wake as he headed for the Qom River. He had to lift slightly once they were enclosed by the sombre rocky funnel. The wind-tossed water was throwing shreds of white-caps skywards, and they were low enough to be catching airborne spray. The reverberating sound of their passage reflected from the steep, fractured walls of the mottled river canyon. Laleh turned to her brother once they'd settled.

"You should have taught me how to use that thing, Farhad. I might have hit the bastards."

Farhad smiled. "I wasn't trying to, Laleh. The pricks weren't revolutionary police. They were air traffic controllers. Frightening them fart-less was enough."

Laleh snorted, but Nick turned towards her with a look of amazement on his face. She could feel his eyes on her and turned with a quizzical look.

"What?"

He turned forward again with a small smile distorting his lips, but it was like someone had opened the flood gates completely. The determination, the commitment, the courage and the logic that helped her climb what seemed like insurmountable barriers to him now made perfect sense. They had decided to escape and nothing would get in the way if she could help it. The ability to go for it was inbuilt, but so too was an ability to change tacks rapidly if that was necessary. She was like a predator guarding her cubs, so maybe her occasional tunnel vision was necessary.

And that revelation was shattering. He had looked for a partner in a half-hearted way before, not sure what he was looking for, and still uncomfortable with the memories of his youth. Also he knew that opposites attract, that there was an ego boost in supplying something your partner was short of, but now he realized he'd been looking in the wrong direction. He needed a partner who had the same warrior instincts as him, someone who would only agree with him if she thought he was right. He needed someone who could cut through the crap and cope with the most pressing problem, even if the solutions seemed risky at times.

In the end, it was about finding a mate who thought and acted mostly the way he did, about someone innately and morally tough enough to travel that rocky road beside him. Someone he could trust to get his back. That was what had been missing, and that was what he had now. It was mind blowing, and the bizarre circumstance in which it happened bemused him most of all.

"Start pulling power now if you're not going to lose speed in the climb, Nick. Your new heading will be 310 when you've cleared the valley."

"310, fine." He manoeuvred through the thin stratus, the wind-screen fogging momentarily as he made his turn.

Two severely frightened air traffic controllers raced back to the small control room. The most senior grabbed for a phone, but had to dial three times before he got it right.

"Mohammed Arak."

Arak sounded bored, but came instantly awake as some of the babbling on the other end made sense.

"Slow down. You said there were three, maybe four, and they fired something heavy at you?"

He sat up quickly and started writing.

"They headed southwest towards the Gulf, you say? Okay leave it with me. I'll get back to you."

Arak scratched a stubbly chin while he read what he had written. Three or four was impossible, there were only two of them, and where would they get heavy weapons from? He felt uncomfortable about passing on something so loose, but then he thought again. How many didn't really matter much, they'd cut the chains and gone, and what they'd fired wasn't that important either. This was above his pay grade. He dialled Tehran. There was a much more agile brain there.

The mullah put half together quickly, the other half he had an hour to think about.

"Mohammed, get to Qalah Murget airfield in the south as fast as you can. There will be an air force Lear Jet waiting for you. I have a team of four who were very useful during the Embassy takeover. We will meet you there."

Arak took off running.

Chapter Forty-Five

"Come ten degrees right, Nick, we're a little off track. The wind is pushing us towards Hamadan. We're coming up to your first hour mark as well."

Nick had weaved around tall, rounded hillocks where spiky grass hardly grew at all, and he'd flown deep into any crevices remotely going his way. Twisting and turning wasn't helping the track much.

"The river on your right is the line to follow, Laleh. It bends sharply to the south soon, so pick a point some way ahead and fly to that. You'll be flying over a grassy plateau once we're over these hills too, so keep close to the deck. The approach radar at Hamadan is sited on a hill and can see up here for about ninety klicks. If you've got all that, you have control."

She grunted. "I have it."

Nick took the map and smiled indulgently when she descended by pushing the speed up with a quiet whoop. "I'd kill for a coffee, Jock."

"Choose your words better when I'm in the bloody thing, Nick. I'm getting more sensitive as I get older."

Nick snorted before opening the map for the next leg. The tension was easing. He looked at Laleh.

"It's spring, and it'll be a lot greener down there, so expect some occupied villages from now on, Lil. They should be friendly, but watch out for sheep and goat herds. We don't want to piss anybody off by scattering them. If you bias to the left, you'll avoid most of them, and we might even see some wild life close to the bigger hills."

Laleh took the machine further to port and tucked in under the shadow of a long, tall ridge. And just as he'd said, the flats were a lot greener. New verdant grasses pushed through dead tussocks, and stunted, gnarled trees were already dusted a vivid lime green. There was no snow on the grasslands either, just a glistening cover on the mountain tops. Thick drifts occasionally reflected in the higher valleys.

Almost immediately after she'd reached the hills, a herd of silver-grey donkeys broke for a canyon dead ahead. They were running hard and fast, looking more ghostly pale than their domestic cousins, and were gone in the beat of a heart. The flyers started chattering. Initially, it had been too tense for that.

And now there were other signs of occupation, but the small sepia villages were few and far between, and mostly snuggled unobtrusively amongst trees and shrubs. They were also cruder than those in Shahabad, squarer and lower, but still built with the inevitable dung-covered adobe. No glass glistened at all, the dark window slits marked only by colourful shutters pinned over gloomy wall openings. Animal pens alongside them were also built mostly of mud brick, although a few were constructed from tortured, weathered branches.

Before Nick had flown in the Zagros hills, nomads evoked images of people following herds with collapsible skin tents. Now he realized that the harsh climate demanded something more substantial than that. Here it meant that villagers owned two or even three tiny settlements, and the whole village moved between them, depending on the animal feed around. The unpredictable climate demanded stouter, better insulated accommodation than canvas or skins could provide for those long, cold springs and autumns. Wintering up there wasn't even contemplated.

Small, wiry ponies with stockmen atop were the only other domestic animals they saw, herding isolated flocks of sheep or goats over the grass flats at a distance, but Nick knew that if they weren't Bakhtaran, they wouldn't be up there. The locals treated strangers with more than average suspicion, and wandering around up there wasn't an easy thing to do. He felt comfortable skimming the waving tussocks. So with the tension bottoming, Nick led a light, frivolous chatter about the animals they saw, and tough way of life of life it must be.

"We'll be crossing the Qezel Owzan River in a few minutes, Lil. It's fairly big, so you can't miss it. Come port twenty when you hit it and climb to about 500 feet AGL. Don't lose speed, do it with power. It mustn't look like a deliberate climb. At that speed we could be any type of light aircraft. The mountain ridges run north-south around here as well, so when we do climb, Sanandaj's radar should paint us a few times on a track south of Lake Urmia. They may not have been alerted yet, but they'll log it for sure. Okay with that?"

Laleh nodded, her concentration unwavering.

Have they got anything to chase us with, Nick?"

"It's mainly a commercial terminal for the area, but it's also got an elementary flying school for their air force, Fred. I don't know what they're flying since they broke with the yanks, but it'll be some sort of light, fixed wing. No-one uses military jets or helicopters in elementary flying. The training area is due east of the base, and aircraft, mountains and students don't mix. We shouldn't see much up here."

Not long after Laleh reached a river that tumbled and bubbled through a winding rocky depression. She turned south and started climbing. Nick gave her ten minutes at the new height.

"Okay, love, down on the deck again and then right to 330. There'll be a tributary of the Qezel on the new track, and a small town called Bijar thirty odd klicks after that. It's probably okay, but keep about fifteen klicks south of it and I'll take over about then." He stretched his arm and squeezed her shoulder. Her flying had been exemplary.

"I know roughly where Sanandaj is, Nick. We've come quite a way in less than a couple of hours."

"It confuses people even at the lower speeds that helicopters fly at, Fred. We've come about 200 nautical miles, but it's in a straight line, so you can't equate it to how long it would take in a car. A half hour or so from now we'll be stopping on the tarn to refuel from the cans, and if we were flying directly to Tabriz, we'd be there less than an hour later."

"Tabriz in just over three hours, though. It would have taken nearly eight by car or train, even though it's fairly straight."

"I don't want to burst your bubble, mate, but Iran has fighters that could be over Tabriz not much more than an hour after leaving Tehran, and their Lear jets would be there twenty minutes after that. They inherited a couple of those from the Shah's royal flight, so I'll wait until we're in Turkey before I breathe easier."

Amini was sobered by the thought. Sinclair said nothing.

"Okay, Laleh. I have control."

Laleh relinquished with a deep sigh and nodded at the Scot to pour from a second flask. She savoured the first sips and then looked at Nick.

"Do you know, I finally understand a pilot's obsession with this stuff, Nickie. This seems like the best coffee I've ever tasted."

Nick grinned. "It's all about keeping the brain charged up, Lil, and nothing does it like rushes of caffeine and sugar. That was the longest you've ever flown in one hit, love, so sit back and enjoy." It was true. He wasn't into inflating her ego anymore, and Laleh sensed it. She felt good as she stretched her lithe body lazily.

They weaved through yet more rounded crags before the horizon dropped dramatically down to another plain, with lilac peaks blending slowly into the hazy distance. Ridges towered endlessly left, right and ahead, but the valley was a lush green and dotted with clumps of taller trees. Bulbous, healthy tussocks leaned drunkenly northeast, away from a strong prevailing wind, and the valley itself was a vast green tablecloth. It stretched for miles before the ground climbed on the far side again. She pointed to a dark, smoky smudge to the right.

"That's Bijar over there."

"Okay. I'm coming left and bringing the speed back a bit. I need to keep really low here. Twenty minutes from stretching our legs, guys."

Arak's private sedan was not that young, and sharp, abrasive sands had been hard on the paint job, but the Qom atmosphere was as dry as it gets. No salt air to hasten the rusting process where he was. The vehicle motored some too, and he was pulling through the mesh steel gates of Qalah Murget in little more than an hour. He flashed his ID without braking fully, knowing that the prominent purple corner ensured he wouldn't be stopped. There was a Lear and a small group waiting for him when he pulled up near the tower.

Even from several paces away Arak could see where the shah's insignia had been sloppily painted over in royal blue. A mullah dressed in drab grey robes and rounded peak-less cap hurried forward with an outstretched hand. Behind him, four religious cops dressed in similar black shirts and blue jeans leaned sloppily on their carbines. Three were thin and hard, like angry whippets, but one was so obese his belt almost cut him in half. That one was already sweating profusely.

"Time is limited, Mohammed, so introduce yourselves later. I need you on your way." Arak looked at the other four. He turned back to the clergyman and nodded.

"Where are we going, Mullah?"

"The air force base at Ardabil. You are expected by the base commander and he knows you carry our authority." Arak raised his eyebrows but the others shuffled their feet. They seemed to know already.

"This seems very urgent, Mullah."

"I will explain, Mohammed. I think there were four in that helicopter and I'm sure I know who they are and where they are headed."

Two of the four troopers looked at each other and smirked. They obviously had been briefed. "So who are they, Mullah?"

He started at a tangent. "I checked the American company files, and Evans has got dual citizenship. He was a flying instructor in the British Navy before he started flying for civilian companies, and Farhad Amini's file indicates he did a lot of his earlier training at the naval college in Britain. Both he and the pilot were there at the same time. It all fits. I don't know where or when it happened, but Evans flies helicopters and there weren't any restrictions until recently. I know he picked Amini up somewhere."

Arak nodded. "Is all this effort worth it for a few people who will probably be able to leave before too long anyway, Mullah?"

"This is, Mohammed. It was one of your people he killed at Abadan, and we can't let that go unpunished. We must make an example of them."

"Is one of his crew the fourth?"

"No. Amini's sister, I think. She was working in the American Embassy when we took it over and hasn't been seen since. There weren't any casualties we don't know about."

It all began to make sense to Arak too. "They were heading to the southwest when they left Mullah. Wouldn't Kuwait be a lot closer?"

"Normally it would be the quickest route, yes, but we are almost in a state of war with Iraq, and Kuwait is their other neighbour. It would be very dangerous to go that way right now, especially with a long track over the sea. I've alerted the Gulf surveillance units just in case, but I think they are flying to Turkey."

"So that's why we go to Ardabil?"

"Yes. Almost all the resources we have in the northwest are up there. And don't forget that two of them were military and Evans has a DFC. They would know not to try the Gulf."

"So when do you expect them in that area? When should we flood it with aircraft?"

"Not so fast. The CO complained that only five of his eight F-14s are flyable, and only three of his helicopters are airworthy. We can't get spares from America anymore and Turkey is close and the border is long. The base commander got quite worked up when he realized what we wanted and won't risk his aircraft until there is something to go on. You will be on standby at the helicopter squadron. Try to talk him into more surveillance if you can."

Arak chose his words carefully. "Those restrictions could change everything, Mullah. They might not even be spotted at all."

"I know, Mohammed, but you must not fail me. That could undermine a lot of things, like giving other people those ideas. The base commander has been authorised to shoot on sight and you should be in the area maybe two hours before they will be. You are in charge, and the others know that."

Arak shrugged. "We'd better get going then."

"I'll make some more phone calls while you head for Ardabil. May Allah guide you, Mohammed."

Arak nodded and shepherded his team up the flight stairs. One sported a large class ring. "When were you in the United States?"

The man was surly. "I wasn't. Someone lost it at the American Embassy."

327

Chapter Forty-Six

A supervisor and two radar operators shared the afternoon watch in the approach room at Sanandaj.

Air traffic was light. It was Iran's Sabbath, but the Islamic Republic of Iran's air force had two trainers out to the east because persistent low cloud had delayed progress for a few of the students. The afternoon DC 9 wasn't expected for another hour.

One controller monitoring the eastern sector read his scope occasionally, while the supervisor and other controller chatted over coffee at the other. The northern quadrant showed up high-flying commercial jets to the northwest, but not much more, so it was ignored more than it should have been. Two controllers and a supervisor were overkill for the Sabbath.

The watch boss had just delivered a punch line and was reaching to put his mug down when movement on the screen caught his eye. He gestured, but there was only the smudge of stationary peaks showing when the operator flicked his eyes up. Then a fuzzy echo blipped again.

The supervisor broke the silence. "What's that?"

"There aren't any high flyers or lighties scheduled through, and nothing has flight planned in the area, boss. Could be a flock of birds."

"It looks too solid. I'll see if the tower knows anything." He picked up the nearest phone, spoke, and then put it down thoughtfully.

"Tehran put out an alert for a helicopter about an hour ago, but wasn't sure if it was headed for the Gulf or through the mountains. It was pretty sketchy and not coming this way so they virtually ignored it. What do you think?"

"The trainers have finished their sortie and are headed back, so perhaps they could have a look. They'll need to refuel first, and the instructors will probably go in one aircraft. They won't want raw students in the mountains with them."

The supervisor nodded and turned towards the other radar screen. "Get them back to refuel and tell them what it's about ASAP."

Over forty-five minutes later, a Swiss Pilotus P3 bored north on supercharger with the squadron training officer in the rear seat, and a new instructor in the front.

"Keep to 6000 feet at top speed around the next peak Hassan, then left to 280. Our target was fifty kilometres northeast, steering 250 at about 100 knots, but that was at least a half an hour ago. Our chances of running it down aren't that good. Air traffic didn't even know if it was an aircraft or a flock of birds, so keep your eyes peeled."

"What did they send us for if there is little hope, Ali? By my calculations, they could be as much as sixty kilometres ahead of us already."

"It's a game we all learn to play in the military, Hassan. It's called coating your ass with tin. Air traffic acted late, but they did react, and now if nothing is found, it's our fault. You'll get used to it. Speed up to max again after the turn and watch the clock. Cut some corners as well. We won't have endurance for more than another 150 kilometres before we go back."

Hassan nodded and opened the throttles to full.

Nick gave control back to Laleh while he checked the map over another coffee. She thundered up a climbing funnel edged by eroded rocks that were some time away yet from becoming valleys. The huge boulders squeezed in tightly as she followed the prominent silver run-offs, and stunted, sickly grasses struggled doggedly to live where any meandering water twisted and gurgled. The surface was more a quagmire. The plateau dropped dramatically lower just ahead and exuberant water now ran quickly down both slopes. Nick drained his coffee as he scanned casually, and then he swore. He dropped the empty plastic mug.

"I have it, Lily. Something flashed at nine o'clock, at about eight miles. I think it's a wind-screen." The others strained to see as Nick flared harshly. He dare not crest the ridge, but eased into a small fissure and landed. His rotor blades were just feet from the unforgiving rock.

"Farhad, climb high enough up that slope to see him. I think he was turning this way. Keep an eye on the bloody blades as well, we're pretty tight."

Amini eased out and disappeared behind the chopper as stress levels went off the clock.

Nick was trying not to show his anxiety, but it went even higher when Farhad climbed in again a few minutes later.

"There's a prop job zig-zagging towards us about six miles south, Nick. It could fly right over us, but if he comes much closer, he'll see us anyway."

Nick sighed audibly. "Fuck it. I'll give it five more minutes and then we'll try a run for it, guys. It's almost certainly from Sanandaj so he'll be on the bones of his ass for fuel by now. The big danger is if he calls it in, but he might have a few radio problems in these hills. We haven't got much choice really, though. We've got to refuel from the containers soon or we're stuffed."

When Nick got going seven minutes later, the P3 was nowhere to be seen.

A placid tarn ahead reflected the azure of a blistering sky, looking as lifeless as a backyard goldfish pond. Neither a ripple nor an eddy disturbed the dark, glassy surface. A variety of silent, deep-green pines stood sentinel for acres around it. They were taller than any they'd seen so far, but the short branches were still ragged and thin, the trunks still knotted and tortured.

It was as if the trees were doing battle with the elements for a right to life. Although the proximity to a copious water supply ensured they did grow, the harsh climate prevented too much familiarity and vigour amongst them. They stood well apart, but the undergrowth hadn't flourished much in those frosty highlands either. The area was lower, the grass greener and the tangled brush thicker, but only where the sun's rays were able to wash the ground frequently.

And a deep, natural bowl captured the tarn. It was surrounded by high peaks on three sides, while a long way south hazy smog and diminutive minarets barely intruded on a paler sky. It was all that Nick could have wished for to refuel and stretch cramped legs.

Nick landed on a pebbly beach on the west shore of the lake amongst mysterious conifers and hefty boulders littering the lake banks. It helped to camouflage without being intrusive. He snapped the throttle closed but didn't follow up with the fuel cock, and used the rotor brake after the blades slowed naturally. There were still a few hundred pounds of fuel left and idling would take very little. The easterly tail-wind had been kind to them, helping to conserve the available fuel, but Nick cursed when he did the sums. They would still need to refuel.

"Can I go for a pee, Nicki? I'm bursting."

"You do it, Lil. Jock and I will stick the fuel in first and Farhad can sort out some grub. I didn't see the prop job either, so maybe he missed us. "

Nick and Jock wrestled out the two white fuel containers and funnel while Fred dug out Laleh's cotton bags. Nick Evans lifted while Jock directed the flow, and the first container was almost empty when they were frozen by a high-pitched scream—then another.

Amini and Sinclair stared around bewildered, but Nick grabbed the Tikka, hit the safety, and charged to where the girl had disappeared. Gasping with effort, he raced around a small rocky outcrop and saw Laleh frozen like a statue, barely upright, her jeans still around her knees. Her frightened gaze was centred close and dead ahead, and she didn't break it to look at him. He swiveled.

Close by a few battered trees stirred gently, while lifeless tussocks waved long, straw stalks in the mild breeze. Other than that, only dark boulders and scrawny bushes hugged the deep shadows.

Nick squinted and concentrated deeper, then one of the larger dappled boulders moved in the sun-washed shadows. A savage pink mouth gaped wide, revealing a throbbing pink throat behind long, ivory incisors that dripped strings of sticky, colourless saliva. Now he was focused, he could see black, pitiless eyes slashed by the vertical yellow of unblinking irises watching the girl intently. The animal hissed as its mouth opened again and its muscular shoulders bunched and raised a foot higher. It was about to charge.

Nick didn't hesitate. He centred between the vicious eyes just twenty yards ahead, knowing the small brain was right behind them. Then he paused. He had to force himself to squeeze, not stab at the trigger, it had to be this shot. If he didn't stop it with the first one, he'd never get another chance.

The sharp crack came just ahead of the other two skidding around the corner. The large leopard reared and half toppled backwards, spitting fiercely as its paws tore at a mangled face. Nick jacked in another cartridge and shot into the whitish chest even before the animal had started to tumble. He probably didn't need it, and hadn't noticed the others arriving either.

By then Laleh had hauled her pants up but hadn't zipped or buckled when she ran sobbing towards him. He held an arm open, keeping the one with the rifle well away from her. She wrapped around him with arms like steel bands.

"Nice one, Lil. I've always fancied a safari," he whispered shakily.

He was trying to make light of it, but Laleh could hear the quiver in his voice and feel every muscle in his body fluttering with shock.

Nick and Laleh walked back to the helicopter, traumatised and beyond being curious. Right then, just being together was enough. Sinclair and Amini moved cautiously to the spotted body and the Scot rolled the carcass with his foot.

It already looked smaller in death, its fur a spotted mantle of matt black dots on what was no longer a shining yellow. It wouldn't be going anywhere soon. They headed back to the chopper themselves.

All four of them perched on rocks, the incident had left them quivering with aftershock. But they didn't have time for it. Nick forced himself to function again, easing his arm from around Laleh's shoulders.

"Fred, give Jock a hand with the other fuel can and Lil pour the rest of the coffee. We go again in twenty." It was what they needed, and they all started to move.

Nick removed the short magazine from the Tikka, fumbling a box of ammunition as he re-replaced two cartridges. He pushed the recharged rifle back under the seat, and then helped force down the remaining food and the last of the coffee. They still needed a catalyst, to do more than just respond. Nick stepped in again.

"Finish everything up, guys, it could be difficult later and we'll need the energy. I'm sorry about the leopard as well, Lil. It was always a possibility now we're further north."

And that opened up the flood-gates. They all tried talking at once, but Laleh predominated in the end.

"Where the hell did it come from, Nick?"

"As we get near the Caspian, we could see more things like that. I just didn't think about it. I should have remembered that there could be the odd tiger, panther and cheetah around as well, and there are even brown bears and wolves a bit further north. A lot have been shot out, but isolated forested areas with plenty of water are naturals."

"I didn't think of it either though, Nick, and it's my bloody country."

333

"Big cats are pretty much a thing of the past now, though, Fred. They must be in most of Iran."

"Well, I could do without any more surprises." Then Laleh chuckled. "I peed on my boots I was so shocked." That broke the ice.

They all grinned and it was easy to get them underway after that. Nick gave Laleh something else to think about.

"You okay to take it from here, Lily?" The girl looked around her, the leopard already receding with more flying to do.

"It's a bit tight, Nick and I dread being the one who stuffs up. You get us out of the clearing. I'll take over after."

"Okay."

They were ready to go again in minutes. Nick towered it out and when he cleared the trees, she took over.

Chapter Forty-Seven

The air force pilot flying the Lear cut downwind and base leg into a tight turn and swooped onto the runway as if it was an air day and he had an appreciative audience. He off-loaded Arak and his team outside the control tower and immediately taxied to return to Tehran.

The tower looked like a military control tower anywhere, its four storeys painted a standard dazzling white, and its outer façade festooned with pipes and windows. The top of the building belled outwards, the panelling up there almost entirely glass, while a variety of aerials and metal frames reached skywards from its bitumen roof. A large painted sign on the bottom floor advertised an ops room. That's where Arak headed while his team shuffled their feet.

Banks of computers, radar screens and wall maps were scattered around the large, air conditioned room, all manned by men in light-blue shirts and slacks. At its centre, a short, muscular older man watched each operation like a hawk. He had dark skin, a shaven head, and gold metallic colonel's insignia on his collar, and looked more Arabic than Persian. As the door squeaked open he turned, his dark eyes slitted and hostile. Arak introduced himself.

"I was told your requests would have priority, Mister Arak, but let me say right now that I'm the commanding officer of this base and I control the aircraft here. I'll decide what my aircraft can or can't do, not you or Tehran, and we've already used up this month's allocation of fuel. I do know the task is to locate and stop a small commercial helicopter in any way we can, but that's all I know. I'll need more before I commit expensive and scarce aircraft resources. There are other issues here besides yours."

It was not the greeting Arak had expected. Right away he knew he needed to be careful. This man didn't like him or the clergy in Tehran, and neither was he cowed. Arak tried tact.

"The decisions about flying are obviously yours, Colonel. I'll give you what I know and you can tell me how we should do it."

That didn't appease the air force officer much either. "Right, Mister Arak. How many people are we looking for, when can we expect them to reach here, and why are they wanted?"

"A pilot and engineer from an American exploratory company, and a male and female Persian. They should reach this area in about an hour and a half and are traitors to Iran. They are implicated in the murder of one of our men."

The colonel wasn't shocked. He even creased around the lips slightly as if he thought it was a good idea. "Your Iran, I presume, Mister Arak. Obviously they are going for Turkey so do they need to refuel?"

"We don't know. They started from Qom, so they'll need more fuel, but they could be carrying it in containers."

The colonel looked skywards.

"I've got two Kiowas with long-range tanks here and basically that's what they're flying. They could just about do that on one fuel load if they are carrying cans. The Turkish border is only an hour's flying from here by helicopter, and it's over 300 kilometres long." The colonel started to pace.

"I'm not getting any spares through for my aircraft, and we've robbed the hangar queens to keep the others flying, so what assets I do have must be handled carefully. If their helicopter doesn't stop, they could be impossible to spot, and if they need fuel, there are a lot of places they could get it from. My Tomcats can't land at any of the smaller airfields, and I don't have enough helicopters to cover anywhere near the number of places they could get it from. It's a vast area, Mister Arak, and keeping in radio contact will also be a problem. You'll have to get Tehran to send a fax authorising the use of the assets and fuel, and we'll see what we can do. Use the white phone." He pointed. "The switch will patch you through."

Even at that late stage, Tehran dithered. It was twenty minutes later before the fax came through. Arak felt his own anger rising. How serious were they about him doing his job? He already suspected it would all come down to him in the end, so he'd better keep the colonel sweet.

"Tell me what we can do, Colonel, and I'll back it up?"

"They should get here around early afternoon, so I'll put an F14 up after lunch. It can sweep from here to the south of Lake Urmia and back, and if the pilot does find something, we'll scramble, but I can't have assets out of place and not in radio contact. The jet can't fly too low either, it eats up too much fuel. The Tomcat will stay at 10,000 feet unless he sees something, and we'll think about choppers then. It would take over two hours for one to get to the southern end of the lake, and I can't risk it being that far out of place if we haven't got anything to go on."

Arak nodded. "I have four men with me, Colonel. What should we do?'

"Well, they won't be cluttering up my ops room, that's for sure." He pointed out a hanger and office complex about 200 metres away through a window. "That's the helicopter squadron. Send them there in case we do have to move quickly and I'll get the squadron CO to range one of his birds ready to go. They can dig up some food as well. You can stay here with me." The colonel turned to a bank of telephones while Arak hurried out to organise his men.

"Head 340 for now, Lil. The Saqqez River is on your left and another feeding the tarn comes in from the right. They've both got roads and small cities on them. I'll keep you about twenty klicks clear so there'll only be a few small villages on your track."

Laleh nodded.

"How far to the refuelling base?"

"About a 130 klicks. After you've crossed that set of peaks ahead, the land drops again and you'll see Mount Sahand standing pretty much alone. It's quite high with several peaks in a group and a lot of snow. It's a lot younger than the hills we've been going through, so the mountains are pretty jagged and Sahand is volcanic so it could even be smoking." Nick leaned over with the map, his index finger on the feature.

"Aim for the southern slopes about there. Azar Shahr is twenty-five klicks beyond that, and the airfield is several klicks southeast of the town. If you reckon you're too close to the bigger towns, sheer away from them. There aren't that many and we've got plenty of room."

Laleh muttered an "Okay."

"Do you know the company manager where we're stopping, laddie?"

"I've only met him once Jock, when the company flew me on a famil: in their fixed wing. He seemed okay. The base control is Norwegian, but he's actually Swedish. He's called Sven and something I can't remember, but all the blokes in these jobs are pretty much the same breed."

"Will he have to get a bowser over?"

"I bloody hope not. It's a bigger operation than ours was, so I think he'll have auxiliary fuel there. Fingers crossed, mate, fingers crossed."

Almost at the same moment there was another quiet whoop from Laleh. The land was still mountainous but lower, and she knew what she was doing. She descended almost in autorotation while Nick studied the map.

"You'll see a big town called Bukan on your left in a few minutes, Laleh. When you do, come right to north and keep us in the hills. If you have to bias between crests, make it to the right."

They both saw the small city at the same time. Laleh came around to north, aiming for yet another depression between two higher hills.

Arak was draining hot water from a squat silver urn when a cream telephone, one of a bank of three, trilled insistently. It got everybody's attention. The base commander fumbled it to his ear and responded in monosyllables, and then cursed. He almost threw the phone back on its rack. He wasn't pulling any punches when he turned to Arak

"That was some idiot in Tehran. They received a report of a low speed contact thirty-five miles east of Sanandaj, tracking south of west some time ago. They sent a trainer up to look for it and the crew saw a chopper right at the end of their search area. He didn't have the fuel to follow it, and he wasn't armed anyway, but it was twenty-five minutes before he could get radio contact. That's over an hour and a half since his sighting. Their track was south of Lake Urmia."

"Is it the one we want, Colonel?"

The air force officer fumed. "How the hell should I know? But if it is them, they could be south of the lake before long. I'll scramble a Tomcat, but don't hold your breath. It's going to take him thirty minutes to get down there." The colonel lifted one of the phones.

Arak's worried frown got deeper. He heard the rumble of big engines spooling up as he moved to a window.

The squadron XO was on first standby and jumped when his boss's telephone trilled. Seconds later, a greying head thrust through the crew-room door.

"Go, heading southwest, brief on ops when airborne." There was nothing else the CO could say right then. He didn't know any more. The XO and a young radar intercept officer started running to join a ground team already swarming over an ugly, twin tailed fighter/bomber. The air start cart whistled into shrieking life as they climbed in, and the crew chief swung onto the wing himself to strap them into their ejection seats.

He was an old hand, and it didn't take long, but he'd hardly reached the ground again before the XO was signalling with a right index finger thrust into a left palm. Starting two wasn't long after it, and the XO waved away the chocks before he could have possibly completed his after start checks. The aircraft crouched as it started to roll, looking mean and nasty as it picked up speed.

Within eight minutes of the scramble, the sinister fighter had switched off after-burners and was trailing a dirty grey plume as it climbed into a pristine clear sky.

"Cobra Two on ops. Sitrep." Flamboyant call signs were almost mandatory for fighter jocks. The colonel grabbed a black plastic microphone on a glowing radar table.

"Cobra Two, command. Your target is a civilian Kiowa, either all white or with blue motives on the rear doors. It should be approaching south of Lake Urmia in about thirty. Seek and destroy, over." There was silence for several long seconds.

"Command, Cobra Two, is that it? There are hundreds of square miles to look at. Can you be more specific?"

"Don't piss me off, Cobra Two. I'm having a bad day."

"Roger command, I hope it gets better. After-burners or not?"

"Don't even think about it. Let me know when you're on station. Over and out."

Cobra Two stayed at 8000 feet AGL as he dashed south. Twenty miles from the lake, the XO managed a grunt.

"For what it's worth, light us up. We're nearly there." There was silence for about a minute.

They had flown together long enough for the RIO to know when he could get a bit familiar. "Not too bad when I sweep at this level, boss, but complete camel crap when we look at the deck. Almost total ground reflections."

"I know, son. The colonel flew these things for a lot of hours and he knows too. That's why he sounded pissed off. Do what you can, but use your eyes. It's probably our best shot."

Nick was close to the mountain, but still eighty kilometres from the rippling, icy water, and not aware of the menacing fighter winging towards the northern edge of Lake Urmia. He knew Iranian resources were limited and he was playing it for all he could. He had only one real shot, but then again that's all they had too.

"Maragheh will come up on your left in about ten minutes, Lily. You can come right if you think you're a bit close. There's a second-class road running from there to Mianeh, but nothing else. I'll take over after that."

"Are they the only towns to worry about?"

"Just Maragheh. The other one's over forty klicks from it. Several run-offs and a few small villages cut into the mountains behind them, but there aren't any roads, only dirt tracks. We'll pick a spot on the western slope and have a look at the base first. That can be a quick wee break as well."

"I can see the city, Nick." She jammed the collective with her knee like she'd seen him do, and looked at the palm of her left hand. "Half passed ten."

He smiled. He'd already seen it, but there was little she hadn't picked up.

"Right, Lil, ten degrees starboard. Fly between those two rivers about five klicks apart." He pointed slightly to his side.

"Got them. Going a bit lower."

They flashed over the secondary road almost immediately, surprising a vehicle rattling towards them two klicks away. Nick shrugged. He couldn't do much if it did report him, but was it likely? They were gone again before it really registered anyway.

"Okay relax, Lily, I have control." She handed over and wriggled in her seat to appease a numbed backside. They were amongst tall, dark-green pines now on a steepening forested slope and he edged port to avoid being sky-lined.

Lake Urmia was huge, the vast, wet expanse stretching hazily westwards, and easily visible from half way up the slope. Further away, in the vague distance, tall jagged mountains marked where Iran ended and Turkey began, while several small towns hugged the rivers in the basin between them. The dirt tracks that linked them were little more than rudimentary, little more than narrow subdued creases on a roughened, rolling surface.

The small city of Azar Shahr stood out, particularly the modern, sealed roads and railway line looping to the west, but south of the town the buildings of the small regional airfield were barely visible. Nick headed for a ragged crag beside the broiling white cascade it overlooked.

"Okay, guys, out and stretch your legs. You take over in ten minutes so I can, Lil."

The big jet was cruising at 450 knots and 10,000 feet when it reached the northern tip of the lake, the most economical speed at that height. The pilot altered to track down the centre of the water.

"Flash it up again, son. See what you get here."

The RIO engaged the forward sweeping dish and angled it towards the lake. There was a distinctive clear return over the smooth water but flickering spikes of nothing on either side.

"The lake's not too bad, Major, especially if I don't angle down too much."

"Okay, leave it there for now. We can't expect to get lucky, but you never know." The F14 thundered on until they were approaching land again and the return over the broad, flat water catchment degenerated quickly.

"I've lost it again, boss, sorry."

"That's all right, Habib, it was wishful thinking anyway. We'll run in towards Sanandaj for several minutes and then reverse up the western side of the lake. We don't have a lot of fuel left, but I'll come down a couple of thousand." There was an angry edge to what he said. A few miles later the major snorted in disgust. "Look at it. They could be anywhere."

Mile after mile of multi-coloured chasms and rounded rolling peaks stretched all around them, some tops still bright with late shafts of sunlight, but lower tracts already dark and foreboding. Deep valleys threw dark shadow haphazardly in every direction, and patches of snow and acres of withered, pied grasses glistened spasmodically in a confusing mix. And at the speed they were flying, it was gone before they could really focus or absorb it anyway.

The XO weaved gently around a base course of southeast for fifty miles, but there was nothing flying below him, and only one set of silver contrails heading west far above. He gave up with a disgusted shrug. He was strapped tightly into his seat, so he didn't actually move much, but his RIO sensed his reaction. The jet pilot reversed course and headed back to the lake again, ordering radar as he tracked back north over the glistening water.

Chapter Forty-Eight

The beige, sandy airfield nestled a good twenty klicks away. Only the two intersecting strips of tarmac were easily discernible from up there. The buildings themselves were nowhere near as obvious, but Jock had thrown in their old Zeiss binos. Nick fished them out of his bag.

A twin light aircraft took off on runway 220, and shortly after, a helicopter droned in from the west. It was bigger than the machine Nick was flying, possibly a Puma, and it headed for a low complex of Nissans and prefabricated offices on the southeastern side of the airfield. The paint job was a dark grey, its shape distorted by a sun now sinking low in the western sky, but what was important was that it was flying at all. Obviously, survey operations that weren't American were still going ahead. A wary look at the sun reassured him. Nick couldn't afford to be too early, but he needed people to be there at the same time he was. He squinted westward.

The distant mountains appeared to be reaching up to drag the glowing ball down quickly by then,, the hazy daylight already muting into a pre-dusk metallic sheen. The sun hadn't slid much lower before Nick made his decision. Even with some fuel, it would be dark in parts of the mountains soon and then he'd have to stop anyway. He couldn't risk flying through the high peaks in the dark and couldn't climb above them either.

And there would be radars on both sides of the border for sure. Nick didn't know where, and it was purely speculative, but even the Turks might splash an unidentified aircraft forcing their borders with Iran. It could be running drugs or arms.

Nick took only enough time to relieve himself before he was ready to go, with fuel his first concern. Without that, they'd be walking through the mountains.

Scanning closer, he saw that a significant gully, carved deep by running water, looped almost as far as the airfield. If he used that, he might not be seen at all. Two small villages on the river banks below were probably of no real consequence, and thick, bushy trees provided cover almost all the way to the depot. It was the way to go.

"It'll start getting rough from now on, guys. I need your eyes swiveled outwards, and nothing is too trivial to report. Look out for wires and fences as well, Lil. I'll be very low if I keep the depot between us and the terminal." He waited for their nods. "Okay. Just you out when we refuel, Jock, and let's hope Sven is still there."

They all grunted.

Nick squeezed off the ledge and tracked down the white water cascading from the peaks above. He flew low, lower than the swaying conifer tops, the tumbling river so close he had to hop over several wayward branches that over-hung it. In less than a minute, his brow glistened with a wet sheen.

Minutes later, they passed the first small village on the river bank. It was deserted as Nick thought it would be, but he was forced up several feet by a flock of doves breaking in panic from the dense trees it nestled in. By then his brow was trickling.

They were only four miles from the base when he hurtled onto the flats beneath the broad skirts of Sahand. Nick scraped the chopper through mottled boulders in the river bed, staying ultra-low all the way in, and by the time they reached the perimeter, the Nissan hangers and office block blanked out most of the airfield.

This close, Nick could see two ground crew wheeling in what was definitely a Puma. One was walking and one towing with a small tractor. A tall, fair-haired male watched with hands behind his back, and shorts, sandals, a polo top and blue baseball cap didn't disguise him. It was the Swede. Nick kept his eye on him and judged his flare so that he didn't balloon. Laleh broke into his concentration.

"High fence, Nick."

He lifted instinctively and was still running forward slightly when he ran the machine onto the concrete. Skids sparked, and the metal tubes screeched, but they were built for it. Sven turned as the steel abraded noisily, a look of incredibility on his face. Nick tugged open his sliding window.

"Nick, isn't it? What the hell are you up too?"

"I need fuel quickly, Sven, and I could do without a bowser being here."

Managers in those remote areas were chosen not just because they are good man managers, but because they were fairly astute. The Swede knew the situation. He didn't need a diagram.

"That cart's about half full. I use it to top up after ground runs. It's got a hand pump though, it's a bit slow."

He whistled to the two stowing the Puma and pointed at the ground cart. They didn't need a diagram either. The Swede showed Jock how to operate it and Sinclair started pumping.

"I'll keep an eye on the terminal from the hangar. If anything happens, I'll let you know." He raced the fifty yards he needed to and the Scot pumped like a man possessed. Nick watched his fuel gauge climb agonizingly slowly.

The Scot hadn't been cranking for more than a few minutes before the Swede shouted, looked back across the flat dusty field, and then ran towards them. Sinclair kept pumping furiously.

"There's a vehicle coming. Close your tank and get out of here."

Sinclair did, and the ground crew dragged the cart back to the hangar. Sven looked over his shoulder.

"Go Nick. There's a truck about 300 metres away."

"What about you, Sven?"

"I'll be all right. I've thought of something to say."

Sinclair was already dragging the door closed.

"Okay, on your way."

As Nick lifted he yelled his thanks.

"Go with your god, Nick." That was said quietly.

The Bell was nearly a mile away, travelling fast and low, when a senior air trafficker and a security guard scrambled out of the truck.

"Who was in that helicopter, Mister Anderson?" The air-trafficker used Farsi.

"A European pilot and two Iranians in some sort of uniform," Anderson answered in the same language.

The air trafficker's eyes slitted. "All flights have to be cleared, and he couldn't have taken much fuel."

"He didn't take any. The helicopter was seconded to look for another one by Tehran. They were asking questions, that's all."

"On whose authority?"

"I don't know. They had a written document of some sort, but nearly all of it was in Arabic and you know I can't read that." Anderson let himself sound uptight.

Azar Shahr hadn't been dragged into the loop, only the larger city airfields, and the controller was fishing. He was suspicious but didn't know why. He looked across to where the ground crew were diligently polishing the Puma, but that didn't tell him much either. Frustrated, he gestured for security and drove back to the terminal, but deliberated before phoning Tabriz. The number he'd been given was for emergencies and he didn't know if this was one or not. Tabriz was in the loop, but they deliberated too before phoning.

"We didn't get as much fuel as I'd hoped, guys, but I think we got enough. I was going around the lake, but now we'll go across it. That should give us enough for

Turkey. There's a large promontory with just a couple of villages on it up ahead, and our water track will only be twenty klicks."

"Do you expect anything nasty, laddie?'

"I've no idea, Jock, but if it's going to happen, it'll be around here."

In minutes they were fifteen miles from the airfield with a greenish land mass jutting out into the rippling lake. He swung to his right, aiming for it, and squeezed down amongst the lighter scrub on the edge of the water.

"Okay, Lily, you have control. The peninsular is about seven klicks ahead. Go due west when you hit it."

She'd done a lot of nodding on this trip.

"I don't think they'd put helicopters this far out on an off chance, so what we should be looking for is a jet fighter. They'll want something they can hit us with if they do find us. It won't be low either, not initially anyway. It's too heavy on fuel. I'll cover port with Jock and you take starboard, Fred. Yell if you see anything. You just concentrate on getting us into the foothills, Lil."

Amini unstrapped and knelt on the cabin deck, to cover the pale, washy sky better.

"We've reached the peninsula, Nick."

"Okay, Laleh. Due west over the water, then bias right. We'll have to get as close as we can to that valley with the road and rail in it. The mountains are too high right ahead. About 100 klicks to go, people."

Cobra Two had descended to 5000 AGL approaching Urmia. The Bell started across the silver lake forty klicks north of it. The young RIO had his radar sweeping, but there was a lot of clutter and the water threw back disembodied ghosts and wavering shadows.

And just when he thought he had a paint, their radio burst into a distorted crackle. They were on an operational frequency so it could only be Ardabil. The XO pushed on power and zoom climbed to 15,000 feet to check in. The RIO was too inexperienced to voice his concerns.

"Cobra Two, command. Tabriz reported some unusual helicopter activity at Azar Shahr, but it's at least twenty minutes old. The idiots procrastinated before they called anyone. Where are you?"

"Half way up the lake. Where was it heading?"

"Towards you from what they said."

"We didn't see anything. They must have changed course."

"It's probably them then. Find it, Cobra Two."

"Okay, command, but be advised, Cobra Two is almost on bingo fuel. I've got a few minutes to search before I return or you've lost another F14."

"Roger that. What's the weather like?"

"The weather's okay, command, but it's getting dark quickly. The mountains already look black in places, but shafts of sunlight are still lighting up some of the canyons."

"Shit. Do what you can, Cobra Two, they haven't got far to go."

"Roger command. Cobra Two out."

Laleh was really smoking. She was over the maximum allowable, but if she hadn't been, Nick would have told her to anyway. She was low as well, lower than she'd ever taken it before. Three pairs of eyes searched the cloudless azure for even a hint of movement, and they were already half way across the stretch of water. It was now only ninety klicks from the border near Orenburc, even closer if Nick risked some steeper mountains in the dark. He flicked his gaze ahead.

"Right 20 to 290 Lily. We'll cut the corner, so there'll be a few settlements to avoid. The biggest is a town called Salmas. Keep well to port and only swing north when we've passed it. It's probably okay, but we're too close to take chances."

"There's one ahead, Nick. I'll come a touch more left, it's clearer."

Amini broke in. "I think all the villages are Kurdish around here, Nick. The border countries in this area have

349

got a lot of them, and they're almost all PKK. They don't like any of the governments, only other Kurds."

"Whatever, Fred, but we're so close we'll try to avoid them all." He squinted at the map. "Go for that ridge ahead, Lily. It's a false one, and the land drops beyond it again, but it's only about ten klicks from the foothills proper. You can come to 330 when you reach it and we'll miss Salmas by a fair bit."

Laleh nodded as she approached dry land again, but their complacency was shattered by an excited yell from Sinclair.

"Fighter bomber about six miles south, Nick. It's climbing hard. I can see two exhaust plumes."

"Fuck. I have it, Lily." The nearest cover was the isolated ridge, now less than six miles ahead.

He squeezed even lower, the skids virtually brushing the thorny scrub, and headed for its crevices.

"What the hell is it, Jock?"

"It's got swept wings, and the only delta twin they've got is an F14. It's turning away at present."

"It won't be for long. Someone at Azar must have phoned and it's climbing to get line of sight. It wants a radio brief and track."

The ridge was only a few kilometres away by then, the land already beginning to buckle and tumble. Nick angled for some eroded, jumbled gullies running down from the crest.

"We can't take a chance with his speed and the weapon load he carries, we're too damn close. We've got to land and clear the chopper just in case. I'll shut down and try to disguise it while you guys take what you can into the rocks. It'll be in about a minute, so get ready." His voice was up an octave, the Welsh sing-song more pronounced.

Nick headed for a wide gully festooned with straggling trees and shrubs. A scree of large rocks nestled half way up from a mini landslide and its irregular surrounds were wreathed in streaks of light and shadow.

Nick flared hard and landed as close as he dared to the stunted trees. The others were out as soon as the skids hit and headed for the rocks. Nick stuffed his map into a pocket and headed for copse.

Nick Evans broke up the chopper's angular lines with dead branches and any smaller live ones he could reach before heading for the crevices himself. The sixty-metre dash seemed more like a marathon. The sudden silence was intense, almost eerie, after long hours of a whining engine. Not even a song bird intruded.

Cobra Two banked steeply over Azar Shahr and aimed for the spit of tawny and green breasting into the lake. He knew they'd go for the shortest water crossing and that was it. The jet jockey started the big fighter down again.

"Anything on radar, Habib?"

The RIO dreaded the question, but knew he had no choice. He anticipated the blast that was about to come.

"Total hash ahead, sir. I thought I might have had a faint echo on the lake just as the radio call came in, but it was very iffy. That was about ten minutes ago."

The XO did explode as expected. "Why didn't you say so, you bloody imbecile, in fifteen minutes we won't be able to see a thing. You've got guard duty for a week when we get back."

Habib took a punt, trying to redeem himself.

"What about a missile, sir. It's pretty cold and isolated down there and the engine must still be pretty hot if they've just landed."

The XO paused. "What the hell does that mean?"

"They're heat seekers, sir. If we get within five or six kilometres, they might warble. They couldn't have gone far in the time they had."

The pilot made his decision. "We'll have to get low for the missile cone to pick them up, but if this works, Habib you've saved your ass. Enable both out-board Sidewinders, and keep an eye on the clock. Five minutes is all we've got."

The jet pilot swung right, dropped to 500 feet, and started flying a search grid.

Nick did a quick check. They had the weapons and two of the four bags, and Fred's black bag with the money was one of them. The other was Laleh's. Sinclair had thrust it at her when he grabbed the Tikka.

The Jet Ranger looked forlorn, obvious and abandoned in the stronger light away from where they were, the geometric silhouette and sharp angles stark and clear. It was too late now though, it was how it would have to be. Amen. Only minutes later they heard the intimidating roar of jet engines to the north. It was obviously very low.

"The bastard's sweeping from our furthest possible position backwards, guys. He must have been here a while though. It won't be long before it's too dark in the canyons for any more searches and he must be getting low on fuel. Fifteen minutes tops and I reckon we've got it made." The optimism wouldn't go amiss, but then Sinclair dissolved it again.

"Fuck it. I didn't latch my door properly. It's swinging in the breeze."

"It's too late now, Jock. He probably won't see it anyway."

"The bloody sun's rays were on it and the Perspex glittered. That's how I saw it myself."

Sinclair brushed Nick's hand away and broke from the rocks. He didn't have far to go.

Cobra Two rolled in for his second pass, side stepping two miles, running south to north. One more and he was out of there. Nothing showed, but when he was four klicks from a narrow, isolated ridge, their headsets filled with a low grade-growl. Both concentrated on the ground ahead as the growl became a higher-pitched warble. Something flashed, concentrating their attention.

"Got it. Switching to guns." That was just one click on a rotary switch, before the XO moved his finger to a trigger on his cyclic. He lined up precisely. The range would be optimum in just thirty seconds.

The chain gun emitted a muted roar like ripping calico, accompanied by a slight, acrid whiff of cordite. The slope ahead jumped and contorted hazily, with decimated shards of earth and rocks hurtling skywards as bullet impacts obscured the target. The XO eased up to avoid the top of the ridge and then rolled and pulled hard into a tight circuit. The 'G' was strong enough to distort their features as compressed air rushed into their flying suits. Both ignored it, staring hard at the ground ahead.

"That's a definite a kill, boss. One skid has collapsed and the rear rotor blade is bent over the fuselage. No fire, but they won't be using it again. I think I saw a body near it too."

"You're right, that's a kill. Allah be praised, because we haven't got fuel for any more. It's too late for a chopper to get here before dark, but they won't get far on foot in this country. No guard duty and I owe you a beer if someone hasn't locked the bloody bar up. Vector us home, son."

Chapter Forty-Nine

Mobile hot tears cascaded down Laleh's face, the running mascara making a mess around her eyes. Nick held on tight, his arms like a vice.

"Shush, Lil, stop it, the jet will be back to see what it's done. Leave it until we know he's gone." She still struggled, but even as he finished talking the ground shook as the fighter bomber did a slow pass. Nick covered her with his body, trying to push her further into the rocks. She stopped struggling even though she was still crying. The engine rumble faded as the jet started to climb, and only then did Nick step out from the rocks. The aircraft was disappearing to the northeast by then. Nick raced to Jock with Farhad and Laleh right up there with him.

Although Sinclair wasn't yet dead, it wouldn't be long before he was. He'd taken one hit, but it was a big calibre though and through. There was a hole in his right chest which he tried to pinch closed with bloodied, twitching fingers, but a slowly spreading pool of gore on the hard, dusty soil told Nick that he was leaking badly from the back as well. The effort he made was pointless. He was bleeding out. Nick's own eyes started to water.

Sinclair's eyelids fluttered, his eyes red and mobile, when Nick checked his carotid pulse. He tried to speak, gasped, and started again.

"No time for any sentimental crap, laddie." He stopped and panted. "In my wallet, the last photo I ever got of my girls. On the back is their granny's address in Stirling." His panting was more ragged. "The number is an account in Edinburgh with the Bank of Scotland and the name Sinclair and the number opens it up. Give it to my girls, Nick. It's a fair bit. Tell them I never stopped thinking about them."

Jock Sinclair was ebbing fast now, but beckoned Laleh with bloodstained, hooked fingers.

"You make sure he does it, Lil." It was the first time he'd shortened her pseudonym. He tried, but didn't manage anything else. The moist eyes glazed in a matter of seconds.

"Command, Cobra Two."

"Cobra Two, loud and clear."

"Command, we destroyed the chopper and think we got an occupant as well." Arak heard that on overhead speaker and hurried to the colonel.

"We must go immediately in a helicopter, Colonel."

The colonel hushed him with an angry slash of his hand.

"Is it worth sending a helicopter now, Cobra Two?"

"Negative command. It's pretty black in the canyons already and a chopper would take two hours to get here, and need fuel from Azar before he could search. It's steep open country though, and they're on foot, so even if they went all night, they would be lucky to make fifteen klicks. They wouldn't dare flag a vehicle down, and the mountains to the west and south are pretty high. They've got to keep going to the northwest, and will still be fifty kilometres from the border in the morning."

"Roger that, Cobra Two. What do you suggest?"

"Get one of the choppers to refuel at Azar Shahr at dawn and concentrate the search to the northwest when he can see where he's going. The FLIR should find them quickly enough. I'll brief you when I get back."

"Roger, Cobra Two. The circuit is clear."

"It had better be, command. I'll be sucking on fumes when I get there."

Nick sat on the ground beside his friend. He was holding a blood-streaked hand that already looked waxy, but he couldn't let go. He was in shock and Farhad wasn't much better off. It was Laleh who stood with tears still filling her eyes. She looked at their ride in the rapidly fading light and could see it was finished. She turned to Nick, her voice urgent, insistent.

"Nickie, we have to get away from here quickly. Jock wouldn't want us to waste any of the time we've got." Both men refocused as if they'd been kicked. Nick wiped wet eyes with his sleeve and seemed to notice the rapidly fading light for the first time.

"You're right, Laleh. We've got to get moving." He shook himself back into the present.

"You two salvage what you can from the machine. I'll look at the map while I can still see it."

Farhad hurried Laleh to the chopper while Nick squatted and opened a topographical map. It didn't take him long to work out a preliminary route and the others were back with the bags as he finished. One of the cloth food containers was shredded by bullets, which further motivated him.

"We can't carry too much if we're walking, so we'll go through what we've got left. We'll take the weapons and just what we can get in your bag, Fred." Nick knew what was in that one. He fished out his pocket knife and gave it to Amini.

"There's a small emergency magnetic compass, starboard side near the canopy roof. It's held on by two small screws. A couple of gadgets on this should shift it." He indicated the rough position with a hand before he glanced at Laleh. "Lily, you go through the bags with me. Only stuff we think is vital goes in Farhad's bag."

They scattered, but were back together in a matter of minutes. Nick forced himself to look at the body.

"The ground is too hard to bury him, and we haven't got anything to dig with anyway. We'll put Jock in a crevice and cover him with rocks. Take him by the shoulders, Fred. I couldn't drag him by the heels." The two men lifted the torso and the girl hurried in and lifted the feet. Getting rid of the body seemed to re-vitalise him.

"Fred, check the weapons and make sure they're fully loaded. Laleh, you empty the bags. We take passports, certificates and important papers and some spare ammunition. Not much more or it will be too heavy."

Laleh dumped the contents in a pile. It was already getting too dark to see properly, and they went through it more by feel than sight. Nick discarded most of it. When he repacked the essentials tightly, there was still some room.

"Nickie, can I please take my clean knickers?" It was plaintiff, almost a plea, and he smiled for the first time in hours.

"Of course, Laleh. Put any spare socks in as well, we'll need to keep our feet dry if we're walking."

She sighed with relief.

"Five minutes for a quick brief and then we go, guys." Nick put the discards back in a bag and stuffed it amongst the nearby rocks.

"We're going for a place called Aslanik tonight. It's an isolated village, close to our route, but not in an obvious straight line. It's about twenty-five klicks away so we'll have to really push it, but that could be a bit further than they expect us to go. There's a couple of villages and a minor road on the other side of this hill too, but we'll by-pass them. There's bound to be some sort of search, and the villagers will be questioned first, so the less people that know about us, the better. Watch where you walk too, we can't afford an accident, but there will be a decent moon up soon. Okay, let's get on with it."

"What is FLIR, Colonel?"

"Forward looking infra-red. It's used mostly in search and rescue. It's designed to pick up body heat, any heat really, but it's only good for about six kilometres. You can be hidden though and it will still sense the temperature difference."

"So it can happen in the dark?"

The colonel had been around long enough to know where this was going. "It does, Mister Arak, but unfortunately it may pick up something warm in the trees, but not that there's something in the way. He needs eyeballs for that. All mammals throw out body heat as well, so a signature isn't necessarily human. He'll need eyeballs to sort that out too. I've got three big choppers flyable out of eight, so I'd like to hang on to what I've got, and attending my men's funerals tends to piss me off. Aviators live with risks, Mister Arak, but the reasons need to be good ones."

Arak could see the expression on the colonel's face and realized it was time to shut up. He was distracted by the Tomcat landing. It wasn't exactly sucking on fumes, but the major didn't ever want to see his fuel gauges that low again either. He was in the operations centre minutes after landing.

"A successful mission, Major. To be honest I didn't think you had a chance."

"It was my young RO, Colonel. I wouldn't have thought about using missiles to look for a heat signature."

The colonel led the major to a large wall map with Arak trailing behind. The XO peered and pointed. "There, on the tip of that isolated ridge."

The colonel made a few calculations. "By the beard of Allah, that's nearly 250 nautical miles away. At least two hours flying, and a half an hour to refuel."

"That's why I suggested a dawn start. If a helicopter leaves here at five, it could refuel at Azar and be searching not long after first light. Our own pilot won't be tired either, but the fugitives will be. They won't get far at night."

Arak was beginning to understand the problems and wisely held his peace. These professionals wouldn't be interested in his opinions anyway.

"You think you hit someone as well?"

"It was all a bit quick, Colonel and I couldn't hang around. Either I hit someone or they dropped a big pile of clothing."

"Good, that should slow them down." Arak was jubilant, but then he stopped smiling abruptly.

Two pairs of eyes as cold as an arctic dawn skewered him from a metre away. It was the colonel who spoke.

"There's a pilot out there and he flew over 500 miles bloody without your people getting a whiff of him. You said he was British Navy as well, Mister Arak, and military pilots are trained in escape and evasion. You haven't caught him yet, and they haven't got far to go. I wouldn't get too cocky until they're in the bag, if I were you."

Arak's gaze slid sideways. This was an exclusive club he would never belong to with an inbuilt sentiment he'd never understand. Aircrew may end up having to fight each other, but now he realized that's not what it was about. Underneath, they were a brotherhood who operated under a different code, who marched to a different drum. They would do what they had to, but wouldn't like doing it, and would remember every aircraft they'd ever splashed. He was about to challenge air force integrity and commitment, but thought better of it. For them, there was nothing personal in this at all. The colonel dismissed the major then spoke into a phone.

"Get some sleep at the helicopter squadron, Mister Arak. You've got a five o'clock take-off. They'll fix you up with some food." He deliberately turned his back.

Nick led up the mini-avalanche to the crest only a hundred yards above. Amini brought up the rear in scrub was juvenile and undeveloped. The lightly crumpled ground made the footing easier, and when they reached the summit, there wasn't much scrub below either. It was Iran, so that was no surprise, but the monochrome views were staggering even though it was rapidly getting darker. A few villages nestled at the foot of the ridge, marked by dim, flickering oil lamps, and a minor road led into them.

Only one set of vehicle headlights wavered drunkenly in the mid-distance, and further away it looked totally deserted. Nick knew there were more villages out there somewhere, but the smoky lanterns didn't throw enough light to mark them.

The rolling ridges of the foothills showed vaguely as ominous dark shadows, but beyond them, the black, foreboding mountains were only noticeable because they blotted out bright stars to the west. Nick pointed out the glowing dot in a sea of grey that was Salmas, and took a bearing from the luminescent markings on the small emergency compass.

Farhad carried the launcher, the girl the much lighter Tikka, and Nick wrestled with the bag when he led off down the slope. The villages at his feet were illuminated enough to see, so Nick headed away from them in case they had dogs. And the footing was easier when they reached the base of the slope, so there he pushed them harder still. A large amber moon had dragged itself up from the eastern horizon by then, and it was doing its bit to help.

Chapter Fifty

The padded, imitation leather armchairs in the briefing room were smothered by a cloying, quiet darkness, but dim light from the passageway spilled though a partially open door. It was momentarily blocked by a young second lieutenant as he pushed through the gap. He shook Arak vigorously. The policeman started, initially confused. There were no curtains on the window and it was still deep night outside, only reflecting the image of the dimly illuminated doorway in the glass. Arak struggled upright, hit a switch, and the lightly sleeping men around him woke instantly.

"There's bread and cheese in the fridge and canned milk for coffee if you want it. The aircraft will be ready for you in twenty minutes." The youngster didn't seem overawed by the team or its collection of weapons either. There was contempt in the way he said it.

One of Arak's men was still chewing when the team trooped outside to an oil-stained concrete hard-standing eerily lit by deck level orange sodium lights. Several ground crew milled around a whining start trolley, their warm, moist breath condensing in the frosty night air. No other lights burned except in the glass-panelled top of the control tower.

A green-helmeted crewman sat Arak's team in the chopper's cheap seats with ear defenders, while the co-pilot scrambled over the transmission platform above. Arak got strapped into the jump seat in the rear of the cockpit. A foam bound wire headset was fitted over the top of his head. They'd all entered through a lowered ramp at the rear, but the machine had a forward door up near the cockpit, and a large sliding panel behind and opposite. It was a big helicopter.

The aircraft captain signaled to start one after the co-pilot settled. There was a quiet rumble above them that initially wasn't very noisy, but when he flashed up two and then the big rotor blades started turning, the noise increased dramatically. The complicated machine padded on the bulbous, black tyres in sympathy with the whistling blades.

A light breeze drifted spasmodically from the north, so the chopper lumbered awkwardly along a concrete taxiway until it faced into it. The pilot flicked on a small overhead spot, had a final check of his map, and then lifted. He accelerated into wind before turning to the southwest.

By midnight they were panting raggedly. Their wisps of breath condensed quickly in the bitter night air, though none of them were near exhaustion. They hadn't slept for some time either, but constant adrenalin rushes had destroyed any desire to anyway. In four hours they'd trekked sixteen kilometres by Nick's topographical, carefully avoiding any villages, and so far it had been uneventful. He was ecstatic.

Over time they did spook the odd flock of sheep grazing quietly ahead of them, but the animals free-ranged and seemed used to humans around them. They made half-hearted lunges if surprised, but didn't trot far before their heads were down tearing at the short tussock again.

Nick squinted at his watch and then signalled a break. All three sank thankfully to the ground, and it was ten minutes before Laleh pulled the last of the food and a water bottle from the black bag. Nick gave them another twenty minutes while they shared.

"Okay, guys, it's time to go again. There's a healthy river only a few klicks ahead and I don't think we can cross it on foot. The map does show the road south from Salmas crossing that river a bit further on though, so there

362

must be a bridge there. Aslanik is only eight klicks beyond that, but left of the direct track to the pass. If anybody is looking for us, they may keep to the east. Let's hope so anyway."

"Do you want me to carry the bag for a while, Nickie?"

"I'm okay, Lil. How about you, Fred?"

"I'm okay as well, Nick. The gun is on a thick sling."

"Right-o. Let's get this over with."

Nick picked up the pace and they were looking at the low rails that edged the bridge within the hour. The navigation was only fifty metres from being spot on.

Distance, not theatrics was what it was all about, so rather than climb a high range at night, the RH52 pilot deviated south at 500 feet until he hit Sarab. After that, he followed a tumbling, silver river which took him all the way to Tabriz. He was there in just over an hour and skirted south of the city.

From there, he could easily pick out the distinctive geometric sheen of steel railway lines fading towards the horizon, and that took him another forty nautical miles further to Azar Shahr. Both line features shimmered silver in the pale moonlight from that height, and now it was only another sixty miles to the site. They had to refuel first, but it was thirty minutes to any sort of decent light anyway.

Arak and his crew took the opportunity to stretch stiff legs while the chopper refuelled at Azar. Now it could operate for four more hours, so the young air force captain ordered box lunches for eight for when they did it again. They got airborne as the eastern horizon was changing from an insipid cream strip to a strengthening pale-blue corona.

Twenty minutes later, the pilot offered Arak the air map. Arak shrugged. He'd never searched from a helicopter before and had no idea how to play it. The captain was unimpressed, and let it show. He took charge of the quest himself.

"There are a couple of villages within a mile of the crash site so we'd better question them first." He stabbed with a finger. "What time they started out and whether any of the escapers were injured will affect how far they get and the villagers may have seen something." Arak nodded but said nothing. Air searches were out of his league and he knew it.

"We'll be keeping the beast running when we do it so don't waste any time either, Mister Arak. If they don't know anything, don't try interrogating them." There was venom in that.

They were questioning the first village thirty minutes later.

Nick moved them in a crouch to the span and watched from the whispering grasses on the road's edge. Kilometres away, the yellowed beams of another car challenged the darkness hesitantly, but it wasn't heading towards them, and the rest of the countryside reflected a cold, eerie moonlight. Nothing was close, no houses showed, and no sentries ambled along the bridge's tarmac either. The group moved forward hesitantly, but the sound of slipping rocks and hollow, ringing footsteps filtered from across the span. Pulse rates raced and hearts bumped. They shrank down again instinctively.

A herd of foraging goats drifted through the low, swirling ground mist, the erect head and gimlet eyes of the leader riveted on them as they cowered. The buck knew they were there, even knew what they were, but he was used to men. They wouldn't be a threat to his charges. He dropped his head again and the animals behind continued browsing contently by the edges of the road. The relief was palpable.

"It looks pretty quiet, so we'll save time by going together. Aslanik is northwest of here so we'll angle left after we cross the bridge and get well clear before I take some bearings. Okay, you guys first."

The three scuttled across the span in an unnecessary but instinctive half crouch. The noise of water crashing and cascading violently under their feet drowned out any sound of their hurried passage. The bridge had obviously been the only real choice. Laleh led down a small pebble and sand shoulder after, before striking out northwest. The goats chewed on, totally ignoring their presence.

Nick stopped again when they were two klicks from the road and peered at the map with a pencil torch and strained, tired eyes. He took a bearing to march on.

"How are you holding up, Lily?"

"I'm okay, Nick, but my legs are a bit tired."

"Jesus, love, your legs are a bit tired! I'm completely knackered. What about you, Fred?"

"Closer to you than Laleh, Nick."

"Would you boys like me to carry your stuff as well then?" She giggled when she said it, and even though he knew it was said in fun, it galvanised him again.

"Right guys, I'm pretty sure these people are Kurds, so we'll try for a guide at Aslanik. It's only thirty odd klicks to the border from there, but they'll know the best way to do it. It's bound to be further north and uphill too, so trust me it won't be quick. You'll be carrying the baggage, won't you, Lil?" They snorted at that, and almost as soon as they started off the land began to rise.

It took a tense two hours before Nick picked up black, more geometrical, shapes on the horizon above. It was still some time from dawn, but the sky was washed a lighter grey by a slowly waning moon, and the ebony houses and low trees contrasted darkly. They moved closer before holing up in a shallow wadi only metres from the dark buildings. Soft, cool sand trickled insidiously into their boots.

They hadn't come across any animals for a while, and now they could hear and smell why. There were extensive animal pens made of tangled, tortured branches around the houses, and quivering, high-pitched bleats came mostly from lambs. Breeding stock were obviously locked up at night. They whispered about what to do next, but it became superfluous in the end.

A weak gleam of lanterns flared through wooden shutters in several houses almost simultaneously, and several doors opened at the same time. The gaping entrances threw weak shafts of light onto the dusty brown surrounds. They realized they hadn't been heard when one of several males moved away from a house to urinate. That close, the village was backdropped by scratchy light, and the baggy pantaloons stuffed into knee high boots and long-sleeved, billowing shirt confirmed he was Kurdish.

"I can speak some, Kurdish, Nick, so you stay here with Laleh until I call. I'll leave the cannon, that may piss them off, but I'll need the bag with the money." Nick passed it across and Amini started walking.

He didn't try to hide his approach and the villagers spotted him instantly. They called out sharply as they moved slowly towards him, and by the time he was near the houses, there were upwards of a dozen males outside. A child's smaller head was silhouetted behind a door jamb.

Whatever talk they talked was animated and vigorous for several minutes before Amini whistled then beckoned with an arm over his head. Nick and Laleh approached cautiously, but it was an anti-climax. Everyone wanted to shake their hands.

"This is Baz. He's the village elder." Amini pointed to one of several large men, all dressed similarly. Broad cummerbunds confined spreading stomachs, and the faces sported dark glittering eyes, large hooked noses and drooping, walrus moustaches. The facial hair on the younger males, although trying hard, hadn't quite got there yet.

Then the ex-commander pointed to a slender youth. "His son Gizko will be our guide, Nick, and wonder of wonders, they're saddling ponies for us. They don't do much on foot around here. Laleh and I can ride, how about you?"

"I've never been on a horse in my life, Fred, but you won't get me off with a bloody crowbar until we get to Turkey."

Amini translated and the males guffawed.

Two males leading four horses appeared shortly after. All the animals looked a sleek black in that light, with saddles of soft sheep's leather, and thick fleeces replaced saddle blankets across their broad, glistening backs. Each saddle had a pommel with a canvas rifle scabbard pinned on the front bracer, and brightly-coloured tassels hung from the bridles and the saddle furniture. The colours were only marginally muted even in that poor light. And by then several women had also joined the group. It was as if they had landed amongst some religious ritual at some time in the distant past.

Amini discarded the cotton bag that had held their food as he went through the grip for a bundle of notes, but one of the women knew exactly what it was. She disappeared into the nearest house and returned minutes later with it half filled. By then, Amini had turned to Baz with a wad. The big man wiggled both hands in front of him and pointed to the woman who had collected the bread and cheese. It was she who accepted the money, and Amini had added a generous bonus to it. The woman muttered something and the whole assembly muttered in approval.

"It's not a huge amount really, Nick, but it's probably more cash than they see in a year. Once they knew that the government was after us, they were happy to do it for free anyway." Amini shook his head gently with a light smile.

Nick smiled too, but knew time was not on their side. He'd been given a docile-looking mare that looked as if she'd been around a while, and it attracted good natured comments as he climbed on. Once up, he looked stable enough with his feet through the stirrups, so a male hung the bag on his pommel.

Laleh slid the Tikka into her scabbard before mounting the skittish horse being held for her, but Fred's rifle combination was big and wouldn't fit into his scabbard. It was strapped to the rear of his saddle instead. He mounted sedately, but Gizko vaulted onto his horse with the exuberance of his youthful years. He led off without looking back. The other three waved.

They'd only gone about three kilometres when they hit a well-maintained bitumen road. Gizko muttered to Amini and held them in a thicket until two vehicles cleared from the west.

"The road goes to Turkey, Nick, but there's a big border post on it and the mountains either side are impassable. It's a few extra klicks, but there's a fairly obscure route a bit further north."

Nick nodded.

He stood in his saddle to eye the fractured bands of primrose spreading swiftly on the eastern horizon. They started to climb in earnest.

Chapter Fifty-One

It was light enough to make out the Bell easily and the religious cops climbed out to poke around. The small chopper was beyond repair, with jagged bullet holes exposing bright, torn aluminum, and shimmering Perspex shards scattered wide around the clearing. The rear rotor blade was also shot through and hung precariously by shreds of jagged aluminum, with the engine also riddled in several places. And to dispel any doubts, the distorted fuselage canted heavily to the left on a crumpled port skid. It had the forlorn, abandoned look of the dead.

They found Sinclair's body quickly enough, but Arak ignored it. A quick glance told him it was European, but it wasn't Evans, and he was the one with the skills and knowledge. The discarded baggage yielded nothing either. The 52 D pilot was studying his map when Arak strapped himself back in.

"Nothing."

"About fifteen Kilometres ahead there's a fairly large river flowing down from the mountains with only one bridge across it. They'd have to cross there, and beyond there's a village called Derik on their route. It's about ten klicks northwest of the bridge, near a smaller river that starts on the border. The pilot would have local maps and he'd see all that. I bet that's the way they went. We'll sweep along the river with FLIR and then visit the village. They'll be looking for a guide, but all the villagers around here are Kurdish so don't expect too much from them."

Arak nodded as the pilot got under way. "Okay, we'll check out the villages over the hill before we get going." A few minutes later they stopped again.

The police scrambled out. The villagers were definitely Kurds, so Arak didn't expect much help, and he wasn't disappointed. Without exception, they were sullen, suspicious and reluctant to talk, but in the end he knew they were telling the truth. None had seen any fugitives. Sure they had seen the big jet pass overhead and heard the gun fire, but no-one had climbed the hill to investigate. It was government business, not their problem.

Gizko kept to the lower foothills for nearly two hours and put ten kilometres behind them on the easier terrain. At the start, they were riding through an eerie half-light, the Zagros range holding back the dawn until it flooded the gullies under the mountains in a startling blaze of contrasting pastels.

The lake changed from dull gun-metal to a dazzling silver with the strengthening sun, while the ragged snow-capped hills to the east showed a pale yellow on the higher peaks. In contrast, the high ranges to the west reflected a shimmering titanium white, looking infinitely colder and much more menacing this close up. Nick knew he was right not to have challenged them.

Their guide reined in shortly after they'd reached another shallow water course that tumbled and swirled across their path. The col leading to Turkey started a few kilometres beyond. "We ford here, it is not deep. But rest first."

Nick understood the gestures and slid out of his saddle with a grateful groan. He massaged sore buttocks as the others followed, before handing his reins to Laleh. He fished around in the bag for the binoculars and swept back towards the misty, isolated spur they had walked from with them.

"Oh shit!" That got everybody's attention.

"What is it?"

"There's a bloody big chopper following the river we crossed. It's not going fast, but it's almost at the bridge."

Amini translated urgently for the guide.

"Mount, we ride." Gizko was aboard before any of them. Laleh held Nick's reins until he was settled then flung herself into her saddle.

With water reaching only just above the horse's fetlocks their guide urged them on, and after they'd cleared the stream, they cantered. Nick stood in his stirrups. It was safer and more comfortable than trying to sit.

He saw the 52 D land near a village not ten kilometres away just as Gizko turned into the mountains proper.

As soon as they had cleared the ridge, the helo pilot switched on FLIR, and pointed out a black square that looked like a small radar display to Arak. Within seconds, the screen faded from black to irregular flickering greys as wavering bands showed up the heat differences in the soils and rocks.

"If there is a significant temperature difference you'll hear a series of beeps, and anything really warm will show on the screen in bright orange blips. Its range is only about seven kilometres though, so don't look too far ahead."

Arak nodded, and his pilot reduced to a more prudent sixty knots to search, and almost immediately there was a series of beeps. Arak leaned towards the screen excitedly. It was covered in deep amber sausages.

"Sheep." The pilot pointed to a flock racing away ahead of them. It happened twice more before the chopper reached the river, and by then Arak's nerves were shredded. The houses threw up beeps and images as well.

A small knot of people congregated beside the houses to watch the helicopter land. Arak rushed forward to interrogate them. There were only women there, the men were already out with the animals, but that didn't matter all that much. The females were just as uncommunicative as the men would be, and the children looked at him with an innate suspicion as well.

For the first few 100 metres, the ravine was steep and narrow, the grass brown and thin, with huge, grey boulders hemming the riders into single file. But not long after that, they reached a grassy plateau that barely sloped at all. It was seventy metres further on before the large rocks elbowed closer together once more. Nick called softly and the other three stopped. The sloping plains had opened up behind them now and he could see the helicopter with the naked eye. Derik was only twelve kilometres below and behind by his reckoning. Nick refocused again.

"Oh shit, it's got FLIR!" The large black half dome was obvious under the machine's chin.

"What's that, Nickie?" He told her, and both the Aminis looked shocked that such things existed.

The guide hadn't understood. Farhad explained then looked at Nick.

"What does it mean, really?"

"Even if we hide it will pick up our body heat, Fred. It's fairly short range, but it won't miss us in these cold gullies, and there aren't many places we can hide."

As he spoke, the RH 52 lifted and tracked up the river into the foothills.

"We can't outrun them, Fred. Show me how to use that fucking thing and get Laleh out of here. I'll try to hit them when they move into this gully. The chopper's got a mini-gun turret as well. I didn't want, Lil to know that."

"How long have we got, Nick?"

"Three ravines before they get to ours. About twenty minutes, mate."

Amini looked wistfully towards the summit. "Laleh's future is with you now, Nick, not me. I know it was a joke, but when you first agreed to pick me up, you said I'd owe you big time. I do, mate, more than you'll ever really know, and it's time to pay up. I've used the launcher dozens of times. I'll do this bit."

Nick started to object.

"Shut it, Nick, we haven't got time. If you move up the slope and show yourself briefly, they'll latch onto you, but have to land to follow up. The plateau is the only place they can do it." He pointed at a jumble of boulders to their left.

"I'll hide in there and hit them when they hover." He dismounted and unstrapped the cannon.

"Take my horse, and put on a good show, but remember that bloody mini-gun. No arguments, Nick— get going."

Amini meant it, it was in his eyes, he wouldn't hear any more arguments. Nick grabbed the reins and turned back up the slope. A hundred metres ahead, he herded the others into a large crevice between huge rough boulders and explained what had to be done. Laleh looked worried as she translated for the Kurd. She lifted the Tikka from the scabbard before Gizko pushed their mounts deeper into the large crevice. Nick squeezed back to the entrance.

He could see most of the sharp, dark rocks that Farhad had indicated although nothing of the Iranian himself. He stepped further onto the path to get a good view of the clearing, and by then could hear the throb of the machine. The big helicopter tracked fairly slowly along the river, but needed a fist-full of power to reach the ridge.

"The crest is the border, but that's all that marks it up here, Mister Arak. I'm turning now, and I'll need to keep the speed up to do it. Air speed and ground speed are different things, and I don't intend running out of power and crashing. Colder, dense air tumbles down from the mountain tops up here, so we'll have to come at each ravine from below. You understand that?"

Arak nodded before muttering a yes. The RH 52 pilot kept his air speed constant as he pulled away from the border, and the cop saw what he meant. The air speed indicator stayed flickering on sixty, but the machine accelerated rapidly over the ground with the katabatic wind coming from behind. He pulled around in a large loop and attacked the next canyon. Half way up, they got beeps and sausages on the screen again and Arak leaned excitedly towards the monitor.

"Wild goats," the pilot grunted, pointing ahead. The next canyon was the same, with probably the same scattering herd providing the beeps. They lined up on the next ravine.

Whilst still four kilometres from it, the unit lit up once more. Arak looked ahead with significantly less enthusiasm, but this time it was different. He picked up a figure on the path made small by distance and obscured by thick cloths and a woollen hat. Then unexpectedly another.

"That must be them, Captain. Can you drop us and then cut them off from above?"

"I can get ahead of them, yes. I'll drop you on that plateau ahead, and move up the slope. If I can hover, I can turn down wind and put the gun on them. We'll be like a vice and I'll try not to shoot you." He smiled and then let his crewman know what he was doing. He rushed through his checks before lifting the nose.

Nick knew the chopper crew had picked him up, but when he turned back, he almost knocked Laleh over. He gathered her in his arms and wrestled them both behind the rocks.

"What the hell are you doing?" There was concern and anger in it.

"Making sure they concentrate on us." She wasn't grinning but she wasn't contrite either.

He shook his head.

"Well, I'll give them one more look, and don't you dare follow me. It'll be very short."

She smiled and pecked him. It was tense and dangerous, and he couldn't believe she'd done that. Nick showed himself briefly again as the big chopper came into a hover, and as he dodged back towards the rocks, he heard three vicious cracks from the 7.62 millimetre. He stopped and looked.

Farhad had stood to take his shots, and even from up there the Welshman could see the wind-screen starred by three crazed epicentres in front of the pilot. Immediately after, he realized that the windscreen must be armoured. The shots hadn't penetrated and Amini realized it too. The heavy crash of the grenade launcher was followed almost immediately by the rip of the mini-gun.

Amini dropped at the same time as a ball of fire and smoke erupted around the forward right wheel of the machine. The chopper wobbled dangerously sideways and nearly hit the deck. But not quite. It recovered within feet of the grass before struggling upwards again, a desperate pilot fighting to get it back under control. Nick raced for Amini and his cannon, but was still a hundred metres away when he realized that he wasn't going to make it. He turned back for the crevice, but he wasn't going to make that either.

The RH 52 had staggered well left during its recovery, but now it was responding and stabilised in a low hover. The right front wheel and oleo dangled uselessly, and a splash of blackened soot smeared the aircraft's chin, but that was all. Nick could clearly see the wolfish grin on the pilot's face through his opened side window. There were other swarthy faces alongside him, and several vaguer figures piled behind that. It all registered in a split second before the mini turret started swivelling smoothly towards him. He dived for a small rock pile just ahead, but knew instantly that it wouldn't do much good.

Chapter Fifty-Two

Nick had pushed Laleh deep into the rocky crevice and it was several seconds before she reacted. He was already fifty metres ahead of her when she took it all in. Then she gasped. The chopper was damaged but still airborne, and its pilot was looking at him intently. Nick skidded to a halt. She could see he wasn't going to make it too.

Everything seemed to slow down. Her brother was sprawled metres in front of Nick, exposed but not moving, and the chin turret was swiveling. Instinctively, she knew what it must be. Farhad was down and her man was about to get perforated, but they hadn't seen her. She didn't hesitate.

The big helo had staggered drunkenly to her right with Laleh on the higher track surrounded by boulders. She and Nick often flew with their side windows open. This pilot did too.

A starred, but intact, windscreen told her that bullets couldn't penetrate it, but she could see the pilot's upper body clearly through the side window. Laleh rested her left hand, reasoning that a rock wouldn't vibrate.

And it was some sort of omen. The thought triggered a subconscious vision of a weather-beaten face that always seemed to be smiling at her, always seemed to be encouraging her. 'Take a breath and hold it.' She did. 'Pick your spot on the target.' The pilot's white helmet stood out through the opened side window against the darker surrounds inside. 'Squeeze, don't jerk the trigger.' She did that too.

Laleh had no idea how far the mini-gun had traversed, but it hadn't got around to firing before she did. After that, she would never know. It wasn't a long or even a difficult shot, just over seventy metres, but even with the powerful scope, she didn't see where the tiny bullet hit. Its effect she couldn't miss.

The pilot's head flew to the left as if bludgeoned with a sledge hammer and his right hand was grasped firmly around the cyclic. It all became inevitable. The clenched hand followed the rest of the upper body and the machine was less than ten feet above the ground. The helicopter rolled heavily to the left, and the huge rotor blades churned viciously into the dirt in a fractured, deadly sequence.

Earth, grass, rocks and disembodied metallic parts sprayed skywards initially, but now the tail rotor was pumping out far more aerodynamic force than the mangled, slowing main blades could ever demand. It swung rapidly upwards, dragging the tail of the machine with it. It paused for a micro-second, and then plunged the last few feet into the turf. A huge red and yellow fireball reaching over forty metres high followed the crash, and thick black smoke obscured the flames within seconds. A low-pitched rumble echoed up and down the canyon for longer than that. She was awed by what she'd done, but there wasn't time for it.

Laleh chambered a round as she raced towards Nick, reaching him as he struggled to sit up. The rocks and his higher elevation had protected him from the blast, so he wasn't injured, but he was dazed and temporarily deafened. When he did focus her face was inches from his.

"Shit!" That's all he could say initially, but the tension eased. That was his response to most dramas. He shook himself and grabbed her. "I don't think I've ever said it before, Laleh, but, Jesus, I love you woman." He hugged her heatedly. It was something she'd always wanted to hear despite the circumstances. She smiled as she dragged her gaze to her brother, but he still hadn't moved. Her hand leapt to her mouth and the tears sprinkled.

Nick followed her stare and dragged them both to their feet. He left the Tikka with Laleh, she could use it far more effectively than he could right then, and instead grasped her hand. And although they were still meres from Farhad, he realized it would be useless.

Nick turned towards Laleh, intending to stop her, but she resisted fiercely even though tears now washed her cheeks. He crouched beside Amini and rolled him over. There was no carotid pulse and when he saw the three big holes in the torso, he knew why. Another round had hit the cannon's breech and the whole of Amini's upper torso was saturated with a red, sticky gore from shrapnel wounds. Nick looked up and shook his head. Laleh's sobs almost choked her.

Nick held her close while she got through the initial grief and slowly the sobs reduced to sniffles. He wasn't stupid. He knew more would follow when they were somewhere safer, but knew this had to be done first. Then she surprised him yet again. Her eyes were still brimming, but she quickly refocused.

"Help me put Farhad's body into the rocks, Nick, he'd want that, but we must get out of here right away. Someone probably saw that fire."

He nodded solemnly, not sure if he could be that strong himself.

They didn't have to lift the body far and rocks to cover him were right there with him. Laleh was the first to start and after they'd finished Nick pulled her to him again. "I'm so sorry it's all happened this close to the border, Lil. Both of them gone in twenty-four hours." He was close to tears himself and missed what she mumbled. He raised her head gently and Laleh started again.

"I loved Farhad dearly, Nick, but you must understand why I'm saying this." She paused.

"Subconsciously he might have wanted it to happen. Some time ago he asked me what an Iranian naval commander could do in the real world with no papers and little more than patrol boat experience. I think it was why he hoped it would work out for us."

"He was being pessimistic, though, Lil. Dartmouth would still have records to prove he was qualified, and he did an overseas staff course as well. We could have sorted something out."

"There's something else though, isn't there? You men in the West may do brave things in battles, maybe even die, but it's usually when you're trying to save yourselves or especially your friends. In the East, it's a bit different and always has been. A lot of eastern men treat their women like crap, almost like slaves; yet go overboard to achieve a glorious, honourable death. But it's all in the mind, really. There's nothing glorious about dying."

"I suppose you're right, Lil. I've never really thought about it much. I do know I've lost a few mates over the years though, and can't think of anyone who wanted it to happen."

"That's what I mean, and this is the sociologist in me talking. Dying when you're doing something heroic for others is one thing. That's selfless. But dying so your mates can call it glorious is selfish. It's more about you and your ego. I'll weep some more for Farhad yet, but not for all that long. It was in his genes to seek a glorious death, but just like Jock's, it was a completely selfless act that caused it in the end. Both of their deaths were noble, they died for us, and that's what I'll always remember." She shook herself. "Let's look at this helicopter before we go." She led off down the slope still sniffling.

Nick followed. He could think of nothing to say.

The RH 52 hadn't burnt much. It was the unused fuel that had caused the huge fireball and pillar of smoke. The cockpit was destroyed, but the rear was less affected, looking more like a scorched cylindrical cavern. It was the enormous and rapid depletion of oxygen that had got them, and in many ways he was glad they'd died quickly.

Fire was always at the back of an aviator's mind. He stretched to look into what had been the cockpit window.

Crisp, blackened corpses were melted into the plastic and upholstery around them, and scorched extremities were little more than blackened, shrunken bone.

Laleh was poking around the ramp at the rear at the same time, and Nick heard her exclaim loudly. He rushed to where she was peering at an almost unburnt body thrown clear of the ramp. The left leg and neck were at weird, unnatural angles and the face was smeared with blood, but it was easily recognisable. She turned into Nick. She couldn't speak initially.

"That bastard was the one who knocked me around at the embassy, Nick. I'll never forget his face." She was still gasping.

Nick brought a gentle hand to the back of her head, and pulled her closer. "That's all you need to know then, Lil. It's gone in a circle. You're pretty much free of it all now."

"If he was here, the other one might be too. I've got to look."

Nick didn't want her in there. It didn't look nice and it didn't smell nice either.

"It's probably not safe, and there's nothing to see, love. It's over. Let's be on our way."

"I must do this. Please come with me?"

He couldn't deny her this final quest. "Okay, but you hang on to me and watch where you walk. You'll see lines of rivets in the deck that have got spars underneath. I'll be walking on them and make sure you do too."

Laleh nodded. He led off, and peered below and above them as she slowly followed. Once they were enclosed, the smell wasn't just unpleasant, it was appalling.

Just inside the ramp there was another half-burned body. Nick stopped so she could peer at it. She shook her head. He kept moving, and when he neared the cockpit, he pinched his nostrils. So did she. They were both fighting the sickly, sweet stench of roasted pork and Nick was sure he could taste it as well. He eased her around him so she could see the awful carnage on the flight deck. He gave her a minute.

"Right, Lil, there's nothing here. Let's go." He was still pinching his nose, and it was more a distorted squeak. The girl nodded and started to turn too, but looked down to navigate around a corpse. She gave a distorted squeak herself, pointing at two black fleshless arms almost at her feet. They were little more than charred bone, but they had a defined shape to them. What they had been was obvious, but the rest of the blackened, flaked heap was unrecognisable. He couldn't see what she was pointing at. Nick kept dragging, and Laleh didn't resist until they were well clear of the scorched machine.

"I'm sorry, Lil, but that was bloody gruesome. I couldn't see anything recognisable and I didn't like the way the metal was groaning. I didn't see what you were pointing at either."

Laleh looked at him with what seemed relief.

"There was a class ring on one of the fingers, Nick. An American one. That was the thing I most remember about the other one. He'd obviously stolen it off someone at the Embassy." She breathed deeply. It was almost a sigh.

When they turned up hill, the Kurd was a few metres away holding onto the four horses.

"I'm ready now, Nick. Let's get on with this."

He was unable to shake images of her in a horned helmet, waving a grisly battle-axe around her head. And someone writing music about her.

Gizko sheathed the rifle and hung the black bag on the spare horse, took up its reins and led off. This time Nick mounted on his own. He waited for Laleh to pull in behind Gizko and then slotted in behind her.

They climbed for another two hours, rarely talking, each sunk into memories of what had happened and what it meant. The metallic ring of the animal's steel shoes on rock and squeak of the harness leather were the only significant sounds.

Chapter Fifty-Three

The track remained narrow with just enough room for them to move in file. Tall boulders and outcrops squeezed in on them from both sides. Nick had expected staggering panoramic views, but they were climbing within a tall mountain range, and it just didn't happen. The slope did ease however, and the grassy clearings got bigger and more frequent, until the ground levelled and then started to descend.

They passed between two lichen-streaked uneven pillars that towered upright like a grand portal, and beyond, the ground spread rapidly into a widening plateau. Their guide reined in and shouted down slope in Kurdish. Nick and Laleh stopped, waiting for a reply. They were still surrounded by rolling hillocks, and jagged peaks still climbed well above, but now Nick could see stunted bushes following the banks of twisted, rocky run-offs. And lower down two men on ponies tended a flock. An answer came in the same sing-song language, but Laleh didn't understand it. Gizko turned to her. When he spoke it was in Farsi.

"My father's brother. He runs his herds on Turkish grass." Laleh turned and started translating for Nick, but when she got to the Turkish bit both their faces registered something bordering on shock simultaneously. They spun to the Kurd as one. A small smile registered on his face, the first emotion he'd shown since they'd started off. He nodded a couple of times and then stabbed a slim, brown index finger downwards.

"Turkey." It was all he said before pulling his pony's head around and setting off again.

Laleh's left fist lifted to her mouth, her eyes brimming, and her right hand shot out towards Nick. All at the same time. His was already on the way, and met hers somewhere in between. Neither could say anything. Gizko kept going without looking back and was fifty metres ahead when Nick cleared his throat.

"We've done it, Laleh." His voice shook with emotion. She still couldn't speak at all. "We're about fifteen klicks from Orenburc, a couple of hours at most." He slapped her pony on the rump, and slotted in behind her again.

Somehow he expected it to look different now, but it didn't. The sun wasn't all that far from disappearing behind the jagged mountains to the west even though it was only mid-afternoon, and their guide was keeping them higher, where the rays still hit. The rocks and hills in the distance had already taken on varying shades of blue and purple, and shortly after passing through a walnut grove, they came to a village that looked exactly the same as those across the border.

Gizko yelled a greeting to the villagers as they rode through and exchanged a few words with a group of males. When they were clear again, he called to Laleh over his shoulder. She turned to Nick.

"Gizko will stay here at his uncle's village on his way back. Twenty minutes to go." She'd looked back at him a few times, sadly, he thought. It was the first she had spoken in over an hour.

Nick had to surmise that she was thinking about the two who hadn't made it, or maybe it was the realization that she'd actually killed other human beings. The first time had that effect on people. But shortly after, their guide reined in on a grass shoulder. It drove it from his mind.

Gizko dismounted and they hopped down with him. They were perched high on a spur overlooking a deep valley climbing gently towards them from the east. A wide bitumen road and railway ran throughout its length, its origins lost in the swirls of white, yellow and orange sands in the distance. The cluttered outer suburbs of a small city nestled close in a basin to the west, with some houses already sprawling towards them on the lower, gentle slopes below. It would be a short walk. The nearest houses were barely a kilometre away.

Gizko pointed out some buildings alongside the railway to the east, and to the city in the west. He muttered something in Farsi again.

"The border post is that set of buildings seven kilometres east, the city is Orenburck." Now that it had happened it seemed an anti-climax.

Nick lifted the black bag off the pommel and rummaged until he located the boxes of Tikka ammunition. Then on impulse, a wad of notes. He pointed to the rifle, then to the guide, before handing him the ammunition and the money. A deal had been struck and Gizko hadn't expected anything more. He looked surprised when he took Nick's offered hand and shook it. When Laleh hugged him, he looked even more embarrassed. He strung the spare reins though a rope, and took off back the way they had come. The three un-laden ponies trotted with heads stretched high behind him, and after he'd called a farewell he didn't look back again. Nick put his arm around Laleh's shoulder, watching him go before staring down the slope.

"Okay, Lil, let's get on with it."

The girl didn't say anything initially, but she didn't move either.

"Have we got a few minutes, Nick?" She was still looking at the city.

"Take all the time you want, Laleh." They had one set of warm clothes each, a half empty bag and their identities, but they were free. She sat on a boulder looking at the city, not at him.

She sighed. "We finally got here, Nick, and it changes a lot of things. You've done everything you possibly could for me, but we only hinted at a future really, and you knew I needed that at the time. I won't hold you to that now. Things are different."

Her reticence and melancholy over the last few hours now made perfect sense. She had grown in confidence over recent months, and slain her quota of dragons, but there was one area that undermined it all for her. He reckoned he knew what it was. Nick dragged the black bag closer and sat beside her while he fished around for his British passport. He extracted a sheet of thick cream paper folded in four.

"This is a formal Embassy letter, Laleh, okay? It's got an address and a file reference number at the top, and this is the meat of what it says.

'To whom it may concern.' Captain Nicholas Evans and Ms Laleh Amini have been recognised as in a de-facto relationship for some time by this Embassy. It was to be made permanent here except that current circumstances in Iran have prevented it. During their time together, they have attended a number of both formal and informal occasions at the Embassy's request, and have also assisted with entertaining visiting guests of the Embassy. The couple are recognised by her Britannic Majesty's Representative in Tehran as being in a permanent relationship and it is requested that their status be recognised should they present this document outside Iran."

The head was up now and she was looking at him intently. The dark expressive eyes sparkled with moisture again. "Does that say what I think it does, Nick?"

"Signed and sealed by the Ambassador himself. It's almost as good as a marriage certificate, and when we get to Istanbul, it will be. You'll just have to decide whether you want to be Ms Laleh Amini or Mrs Laleh Evans on the passport they issue you. When we get to London, we can have a religious or more formal civil ceremony if you like, but we don't have to. It's entirely up to you."

By now the moisture had spilled over the eyelids and was gently tumbling down her cheeks. "I like Mrs Laleh Evans, Nick. It sounds as if I really belong somewhere again." She was smiling through the tears now. "Just a couple more things."

Nick took her hand. "Okay. Keep going."

"Jock told me a bit about your childhood, and thought you might be against having children, but I would like us to make babies, if we can." She was looking earnestly into his eyes now and seemed slightly disconcerted when he didn't answer immediately. He was thinking how best to put it.

"I want that too, Laleh, and believe me I've thought about it a lot. Jock said a few things about this to me as well, and I swear on his grave that our kids will never be brought up the way we were. They will never get farmed out with anyone, nor be sent off to a boarding school, nor be looked on as an asset either. Wherever I end up, you'll be there too and so will our kids. If there aren't any schools around, we'll educate them ourselves." His jaws were clamped and there was a determined look in his eye.

"I'm so glad you said that, Nickie, and I know you mean it." She smiled shyly. "I missed a moon three weeks ago. I think it's already happening."

She couldn't meet his eye initially, but the way he grabbed and hugged her left her little choice.

He looked bewildered even though he was grinning broadly.

"None of this is any different than what I wanted, Lil. I'm surprised that you didn't see it before."

"I think I did really, Nickie, but things in the past have made me insecure. I love you so much but still find it difficult to believe you could feel that way about me."

"It works both ways, Laleh. I honestly didn't think I would meet someone I could love, respect and be a little in awe of all at the same time, but here you are and you feel that way too. That's pretty rare, my love, and I would never jeopardise it. Is that it or is there something else?"

"If things had gone differently I would have found Jock's girls on my own, Nick, but I'm not worried about that now. We'll do it together. I just need to read something to you too."

She smiled coyly, rummaging in the bag for the buff envelope that held her degrees and certificates. "It's the letter that Minu sent. It's girl stuff really, telling me what I was afraid to see for myself. She's obviously very fond of you and told me to trust in us and things would be okay. It's just the post script really. It says: 'Lyons Coffee House, Piccadilly Circus, Valentine's Day 1982 at 11 o'clock." She looked up at him.

He nodded. "I'd love to see them again myself. We'll make a shopping weekend of it, and take in a show." Nick was being deliberately casual for her sake. "Don't worry, Laleh. They'll make it."

"That's it then, Nickie. I've got nothing more to bring up, and I feel so much happier now. I couldn't say any of this until I knew we were free." She paused before grinning wickedly herself.

"As we British say, this should all be set in concrete, right?"

He smiled quizzically and nodded.

"Okay, but we'll have to wait until we get to the hotel. It's too bloody cold up here."

Epilogue

They stayed at a small, clean hotel in Orenburc that night and caught the bus that linked to the railway station at Vantat the next morning. There was only one sleeper car on the afternoon train, but then again they were the only takers anyway. There were no dining cars that far east either, but most of the stations they passed through had cafés of a sort, and Nick had American dollars on him. They didn't starve and they made Istanbul the middle of the following morning.

It took several days for the British Consulate to process them fully, but now that Nick had Laleh with him, he found he'd developed a taste for ancient buildings and religious artefacts. He saw parts of the city he'd never seen before and treasures he'd never heard about, but by the following weekend, they were heading for Heathrow as the nucleus of a family.

And their first weeks in London were also hectic. Laleh had been disconcerted by the brief, clinical ceremony at the consulate in Istanbul, and felt more comfortable after a more elaborate civil ceremony in London.

Nick met an old flying mate looking for a job with Bristow's too, and with him and his wife as witnesses did the nuptials thing again. A decent registrar's ceremony, a healthy, fragrant bunch of flowers, and an up-market dinner date for the four of them, and Laleh felt properly married. Nick re-established his Australian Citizenship at Australia House on the Strand next, and added Laleh as family.

And helicopter pilots were still in big demand, so within a few days, he was also contracted to Bristow's. They were just about the largest helicopter operator in Europe, and he would be flying S61s, the civil version of the Sea King he'd flown in the services, but the destinations this time were the big oil platforms in the North Sea.

And Bristow's turned out to be quite extensive. Its North Sea operation in Aberdeen, Scotland, serviced the rigs in the North Sea, and when they got there, Nick met several pilots he'd known in the services. Other, mostly ex-military pilots who'd been to exotic overseas areas filled in the gaps, and not surprisingly, several of the wives had their origins in exotic places as well. It was not that unusual amongst such a well-travelled crew.

In a country that was already cosmopolitan, it was one of the most racially diverse corners in the United Kingdom, and the atmosphere was like a large naval squadron. They fitted in instantly, adding significantly to an already extended family.

It was a few months later before Nick was rostered off for a long weekend, and by then the highlands were well into a vibrant, colourful autumn. Laleh's bulge was long beyond being just noticeable.

"Stirling is a Sunday drive from here, Lil. About one and a half hours each way. You up for it tomorrow?"

"If you hadn't suggested it, I was going too, Nickie. Should we try to find a phone number for them first?"

"I thought about that, and I don't think so. The first half hour is probably going to be touchy, and if we phone first, they could tell us to push off and that would be the end of it. If we turn up unexpectedly, they're almost certainly going to talk to us for a while, and that could make the difference. If they aren't there, we would have probably gone for a drive anyway, so it's no big deal."

"Okay, let's do it. I'll drive down, you drive back. I won't be able to get behind a bloody steering wheel for much longer."

They didn't hurry, enjoying the drive south along the east coast of Scotland, but were still in Stirling by mid-morning. The address was a small, red-brick semi-detached, sporting a large yard and driveway, in an outer northeastern suburb. Mature evergreens, the inevitable sprawling Scots pines, partially screened the houses. Nick rang and the chimes were answered by a short grey-haired woman, probably in her early seventies, who was wiping her hands on a floral pinafore.

When he introduced himself, her eyes slitted fractionally, but then she saw Laleh's bulge. It was a thing that probably only another woman would completely understand, but she stepped back immediately and invited them in. The husband she introduced was shod in carpet slippers.

He chatted to them while the wife boiled a kettle, but Nick could barely understand his thick accent, and Laleh couldn't at all. She nodded and smiled when it seemed appropriate, but fortunately the wife didn't take long with the tray. She pushed a large decorative plate of chocolate biscuits and rich, dark Dundee cake towards them, and took charge of the conversation. But from then on, it was Nick and Laleh who did most of the talking anyway.

Nick talked about a Sinclair that neither had ever known, with Laleh embellishing with little personal touches, and the regrets, intrinsic strength of character and insights got to the mother in the end. She had tears in her eyes by then and leaned across and put a trembling hand on his knee.

"Stop there, Nick. I'll make some sandwiches for lunch, and I have something else to do as well. Father, take them out for some fresh air. Show them the back garden." That was an order. He dutifully dragged them out with him and showed them his prolific veg patch and the swings and cubby for the grandkids. He got around to the low green hills behind the back fence and the ancient castle that dominated everything shortly after.

And when they moved towards the back door again, his wife was watching. She'd poured another coffee before they'd stomped the mud off, somehow knowing they would be ready for it.

"Do you two mind going through all this about Alistair again? I really want to hear it, and I know the girls will too. Neither knew any of this, and I think that they've both wondered about it ever since. They both live in Stirling and aren't far away. They'll be here shortly." She stopped to wipe her nose with a tissue, and almost immediately the bell chimed and the front door opened at the same time. The girls had travelled over together.

They were handsome girls, resembling each other closely, and vaguely their gran as well. By the time he and Laleh had finished their story again, their eyes also glistened, and when he brought up the numbered account in Edinburgh, there was hardly a dry eye in the house.

Nick and Laleh Evans were talked into staying overnight and as guests at the traditional family roast on the following day. The grandmother was delighted. It would even be a Sunday.

But it was the next one they were apprehensive about. February 14th, 1982 was cold, wet and blustery in London, as English winters always seemed to be. Random sheets of drizzle lashed through every open space and trickled unpleasantly down any gaps in exposed neck lines. The chipped pavers were rendered dark and slippery. Things had certainly changed in Iran, and also in the rest of the world, but where and by how much was still conjecture.

The American hostage crisis was long over, but Iran's relationship with the west was still hostile, and suicide bombing by Islamic radicals was all the rage in many countries.

Nick even had a female co-pilot by then, and a number of women in the military were now being trained to fly. Other hitherto exclusively male domains, including the operation of weapons and front line operations were also open to females. His co-pilot was in some ways a pathfinder, but other females were following close behind.

Laleh had wanted to, but she hadn't contacted Iran in the nearly two years since they'd got out, just in case. If overseas mail was being opened, she could destroy everything for Abdul and Minu, leaving them with no options at all. Going to London on that holiday was a giant leap of faith, and neither had a clue about what they would find.

Nick and Laleh were heads down, hurrying passed theatres and the ticket agents, eager to get out of the frigid drizzle. He pushed a stroller and her left hand helped, but it was covering his rather than resting on the push bar. The toddler inside strained constantly against a waterproof covering. He was more interested in passing people struggling against the elements with lowered heads, and ignored the string of brightly coloured plastic ducks unless they got in his way.

When they reached the walnut and brass revolving doors, Laleh plucked the infant from the push chair and headed in. Nick collapsed it first, and he was still in the revolving door when he heard the shriek. Nick smiled automatically. Although he couldn't see passed the ornate walnut desk that guarded the austere, grim entrance, he knew what it had to be. The British were too reserved to vent their joy noisily in somewhere like the Lyons Coffee House.

Laleh had stopped by the entrance desk and Abdul and Minu had nearly reached her when Nick struggled through. Except for a little more grey hair, they looked no different at all. All three met in a bear hug, a smaller head looking out curiously from the middle.

Abdul moved to Nick with both hands extended, first gripping his hand, but then hugging him, and by the time he surfaced, Minu was on him too. She already had Alistair Farhad in her arms, but somehow she got close enough to hug and kiss him as well. There were two younger men standing at the table they'd just left, and women and children too.

A relocation wasn't quite what Abdul had in mind, but he didn't have a lot of choice.